Darker
Trina M. Lee

Published 2013

ISBN 978-1482651683

Copyright © 2013, Trina M. Lee

All rights reserved. No part of this publication may be reproduced, stored in a retrieval system, or transmitted in any form or by any means, electronic, mechanical, recording or otherwise, without the prior written permission of the author.

Manufactured in the United States of America

Published by Dark Mountain Books

Editor
B. Leigh Hogan

Cover Artist
Michael Hart

This is a work of fiction. The characters, incidents and dialogues in this book are of the author's imagination and are not to be construed as real. Any resemblance to actual events or persons, living or dead, is completely coincidental.

Chapter One

Sin and sacrilege. From fornication and bloodletting to death and obsessed addiction, those two words summed up the vampires' world quite nicely. The Wicked Kiss was all of that and more. It was also the only place I felt comfortable with myself these days.

Blood dripped into my mouth, taking me away to a place where right and wrong ceased to exist. The scent of desire accompanied the steady pulse of arousal deliciously coating the atmosphere. I drank it in, savoring the heady sensation of spiraling headlong into euphoria.

"Bleed for me, my dear." Arys's throaty murmur was thick with yearning. He nuzzled the neck of the woman sprawled on the bed between us, driving her wild for him.

I lay back, holding her bleeding wrist above me so the scarlet nectar dripped from the vampire-inflicted wounds into my mouth. The irony wasn't lost on me. Both Arys and I were doing the very thing we'd sworn never to do, feed from the willing victims at The Wicked Kiss. I wasn't proud of myself. In fact, I'd be downright disgusted with my actions when I came down from the high.

If I'd been alone, I likely would have killed her. Arys kept me from doing something I'd hate myself for. As the dark power inside me grew, so did the hunger. I was still mortal, a werewolf with a twin flame connection to a vampire. However, the balance of our yin-yang bond was shifting.

Arys believed his darkness would consume me. Two witches had warned us of the dangers of our connection. One had gone so far as to show Arys a vision of our future: my death at his hand. There were too many possibilities and not enough concrete answers. All we could do was take it one day at a time. In the meantime, I needed to sate the bloodlust, preferably without adding to my death toll.

Our victim writhed in pleasure as we fed upon her. The club was constantly crawling with willing victims because they got as much as they gave. Arys easily stirred her longing. The right words whispered in a low, seductive tone or a carefully placed caress or two, and she was a swooning mess. Perhaps watching my lover so easily seduce another woman should have bothered me. Instead, I found it enticing.

Watching Arys in action was mesmerizing. It stirred my hunger to life as well as my libido. He wasn't always like this though, a careful predator manipulating his prey into bliss. The things Arys did when he wasn't with me were far more horrific. Screaming, begging and fighting, that's what Arys loved in a victim. There lies the essence of our differences. He was a monster who loved every minute of his curse.

"Alexa, my love." He beckoned me with a finger.

I dropped the woman's wrist and sat up. At Arys's command, I joined him near her head, watching as he sank fangs into her throat. Blood welled up from the wounds, spilling down her neck and chest. She moaned, clinging to Arys with a desperation that bordered on fearful.

He disentangled himself from her and turned to me with a devilish glint in his midnight blue eyes. Pulling me into his arms with a demanding aggression, he kissed me hungrily. Blood dripped from his mouth into mine, tangy and hot.

With a low growl, I slipped a hand up into his unruly thick black hair. A crimson drop escaped the corner of my mouth to slide down my chin and neck. Arys quickly captured it with his tongue, warm and moist against my sensitive flesh.

I quivered at the sharp sting of fangs scraping over my skin. I wanted him to take me right then and there. He would have gladly done it, too, but I wasn't willing with a stranger present. Most certainly, I didn't want someone watching who we were using as a food source.

"Arys, stop," I gasped when he buried his face in my cleavage. "We can't do this here."

"Like hell we can't." Ignoring my protest, he sought to free me of the tight black top I wore.

I shoved his hands away. "I can't do this with you. In this place. I feel dirty."

Annoyed, I left the bed and stood awkwardly near the door. Glancing around the room, I felt suffocated by its close confines. The back rooms at The Wicked Kiss were private enough for those seeking a place for some dirty fun. However, they were no less sleazy than any cheap motel room.

Four weeks, three days and sixteen hours. That's how long it had been since my wolf mate had left town. Shaz Richardson, the one person that fully understood me. Or, so I'd thought. Recently there hadn't been enough understanding between us. We both had issues that we chose to hide rather than share with one another. I'd thought his absence would get easier with the passing of time; I was wrong.

Turning away from the sight of my vampire on the bed with a bleeding, quivering victim, I left the room to stand awkwardly in the hall instead. I'd been feeling sorry for myself lately. It was ridiculous and time to cut that nonsense out. I had also been looking over my shoulder far more often than usual since a cursed demoness tried to have me killed. Self-pity and cowering wasn't my thing; I was ready to snap out of it.

A scream rang out, muffled slightly by the door I'd just closed. Arys's devious laugh followed, sending a chill down my spine. I walked away; I had to. When the bloodlust rose, I walked too close to the edge of sanity. Knowing what he was doing was as horrifying as it was alluring. I clung hard to what remained of my humanity, but every night I felt it slip further away. I could mourn it, or I could accept it. I had yet to do either.

Making my way down the hall, back to the main entrance from the club, I found myself overwhelmed by the onslaught of metaphysical energy leaking from every occupied room. Sex, blood, violence and pleasure oozed through the atmosphere like a metaphysical gas leak. The tantalizing blend of vampire and human essence called to me, beckoning like a wanton lover.

My pace quickened. I reached for the door that separated the nightclub from the back playground. The sound of a commotion beyond greeted me before I turned the knob. I almost collided with Josh as he rushed toward me.

"I don't know who you pissed off now, but we've got problems," he shouted over the noise. The panicked bartender pushed by me, heading for the back exit.

I couldn't say that I blamed him; I'd have loved to vacate, too. As it was, the other owner of the club, Kale, had been missing for weeks so I was the only one left to deal with this shit. Once I got a good look at what exactly was going on, I wished I'd stayed in the back.

A gang of vampires were happily trashing the place. Like a bunch of delinquents, they overturned tables and smashed liquor bottles. However, it didn't take them long to target the patrons. Total hysteria broke out as they savaged stray humans. People stampeded toward the door.

The vampires that frequented the place as well as the few on my security staff attempted to fight back. The invaders were quickly tossed aside or dealt a deathblow that left them in piles of ash and dust.

I leaped into the fray, dodging a flying table and fighting to avoid being trampled by the crowd that rushed against me like a powerful ocean wave. I gathered my power but couldn't use it with so many innocent people in the crossfire. When I had a clear shot of one of the vampires, I let loose with a psi ball that threw him hard against the wall. Guiding my focus, concentrating hard, I flooded him with enough power to make his head burst.

Sating the bloodlust had honed my senses, sharpening them to a delicate point. I was able to take out another vampire and slash the throat of a third before taking a heavy punch. I would have given just about anything to have my dagger then.

Forged by a demon, the Dragon Claw had the ability to kill a vampire with just a nick of the blade. It didn't even need to pierce the heart. Unfortunately, it was sitting tucked away in its velvet-lined box in the trunk of my car. Real helpful.

I stumbled backward and fell gracelessly over one of the lounge-style couches. Before I could get to my feet, a large vampire with a meaty hand grabbed my arm and dragged me up. I didn't hesitate, shoving power into him with my focus on his heart. Blood burst from his eyes, ears and nose seconds before he exploded in a shower of dust.

I expected further attack, but nobody grabbed for me. The remaining vamps hung back, looking to a shadowed figure standing mostly unnoticed near the entry.

Brook stepped into view, oblivious to the people shoving past him in their haste to escape. Some mysterious illusion hid the demon's black wings from sight. His eyes were void of any emotion. Brook was lower on the demon hierarchy but still no one to be messed with lightly. I'd been brushing up on my demonology since Lilah had decided I was a problem that she needed to eliminate.

"Back off blood suckers," the demon barked. "That's enough brainless destruction. Don't we have something for Ms. O'Brien?"

"Whatever it is, I'm sure I don't want it." What I wanted was to kick Lilah's ass for sending him, but she had been lying low since our last encounter.

"Why, of course you want it. It does belong to you after all." Brook gestured to a vampire who came forward with a box big enough to hold many things. I knew I didn't want to see what was in there.

The vampire placed the box on the bar, never once taking his eyes from me as he backed away. I couldn't resist. I focused on him and unleashed my energy. His head exploded first, his body quick to follow. The sense of satisfaction that followed was short lived.

"Disposable," Brook said with a shrug. "That's why she sent them. We came to deliver a message. This is my queen's territory, wolf. You're nothing. Not even worthy of the power you have. Lilah needs something from you. She wants to make sure you know she's going to get it."

With the help of Shya, a demon I truly loathed, I'd played a part in binding Lilah's power. She was a demon cursed into the form of a vampire. I'd stripped her vampire power, leaving her vulnerable enough for Shya to bind her.

Clearly, it had worked. She was relatively powerless, or so it would seem since she had sent another here in her place. Unfortunately, to break that curse, Lilah needed my blood. So, here we were.

"Get out of my club." I held Brook's solid black gaze, refusing to be intimidated.

"And, miss you opening your gift? Now that would just be rude of me." He gestured to the box sitting untouched on the bar. "Lilah owes you a little payback for that damn binding stunt you pulled with Shya."

I considered reaching out to Arys through our mental connection, then decided against it. Things were tense, but nothing I couldn't handle. I strode to the bar, keeping Brook in my sight. The stench hit me immediately. Death.

I didn't pause, didn't so much as hesitate with his eyes upon me. I tore open the box, knowing what I'd find before I looked inside. I just didn't know whom.

Double take. Then another. This couldn't be real.

Staring up at me with vacant dead eyes and a look of frozen horror etched permanently on his face, was the severed head of my fellow pack wolf, Zak.

Brook oozed satisfaction. "Consider this a warning. You have something she needs. All you have to do is provide it. Or, this won't be the last wolf."

He took advantage of my stunned silence. Slipping away with Lilah's remaining minions in tow, he left me there staring down at what used to be one of my wolves. Hot, angry tears filled my eyes. I clenched my teeth, gripping the side of the box with clawed fingertips.

I'd taken enough shit from manipulative vampires and demons. The time had come to cut the puppet strings that held me. I wasn't like them, wasn't one of them. As a creature of the light, I intended to hold tightly to that. Lilah thought she could play me, but she didn't know me. She had no idea what I was capable of doing. In many ways, neither did I.

We were both going to find out.

Chapter Two

"Close the doors for the night. Don't let anybody else in." I gazed around at the mess.

At least half a dozen bodies littered the floor. They had all been taking a risk by coming to The Wicked Kiss. Still, not one of them deserved this. Lilah had her goons kill them for no other reason than to hurt me. Same with Zak. It had worked.

It did hurt to see that these people were dead because someone wanted to take a shot at me. Lilah needed me alive. What better way to stick it to me than to start picking off those around me?

Justin approached with anger sparkling in his eyes. Tall, dark skinned and built like a football player, he was as mean as he looked. "They never should have made that demon bitch a vampire. I'd die before I'd play lapdog for her."

"That makes two of us." I closed the box, unable to look at Zak's remains. I regretted each of the casualties of the night, but Zak was special. He was my wolf. Mine to protect. I had failed him. I couldn't let it happen again.

"What's her deal with you? Or, is that something that will get me killed if you tell me?" Justin shook his head and bent to pick up an overturned table. "Never mind. Forget I asked."

"She needs my blood to break her curse," I spilled the truth. There was no sense lying. "She wanted to kill me because she felt threatened by my power. Then, she discovered that I could set her free. Now, she wants to force me into giving my blood willingly."

Justin glanced at me with a thoughtful frown creasing his brow. "I've seen what you can do. Why not just kill the bitch?"

"I'm gonna have to. If only it was just that simple."

Together we tidied up the broken glass and furniture. The place was empty other than the remaining staff. My vampires waited for me to throw cash at them to have the bodies removed. I wasn't sure we could just dump them in the river or wherever else the vamps might have in mind; we were dealing with several bodies. If the FPA caught wind of this, they'd be all over me like shit on a blanket.

Everyone lost in the throes of wicked ecstasy in the back of the building were either clueless to what had happened here or entirely apathetic, Arys included. It didn't sit well with me that a demon had been in here, and he'd been unaware or, worse, merely more concerned with the woman bleeding for him. Was existing night to night for the pleasures of blood and violence really so exquisite that it was worth blinding oneself to true danger?

No sooner had I finished the thought than a cold wave crashed over me. Arys swept through the door from the hall with the grace of the undead. He exuded the amped up energy of one who had just drained his victim dry. A devilish smile lit up his features in a macabre light.

He paused, taking in the disastrous surroundings. "What happened here? Did one of the self-neutered vamps finally lose it?"

I turned on him with an ice-cold glare. "Brook was here. Lilah sent him. He didn't come alone. I guess you were too busy playing to notice."

"Why didn't you tell me?" Curiosity drew him to the box sitting atop the bar. He opened it before I could respond. There was no sense of surprise. The things that shocked me were merely shrug-worthy to Arys.

"I considered it," I admitted, fetching a broom from behind the bar in order to sweep up the broken glass. "I figured adding you to the mix would make things worse, not better. Her goons trashed the place, killed innocent people and then left. After promising me that Zak was just the beginning. If I don't strike a deal with her for my blood, she keeps killing my wolves."

Arys's grin faded. "She's smart to start with your wolves. She knows how deep that cuts. And, she won't quit there. The angels built a cage for her for a reason. It's time she goes back."

Broken glass clinked loudly as I swept the shattered remains of a vodka bottle into a pile. Shya hadn't wanted to send Lilah back when we had the chance. He thought she'd break free of the cage the angels had made for her and come back for us with a vengeance. Apparently, she was getting an early start on that.

"And, if it doesn't hold her?" I questioned Shya's motives in keeping Lilah here with us, but what if he were right?

"That's the angels' problem."

Justin interrupted. "I'm going to take care of those bodies. Do you want me to do something with that as well?" I followed his pained gaze to the box containing Zak's head.

I swallowed hard. *Shit.* "No. That's fine, thanks. I'll deal with it." Zak was mine. The least I could do was properly bury his head, seeing as I'd likely never see the rest of him again. "What will you do with them? There's got to be six bodies here."

"Make that seven," Arys added, looking chagrined, but it was forced. Remorse wasn't one of his personality traits.

"Arys, what the hell? You promised."

"Oops." It was as close to an apology as he was likely to get. "You shouldn't have left. I got carried away."

"Of course. It's my fault that you killed someone." I rolled my eyes and sighed. Why did I bother arguing with him?

Looking uncomfortable, Justin edged away. "It's no problem. I can handle one more. It's really not hard to make them disappear." He hesitated, glancing from Arys to me. "For what it's worth, the last thing I want is trouble. But, if I have to choose sides, I'm on yours."

"Thank you," I murmured. I didn't expect the vampires of the city to start proclaiming their loyalty; however, Justin's declaration meant a lot to me.

He and Arys exchanged a look. Arys nodded his thanks, a brief but expressive action. Justin left the two of us alone and set to work giving orders in regards to the cleanup. I couldn't watch. I didn't particularly want to turn my attention to the gruesome box contents either but had little choice.

I tried to picture telling Kylarai and the rest of my wolves about this. My stomach turned. Arys was silent, watching me stare at the box. I wished he would spit out whatever he was thinking. So, when he didn't speak up, I did.

"You shouldn't come in here anymore." I rushed on before he could reply with something that matched the dark frown he suddenly wore. "You've always hated this place, Arys. You come here out of obligation, and then you do things like kill willing victims and intimidate the staff. I don't need you hovering over me, though I do appreciate it. I like it better when I don't know what you're up to and who you're killing."

"You don't need me here? This place is a disaster waiting to happen. If anything, it's you that needs to stop coming here." He inclined his head pointedly toward the array of death and destruction. "Besides, I only account for a small percentage of the missing person reports in this city. I don't kill nearly as often as you assume I do."

"How often is that?"

Our eyes locked. The smoldering heat in his gaze promised wonderfully wicked things. I tried to ignore that familiar flicker of vampire energy low in my core. It whispered through me, enticing me to fall into his eyes and abandon the annoyance I felt. It almost worked.

"Not often enough," he said with a flirtatious smirk. "Give me some credit. I can restrain myself." At my harsh laughter, he added, "I'm doing it right now."

He pulled me close and kissed my neck. The telltale sting of his fangs followed as he dragged them roughly across my skin. Against my will, I quivered.

"Cut it out." I shoved him away before he could get inside my head again. I had another role to play before I could play the role of smitten lover.

The vibration in my back pocket alerted me to an incoming call. Hoping it would be Shaz, I still grabbed the phone with a trickle of anxiety. Fan-fucking-tastic. It was the FPA, or more specifically, Agent Briggs, who had already decided he didn't like me. I was bad news, valuable only for the information I might have.

"What?" I answered in a short, clipped tone. The anxiety didn't leave me, but the reason for it changed.

"O'Brien? We've got a body here that we think you should take a look at. Pretty sure it belongs to you." Crime-scene background noise accompanied Briggs's snide remark.

So, they found the rest of Zak. *Thanks, Lilah, you bitch.* "Care to elaborate?"

"Headless werewolf. Strange markings on the torso, possibly ritualistic in nature. Prints match with a Zachary Benz. His home address is in Stony Plain. Any of this mean anything to you?"

Since the Federal Para-Intelligence Agency had introduced themselves to me by accusing me of murder and revealing that I was on their watch list, they had been a real thorn in my side. Discovering my dead sister was actually alive and employed by the covert government sector really rubbed salt in the wound.

After surviving the wolf attack that turned us both, a vampire recruited me to hunt supernaturals that risked public attention. I later learned it was a front for Shya, a demon who sought people with power for his own agenda. The government had lured in my sister, Juliet. Now, we worked for opposing sides, or at least, that's how the FPA chose to see it.

I wasn't naive enough to believe I wasn't one of the bad guys. However, that didn't make the FPA the good guys. I'd definitely done my share of shady things I wasn't proud of, but that didn't define who I was.

"What's the address? I'm on my way."

Briggs rattled off a south side address, demanded I hurry my ass up and then promptly disconnected the call. I locked eyes with Arys who regarded me thoughtfully. Keen senses and the absence of regular club noise allowed him to hear the conversation.

"Don't let him know about that." Arys pointed to the box containing Zak's head. "The less they know about any of this, the better."

"Easier said than done. He's going to have Juliet there to sniff out a lie." I shook my head and stared at the mess. That Vegas vacation Jez had been talking about lately was starting to look tempting.

The entire drive to the scene was painfully tense. I had to pry my fingers from the steering wheel and drag myself out of the car. Arys appeared perfectly composed, but his energy hummed with excitement.

Voices drifted to us, coming from behind the old warehouse located at the address Briggs had given. With no flashing lights or sirens, a whole lot of suits were taking pictures and asking questions.

"Let's get this over with," I muttered as we made our way around the building.

A dark suited agent stopped us with one hand held up in an unspoken command; another reached for the gun at his hip. "Are you Alexa O'Brien?"

"Yeah, that would be me."

"I.D. please."

"Seriously?" I stared at his outstretched hand. "Where's Briggs? Or Juliet. They know who I am."

He opened his mouth to refuse, but Briggs cut him off. "Let them by, Agent James."

The man I dreaded seeing stood behind a line of caution tape with several other agents. He watched our approach with a narrowed gaze, scrutinizing our every move.

Briggs was a tall, black man with a taut physique that bragged of hours in the gym. With his dark suit and government agent persona firmly in place, he was both a bit of a cliché and a tad scary. I wasn't entirely sure what he and the FPA were able to do, but from what I'd seen so far, it wasn't good.

I ducked under the tape, followed closely by Arys. I scanned the area for Juliet, finding her over by the body. Our eyes met across the distance, and she quickly averted her gaze. Nice to see you, too, little sister.

"Thanks for coming," Briggs drew my attention back to him.

"It's not like you gave me a choice," I said pleasantly, beaming a phony, see-through smile.

"You had a choice." Turning his dark gaze on Arys, Briggs stuck out a hand. "I'm Agent Thomas Briggs. Nice to meet O'Brien's other half. I've heard so much about you."

"Arys Knight." Arys accepted the other man's hand, and they took a moment to size each other up. "I'm sure whatever you've heard is only scraps of the truth."

Briggs lingered on Arys as if he didn't dare take his eyes from the vampire. Finally, he extended a hand toward the cluster of agents gathered around Zak's remains. "Well, have a look. Tell me what you think."

He led the way, the agents dispersing like flies at his approach. When only Juliet remained, we shared a look, brief but poignant. A spark flickered in her dark eyes revealing a remnant of the girl I remembered.

"Hey, Lexi. Sorry we have to meet again under these circumstances." Juliet gestured to the headless corpse. "Do you know him?"

I studied the remains of my pack wolf. It was hard to look at but not quite as hard as it had been to see his head in that box. Zak's body had been stripped naked. As Briggs had said, a large ritualistic looking symbol was etched into the flesh in the center of his chest. It was a triangle with what appeared to be an eye in the center, surrounded by an inverted five-pointed star. *Great.*

I closed my eyes, concentrating on the residual energy surrounding us. Zak's body was tainted with a black, inky energy that reeked of demons. It was faint, telling me very little about what happened to him. He hadn't been killed here.

"Yeah," I let out the breath I'd been holding. "I know him."

Briggs turned his scrutiny on me. "How do you know him? Or, should I say, how well do you know him?"

"He was one of mine, if that's what you're driving at. A member of my pack. A friend." I met Briggs's cold stare with one of my own.

"Any idea why someone would do this to him?" Briggs raised a dark brow, daring me to deny it.

I glanced back at the cryptic symbol. "Looks like a demon ritual to me. Possibly to raise one. Maybe bind one." *Or, break a binding on one*, I added silently.

"Uh huh. But, why choose this werewolf specifically?" Briggs was like a dog with a bone.

I crossed my arms and tilted my head, studying him intently. "Is there something you'd like to say, Agent? Just spit it out."

Juliet stiffened but said nothing. Her silence spoke volumes. She was uncomfortable but forced a relaxed front.

Briggs swung his gaze over Arys and then me. "I'd say it looks like someone's trying to send you a message. Like you've pissed somebody off."

"Yeah? That's what you think? Is that why you're sniffing around here? Because you sure as hell don't want to meet the demon responsible for this. If I were you, I'd wash my hands of the whole thing before you endanger your people." I tried not to look at Juliet but was unsuccessful. The further she stayed from this situation the better.

"We've dealt with demons before. Don't patronize me, Ms. O'Brien. I can assure you, I've been doing this since you were in diapers."

If that was true, Briggs looked pretty good for his age. I wondered what he was up to that gave him access to the fountain of youth. With a shake of my head, I dismissed his comment as ignorance.

"I don't give a rat's ass what kind of demon you think you've dealt with, none of them even compare to this one. Do yourself a favor. Get acquainted with their hierarchy and stay the hell away from the ones at the top. Now, are you going to release my wolf to me, or do you have other, more unsavory plans for him?"

The agent and I glared daggers at one another. Briggs was used to calling the shots. Well, so was I. At least I was when Arys was willing to let me.

"I'm not authorized to give it to you. It's evidence of some obviously serious activity going on in the city. We'll be keeping it." Briggs was unapologetic. "We haven't found the head yet. Hopefully we will before a civilian does."

Without asking for permission, I whipped out my phone and snapped a photo of the body before Briggs could tell me not to. I wanted some kind of evidence of that symbol. I had the sinking feeling I'd need to see Shya about this. I'd been avoiding the demon for weeks despite his insistent demands that I speak with him.

Juliet cleared her throat, drawing every eye. "Alexa, is there anything you can tell us about the demon that did this? Maybe we can help you if you're in some kind of trouble."

A chuckle spilled forth, earning me a dirty look from Briggs. An offer of help from the FPA was beyond ridiculous. They'd tortured someone dear to me, and now, he was missing. Without a doubt, they would have done the same to me if Kale hadn't taken the fall. I would never trust the FPA. If that meant never trusting my sister again, so be it.

"I'm always in trouble, Juliet. All I can tell you is to stay away from this. Messing with this demon would be suicide." I turned my gaze on Briggs who regarded me like a bug he wanted to squish. "If you value the lives of your people, you'll stick to entrapping and torturing vampires. You all seem so good at it."

I turned to leave; I couldn't do anything more here. What had happened to Zak sparked a fire in my core. It would burn until I sent Lilah back to where she belonged, to the cage the angels made for her.

"I'm sorry for what happened with Kale Sinclair." Briggs's forced apology stopped me in my tracks. I faced him with a new rage burning within.

"Too little too late, Agent."

"We have a proposition for you. If you would hear me out."

Arys's wicked laughter sent a lovely tingle down my spine. It didn't have quite the same effect on Juliet or Briggs, who both stared at him suspiciously.

"I don't think so," he said. "What you did to Sinclair, you would have done to Alexa. You'd be wise to stay away from her." Arys's mood changed, going from grim amusement to deadly calm. "I'm not asking."

"No," Juliet replied vehemently. "She's my sister, dammit. I'd never let that happen to her."

Arys moved fast, a blur of motion. He was dangerously close to Juliet, scowling down into her face. "You led the fucking team that came to get her."

Briggs pulled his gun and trained it on Arys. That might work on some vampires but not on my vampire. Arys never took his eyes off Juliet. He merely snapped his fingers, and Briggs's gun flew from his hand and skidded across the pavement.

I laid a hand on his arm. "Arys, please."

I didn't have to say anything else. Reluctantly, he backed off. Juliet's eyes were wide, and the scent of fear rolled off her. She wasn't foolish enough to try pulling a weapon.

Agent Briggs was fuming. He was also looking at Arys with a new sense of intrigue. Showing even a small display of power in front of the FPA was a bad idea.

"Would it be too much to expect you people to sit down and have a civilized discussion?" Briggs stooped to retrieve his gun. He stuffed it back in the holster but rested a hand atop it.

"You people?" I rounded on him with a snarl. The urge to bare my four vicious fangs at him was strong, but I held the wolf back. "We're just monsters to you, aren't we? You don't see us as human in any way. We were once, you know. Human. Like you."

Briggs looked down his nose at me, haughty and self-assured. "You are a monster, Ms. O'Brien. That's just a cold, hard fact. But, I don't believe that makes you void of any humanity whatsoever. I meant no offense."

"I think we're done here. I have nothing further to say to you."

I didn't want to give Briggs a chance to coerce me into staying; I couldn't count on Arys to behave himself. He was eyeing up Briggs with a devilish glint in his eyes.

"We need your help, Ms. O'Brien. You want to talk about dangerous demons? Let's talk about Shya." The agent's face softened. "That's not even his real name. Demons don't give their real names if they can help it. He's up to something, and we need to stop him. You're the closest one to him that can help us."

Arys's energy was hot and scattered. His growing frustration was palpable, teasing my senses. I wanted to get him out of there before he did something I'd regret, but I was curious as to how much the FPA knew about Shya that perhaps I didn't.

"Clearly you're misinformed about my relationship with Shya." I kept my voice low so it wouldn't carry outside the four of us. "I don't have one. I never did. He never interacted with me personally until recently. He sure as hell hasn't shared any of his big bad plans."

"Yet he trusted you to help him bind a demon goddess that he is supposed to bow down to. Sounds personal enough." Briggs smiled slightly, as if sure he had me there.

"Shya and I both had our reasons for that. They were entirely selfish. We weren't doing each other any favors." I wasn't happy to hear that they knew about that. "I want to make it very clear to you that I have no alliance with that demon. Whatever he's up to, I don't know about it, and I sure as hell have no part in it."

Briggs didn't believe me. Skepticism colored the grimace he wore. "Would you be willing to help us gather more information?"

I wanted to tell Briggs to sit on it and rotate. The words were on the tip of my tongue, but I saw a chance to learn more about the FPA and what they were up to, so I reconsidered. Could I make this work to my advantage?

I exchanged a glance with Arys, sharing so much with just a look. Tilting my head, I gave Briggs my best smile and purred, "What's in it for me?"

Darker

He couldn't hide the relief that swept over his hard features. Relief quickly gave way to a cryptic grin that didn't sit well with me. My stomach flipped a few times. Briggs's grin grew until it was downright unnerving.

"I'll tell you what really happened to Kale Sinclair."

Chapter Three

"Are you fucking kidding me?" The words spilled out, driven by a crash of emotion. A growl rumbled in my throat, and I was all fangs and claws.

Briggs raised his weapon. Uncertainty replaced his smug smile. So much for negotiating with the FPA. Briggs had uttered the magic words that were stronger than my rein on sanity.

I timed my attack perfectly. Sudden and instinctive, I hit him dead center in the chest, grabbing his gun arm in a bone-shattering grip. An audible crack brought me a shred of satisfaction but not quite as much as his pained shout. He hit the ground hard with me atop him. Briggs grunted as I knocked the gun from his hand.

Wrapping a hand around his throat, I snarled down into his face. Commotion broke out as nearby agents rushed over with guns drawn. Juliet yelled for them to hold their fire. I looked up to find myself staring into the barrel of her gun.

"Do you really have it in you to pull that trigger?" I snapped, refusing to loosen my hold on Briggs.

Juliet's eyes were wild, all wolf. "How bad do you want to find out?"

Little sister had a backbone after all. A chuckle spilled between my lips. I was proud of her. She held the gun on me, but her wary gaze flicked to Arys. He watched me with a mischievous smile.

At a time when Shaz would have dragged me off Briggs, Arys merely watched with amusement. It was a sobering realization. I had to keep my rash actions in check. My white wolf wasn't here to keep me from doing something I'd regret.

Ignoring Juliet, I leaned in close to Briggs. Sniffing deeply of his scent, I savored the delicious smell of fear. It was tantalizing, calling to my bloodlust the way the scent of fresh bread called to a starving man. I gazed at the man beneath me and saw only prey.

"Tell me what you know about Kale Sinclair." I focused on the clean after-shave scent of Briggs, trying to block out the enticing aroma of human and terror. I couldn't lose control. Not here, not now.

"Get the hell off me," he grunted, struggling for breath.

"Try again." I tightened my hold on his throat, choking off his air supply completely.

A sudden surge of panic had Briggs flailing. As well muscled as he was, he still didn't have it in him to fight a pissed off werewolf. He had no idea how lucky he was that I purposely held off using power on him. I wanted him to talk; I didn't want his head to explode. At least, not just yet.

Briggs stared up at me with wide eyes. The fear in their brown depths faded, replaced by a growing fury. He shook his head as much as my grip would allow. Total refusal.

I smacked his head against the concrete hard enough to rattle his pearly white teeth. "Tell me, goddammit!"

"Alexa, that's enough." Juliet stepped closer, her gun inches from my face. "Let him go."

I didn't look at her when I held up a hand and, with a push of power, threw her back. Before the remaining agents could rush me, Arys surrounded us with an energy circle. Briggs was trapped inside, entirely at our mercy.

"Start talking before I decide you smell just a little too good," I growled. I eased off just enough so he could speak. "Where is Kale?"

He gave a strangled cough. With a murderous light in his dark gaze, Briggs said, "He's dead."

"Liar," I shouted. The punch I threw was automatic. I wanted to make him hurt for that.

"I gave the kill order," Briggs roared back at me. His words cut deep because I smelled no lie on him.

"What?" I whispered more to myself than to anyone else.

"When I told you he escaped, it was a lie. We had him all along. Keeping him alive wasn't a risk worth taking." Briggs might have been in a bad position, but it didn't diminish his arrogance. "Go ahead and kill me. The entire agency will be on your ass, and your demon problems will be a cake walk in comparison."

I glanced around at the waiting agents, each of them with guns drawn. Juliet was back on her feet, watching me with a guarded expression. Killing Briggs was exactly what I craved. It was the least I could do after what the FPA had done to Kale.

Kale... how could I not know that he was dead? My instinct had told me he still lived, and yet Briggs's words rang with truth. A scream built within me, threatening to burst forth.

My wolf stared out of my eyes, gazing down into Briggs with a fierce hunger that had nothing to do with appetite and everything to do with vengeance. He was right. The FPA already had me on a watch list. If I tore his throat out the way I wanted, I'd never be free of them.

I landed one last blow, connecting with his face hard enough to make my hand throb. Then, I got off him and stepped back. Briggs would get his alright. His time would come, and I'd be there to see it.

"Stay the fuck away from me, Briggs," I warned. "I may not know what Shya has planned, but I hope it involves making you his bitch."

I was thrumming with power. Holding it contained inside had me visibly shaking. I had no parting words for my sister. There was nothing to say.

Arys dropped his circle, and we turned to the cluster of agents standing between our car and us. Despite the weapons they held, not one of them appeared confident enough to use them. With a slight wave of my hand, I knocked them aside, creating a clear path to pass through.

I anticipated a shot or two, but Briggs told them to let us leave. Upon my last glance back, he was sitting up, holding his head with Juliet silently watching us go. I hated myself for thinking it, but I couldn't help but wonder if it would have been better if she'd died the night Raoul attacked us.

A smile tugged at Arys's lips. "Watching you get rough like that drives me wild. You're a goddamn force of nature, and it's beautiful."

He reached for my hand, and I gasped as our power joined with the electrical burst of a lightning bolt. It was exciting, arousing and comforting. Yet, it didn't shake the growing sorrow or the urge to cry.

I shook it off and sucked in a deep breath of night air. Maybe Briggs was wrong, or just a damn good liar. He had to be. I refused to believe otherwise.

"Hey, don't worry about Sinclair," Arys's velvet smooth tone was soothing, promising false assurance. "That was a lie. An attempt to gain some kind of control over you."

Knowing Arys didn't give a damn about Kale made me appreciate his effort to ease my fears. It didn't work though.

"His words stank of the truth." We reached my car, and I dropped into the driver's seat with a heavy thud. As Arys slid into the passenger side, the weight of his gaze was crushing. "Not even a hint of a lie."

Briggs hadn't had the pungent, acrid aroma caused by the change in brain chemistry during the telling of a lie. Of course, smarmy, manipulative liars could tell a lie so convincing that they themselves believed it to be true. I had known a man like that, Raoul. The first man I'd ever loved.

Arys was quiet, watching me as I started the fire-engine red Dodge Charger and pulled away from the FPA crime scene. I stared straight ahead, fighting the wave of fear and worry. The thought of losing Kale made my stomach flip in a very bad way, but I didn't want to show it in front of Arys. My twisted entanglement with Kale was just one of several touchy subjects between us.

"Why are you trying so hard to hide how much this is killing you?" Arys broke the silence after several strained minutes. "I can feel it. Like my own heart is breaking."

"I'm sorry." My fingers tightened almost painfully on the wheel.

"I'm the one who should be sorry," Arys replied, averting his gaze when I glanced his way. "You're in pain, and I can't help but feel relieved."

I stifled a gasp. It shouldn't have surprised me, but it was an admittance I'd have rather he'd kept to himself.

"You wanted this," I muttered bitterly. "Can't say I blame you."

I crossed down a side street toward the downtown core, heading back to The Wicked Kiss. I wanted to retrieve Zak's head and take it home where the pack would bury him properly. I imagined his body would wind up in an FPA lab where they'd do God only knew what to it.

"I never wanted this, Alexa." With a shake of his dark head, Arys laid a gentle hand on my thigh. "Anything that hurts you could never bring me pleasure."

I wasn't so sure about that, but I wasn't willing to give voice to the thought. Arys meant well and I knew that, so I nodded tightly and focused on my destination.

My plan was to get to The Wicked Kiss, get in and get out. Things so rarely go as planned. Why should it be any different now? So, when I walked into the club to find Shya seated at the bar with a glass of red wine, I merely groaned. It wasn't worth the effort to muster a more emphatic reaction.

The demon looked up at my approach, tearing his gaze from the box on the bar. A small half smile curved his thin lips.

The club was now free of bodies and overturned tables though it was still far from clean. The scent of blood clung to the air, metallic and sweet. It stained the floor in several places like a lurid decoration. Closing the doors for a night or two might be the best plan at this point. I'd do it if it weren't so likely that the number of street kills would skyrocket overnight.

"What are you doing here?" I cut Shya off before he could slip out a snide greeting. "If this is a follow up to Lilah's little goon squad, then save yourself the trouble. I'm not in the mood."

Shya raised a brow and gave me a critical once over. He was attractive with an Asian appearance, clad in the dark suit he usually wore. I didn't know his real face, but I imagined it was something I never wanted to see. The demon was smooth and calculated, as untrustworthy as they come.

"Don't flatter yourself," he scoffed, eyes flashing in annoyance. "You're not the only one Lilah has made her enemy. Binding her power has done nothing to stop her from being a royal pain in the ass. I think it's fed her madness."

"She killed one of my wolves and threatened to keep doing it unless I willingly give her my blood. As far as I'm concerned, this is all your fault."

"Our fault," Shya insisted, sniffing the wine in his glass.

"It was your genius idea to bind her," I retorted, my fuse short. "I wanted to send that bitch back to imprisonment where she belongs. It needs to happen. Better late than never."

Darker

Arys didn't give Shya a chance to reply. He loomed menacingly over the demon. "What are you doing in here anyway, Shya? Come to make good on your threats?"

Shya gazed up at Arys from his seat and shrugged. "Not tonight. I've come to apologize to Alexa. No need to get all puffed up, Mr. Knight. I come in peace."

"I'll just bet you do."

"Apologize?" I cut in before Arys could initiate violence. I feared he would let that feisty vampire temper start a war I wasn't sure we could win. "You really are out of your damn mind."

Ignoring Arys's glower, Shya fixed me with a cool crimson gaze. "Hear me out?"

Those blood red eyes were eerie, downright chilling with the snake-like pupils. Not so long ago, those eyes had instilled a deep-rooted fear within me. I'd be lying if I said I wasn't afraid of Shya, but that instinctive wariness was now colored with absolute abhorrence.

"Fine," I relented. "Make it fast."

"I am genuinely apologetic for my behavior the last time we were together." He paused to take a sip of wine, a melodramatic action. The demon seemed to be fond of drama. "It was a choice I have come to regret. I should have been more respectful. As one of the revered Hounds, you deserve much more than that. Please forgive my selfish nature."

Shya swirled the wine in his glass, looking pleased with himself. He apparently hadn't just heard the same crock of shit I had. Demons might be many things: clever, powerful, frightening. Above all things, I believed them to be exceptionally delusional.

"So what you're saying is, you came here to waste my time," I said. "You threatened to kill me. I'm not pretending that never happened. We're done, Shya. I'm not one of your pets. Whatever it is you want from me, forget about it."

Shya's smile disappeared, replaced by an ugly sneer. "I've never looked upon you as a pet. I see the potential in you. The power of life and death joined in a rare and unlikely union. You could be a great ruler, you know."

"Good Lord, you are out of your mind."

"Am I really though?" he challenged. "You feel it, don't you? The power burning in your veins. You've watched how it makes others fall before you. Have you not felt the glorious sensation of bringing your enemies to their knees? Can you tell me it doesn't feel like paradise?"

The crazy talk was giving me a horrible feeling. It was ludicrous. I didn't understand the demon's need to rule over others or his hunger to be any more than what he was now.

Arys's sapphire gaze held a knowing look. He regarded Shya with a pensive stare. "Get to the point. Why are you really here?"

"Fine," Shya snapped, both his patient demeanor and his forced charm vanished. "Lilah is intent on reclaiming her throne. To do that she has to break the curse. And, that starts with you. She is determined to once again be queen at any cost, which I'm sure you've already noticed. You need protection."

"I'm not accepting protection from you," I retorted. "What kind of an idiot do you think I am?"

"It's your blood she wants. She's started with your wolves. What about when it spills over into your precious human world? You think the monster police at the FPA can contain something like her? I can't even do that. Not anymore."

I pursed my lips and stifled any reaction I might have had. Shya's words scared me, but I couldn't let him get inside my head. I pulled out my phone and brought up the picture of Zak's body.

"What does this symbol mean?"

"It's a summoning mark. Blood sacrifice in exchange for having her binding broken. If it had worked, we'd know. Whoever she summoned must have refused her request."

This tidbit of information brought Shya's smile back. I couldn't muster one myself, but I was relieved to hear her binding was still intact.

"How many other demons can break the binding you created?" Arys asked.

"Several. Of course, most won't be willing to help a cursed demon lest they too fall under her curse. It won't be easy for her. That isn't going to stop them from siding with her. They will still serve their queen."

I groaned. All I wanted to do was go home and mourn the loss of Zak and Kale. One night to myself to cry it out before I had to face what Shya was telling me. Just one night. Was that too much to ask?

Darker

I watched as Shawn and Justin cleaned up the rest of the mess. The scent of bleach quickly filled the place with a brain-smashing odor. If this were just the beginning of what Lilah had planned, how much worse would it get? She had to be stopped.

"So we kill the bitch. Problem solved." Arys stole the words right out of my mouth. "And, we don't waste time doing it."

"It could never be so simple." Shya shook his head. "She'll be expecting that. She won't be foolish enough to let down her guard. I imagine she has both vampires and demons with her at all times. Getting close enough to harm her will be difficult."

I ran a hand through my hair in frustration. The motion made me think of Shaz. I would have given almost anything for him to be here right now.

"Then what do we do?" I asked, exasperated. "Your last brilliant idea didn't work out so well."

"We ready ourselves for what may come," Shya paused to look at each of us in turn. "And, we keep her from getting her hands on you."

"We?" I scoffed. "I don't think so, Shya. Your sudden interest in apologies and teamwork comes solely from your desire to save your own ass. You fucked up and you know it. Binding Lilah didn't give you any more control over her than you had before. All it did was piss her off, and now, she's gunning for us. If she gets my blood somehow and breaks the curse, it's all over for you. You must be scared shitless."

I allowed myself a grin, feeling for the first time that I had leverage where the demon was concerned. I figured it was temporary so I'd enjoy it while I could.

Shya's eyes narrowed, but he appeared otherwise unruffled. "I'm aware of how this appears. We have no choice but to trust one another for now. I promise you, I will do nothing to harm you. You have my word."

Was he for real? I'd never trust Shya again. A glance at Arys's reaction made me do a double take. I knew that set to his jaw and that curious glint in his eyes. Was he falling for Shya's smooth-talking charm?

"I'm not making any agreements with you." I let Shya see the wolf in my eyes, demanding he take me seriously. "You screwed me. Now, you're on your own."

"You're one of my best assassins. You're good because you really believe you're taking scum off the streets. Keeping yourself safe and taking Lilah out would be doing humanity a favor." Shya was persistent; he clearly wasn't used to being denied. "You are the protector of mankind, aren't you?"

"Since when do you care about humanity?" I frowned, shaking my head and ignoring his reference to the meaning of my name. "You're a demon. Don't insult my intelligence."

Anger flashed in Shya's red eyes. A pulse of searing energy rolled over me.

"I'll level with you, Alexa," he snapped suddenly. "The human world is an amusement park for demons. We control them by keeping them oblivious to what's really going on around them. People like you and Sinclair help me do that here. I have an agenda, as do you. We all have our own reasons for doing what we do, but don't you dare make the mistake of thinking your reasons are not selfish."

Shya stood abruptly. The atmosphere around him was unbearably hot. With a scowl, he sneered, "If you decide stopping Lilah is more important than your personal vendetta, you know how to find me."

* * * *

"No." My voice echoed throughout the silent house. "A thousand times, no."

"It's not such a bad idea, Alexa. Think it through. As long as Lilah is cursed, she's desperate to get her hands on you. Right now, Shya has more power than she does. And, so do we. Partnering with him on this is in everyone's best interest."

"That," I snarled, my fists clenched, "is the dumbest thing I've ever heard."

Arys gave me one of those looks I hated involving a slight roll of the eyes and a quirk of his lips that indicated he found me absurd. From his place on the couch, he watched me pace the open length of the living room to the adjoined kitchen and back again. He patted the cushion beside him, a gesture I ignored.

Darker

I didn't want to pace around the house arguing with Arys. I wanted to tear off my clothes and race across the backyard on four legs. I'd moved into the new house on the edge of town just two weeks ago. It still didn't feel quite like home, but I liked it. The location was perfect for a wolf. Jez insisted on a housewarming party, but in light of recent events, there was no telling when that would actually happen.

"I don't trust him, and I don't want to play nice with the same demon that tried to sell me out to Lilah." I gazed at the patio off the kitchen, aching to escape the confines of the house and run. "I'm shocked you'd ever suggest such a thing. Shya's just pissed that she refused him. Don't you find it suspicious that he's trying to include us in this?"

"I'm not suggesting we blindly follow Shya into anything, but playing along seems like the safest way to deal with this for now. Lilah's going to continue putting the squeeze on you."

"She wants my blood to break her curse. Shya can't protect me from that. Not when she's targeting others."

Arys studied me, an unnerving darkness in his eyes. "She just needs a Hound of God. It doesn't have to be you."

I stopped dead mid-pace. Unease crawled up my spine like a giant spider. "You better not be saying what I think you're saying. Tread carefully, vampire."

With an unapologetic shrug, Arys said, "Have you wondered yet if it's just you? Little sister might be a Hound, too."

My initial reaction was territorial rage. What he was suggesting was so wrong, so vile, so... Arys. I was momentarily flustered by a tangle of angry words snagged on the tip of my tongue.

Juliet couldn't be a Hound. It couldn't be a running bloodline unless Raoul was one, too. As far as I knew, we were chosen, not made. Either way, I'd die before I'd let anyone harm my sister.

"Let's get one thing straight right now. Nobody touches Juliet." My words came out a growl. "How can you possibly think it's a good idea to help Lilah break her curse? What's going on with you, Arys?"

A muscle twitched in his jaw. Despite his calm appearance, I knew he was fighting his short temper. Heated arguments were a regular part of our relationship. As twin flames, we were guaranteed to have conflict with one another. At times it was sexy, lending fire to a rough bout of lovemaking. Nevertheless, it could get ugly, driving a wedge between two beings who were destined to share everything. We were each other's greatest strength and most formidable weakness.

"I just want to keep you alive, my beautiful wolf. I'm seeking the best way to do that without incurring the wrath of a demon goddess."

"There's more to it than that, I know you. What is it you're not saying?"

"Nothing," he insisted. "You are my priority. Keeping you safe is what matters most to me. Especially with the wolf pup out of town."

I turned away so he wouldn't see the emotion fill my eyes. Arys's pet name for Shaz had stuck despite Shaz's protests. Eventually he'd simply accepted it. Damn I missed my white wolf. I swallowed hard and crushed the swell of feelings, forcing them back down where they belonged.

"I'm not doing it, and I'm not going along with anything Shya has planned, either. It's never what it seems no matter what he makes you think," I said, shaking my head.

Arys watched me with uncertainty, ultimately deciding the risk was worth taking. "What if I'd like to go along with it?"

My jaw dropped. "Has everybody taken a big fucking dose of insanity tonight?"

"It's risky, but playing nice with Shya might give us an advantage that we wouldn't have if we told him to fuck off. It's a strategic move, one that could keep us from having our asses handed to us by a nut job demon goddess."

He had that look in his eyes, the glint of assurance when he knew he was right. I wasn't folding this time. As often as Arys was right during these disputes, this time he was dead wrong.

"Hell no," I murmured. "I don't know what's going on in your head, Arys, but it's scaring me."

Much to my surprise, he averted his gaze, suddenly unwilling to give me his famous stare-down. I was sure it wasn't because he had no fight left in him. Arys was always spoiling for a good fight. A sick sensation gripped me.

I slid the patio door open and stepped outside for some air. The confines of the house were making my wolf crazy. That in turn would eventually drive Arys crazy. Plus, I needed a moment to think this through.

Darker

There was no sound, no sense of movement, but I knew when Arys stood behind me. I anticipated his touch when he placed a hand on my waist. His mouth was hot on the back of my neck. He emanated the heat he'd stolen from his victim tonight.

"Please, trust me?" Low and smooth, his voice made my knees weak. "I only want what's best for both of us, but especially for you. I can't bear to lose you now."

I turned to face him, gazing up into blue eyes filled with concern. "Where is this coming from, Arys? Paranoia has never been quite your style."

Again he glanced away, staring into the darkness beyond the glow of the patio light. I barely resisted the urge to shake him.

"You're powerful," he said. "Not invincible. I've watched you taunt death enough times to know that it's only a matter of time until it comes for you."

"You made sure I'd rise as a vampire after death. You called my mortality a burden to be cast off. Now, you're afraid it will actually happen. What's your deal?" I touched his face, gently guiding his gaze back to mine. "Is it because you think you'll be the one to do it?"

His lips were warm against my skin as he kissed the side of my face. "It's because I know it. And, so do you."

A chill crept through me. I'd felt my own death in Arys's hands many times, most often when passion drove us into a frenzy of bloodletting and power-fueled sex. I had never voiced this to him. Since discovering that a witch had shown him my death at his hand long before I'd even been born, I intended never to share my sense of foreboding.

"Then why are you concerned with Lilah? She won't be the one. No big deal then." I sought to downplay his worry. My hollow voice betrayed me.

Arys stiffened. He captured my hand in his and gave it a desperate, almost painful squeeze. Anger crashed forth from him, dousing his energy in flames. Power sparked in our joined hands, a flash of blue and gold.

"It's not just about Lilah. I know you asked Shaz and Kylarai to kill you when you rise as a vampire. I knew you'd regret the blood bond, I just didn't think it would be so soon."

I was stunned, but I also felt a little betrayed. Kylarai would never have shared my secret request with Arys. How could Shaz do this to me?

"But, I didn't," I protested. "That was only if I were to lose all control, if the bloodlust were to consume me to a point where I wasn't myself anymore. It was a safety net."

With a storm brewing in his eyes, Arys jerked back from my touch. "You don't trust me. Do you think I would let you face that alone? Do you have any idea how I've wrestled with the guilt of binding you that way? To hear you've asked your wolves for a way out... that hurts."

The atmosphere grew increasingly uncomfortable as we stared at one another. Arys's sire had forced us into the blood bond. Perhaps we shouldn't have rushed into it, but Harley's intent to bond with me had left us no choice. He'd unknowingly played an important part in bringing Arys and I together. Upon discovering this, he'd grown desperate to have us both for himself. Jealousy will drive people to madness.

The blood bond is the vampires' way of binding mortals to themselves through a deep exchange of blood. Though not enough to turn a mortal immediately, it ensured they would rise as a vampire upon their death. To prevent Harley or anyone else from binding me, Arys had done it. Now, his darkness grew in me in a way that threatened the balance of our twin flame union.

"I'm not looking for a way out." I heard the pleading note in my tone and cringed. "I just can't allow it to consume me. It's already starting to. I may be a killer, but I don't have to be ok with it. I can't be like that."

My voice rose dangerously, a near shout that bordered on hysteria. Arys flinched, a rare crack in his armor that allowed me to see the wound I'd inflicted.

"Like me. Isn't that what you're really saying?"

It was my turn to look away. I didn't want him to see it in my eyes, the truth, that the thought of becoming a vampire terrified me in ways I couldn't describe. Vampires were ruthless, cunning and powerful. Ultimately, they existed for the thrill of the hunt, the euphoria of the kill. They felt no remorse. Arys was all of this and yet still human in so many ways due to his connection to me. I didn't want to hurt him.

"I'm scared," I admitted. "I'm not ready to let go of my human side."

"Will you ever be?"

The weight of his stare grew heavy. I forced myself to let him see the fear in my brown wolf eyes. The wolf was my safe place.

"I don't know."

"You should go, be wolf," Arys said, gesturing toward the dark field and the forest beyond. "We don't have to do this now."

My beast leapt against my insides, demanding release. I didn't feel good about leaving this unsettled, but was it even possible to settle? I felt ill.

"Arys, I love you. You know that, right?" I needed something, some kind of reassurance.

A sinking sensation gripped me. I knew Arys had been on edge lately. He had known the blood bond would afflict our twin flame tie, tainting me with his darkness. This was worse. He now believed he'd condemned me to a future I no longer accepted, which made it easier to understand why he was desperate enough to strike deals with demons. I understood his need to protect me from Lilah, but did he really think he could save me from himself?

I resented a choice I had willingly made. This was my burden to bear, not his. If he did something reckless, it might come back on us with a vengeance. I couldn't let it come to that.

"Of course. And, I love you, my wolf." He smiled, a sensual flash of fang that lacked genuine warmth. "After a century of believing I may never find you, I won't lose you now, to anyone or anything. I'm willing to do whatever it takes to protect you, Alexa. Whatever that happens to be, I hope you can learn to live with it."

Chapter Four

The Big Book of Love Spells held my attention while I waited for Toil and Trouble to close for the night. Brogan was finishing up with a few remaining customers. The people I saw in her magic shop, soccer moms, businessmen, little old ladies with walkers, always fascinated me. Looks sure are deceiving. I doubted I looked anything like what one would expect a werewolf to look like, particularly not one with the power of a vampire. With my long, ash blonde hair and brown eyes framed with smoky dark makeup, I probably looked much like any average twenty-something woman. Petite and casually dressed in blue jeans and a tank top with a rainbow colored peace sign, I was sure nothing about my appearance screamed supernatural. Of course, those who could work magic or possessed power of their own saw right through my outward appearance.

As if on cue with my thoughts, the shop door opened, and Gabriel slunk inside. Gabriel was tall, lanky and drenched head to toe in Goth attire. From the spiked collar to the thick eyeliner to the metal band t-shirt, he looked more like the type one might expect to see in a magic shop. However, this kid had serious power. I'd felt it myself, and my curiosity had been piqued.

Relief swept through me. After the look of horror he'd given me the last time we'd both been here, I was surprised he'd shown up. Brogan had arranged this meeting. I had some magically encrypted files that I desperately needed to get into, and she'd been sure Gabriel had the talent to do just that. He shuffled over to the other side of the store without so much as a glance my way.

Shaking my head at some of the silly love spells, I returned the book to the shelf. Did people really think that a few herbs and the right words would make someone love them? Even more disturbing was the possibility that one's will could be bent that way. I suppressed a shudder and moved on to a rack filled with chalices and crystal balls.

"Finally," Brogan announced after she'd locked the door behind the last customer. "Are you two ready? We can go in the back."

I followed her into the back room where several large storage shelves lined the wall, laden with various spellcasting items. In the center of the room was a large round table covered with a red cloth. It sat inside a big circle painted on the bare floor. Gabriel joined us a moment later, sitting opposite of me.

"Gabriel, have you met Alexa?" Brogan was all smiles, clearly used to his sullen teenage behavior.

At last he met my eyes. With a half nod, he said, "You have a pretty wild reputation. How much of it is true?"

"I guess that depends what everyone's saying about me." I shrugged. He was curious and trying hard to prove that I didn't intimidate him. I had to admire his grit.

"Did you really make a vampire's head explode?" He asked with undisguised interest.

I stifled a laugh. "Yes. Several."

"And, did you really kick a demon's ass?"

"That's a bit of an exaggeration." My expression turned sour. Hoping to redirect the conversation away from demon talk, I pulled my laptop out of its bag and slid it across to him. "So, you think you can do this? I'm completely lost."

"I'll give it a shot." Gabriel's mood lightened, and he grabbed the laptop eagerly. "Let's see what we're dealing with."

He peered through a fringe of long, dyed-black hair. I waited impatiently while he clicked around on the keyboard. I had swiped those files months ago. Judging by how heavily encrypted they were, there had to be something worth finding on them.

"Oh yeah," Gabriel murmured after several minutes had passed. "These are definitely spelled somehow. It doesn't feel like serious magic, though. I'm sure I can break it."

"What do you need?" Brogan asked, awaiting instruction.

"Maybe a gemstone. Lapis Lazuli should work."

Brogan grabbed a large black box from a shelf and began to dig through the padded display boxes inside. I watched her with a knot in my stomach. Close to finally finding out what information Veryl had been hoarding, I was as excited as I was anxious since I expected to discover something I would rather not know.

"Here." Brogan placed a royal blue stone next to Gabriel. It was the size of a small egg, streaked with gold that glinted brightly despite the low lighting in the back room.

"What does that do?" I asked, eyeing up the stone.

"It's a truth stone," Brogan explained. "It helps set the truth free."

Gabriel ran a hand over the smooth edges of the stone. It responded to his touch by glowing a deep but vibrant blue. The room grew warm with Gabriel's strong energy. I was drawn to it, unable to tear my gaze from him as softly spoken Latin tumbled from his lips.

After a moment, he paused, staring at the computer screen. I grew restless. I wanted to see it for myself. He shook his head and muttered a few obscenities.

"I'm surprised that didn't work," he mused. "The spell that was used is stronger than I thought. Let me try something else."

Tapping his fingers against the tabletop, Gabriel's thoughtful gaze fell upon me. I raised a brow in question, but his expression remained unchanged. He began to speak the words again, slower this time. Again, the stone glowed, brighter this time. I sensed a shift in the atmosphere, the build-up before a transfer of energy. Was it working?

Without so much as a stutter or a stall in his words, Gabriel leaned across the table and grabbed my hand. He uttered the last word, and an intense ticklish sensation shot up my arm. Our energy merged into one, directed by Gabriel's spell. The crystal responded with a bright cerulean light that was nearly blinding.

"Sorry," he said with a sheepish grin. He released my arm and turned the laptop toward me. "I needed a bigger energy source than myself. You're obviously the natural choice. But, I think it worked."

I dragged the computer over with the eagerness of a kid on Christmas morning. Holding my breath, I clicked the first file of the dozen or so. It opened without issue. I almost squealed with glee.

"Thank you," I gushed. "You're a lifesaver. I owe you one, Gabriel. Seriously."

Darker

He sat back in his seat with a nonchalant shrug, but I could see that he was pleased with himself. "Sure. It was no problem. With power like yours, you could easily do stuff like this on your own. If you learned a few spells."

"No thanks." I smiled. "I'll leave that to you guys. Spells are really not my thing. I'm more of a point and shoot kind of gal."

I poured through the file, finding a blueprint of the FPA building as well as information on how to access the various entrances. That could be handy, as long as the FPA remained in that building. Clicking on another file, I was surprised to discover a copy of what appeared to be a contract. Raoul's signature caught my eye, and my heart began to pound.

Without another look at the document, I backed up all of the files online and closed the laptop. This stuff was better viewed in private, where I could freely exhibit an emotional response to whatever I might find.

"I should go." Gabriel stood up and stretched his lanky body. "If I'm late again, my mom is going to shit a brick."

"How is she taking everything?" Brogan asked with a gentle smile. "Any better?"

"Nah, not really. I'm forbidden to do magic in the house. She's been pretty freaked out since she caught me floating the cat." Gabriel chuckled. "I'm glad that's all she caught me doing."

Brogan's smile faltered, but she carefully twitched it back into place before the boy could notice. "Well, be careful. She's freaked out because she cares about you. Don't give her a reason to worry, and she'll come around."

Gabriel opened his mouth to reply when a crash from the front of the store cut him off. Brogan and I gasped in unison. Before we could react, a figure appeared in the doorway. It was Falon.

He didn't so much as glance my way; his angry pale gaze was locked on Gabriel. Falon crossed the room in a motion too fast to follow. He grabbed Gabriel by the throat and shook him violently.

"You little shit. Did you think we wouldn't find out?" Falon shook the frightened teen so hard his teeth rattled. "You can't lie to a demon and get away with it."

"I didn't see anything," Gabriel choked out. His face turned a dangerous shade of red. "I couldn't. I tried."

I was on my feet, confused but ready to intervene. "Falon? What the hell is this about?"

"Not a word out of you, wolf. This doesn't concern you."

Falon lashed out at me without a move or look my way. I rolled ass over teakettle until I landed splayed against the heavy-duty rear exit. Before Brogan could act, Falon hit her with a slap of power as well. It held her frozen in her chair, unable to come to Gabriel's aid.

Rubbing the back of my head, I grimaced as pain shot through my skull. I got to my feet slowly, wary of Falon's temper. I didn't want another taste of it. Though I loathed the fallen angel with abundance, I'd seen enough of his abilities to know I didn't want to tangle with him. Still, I couldn't just stand by while he throttled a kid.

"You had only to tell the truth," Falon stated, his tone low and malicious. "You're either incredibly brave or unbelievably stupid."

"Please." Gabriel struggled violently. His eyes bulged, and he fought for air. "I'll try again. Even if I can't see anything, I can still do the spell."

"You're damn right you'll do the spell. I still think you saw something. Ready to start talking?" Falon shoved Gabriel hard, sending him sprawling in a heap of flailing limbs.

Blood trickled from Gabriel's forehead. He gulped in deep breaths, watching the fallen angel with terror-filled eyes. Falon didn't move. He was just suddenly there, standing over the quaking teenager with a macabre light in his eyes.

"Come on, Falon," I tried again, willing to risk another bitch slap of power. "He's just a kid. Take it easy."

I got Falon's attention easily enough. A frown creased his brow, and he wore his usual sardonic expression as he sauntered toward me. I braced myself. Falon's asshole extraordinaire persona wasn't new to me, but it was, however, a pain in the ass.

"Listen, you filthy little beast," he oozed contempt. "I didn't come here to be pummeled by your pitiful hybrid powers or to offer you an explanation for my actions. So, save the superhero act. The kid and I have business. Which is none of yours."

The angel was as smarmy and arrogant as ever. He brought my wolf roaring forth with a snarl. My fangs filled my mouth, two on the top and two on the bottom. My fingernails lengthened into claws, and I stared at Falon through wolf eyes. He smirked, enjoying my defensive rage.

"So this is how you get your kicks now?" I demanded. "By bullying innocent kids? I knew you were a worm, but this is really low."

Gabriel coughed as he caught his breath. His eyes were wide as he took in my wolfed out appearance. "I'm not a kid. I'm nineteen."

"He's also far from innocent," Falon replied, continuing his slow advancement on me. "Don't be naive, Alexa. Nobody is guiltless. You should know that."

"I'm not going to keep quiet while you rough him up, Falon." I spat his name with as much venom as he'd injected into mine. We certainly had no love lost between us. I couldn't think of anyone I loathed quite so much.

Falon stopped short of touching me. Invading my personal space in a blatantly rude way, he spread his great silver wings. They were huge, cloaking him from shoulder to ankle and wider than his arms were long. It was an attempt to intimidate me, which didn't work anymore. I was wary of Falon, but I wasn't truly afraid of him.

"Fine," he quipped. "Make all the noise you like while I rough him up then. Just stay out of it. I came for answers, and I'm not leaving without them."

As he looked me over, his pale silver gaze became scrutinizing. Then, he added as an afterthought, "Actually, maybe you could be useful."

Before I could fend him off, Falon grabbed my arm. He dragged me over to Gabriel despite my attempts to shake myself free. Falon's hand was cold and clammy. It made me fight harder, but he held tight. I was no match for his immortal strength.

"Dammit, Falon, let me go. I'm not doing a damn thing for you." My power crashed over me, rising in response to my urgency.

"Oh please, do it. I dare you." Falon's laughter echoed through the room. "You may be a big fish with the other blood feeders, but you're an insect to me. Now, I'm going to ask the kid here a question or two, and you're going to tell me if he's lying."

"So there *is* something I can do that you can't," I scoffed.

Falon released his hold on me but stood invasively close. I leaned away as if that would make a difference. He was a foul creature, and I wanted him to know how pathetic he was.

"Gabriel here is a precognitive clairvoyant. He can see the future for those he touches. You didn't let him touch you, did you, wolf?" The fallen angel's mocking laughter continued. "He touched Shya and lied about what he saw. Now, he's going to tell the truth." To Gabriel, he said, "Start talking. What did you really see?"

"I told you." Gabriel faced the angel with a brave face that was betrayed only by the scent of fear oozing from him. "I couldn't see anything. Nothing. It doesn't work on immortals."

The acrid scent of a lie mingled with his fear. So, he was lying after all. I forced my best poker face into place so I was ready when Falon's attention returned to me.

"So?"

I met his gaze evenly. "He's telling the truth, Falon. Why is that so hard for Shya to accept? I'm sure there are other ways he can sneak a peek at the future."

I crossed my arms and tapped a foot impatiently. The sooner Falon left, the better. I had a few questions for Gabriel myself.

"Of course there are," Falon replied, studying me a little too closely, "but they tend to involve rather heavy sacrifices. Are you volunteering?"

"Why did he send you?" I changed the subject. "Can't Shya do any of his own dirty work?"

"What can I say? I enjoy it."

Falon took a few steps back. He pointed a finger at Gabriel. The air around him hummed with a heavy energy that made it hard to breathe.

"I'm watching you, kid. I'll be back when it's time to do that spell." With a glance my way, he added, "Shya's waiting to hear from you, Alexa. You should follow your twin's lead and make staying alive your priority."

Before I could make sense of his comment, he was gone. The pressure on my lungs decreased, and Brogan was freed of his hold.

"Well, I really gotta run." Gabriel darted for the door.

Darker

I blocked his exit. Shaking my head, I forced him to look deep into my eyes. He flinched, apparently uneasy with my wolf looking out at him.

"You owe me an explanation," I demanded. "I lied for you. Now, tell me what you saw when you touched Shya."

He looked nervously to Brogan who only shrugged and nodded. Swallowing hard, Gabriel shoved a hand through his long, tangled hair.

"I've been trying so hard not to think about it. It was just a glimpse, but it was so awful." He paused as if he had to gather the strength to say it. "I saw his real form. And, it is not human. Not even close. He was standing in the center of a circle, performing a ritual. A sacrifice maybe. Whatever he was doing, he failed. There was a flash of light. It took him out. That's all I saw. I swear. But, I lied. I told him what he wanted to hear. That he would rise to greater power."

"How long ago was this?"

"At least a month or so."

That was before the incident with Lilah where she told Shya he'd never be more than underworld scum. He'd been so sure that he could exchange my blood for a place as her second-in-command when she returned to her dark throne. She had spurned him like he was dirt. He likely wasn't taking that so well.

"Do whatever it takes to keep him away from you," I said, gesturing to Brogan. "Maybe Brogan can help. Get your house blessed by a priest if you have to. I don't care. But, don't let your guard down. Shya's already decided you have power he's interested in using to his advantage. He'll be back for you."

"I know." The color drained from Gabriel's face.

"Shya's a collector of people with power, especially rare power. Trust me, I'm one of them." I dug in my bag for the cross Kale had given me as a birthday gift. Maybe it was time to get it blessed. A thought gripped me, and I turned back to Gabriel nervously. "When you touched me earlier, did you see something?"

His gaze dropped to the floor, and he shuffled his feet. "I really need to get home and make sure my mom is alright."

My heartbeat quickened. "Tell me what you saw."

He couldn't bring himself to meet my eyes. Bracing himself, he shoved by me and ran for the front door calling back over his shoulder, "You don't want to know."

* * * *

I stared up at the church. It was overwhelming in its size and structure. Large white pillars stood at the top of a high stone stairway. A set of wooden double doors beckoned as I made my way up. Several cross-topped steeples perched atop the brick building. It emanated a palpable energy that both welcomed and intimidated me.

The stone steps beneath my feet hummed with vast power. The ambiance was light and breathy, like an unseen breeze that promised cleansing, and it drew me like a caged bird catching my first glimpse of freedom. Could I find a way to ward off Shya and withstand Lilah in a place like this, or was it just wishful thinking?

I grabbed the door handle and gasped. My entire arm lit up with pins and needles until I swung the door open and stepped inside. Shaking off the strange sensation in my hand, I took in the immense interior of the church.

It was breathtaking. I stood in a foyer that looked into the sanctuary of the church. Taking slow, steady steps, I moved beyond the foyer to gaze in wonder at what lie beyond. Paintings of saints and angels adorned the place from floor to ceiling. An elaborate crystal chandelier drew my gaze. It seemed to sparkle with an iridescent shimmer.

"Can I help you?"

A man sitting in the front pew stood up and raised a hand in greeting. A fair distance separated us. I made my way down the aisle toward him. He wore a priest's white collar and dark attire. I judged him to be about fifty. Though physically he was in good shape, his eyes aged him. As I drew closer, I saw the deep lines and shadows evident of a man who has known many sleepless nights.

"I hope so." I smiled, fearing just a little that he'd see right through my human exterior to the monster within. "I came to ask about getting an item blessed."

I withdrew the cross from my shoulder bag, hesitant to hand it over. He accepted it with a raised brow.

"Fascinating." He turned the cross over in his hands, studying it closely. "This looks very old. It must be quite valuable to you."

"Sentimental, mostly."

Darker

"May I ask why you're seeking a blessing?" Curiosity shone in his eyes.

How much should I tell him? Could I trust this man? He was a stranger to me but a stranger who just might believe me if I told the truth.

"I'm experiencing a dark time in my life. Dark forces," I offered. "I could use a touch of light." I cringed inwardly. The same light I sought was supposed to live inside me, but all I felt these days was Arys's darkness.

The priest's face lit up in a gentle smile that radiated kindness. "I'm Father Andrew. Would you like to sit down and talk?"

He sat down on the pew, and I reluctantly joined him. In the grand building, I couldn't shake the expectation of bursting into flames. I sat awkwardly beside him as he said a prayer over the aged necklace. It struck me then that it might be all that I had left of Kale, and hot tears pricked the back of my eyes.

After passing the cross back to me, Father Andrew sat quietly. "Are you all right? Anything you say will be completely confidential. If you're in trouble or something…"

"Oh, Father. I'm not sure you'd even believe me if I told you."

"Try me."

For a moment, I was tempted to take him up on that. Instinct demanded that I keep my mouth shut, so instead I mumbled my thanks and rose to leave. Father Andrew's hand snaked out to grab my arm. I turned quickly, defenses ready. My gaze fell to where his shirtsleeve had ridden up a few inches, exposing the tip of a dragon tail. A dragon tail that perfectly matched the one I also bore.

I met Father Andrew's eyes and saw the knowing glint within. Jerking my arm from his grasp, I stepped back and gathered my power. I was ready to use it, man of the cloth or not.

"You're one of Shya's corrupt priests," I hissed. "I should have known. Is there any place in this city that he hasn't tainted?"

I walked backwards down the aisle between the pews. Killing a priest was something I'd rather not do. If he insisted on giving chase, I'd do whatever I had to.

"Alexa, wait!" He called, advancing on me slowly, hands held up in surrender. "It's not what you think. I got sucked into his games. Just like you. I'm a victim."

The truth of his words was undeniable. I slowed my pace, glancing around suspiciously. Could Shya pop into a place like this? I'd seen him in a church before, but it hadn't felt the way this one did.

"How do you know him? What do you know about me?" I demanded. Was there anyone in this damn town that Shya wasn't after?

"I know you're a Hound of God. A creature meant to combat evil." His voice echoed throughout the church. "Rare and absolutely vital."

"I don't want to talk about that." My voice wavered. "Tell me why you have Shya's mark."

Father Andrew stopped several feet away. Guilt and confusion curved his features into a frown. He tugged the sleeve back down over the dragon's tail.

"I made a deal with him to save a friend," he said bitterly. "But, I was too late. The demon was already inside his head. He took his own life."

"I'm sorry. That was very selfless of you. Something a true friend would do." It was something I had also done for a friend. Taking Shya's mark to save Kale had done neither of us any good. I had done it so Shya would spare his life, but he was dead anyway.

I gave myself a shake and fought back another threatening surge of tears. Crying blood in front of the priest was hardly going to fit his expectations for a Hound of God. I didn't ever want to let myself cry over Kale; then I'd have to admit he was gone. That it was real.

"It didn't save him though." Father Andrew shook his head; the weariness in the hunch of his shoulders conveyed more than any words.

"What is it that Shya hopes to gain by making a deal with you? I know he doesn't do anything unless it benefits him."

There was a moment of quiet while the man gathered himself. He looked so forlorn and frustrated when he forced out, "Access to a relic meant for no demon. Something secret that needs to stay that way. Powerful and deadly. That's what Shya wants from me."

"Holy shit. Sorry," I added, suddenly self-conscious of my potty mouth. "Do you know where it is? Or, what it does?"

"There is plenty of speculation about what it does. Nobody seems to know for sure. If a demon wants it, it can't be good. It's here somewhere, in the city, hidden. I have no intention of helping him find it. I'll let him kill me first." Father Andrew shrugged, resigned to his fate.

My mind raced. "He wants something from me, too. But why? What's he up to?"

"He's building an army to serve him. People like you are his link to the human world. If he controls you, he controls it. Watch out for him and the fallen angel." His tone became pleading. "Don't let them corrupt you. You're a Hound. One of the last."

I threw my hands up and turned on a heel to go. "I can't listen to this. I'm sorry. I'm a killer. A monster. That's all."

"If anyone has a chance to stop him, it's you."

Father Andrew's voice followed me out of the church, but I didn't look back.

Chapter Five

"I don't believe it," Jez announced. "I refuse. Kale can't be dead."

Her red lips twisted into a scowl. With a vigorous headshake, she huffed. I had anticipated her reaction. Disbelief still held me in its grip as well.

We sat on one of the couches at The Wicked Kiss, looking on to the near empty dance floor. After the disturbing evening I'd had so far with Gabriel and the priest, I decided to follow through with my plan to close the club for a few nights. Only regulars were allowed in, which meant more action in the back than out front.

"Briggs can't be that good of a liar," I replied, watching a middle-aged man offer himself to a vampire. The man had more visible bites than I could count. These people must get damn good at hiding the truth behind their daytime personas.

"Says who? He's a government drone. They mess with mind control. Just because he believes it doesn't make it true." Jez's haughty green cat-like gaze landed on me. "You don't believe it either. Otherwise, you'd be a total mess."

I scoffed. "Give me a break. I care about Kale. The last thing I want is for anything bad to happen to him. But, I'm not this lovesick puppy you insist I am."

"Bullshit."

I turned my attention to a loose thread on my sleeve. I'd been wearing a lot more long sleeve shirts than usual these days in order to cover the dragon etched into my forearm thanks to Shya. The ugly demon mark drew a lot of unwanted interest.

"If he's not dead, then where the hell is he? He's been missing for too long. It can't be good." My stomach flipped a few times in response to the anxiety-riddled scenarios that played out in my head.

"I bet they still have him," Jez mused, chewing on a long, tapered fingernail. "Locked up somewhere in that hospital of horrors. We have to know for sure, Alexa."

"Are you saying you want to go in there? Jez, trust me, you don't want to see the inside of that place."

She fixed me with a pointed look. "Let's just say there's a possibility he's in there. How can you live with not knowing for sure? He would go in after either of us. If he is alive, we can't just leave him there."

Such seriousness was rare for the fun-loving leopard. Jez was far more worried about Kale than she let on. Of course, it was possible. I'd entertained the idea more than once myself, but trespassing on FPA turf wasn't going to go over well.

"The chance of getting in there undetected is slim to none," I warned, but I could see the determination in her eyes. She was set on this.

"Then let's not go in undetected. They want you to become an informant so use that to get us in. Tell them you're willing to negotiate."

"That would be a lot more believable if I hadn't attacked one of their agents."

"Your sister is there. That gives you some leeway."

Jez wasn't having a hard time convincing me. Perhaps I didn't need much encouragement. I wanted to believe Kale was alive. Going into FPA headquarters was dangerous. No matter what I told Briggs to get in the place, he still wasn't going to let me search the building.

"Fine," I relented. "I'll try to get us in there, but let's not do anything rash. I don't want to give the FPA any more reasons to keep me on their watch list." After my last experience inside the haunted old hospital that the FPA used as their local headquarters, I was reluctant to go back.

I reached for the bag containing my laptop, itching to get cozy with Veryl's secrets. Butterflies beat a steady nervous rhythm against my ribcage as the computer went through the start-up process. I looked longingly at the bar. Having a whiskey in hand would be nice. Staying alert meant staying alive, so I dismissed the thought immediately.

"The moment of truth, huh?" Jez fidgeted in her seat. "Think there's anything on there about me?"

"We'll find out in a matter of minutes."

I stared at the list of files, unsure where to start. So, I started at the top. Most of the folder names were random letters and numbers. Others had a name mixed into the mess. Kale's, Jez's and mine all jumped out at me right away. My palms grew moist as the first one opened.

It was a brief bio on Falon, of all people. I was intrigued. Unfortunately, it wasn't as juicy as I'd have liked. Falon took his leap of disgrace long after Lucifer's exile. There was much speculation as to what drove Falon to it. Some believed it was a human woman. Other studies concluded that he'd strayed on the promise of power and glory. Regardless, his reputation had always been shady. Nobody but Falon knew why he fell. Whatever it was, it had made him a nasty thing alright.

"Can't say I'm surprised Falon is documented as an asshole," I commented after both Jez and I had read it.

"He makes my skin crawl." She visibly shuddered and made a sour face. "There's something really not right about him."

"There's something wrong with anyone that willingly chooses to embrace darkness after once being light." The words left a bitter taste in my mouth; they hit a little too close to home.

"Open mine next," Jez said in a hushed tone. "Wait, one sec." She slipped out of her seat and went to the bar where she proceeded to pour white rum into a glass of ice. I'd never seen her go for a drink that wasn't sparkly or fruity. She returned to the couch, took a long sip of rum and nodded. "Ok, open it."

With a small laugh, I clicked on the file. Like Falon's, it was a rundown on Jez. For the most part, there was nothing in there I didn't already know. Then, I reached the paragraph regarding her parentage. My eyes widened, and I quickly looked to her for a reaction.

Another silent nod and then she drained the entire glass of its contents. "Looks like my mother's dirty little secret isn't really a secret at all."

"So it's true?"

"Yep. My father is a demon." Her emerald green eyes downcast, Jez gazed longingly into the empty glass. "My mother was terrified I'd turn out just like him. She did her best to beat the demon out of me. I'm still not sure it worked."

I was stunned. Falon had referred to Jez being of mixed blood, but I never would have guessed what he meant. I'd known Jez had experienced abuse in her past, but the raw truth of it was horrifying.

"Jez, I'm sorry. I can't imagine."

"No, it's cool. I've had years to get over it. I didn't even know him. Sometimes though, I wonder how much of him is in me." She met my eyes then and forced a smile. Raising her glass she added, "I hope that's all Veryl had on me. I'm not sure there's enough rum here for me to face anymore of my past. How about you? What does yours say?"

I laughed nervously. "I'm afraid to look. I'm tempted to leave it for last."

"Just get it over with. It's going to drive you nuts until you do."

That was an understatement. It had been driving me nuts since I swiped the files from Veryl's computer the night I'd killed him. Putting this off might be for the best since I had yet to process the events of the past two nights. Of course, it might be best just to get it over with no matter how harsh.

Screw it. I clicked on my file before I could change my mind. I held my breath as I read through it. Jez leaned in close, reading along with me.

At first, nothing immediately stood out as unusual or unexpected. Once I got past the basics, that started to change. Apparently, Veryl had reason to believe my parents were not the people I thought they were. Instead of good ol' hard working, taxpaying Mom and Dad, Veryl had them listed as FPA agents.

I sucked in my breath, holding it until I was sure my lungs would burst. I scanned the rest of the document with growing trepidation. The FPA had recruited my parents shortly after my birth. The government organization was after me from the start, somehow knowing I'd been born with a link to dark power. My father was against allowing them access to me while my mother saw no problem with it. This was when their marriage began to break down.

Soon after Katie O'Brien became the lover of werewolf, Raoul Roberts. This turn of events allowed us the opportunity to prevent the FPA's claiming of the first-born O'Brien girl. By manipulating Roberts's emotions, the FPA were successful in eliminating the O'Briens. The girls were injured and turned in the process. Alexa fled, certain her family was dead. The FPA took the youngest girl into custody from the hospital. We approached Roberts and succeeded in convincing him to take Alexa into his home, protecting her until she was ready to join us.

There was more, details that jumbled together. I blinked a few times, but the words on the screen remained. My mind was a mess as several thoughts struck me. My parents were FPA. Raoul had been a pawn in Shya and Veryl's plan to keep me from the secret organization. My mother had been willing to hand me over to be groomed into a good little government weapon. Dumbstruck didn't even begin to cover it.

"Wow," Jez said softly. "Our mothers could go head-to-head for the worst parent ever award. I'm sorry, Alexa. Judging by the look on your face, you didn't already know this."

"No, I didn't. I'm not sure if I should be grateful to Veryl for keeping me from the FPA or pissed because I don't know why he did it."

"I'm willing to bet the answer is in here somewhere." Jez gestured to the computer.

I closed the file, going so far as to close the laptop. "It has something to do with whatever Shya's up to. He's been collecting people like me for years. People like you."

We shared a look. There was nobody else quite like us. Even Gabriel and the dreamwalker Shya sought, we all had something to offer that almost nobody else had. What the hell did he want with us? It had to be bigger than merely helping him control the supernatural community. And, if Shya was targeting those with specific abilities, what did Kale have to offer that set him apart from any other vampire?

"My brain hurts." I rubbed my temples, unable to read through the rest of the files just yet. "I'll finish going through these at home with a stiff drink in hand."

"Did someone say stiff drink?" A husky male voice rang out behind me. "Don't mind if I do."

Willow appeared behind me with a ripple of air and the sound of feathers being tucked away from sight. He dropped into a nearby chair and promptly offered a hand to Jez in greeting. She eyed him suspiciously while I made the obligatory introductions.

Another fallen angel, Willow was nothing like Falon. Willow had fallen because of his forbidden love for a human woman, a prostitute. His love story didn't have a happy ending.

"Help yourself," I told him, pointing to the unmanned bar.

He paused, a pensive expression on his face. "What happened? Where are all the spooky kids tonight?"

I chuckled at his choice of words despite my dark mood. "We're closed tonight. No spooky kids allowed. Other than the ones with fangs fucking and feeding in the back rooms."

I caught him up on Lilah's unwelcome gift as well as Shya's insistence that I was better off partnering with him. Willow listened closely while relieving the bar of some of its tequila supply.

"Never take anything a demon says as truth. Even if it is the truth, they only use it to manipulate." Willow chewed on a slice of lemon. "Lilah has a weakness. Forget about Shya and find it."

"It might be in those files," Jez said with a shrug. "If I were you, I'd read them sooner than later."

Willow raised an inquisitive brow, his gold-flecked green eyes filled with interest. "You got into the files?"

"Yes, she did." The leopard cut me off before I could speak. "We found some dirt on the FPA that makes me even more confident they have Kale. We need to go in there and find him." She turned to me with stone cold seriousness. "Tonight."

"No way. You don't want to go in there, Jez. Trust me."

"Why not?" Willow's curiosity was piqued. "I'm up for making a little trouble for the FPA."

"Really?" I was skeptical. Could the three of us achieve anything by sniffing around the old haunted hospital?

"Come on, Alexa," chided Jez. "I know you're thinking the same thing. It must be driving you nuts. I'll bet you haven't slept since you heard Kale was dead. You probably paced the day away, bottling up your feelings. Like usual."

"I don't bottle," I insisted with a glower.

"Like hell you don't. You bottle until the pressure blows the lid and bathes everyone around you in a fiery explosion. If we go in there, we'll know for sure. Then, you can mourn him. Or, save him. He would do it for you."

Ouch. That stung. Jez was hitting below the belt now.

"Fine," I relented, albeit grudgingly. "But, don't say I didn't warn you."

I was letting Jez and Willow call the shots, something that didn't come naturally to me as a control freak. The fallen angel was eager for some mischief. I hadn't known him long, but he'd proven to be a loud-mouthed, booze-swilling, self-deprecating yet fun-loving soul. He'd also saved me from a beating that would have left me a bloody pulp. He'd earned my trust. If he wanted to accompany me into the FPA's house of hell, I'd be grateful for it.

Twenty minutes later, we sat parked in Jez's beat up Jeep Liberty a block away from the Charles Camsell Hospital. It loomed in the distance, a dark mass against the night sky. I suppressed a shudder.

"I can feel them watching already." Jez's voice was hushed, as if she feared the disembodied spirits within the hospital could hear us.

"Just wait until you get inside." I laughed, bitterness creeping in. "If we can get in without being swarmed by agents that is."

Willow's gaze stayed on the haunted building. "That's where I come in. I shouldn't have a problem freezing their security system. They won't even know we're in there."

"Until we run into someone," I added. If Briggs caught me in there, I'd never hear the end of it. "Of course, the scariest thing in that place is far from human."

"It feels heavy. Evil. Something that isn't new to any of us. No worries." With a mischievous grin, Willow swung his door open and hopped out.

With an inward groan, I followed suit. This was easily one of the most terrifying places in the city. As we walked down the street, drawing closer, I felt the ghosts of so many who had died horrific deaths, watching us with eagerness. The hospital had many floors, each of them occupied by the dead. From soldiers to children to the insane, the hospital was home to many unable to find rest.

"Where do we start?" Jez asked. "Where did they have Kale last time you saw him?"

An image sprang to mind, one that brought with it a rush of fury. The last I'd seen of Kale, he had been a tortured, naked mess, held captive by humans who had no idea how large the forces they tried to command were. *I should never have left him.*

Briggs had struck a deal with me. He would free Kale, and I would give the FPA access to Veryl's files. Instead, Briggs called to tell me Kale escaped and the deal was off. Lies. Perhaps that was a blessing in disguise; those files should never be in human hands.

"He was in a torture room that could be viewed through one-way glass. It's on the top floor. Heavy agent presence. But, that's not where I want to go." A trickle of fear slithered through me. "I have this feeling we need to go down. Into the basement."

The basement held the morgue, which was creepy enough in its own right. However, the basement also held something sinister, something that had driven Arys crazy. Having to be saved from my vampire's attack by Falon wasn't a fond memory.

We reached the perimeter where a twenty-foot fence topped with razor wire stopped us. That was new. Large signs warning of prosecution for trespassers decorated the fence in various places. Ignoring them, Jez had little trouble peeling back the fence near the bottom. We slipped through with ease.

I would have expected higher security from a government agency. Except their goal was to appear as if they weren't housed within the abandoned hospital, so the real security didn't begin until one was already inside.

I led the way to the far end of the structure, opposite the entrance used by agents. That left us with little more than a broken window to enter through. I wanted to come in close to the stairwell since the FPA had no surveillance on the stairs.

"I'm not sure what's in the basement, but it unhinged Arys," I paused, looking from Willow to Jez. "I think the FPA has something really shady going on down there. Be ready for anything."

Willow didn't seem concerned. If anything, he was excited. Being immortal clearly had its advantages.

The second I dropped through the busted out window into the hall, I was frozen with fear. My heart pounded so loud in my ears I could barely hear Jez's soft whisper.

"What the fuck is that?"

I followed her gaze to the shadow creeping along the wall behind me. In the nearly non-existent lighting I watched it morph as it moved, taking on different shapes. It grew and stretched, becoming a heavily muscled cat. It continued to writhe and ripple, changing into a wolf with bared fangs. Wings sprouted from the wolf's back moments before it shifted into the form of a man.

"It's mocking us," I said in both awe and apprehension.

"It's a shadow weaver," Willow announced, utterly fearless next to us two fidgety mortals. "A demonic force that preys on restless spirits. Harmless to the living, for the most part."

I edged toward the stairwell. Debris littered the floor. From broken boards with nails jutting through to drug paraphernalia and broken glass, the place was a hazard. It hadn't changed in the month since I'd last been inside.

Several ghosts drifted over to check us out. I couldn't see them, but I could feel them darting out to grab my clothing or tug my hair. It wasn't as startling this time around.

"I knew it would be like a horror movie in here," Jez stated, her voice loud in the silence.

"On the bright side, you don't have to see the psych ward upstairs." I picked my way through the graffiti-riddled hall, stepping carefully to avoid rubble.

I kept expecting an alarm to sound as agents surrounded us. So, when we reached the basement door and nobody had stopped us, I started to get an ill feeling.

Willow came to an abrupt halt. "There aren't many places that hold this kind of darkness. It could be dangerous for you."

"Oh God, Lex, please tell me you're not going to vamp out on us." Her tone was light, but Jez wasn't kidding. "Make that me. Tell me you're not going to vamp out on me. I'm sure the angel will survive it."

I was conflicted. Last time, the basement had done a hell of a number on Arys. If Falon hadn't shown up when he did, Arys might have killed Shaz or me. The place might do something similar to me.

"I feel fine, Jez. I'll let you know if that changes."

She nodded, but I noticed she was careful not to have me at her back. I couldn't say I blamed her. She'd survived one of Kale's attacks, so she had every right to be wary.

The basement door was secured with a heavy-duty deadbolt and a security-card clearance slot. Before I could wonder aloud how to get by it, Willow vanished; within seconds, he opened the door from the other side. I waited for some evidence of a security breach to ring out, but again, silence. It was too strange, as if something wasn't right.

"Hot damn you are a handy thing to have around," Jez commented with a smile. "Is there anything you can't do?"

The light in Willow's eyes faltered for just a moment. "There are many things I cannot do."

The stairs were cold, hard concrete. Dimly lit by a dusty, low-watt bulb, it was impossible to see the bottom due to the slight spiral in the staircase. Stone walls lined each side, giving it a small, claustrophobic sensation.

Willow took the lead, which was fine with me. Feeling a curious blend of fear and anticipation, I descended slowly behind him. I shielded tightly, afraid to allow any of the energy down there too close. In my mind, I kept seeing what it had done to Arys.

He'd be livid if he knew I was here without him, but I'd never allow him inside the old hospital again. Never. I had thought for sure he would kill me that night. Stripped of all self-control, he had been reduced to the essence of the vampire without the man, a killing machine.

In all honesty, I had been hoping to avoid Arys. I wasn't in the mood to continue our conversation about Shya from last night. It was far from over. Of that, I was certain.

Jez hovered close as we rounded the bend in the stairs. Her perfume tickled my nose, and I had to fight back a sneeze. That would be a hell of a way to announce our presence to anyone down there. Of course, anything other than human likely already knew we were here.

I expected to see something at the bottom of the staircase. Instead, absolute black greeted us. My chest tightened, and the fine hairs on the back of my neck stood on end.

"And, if you gaze into the abyss..." Willow murmured.

"The abyss gazes also into you," I finished the Nietzsche quote, and my skin began to crawl. Whatever lay below us, it found its new visitors intriguing.

Jez made an irritated noise. "That's really calming, guys. Thanks."

As good as my night vision was, even I couldn't see in absolute darkness. I momentarily wrestled with the decision to drop my shields in order to use my power. Holding my palm up, I took a deep breath, said a small prayer and formed a psi ball that glowed with visible blue and yellow fire. It lit up several feet surrounding us, and we moved forward.

A lengthy corridor kept us moving for what felt like ages. The dark behind us swallowed up the stairs, and we still had nowhere to go but straight ahead. Every step I took was like treading deeper into murky, cold water. The atmosphere grew thick with the presence of evil. I felt like I was choking on it as I struggled for each breath.

A pale blue glow drew our attention to a large room to the left. Double swinging doors blocked the entrance. Willow pushed through without hesitation. Metal tables lined the room, and rows of openings made a grid on the back wall. So, this was the morgue.

It wasn't as creepy as I'd expected, but that did nothing to ease my mind. All that meant was the morgue wasn't the big bad down here. We had yet to find that.

"Oh, disgusting." Jez clasped a hand over her mouth and nose. She was staring at a body on a nearby table.

It wasn't covered very well. An arm hung down, pale and lifeless. The stench of death and decay was overwhelming, assaulting my sensitive nose. I shared Jez's revulsion. I wasn't a fan of this place.

"I don't think there's anything in here." As Willow scanned the room, he seemed to grow somber.

"Are you ok?" I asked, unsure how a place like this would affect someone like him.

"Yes. It's just that I can feel the joy it has, the evil in this place. It thrives on death."

I turned to leave, but a shelf lined with jars caught my eye. Against my better judgment, I leaned in for a closer look and came face to face with a severed head. It floated in a jar of liquid, eyes wide and mouth agape. It was impossible to tell if it was male or female. Next to it was a smaller jar filled with hearts. I gasped, inhaling a lungful of the musty, putrid air. Immediately, nausea threatened, and I fought back the urge to heave.

Darker

"What are these sick fuckers up to?" Jez spied the jars and pulled me away. "And, they say that we're the monsters. I sure as shit don't have anybody's head on the mantel at home."

Vacating the morgue, we returned to the black hall, following the light of my fireball until we reached another room. As I crossed the threshold, a violent, greedy force slammed into me, seeking a way inside. I resisted, struggling to fight it off.

'So lovely,' it whispered in my ear. 'I've been waiting for you. The lost wolf's come at last. Into the darkness where you belong.'

"Did you hear that?" My voice shook, and my whole body vibrated with fear.

"Hear what?" Jez gripped my arm with clawed fingernails.

Willow shook his head; his dirty blond hair reflected the flicker of gold and blue power dancing in my hand. "No, but I can feel it. Entities like that thrive in madhouses. It preys on those with a fragile grip on sanity. Whatever it says to you, don't listen."

A bitter laugh escaped me. "Should I be offended by that? I know I have control issues, but I'm not slaughtering people in the streets."

"Yet," quipped Jez, shrugging when I made a sound of protest. "Sorry, Lex."

The silence was so heavy that the slightest noise was startlingly loud. When a keening wail echoed down the hall toward us, adrenaline crashed through me. I knew I wasn't going to like what lay ahead.

A menacing energy pulsed all around us. It brought my wolf forward as I prepared to defend myself. The disembodied voice had ceased to whisper. It didn't have to. I was already wrapped in a cloak of darkness, feeling the persuasive pull of its influence. It called to the vampire power coiled tightly in my core.

The unmistakable scent of blood hit me like a slap in the face. The distant wail gave way to an ear-piercing shriek. It was hard to tell if it was male or female. Whoever it was, they were suffering.

My stomach clenched. I considered turning back, but it was a selfish urge that I squashed. The closer we drew to the noise, the harder it became to suppress the vampire side of me. My control was being stripped away faster than I could fathom. The last thing I wanted was to prove Jez's suspicions right.

The bloodlust dominated my focus. I let my gaze wander over Jez and Willow in turn, wondering what they would taste like. A naturally born shifter had to be a delicacy. The angel, that could be heaven right there.

No. None of that. The constant battle between wolf and vampire warred on inside me. This was no time to lose it. Even as I refused to give in, the hunger burst forth to drown me in a wave of illicit desire. Wicked thoughts danced through my head. They didn't belong to me. It was Arys's darkness, and I had to remember that.

Jez seemed to be unaware of the battle going on inside me, but Willow was looking a little too intently in my direction. I gestured for him to lead the way, and we continued toward the eerie sounds. My apprehension dissipated with each step. I was eager to see where the tangy aroma of terror came from.

"Oh, shit." Jez's two words summed it up perfectly.

The interrogation room we came upon was like nothing I could have imagined. The morgue was child's play compared to what we saw through the window in the large double doors. My jaw dropped.

Steel chairs lined the room in neat rows of five or six. Most of them were currently empty. Torture devices, sharp and wicked, lay on a tray close to a man in a white lab coat. A green-tinted light cast the large room in a sickly glow. Two agents flanked him, their backs to us. One of them I recognized as Agent Asshole, the prick that had come with Juliet to The Wicked Kiss for Kale and me.

They had a woman shackled to a chair. Her dark hair was plastered to her forehead with blood and sweat. Her head hung limply.

Agent Asshole leaned in close to her, slapping her face. "The sooner you tell us what you know, the sooner this will all be over. That's what you want, isn't it?"

"The tests all reveal that she's human." The doctor concluded after a look at the computer in the corner. "Maybe she doesn't know anything. If she were just a victim, he would have no reason to share anything of importance with her. Leaving her alive may have been a mistake on his part."

It was difficult to get a good look at the woman with the men blocking her, but I was sure I caught a glimpse of a vampire bite decorating her pale neck. The sinister energy that had been hovering pressed closer, forcing itself on me like an unwelcome lover. I pushed back, refusing to bend to its will. I was not going to be its bitch; I was stronger than that.

The agent shook his head. Snatching a scalpel from the tray, he pressed it to her throat and snarled into her face.

"I happen to know Arys Knight doesn't leave his victims alive. I want to hear anything and everything you know about him. Start talking, or I'll send you back to your family in pieces."

Fear shone in her eyes as she rolled them up toward him. "I told you already. I don't know a damn thing about him. I didn't even know his name."

I cringed. My heart dropped into my stomach with a painful thump. They were interrogating one of Arys's victims. That I had not seen coming.

"Is there anything you can remember? Any names he may have said? Anyone else present? A blonde perhaps?" Agent Asshole was aggressive. The scalpel bit into the woman's flesh, and she shrieked.

Jez and I exchanged a look. So, the dirtbag wanted me, did he? He was about to get lucky.

Anger burned in my gut. The malevolent entity preyed upon it, and I found myself wanting to give in to the wicked urge to spill human blood. I'd start with the agent. Even as I thought it, I knew I was slipping into that dark place with no way back until the hunger had its fill.

"No," the woman sobbed. "There was nobody else there. I told you. Please. I just want to go home."

Agent Asshole glowered. It looked strikingly similar to a pout. "There's got to be a way to get a lead on those two," he snarled to the others, "before Briggs does. I want that promotion to Captain."

The doctor shuffled about, gathering papers and tidying their instruments of terror. "Briggs is busy chasing demons. You probably won't have to worry about him much longer. The dumb bastard will get himself killed."

"Let's hope so."

I held my breath. The scent of blood was stripping away what was left of my composure.

"You should go," I whispered to Willow. "Get Jez out of here. Find Kale. Or try."

"We can't just leave you here." His green eyes were filled with curiosity. "Are you alright? Your eyes are a really messed up blue."

Solemnly, I shook my head. "Don't worry about me. If you can't find Kale, just get out. I don't want them to catch you guys here."

Willow didn't question my decision the way my lovers would have. He trusted that I could take care of myself. Jez gave my arm a quick squeeze before the two of them disappeared into the dark.

Agent Asshole was getting impatient. His cheeks were red, and his breath came fast. He was full on shouting at the quaking woman.

"This is your last chance to give me something I can work with."

I burst through the double doors, my hands blazing with power, but I had only a second to enjoy the shock on each man's face.

"Can you work with this, asshole?"

Chapter Six

"What the fuck?" The doctor muttered.

Both agents reached for their weapons. I didn't think twice before unleashing the power I held. The nameless agent flew backwards, crashing into a table laden with saws and scalpels of varying sizes. His gun skittered across the floor, stopping when it hit my foot.

I didn't give the asshole agent a chance to use his. With careful focus, I tore it from his hands with little more than a thought. Satisfaction thrilled through me.

"Did you come to save her or to keep her from talking?" Agent Asshole smirked. He appeared a little too happy to see me.

"Neither. I'm here for someone else."

"Well, then I guess I have no further questions." With a vicious cackle, he slashed the scalpel across her throat.

Blood gushed from the fatal wound. It poured down her chest, dripping to the floor where a puddle quickly formed. Every breath I took stripped away what little remained of my self-control. The basement's unholy occupant encouraged my dark side to reign.

I was fast learning that the FPA weren't the model citizens they painted themselves to be. The more I saw of them, the more I believed I'd gotten the better deal by ending up with the monsters.

"You just made things very easy for me," the agent sneered. "No need to waste time with transients when I can go to the source."

"Come on, then."

He approached me as one might advance on a snarling dog, cautious but ready. I was aware of the scalpel in his hand and the Taser on his hip. I'd have to make sure he never got a chance to use it. With great effort, I forced the wolf back down. If I injured this prick with fangs or claws, he would turn. No way was that happening.

"You were pretty stupid to sneak down here. There's no Briggs or Juliet to save your ass. They never come down to the basement. Then they'd have to get their hands dirty."

"Just keep talking."

I was ready when he tackled me. It didn't stop the cold hard floor from knocking the breath from me as my back took the brunt of the fall. Bringing my feet up, I used his weight and momentum to throw him over my head. He crashed against a chair that turned over with a loud crash of metal.

On my feet first, I jumped on Agent Asshole, pinning him to the floor. He fought to dislodge me, but I held tight. The strength of a werewolf far outweighed that of a single man. I landed a few punches before he brought his cast-bound arm up to block me. Just a month ago Kale had broken the man's arm, and I was more than happy to re-break it for him.

His bitter coffee breath puffed into my face as he struggled to overpower me. Instinct commanded that I tear his throat out. I ached for the hot splash of blood on my tongue. I hadn't come with the intent to kill anyone, but resistance was fast growing futile.

I wrapped my hands around the agent's throat and squeezed until his face turned a horrid shade of purple. A noise behind me had me whirling to blast the other agent before he could use the Taser in his grip. Unfortunately, that allowed the doctor to approach from the other side. The telltale click of a hammer being cocked held me frozen.

"Stand up. Slowly." He pressed the cold gun barrel against my temple.

I did what he said, sure I could blast him before he could pull the trigger but unwilling to take the risk that I was wrong. Caution had me doing what he said though I wasn't as afraid as I was mildly amused. Playing along was best for now.

Agent Asshole wielded his Taser like a man on a mission. He hit me with it before I could brace. The shock of electricity slammed through me like a sledgehammer, dropping me like a sack of meat. My limbs seized, and I twitched on the floor like a drunk on *Cops*. Fabulous.

"You twisted bitch," the agent spat. He rubbed his neck, which was red and welted in the shape of my fingers. "You want to see the basement? Oh, I'm gonna show you the basement. Get up."

I gasped, struggling for each painful breath. My entire body shook as I tried to get up. I was unsteady on my feet, my limbs numb. With a gun in my face and a Taser-wielding asshole behind me, I suddenly wasn't feeling so confident anymore.

"Take a good look around," Agent Asshole said. "Because you're never getting out of here."

Recovered from my attack, the other, quieter agent stepped up, yanked my arms behind my back and slapped cuffs on me. I was familiar with these cuffs. They had the ability to reflect my power back at me with a negative charge, rendering my power useless.

The agents shoved me along through the door. The doctor remained to clean up. Both agents flanked me, hovering dangerously close.

"Got nothin' to say?" The loud jerk poked me in the ribs with the gun he'd retrieved. "That's fine. You'll be screaming in no time."

Wherever Jez and Willow were, I hoped they were far from here.

As we walked down the corridor, we reached a row of wall sconces that cast the hall in a dim light. The further we got from the basement entrance, the brighter the light became. Harsh fluorescent bulbs flooded an adjacent hall lined with solitary prison-style doors. This was just getting better and better. I went along willingly as they steered me down that hall. I didn't have much of a choice. Agent Asshole shoved me against the first door we encountered.

"Look."

I didn't have to be told twice. Curiosity drew my attention to the small pane of glass in the center of the heavy iron door.

Inside was a man sprawled on a double bed. The mattress was fluffy, the blankets thick but aged. The concrete walls were decorated with drawings depicting buildings, scenery and an array of people. The man scribbled furiously in a notepad, bringing another image to life by the light that a reading lamp provided him.

"He's precognitive." Agent A informed me. "We promise to take care of his family. In exchange, he shows us likely outcomes of events and decisions."

"Looks like he's lost his mind," I muttered. The poor bugger was oblivious to anything but the image he was creating. "So what you're saying is he's a prisoner. Forced to be a tool for the government until it drives him mad. I wish I could say I was surprised."

Agent A tugged his tie loose, careful not to take an eye from me. "Hey, his daughter can afford to go to Harvard now."

A cold, sick feeling spread through me. The FPA was no better than Shya. Their shady deals worked out only to their benefit no matter what they bartered away. Sickening.

"He doesn't speak anymore," the other agent spoke directly to me for the first time. "It won't be long before he's on his way to the end of the hall. They all end up there eventually."

I turned sharply toward the agent, but Asshole jabbed me in the ribs again, forcing me on.

"Shut up, Hastings," he snapped. "There's a reason I do all the talking."

"You mean other than you simply love the sound of your own voice?" I asked with a sour smile.

Agent Asshole responded by slamming me into the next door we came across. My teeth smacked together, and my head bounced off the glass. But, the pain was quickly forgotten when I saw what was on the other side.

A little girl lay curled up in the center of the bed. Surrounded by stuffed animals, with her golden locks spread out on the pillow, she looked so tiny and innocent. She couldn't have been more than eight years old. Fast asleep, the sound of my head bouncing off the thick door had failed to wake her.

"You fucking monsters," I breathed, unable to tear my gaze from the child's sleeping form.

Agent Asshole chuckled and nodded his greasy head. "Looks can be deceiving. Ain't that right, werewolf? That kid may look sweet and pure, but her parents begged us to take her."

"Why? What can she do?"

The chuckle continued. The bastard enjoyed giving me the grand tour. I turned to him with a glare.

His shit-eating grin vanished. "She summons demons. And, it ain't for tea parties."

My jaw dropped. She was just a child. "But how? Why?"

Darker

"It doesn't matter," came his flippant reply. "As long as we can use it."

"Is that all you see her as? A tool? An object?" I resisted him when he tried to shove me away from the window. The result was another Taser blast that had me seized up on the floor. I bit my tongue, and blood filled my mouth.

Agent Asshole stood over me. "A weapon, actually."

It was several minutes before I could get up. As I struggled to get my stiff muscles to move again, I thought of all the ways I'd love to kill him. One day the FPA agent would look back on this night with regret. So much regret. He was my victim; he just didn't know it yet.

"Alright, enough with the dramatics," he barked, hauling me to my feet. "Keep moving. We're not there yet."

I held my tongue, knowing if I opened my mouth a growl would come out. My wolf itched to bury my thick fangs in his throat, but she would have to wait.

Though we skipped several doors, he showed me a few more of the FPA's prisoners. From a seventeen-year-old pyrokinetic to an elderly necromancer, it was like taking a walk through the living museum of hell.

"Dreamwalker," Agent A boasted as I looked in upon a middle-aged woman reading and doing her best not to acknowledge us. "Ever seen one? They don't sleep much."

Still I said nothing. Within that room lay my key to the lock that held me bound to Shya. The dragon etched into the flesh of my forearm burned. I owed Shya a dreamwalker. Only then would he release me from our deal and remove his mark. I knew I would never do that. Handing over a human being to Shya would make me as evil as he was. Though I might be many things, that could never be one of them.

I gave a wistful sigh which Asshole mistook for fearful acceptance.

"Ok, that's enough," he announced. "Time to show you to your cell. I mean room. This will be worth it even if I never make Captain." Again with the cackling chuckle. "If you live through the night, maybe you'll prove to be useful after all."

"What are you talking about?" I studied Hastings, finding his solemn expression unnerving. He wouldn't make eye contact, focusing instead on a door near the end of the hall.

I gasped when Agent Asshole began to aggressively frisk me. He relieved me of my phone, the only personal belonging I had on me.

"I suppose I'll have to report this." He sounded disappointed. "Maybe I'll forget for a day or two. Give you some time to get reacquainted. If you survive the reunion."

Hastings pulled out a set of keys that included a swipe card with each one. He unlocked the deadbolt, ready to follow up with the swipe card. "Ready?"

"Are you going to leave me in these things?" I indicated the cuffs.

Agent Asshole considered it. I willed him to free me. Cut off from using my power, I felt naked and helpless.

With a nod to Hastings, Asshole trained his gun on me, inches from my face. Ignoring my request, he watched as Hastings opened the door just wide enough for me to enter. Then, he shoved me through the dark opening so hard that I fell inside. Unable to catch myself, I landed painfully on my back with my bound arms beneath me.

"Hey, werewolf," Asshole spat. "Welcome to the execution chamber. This is where we put the trouble makers. Found a use for your vampire after all."

With that, the door slammed. There was a thud as the deadbolt slid into place. I rolled over and pushed to my feet. The strong, honey sweet vampire energy swept over me, and my heart stuttered.

I turned to take in the room. Hope gave way to relief and then renewed fear. My gaze slid over the double bed, the nearby writing desk and the vampire standing in the center of the room.

With five centuries of bloodlust in his mismatched eyes was Kale.

"Not you," he said in a broken whisper. "Dear God, not you."

Chapter Seven

Kale stared at me, uncertain and confused, as if he couldn't be sure I was real. Something passed behind his eyes, a glimpse of someone I knew. Then, it was gone.

I had wanted so badly to find him here. I hadn't really allowed myself to believe I would. Before I could react or speak, he moved in a blur, shoving past me. With both fists, he pounded on the window.

"Not her, you mother fuckers! Anyone but her."

The rage emanated from him. It swirled around me, a cloud of anger that I responded to against my will. I was burning with the urge to reach out to him with my power, to draw in his sinfully sweet energy. It called to the part of me that was all vampire; that side of me recognized him as mine.

Slowly, he backed away from the door, away from me to the opposite wall. His fists clenched and unclenched. His eyes darted around, settling on me in brief intervals.

"You need to get out of those cuffs. You have to be able to fight." Squeezing his eyes shut, Kale shook his head vigorously, battling a hunger that wouldn't be denied.

When at last he dragged his gaze to mine, I saw the eagerness for blood and death burning in his gorgeous eyes. One brown, the other blue, it was a mesmerizing feature that promised to enchant his victims as he killed them.

"I don't think I can. The cuffs are on too tight." I concentrated on slow, steady breaths, knowing my fear would only entice him.

"Try." His pupils dilated, a dangerous sign of excitement. "Try hard."

I strained against the cuffs, testing their limits. They were damn tight. My only chance of slipping them would be to shift. I could potentially slip them during the change. Being wolf in this place couldn't possibly be a good idea. It would also mean being nude in human form once the change shredded my clothing. Decisions, decisions. If it meant surviving Kale, I'd do what I had to.

"Kale? Talk to me. What have they been doing to you?" If I could keep him talking, I might buy myself a few minutes before he tried to kill me.

He didn't answer. Instead, he stared at me as if he was seeing someone or something else. A stranger. A victim. He might have seemed coherent, but I was fast realizing he wasn't all there.

"Kale?" I tried again. My big plan to find Kale and bust him out of here couldn't have gone more pathetically.

"This can't be real," he said more to himself than to me. "I've been waiting for it too long."

A frown creased his brow. His dark brown hair was dishevelled. Shirtless and barefoot, he wore only pants. He had a primal appearance that triggered every one of my defenses. I understood Agent Asshole's remark about the execution chamber. He'd thrown me in here expecting Kale would kill me, and judging by the bloodlust's madness lurking in the vampire's gaze, I was as good as dead. Once he snapped, it was all over. I had to get out of the cuffs.

I slid down the wall to the floor. I stretched my arms as far as I could, trying desperately to slide my cuffed hands over my butt so I could pull my legs through and have my hands in front of me rather than behind. I'd still be bound, but it would give me a better chance to defend myself physically.

It was a tight squeeze. My hands nearly became stuck beneath my rear end. Gritting my teeth, I forced them to move. Something pulled in my shoulder, but a moment later, my hands were in front of me. I stood up quickly, keeping my back to the wall and Kale in my line of sight.

Kale began to mutter to himself, something low and hard to make out. To me he said, "This is all your fault."

Before I could tell him to snap out of it, he was on me. I brought my hands up to protect my throat, but it was useless. He grabbed the handcuffs and used them to slam my hands against the wall above my head. Pain shot through my wrists, and I whimpered. No matter what he did to me, I wouldn't scream. That's exactly what he would want.

With his free hand, he grabbed my chin and forced me to look into his eyes. It wasn't difficult for him to draw me into his thrall. With my power cut off, I was unable to combat the strong pull.

"Why can't I escape you?" His words dripped both venom and wonder.

My instinct was to tap my power and toss him across the room. Unfortunately, the mere act of reaching for it ricocheted it back at me with searing intensity. I gave a startled yelp. Having my power tied was unnatural and agonizing.

"The tables finally turn," Kale murmured, leaning in to press his face to my hair. Inhaling my scent, he ran a finger down my neck, dragging it over my jugular. "I'm not the one at your mercy this time. I'm going to enjoy this."

Sweet, soft-spoken Kale was absent from the creature caressing the throbbing vein beneath my skin. My mouth was as dry as cotton when I tried to speak. Nothing I could say would stop him. The FPA had done a good job of breaking what was left of his already fragile hold on sanity.

"I came for you," I said quietly, fighting to stay calm.

"You came for freedom from the guilt. You put me here when you refused to release me from your clutches." Kale brazenly ran his tongue over the vein he'd touched. "Time to finish what you started."

I cowered against the wall. If he bit me, he was getting my knee in the groin. The touch of his mouth on my flesh was alarming and unwelcome. Hungry and possessive, his intentions were clear. This was not the lusty touch of a forbidden lover; it was the predatory manipulation of a killer.

"You're out of your mind. This isn't you, Kale." I tested his hold on my hands, but he held tight. "It's this place and these people. There's something evil here."

In response to my words, the small desk lamp flickered a few times. The murky sensation of the basement dweller was stifling. It was influencing Kale as it had Arys, as it had tried to do to me. From what I'd seen, vampires were more susceptible to it. Good for me earlier. Bad for me now.

"There are many evil things here. Including you and I." He sucked at my sensitive skin, his fangs scraping over the fount of blood beneath the surface.

A pulse of dizzying energy caught me in his trap. Despite my growing fear, my body responded to him, betraying my mind and confusing my heart.

"Please, don't do this." Inwardly, I cringed. Begging would only feed his fire, yet as my panic rose, my rationale failed me.

His head snapped up, and his eyes blazed with wicked hunger. "I'm not ready for you to beg yet. But, I'd love to hear you scream."

His free hand slid around my throat, tightening just enough to limit my air intake. "Pain?" Kale taunted with a vicious grin. "Or pleasure?"

Before I could feel relieved that he so quickly released my throat, he slid a hand between my legs. A fresh flood of adrenaline hit me. I wouldn't have thought I had any left to spare, but the uncharacteristic action had me ready to fight.

I bared fangs, and a snarl slipped from my lips. This couldn't be happening. Not like this. Not with him.

"Don't worry, Alexa." He oozed mesmerizing charm. "I'd never force you. I don't have to. Because you want it."

"Like hell I do. Stop this now before you do something you'll regret later. I can help you, Kale." Even as I spoke, my will was being manipulated.

The alluring draw of his heady vampire essence stirred my desire for him to life. I always wanted him but not like this, as his victim. As hard as I fought, I was falling under his spell. My will faded fast. With little more than clothing between us, his teasing fingers coaxed forth a groan.

"You said once that you never wanted it to happen like this," I accused. I was running out of time.

"That was before you abused your power and made me your bitch." Bitterness colored his words. He stroked my sweet spot, smiling when I gasped.

Kale was high on the thrill of the hunt. I couldn't get through to him. It was just a game, one he would inevitably win. What would Arys think when it was Kale who killed me?

The warm rush of arousal chased away what little remained of my resolve. Kale had five centuries of seduction and bloodshed driving his careful strategy. We had shared one hurried, wild rain swept encounter, yet he had never touched me intimately like this. I longed for him to devour my body and blood.

With a sudden fright, I realized how strong his influence was. A final surge of desperation forced me to act. I brought a leg up between us and shoved my foot into his midsection. I shoved with all the strength I could muster, launching Kale across the room. His grip on my cuffed hands slipped but pulled me forward in the process. I caught myself before falling. With hands clenched into fists, I braced for his retaliation.

Kale wasn't put off for long. He picked himself up and eyed me with a spark of malevolent glee.

"Alright then. Pain it is."

Shit. I didn't wait for him to come at me, not after a comment like that. As awkward as it was with my wrists attached, I succeeded in landing a blow that left my knuckles hurting. After landing a few more, it dawned on me that he was allowing it. Never a good sign.

I backed off, putting as much space between us as possible. Kale swiped at a dribble of blood dripping from his bottom lip. Then, he laughed, a sound so tainted with evil it made my skin crawl.

"Last chance to change your mind," he offered, taking slow steady steps toward me.

"Here's an idea. How about you change your mind, and instead of trying to kill me, you help me find a way out of here."

"Tempting. Though honestly, I've spent weeks locked in this hole thinking about what I would do if I ever got my hands on you again."

He threw me before I saw it coming. I crashed into the desk and hit the concrete floor. It skinned the palms of my hands and caused the cuffs to dig into my flesh. I did a quick check to see if I was bleeding but didn't think so. Blood would be very bad.

On my knees, my hair in disarray around my face, I peered up at him. No semblance of anything that had ever been human looked back at me. Kale was all vampire. I was going to die in here with him. The FPA had gotten what they wanted all along: me at their mercy. I should never have come here. I could almost hear Arys in my head scolding me for such a dumbass move.

No sooner had I thought of him than I felt his presence in my mind. The waves of his worry reached me and guilt struck.

'Where the hell are you? I'm looking for you.' Arys's annoyance translated just fine through our mental connection.

Instead of trying to form a coherent thought, I allowed him to see through my eyes. Together, we watched as Kale dragged me to my feet.

"He's here, isn't he?" Kale asked, holding me tight. "I can feel him. Good. He can watch."

I fought to get away, but he was stronger than I was. My power gave me an edge over Kale. Without it, I was a flailing, panicking mess.

'Oh, hell no.' Arys's sudden fury burned inside me as if it were my own. 'He's a dead man.'

Arys's intent to come for me had my panic going into overdrive. 'You can't come in here,' I told him. 'You know what it does to you.'

Kale shoved me down on the bed. The squeak of springs was loud, and his weight atop me was suffocating. I thrashed violently, doing all I could to escape. He pinned me easily. Pressing his groin against mine, Kale shoved my hair aside and bit into my neck with a vicious snap of fangs.

It hurt dreadfully. I screamed, unable to hold it back. Blood poured from the wound. Kale swirled his tongue over the bites, making a strangled sound of pleasure as he did so. He was getting off on the fact that Arys was present for this.

I felt Kale grow hard against me, and my heart leaped into my throat. The more I fought, the more persistent he was. He jerked my pants down, taking my underwear along as well. The muggy basement air caressed my exposed flesh, and for a moment, I thought I heard disembodied laughter. This place thrived on such acts of terror and violation.

'Fight him, Alexa. You have to.' Arys wasn't able to hide his panic.

"Kale, please," I shouted, my voice bordered on hysteria. "Don't do this. It's not you. I know it's not you. Please."

When he looked into my eyes again, I fell silent. His delicious energy rolled over me, trying to drag me back under. I saw my way out, and I took it. Kale forced two fingers inside me. With a soft moan, I allowed it to happen. I invited it. Playing the wanton victim wasn't hard.

Arys was a silent witness. What he saw, what he felt through our connection, repulsed him, not because of what Kale was doing to me, but because I was allowing it and even enjoying it.

"Kale," I purred like a sex hungry seductress. "Kiss me."

Without hesitation, he pressed his lips to mine. I drank in the scent of him and the taste of my blood in his mouth. It mingled with the blood coming from his cut lip. It was bittersweet. As our blood taunted my lust for him, our violent reality crushed that secret dream where Kale and I made sweet love the way we never would. Arys's presence gave me the strength to resist Kale's vampiric charms. It was both a blessing and a curse. I clung to our twin flame connection, seeing it for the rare and wondrous thing it was.

Kale's attention returned to my bleeding neck. He sucked at the bloody bite while exploring me with his fingers. Though I was faking the glamoured victim act, I couldn't deny the pleasure he stirred within me. That was real.

I counted to three and brought my knee up into his groin as hard as I could. He cried out in pain and rolled onto his side. I grabbed the lamp from the desk and smashed it over his head. It slowed him but didn't put him down like I'd hoped, so I went for the chair next. It was heavy and wooden, slamming into his skull with a sickening thud.

I held it ready to bring down again, but Kale didn't move. I nudged him just to be sure he wasn't trying to fake me out. I set the chair down but kept it close while I fixed my clothing. Thank God for having gotten my hands in front of me. I wouldn't have stood a chance with them behind me.

'I really don't give you enough credit,' came Arys's relieved thought.

'Isn't that what I've been saying for a while now?'

I pressed a hand to my neck. Blood streamed through my fingers to drip on the floor. Kale hadn't taken it easy with that bite. This could be bad.

'You need to get out of there. I'm coming for you.' His insistence was worrisome. This place would eat him alive.

'Don't be an idiot, Arys. This place will kick your ass. Again. If the FPA don't do it first.' I glanced around the dimly lit room. The lamp base had shattered, but the bulb remained lit.

I didn't think Kale would be out for long. I went to the door and stood on my tiptoes to look out the window. I saw only the door across from me. A faint light glowed beyond, but I couldn't see the occupant.

I banged on the window a few times, fearful of rousing Kale. If he started to move, I might have to hit him with the chair again. I banged again, adding a shout along with it. It was futile I knew. If anyone heard me, it would likely be Agent Asshole and his pitiful excuse for a partner.

'Don't come here, Arys. Get a hold of Juliet. Tell her I'm here. And, find Jez if you can. I need to know her and Willow made it out.'

'Of course, you had accomplices.' His disdain was evident.

A shadow moved in the hallway. Someone was approaching. I tensed. The surprises kept coming. It was Bianca, and she was in a hurry.

I backed away from the door and grabbed the chair. I'd let Kale kill me before I let Shaz's lover lay a hand on me. She opened the door and slipped inside, closing it fast.

"I'm here to get you out," she said in a rush, eyeing the chair in my grip and Kale's prone form on the bed. "We have to hurry."

"Are you kidding me? I don't trust you."

"I don't blame you. I wouldn't trust me either, but you've got to believe me; I'm sorry for what happened with Shaz. I respect you, and not just because you kicked my ass." She glanced furtively toward the door. "But, we really don't have time for this now."

"I can't leave without Kale. He's the reason I'm here." The prospect of freedom was promising. However, the thought of leaving this building for the second time without Kale was crushing.

Bianca's long black ponytail swung as she opened the door and peeked into the hall. "I'll come back for him later. We've got to go. Briggs doesn't know you're here yet. Trust me when I say you want to keep it that way."

I was torn. Could I trust Bianca? For all I knew she could have unsavory plans for me. Despite what he'd just done to me, I didn't want to leave Kale.

'What are you waiting for? Get the hell out of there before Briggs knows he has you,' Arys warned.

I cast one last glance back at Kale and followed Bianca into the hall. "How did you know I was here?"

Instead of heading back the way I had come in with Jez and Willow, Bianca led me through a maze of halls in the opposite direction. She paused to remove the horrible handcuffs. I rubbed my bruised wrists and gratefully tapped my power. It surged through me, a comforting sensation.

"I ran into your friends. I recognized the leopard. She told me about Hunter. The man is an oversized child with a gun. It's ridiculous."

"Hunter? You mean Agent Asshole?"

Bianca laughed, a short clipped sound. "Yeah, that'd be him."

A tall, leggy thing, Bianca had ebony hair and eyes that glittered with sensuality. She'd seduced my wolf mate, making him her willing blood slave. I hated her. That she sprung me from Kale's prison rubbed salt in a wound that might never fully heal. It was one of life's little kicks in the teeth.

"So, where is Jez now?" We passed a wing of empty rooms rife with spiritual unrest. The residual energy screamed of violence and death. Spirits swarmed me. They pulled at my clothes and whispered obscenities in my ears. I shielded against them, forcing them back.

"She got out. With the angel, who called me a harlot." Bianca slid a sidelong glance my way. "I suppose I deserved that."

"I don't want to talk about it."

If we dredged this up, I wouldn't be able to censor myself. I wanted to blame her for taking Shaz away from me, to tell her she's the one who turned him into a junkie and drove him out of town. It wasn't true though. She had merely taken advantage of Shaz's weakness, but it had started with Arys and me.

"Fair enough. I get it. I'd hate me, too. But, I was just taking what he was freely giving," she said, leading me to the left when we reached a T in the corridor. "This way."

We rounded a corner, and I was happy to see a stairwell ahead. I wanted desperately to escape the truth lurking behind her ugly excuse. My adrenaline had long since run out. I forced myself to keep moving, shoving aside the blood loss and exhaustion of having my ass kicked.

My short-lived imprisonment was almost over. I couldn't wait to get away from the writhing black mass plaguing my every step. I cast a wary look at the vampiress, curious as to how it was affecting her. The last time I saw her here, she had been on the top floor, far from the basement.

As blessedly short as my stay had been, I was ready to get out. So, when Agents Hunter and Hastings stepped into our path, I groaned in exasperation. Without hesitation, I slammed them both with the power pent up inside me. It felt so damn good to unleash it.

"Bianca, what the fuck are you doing down here?" Hastings grunted. He gasped for breath and reached for his weapon.

Bianca was on him before he could aim it. Her guttural snarl echoed in the dank, empty corridor. The atmosphere hummed with her savage hunger. She bit into Hastings with the intensity of a rabid dog. That answered my earlier question. She couldn't handle it down here either.

I fixed my attention on the asshole I now knew as Agent Hunter. He stared up at me with terror-filled eyes. The force of the blast I'd hit him with kept him pinned to the rubble-littered floor. I stood over him, savoring the way his human energy so easily bent to my will. I could feel his fragile heart, every beat palpable. So easily, I could crush him. I bent down, retrieved my phone from his pocket and gazed deep into him.

"Agent Hunter, you've made a very big mistake. I'm going to leave now, but I promise I will hunt you down and kill you slowly. And, you will love it even as you're screaming for your pathetic life."

Anger flashed in his eyes. I didn't hang around long enough to hear his retort. Leaving Bianca to have her way with the agents, I sprinted up the stairs with that disembodied voice begging me to stay. I didn't stop running until I had escaped the haunted hospital, leaving Kale behind for the second time.

Chapter Eight

"Ok, we're not doing that again." I collapsed in the passenger seat of Jez's Jeep. "Not only did I get my ass kicked by two humans, but I have Shaz's playmate to thank for springing me from Kale's private prison."

"You saw Kale?" Jez turned to me excitedly, almost side swiping a parked car as she drove us away from the hospital. "You're bleeding. Are you ok? Is he ok? What happened?"

I sucked in a deep breath and slowly let it out. I turned in my seat to look at Willow who watched me with an expectant expression.

"He's far from ok," I said, reluctant to tell them everything. "That place has driven him mad. He bit me. Obviously."

"And?" Jez prompted. "Come on, spill it."

"What happened, Alexa?" Willow spoke up, a knowing look in his gold-flecked eyes.

I gripped the door handle tight as Jez took a sharp corner. "They cuffed me and locked me in a room with him. He attacked me. And, he tried to take more than my blood. He didn't get far."

My cheeks flushed hot. I stared out the window, wishing I could forget the entire thing.

'I won't be forgetting.' Arys's unbidden thought added to my unease.

'Can we talk about this later? I'm safe now. I'm going home.'

'I'll meet you there.' He slipped away, closing the mental door between us before I could either agree or refuse.

"Wait, are you saying he tried to...?" Jez was aghast, leaving the question unfinished. "Son of a bitch. I knew we shouldn't have left you alone."

Willow showed no surprise. "Are you alright?"

"Is it still a violation if you like it?" I asked bitterly. "I'm fine. I'm not sure I can say the same for Kale. Arys knows and he's pissed." I waved a hand, dismissing the subject. "Did you guys find anything after we split up? Because I saw something I can't ignore."

As Jez drove through the city, I held a tissue to my bleeding neck and told them about the people that the FPA kept in the basement. They in turn told me about the lab they had discovered deep within the maze of halls, where gruesome experiments were being performed on live supernaturals and humans.

"I've never seen anything so fucking scary." Jez shook her head, remembering. "They're up to no good in there. It's like the shit that nut job conspiracy theorists talk about. Everyone thinks they're full of crap, but they're not."

As she spoke, I went cold inside; I was relieved that I'd only had to contend with Kale. It took a lot to truly scare me, but the things Jez went on to describe were deeply disturbing. Some experiments caused human and supernatural mutations with grotesque malformations; others seemingly compared disease or poison progression between mortal species, leaving the limp victims slowly dying. One restrained vamp even had an assortment of shifter limbs grafted onto his body.

Did they take samples from Juliet? My ill feeling grew. It was no wonder the spirits in there were so restless.

"Humans playing God," said Willow. "It happens all the time. Still, it's worse when the demons do it. In every generation humans try in one way or another to harness the power of the supernatural for their own gain. It never works out well for them."

He didn't elaborate and I didn't ask. That conversation would have to wait for another time, preferably one with copious amounts of alcohol. After what I discovered in Veryl's file on me, I'd be having a chat with Shya soon. Until then, I didn't want to entertain thoughts of what the demons might be doing.

"I don't know what to do about that place," I muttered. "I don't feel right just leaving all those people locked up in there."

Darker

Jez's tight smile was sympathetic. "If you keep going in there, one of these times you won't come out."

* * * *

The plentiful scents of the forest were a great comfort. I paused to sniff at the earth, savoring the many things it told me about the creatures that called this place home. A doe and her young had passed through earlier. The rich foliage emanated purity. It washed away the remnants of the city and its obnoxious sounds and odors.

Sunrise was an hour away. I hadn't wasted any time vacating the city and heading for home. I was in need of some time to myself, in my town where I could run free in the surrounding forest. I made it to my house before Arys did and took the opportunity to abandon my human form and the life that went with it, if just for a while. Maybe I was avoiding him, but the freedom I found in being wolf was comparable to none. I needed it.

I loped through the trees and brush trying to shake the things that plagued me. I wouldn't let myself replay what had happened with Kale. He had victimized me. I'd both loved and hated it. I knew better than to trust the monsters, even those who claimed to love me. Love didn't stop a vampire from being what they were. If anything, it made it worse.

Slowing my pace, I slipped into a copse of trees that had come to be one of my favorite places. In amongst the trees was a small pond. The sound of crickets and croaking frogs greeted me. An owl peered down at me from his perch in a nearby spruce. We shared a look, a brief acknowledgment of our mutual acceptance and respect. Nature got it right. What the hell was wrong with everyone else?

I padded over to the pond and sat beside it. My tongue lolling out, I gazed into the water at the tiny creatures that called it home. My ears twitched, picking up the many sounds of the forest right before night retreated to allow the dawn. I felt safe. I belonged here. There was just one thing missing.

I raised my nose to the sky and howled. The sound echoed in the stillness. I waited, knowing I wouldn't hear the reply I ached for but hoping anyway.

Shaz should have been by my side. I longed to see his white fur shine just a little brighter in the moonlight. He didn't even know about the new house. I was happy to have my own little piece of forest near my backyard, but I wanted to share it with him.

I stayed there beside the pond until I felt Arys's insistent nudge in my head. 'Get your furry ass back here, Alexa. You can't avoid me forever.'

'I can try.' I let a glimmer of amusement show; I enjoyed antagonizing him.

'I'm waiting for you.'

As much as I would have loved to welcome the sunrise there amid the calm and comfort of my forest home, my lover called, and I could only avoid him for so long. I headed for home both eager and reluctant to see Arys.

A great span of field separated the forest from my backyard as it did with most of the houses in the outlying area. My house was a little better because it was beside a cemetery, where very few wanted to live. I had just one neighbor on the other side of the graveyard, hidden from sight.

Arys stood in the backyard with his arms crossed over his chest. He watched me approach with a haughty arrogance that quickly turned to appreciative wonder. I sat back on my haunches, staring up at him.

"You're magnificent." He moved closer, a flicker of vampire fire in his midnight blue eyes. "And, as much as I love to see you as wolf, we need to talk."

I simply stared at him. He could talk; I would listen. That way this couldn't blow up into a fight. I knew that look in his eyes. Arys was going to say something I wouldn't like, and he was bracing for a clash of wills.

"Really?" He prompted after a few minutes of staring at one another. "Is this how you want to do this?" When I didn't move, he nodded. "Alright, fine. Have it your way. I shouldn't have to tell you how stupid it was to go back into the FPA building, but apparently I do. Briggs could have caught you. It's bad enough that anyone caught you. And Sinclair... I don't even know where to start."

He paced the length of the yard, waving his hands in a grand gesture of ire. "He was going to fuck you and kill you, Alexa. You know why? Because you're so deep in his system, it's the only way he'll ever be rid of you. If he gets out of there, you'll never be safe from him."

I wanted to argue, which was exactly why I'd stayed in wolf form. Being patient and allowing Arys to vent first would be better for both of us. Yet, the fire had already sparked within my belly. We shared the need for a good fight. Though my instinct was to tell Arys he was wrong, that Kale would never hurt me, I knew I could no longer believe that.

"He's not going to get away with what he did tonight," Arys declared. "I can't let him."

A muscle twitched in Arys's jaw. He ran a hand haphazardly through his black hair, making it more of a sexy mess than usual. The mixed scent of cologne and hair products, an aroma that was solely his, reached me. It made me itch to bury my face in his neck and savor the many sensations of him.

"The last thing you need to deal with is a psychotic vampire with an incurable obsession. It will distract you from the real issue, Lilah. She's going to do everything she can to force your hand. She'll keep targeting those you've sworn to protect. Those you love." He sat heavily on the small concrete wall encircling the fire pit in the center of the yard. "We have to stop her."

We sure did. I agreed with him there, but I still didn't believe playing nice with Shya was the way to do it. I considered shifting back to human form but decided to hold off a little longer. Arys was doing just fine spilling his thoughts and feelings with my silence.

"She won't stop until you willingly surrender your blood to break her curse," he continued with a shrug. "I don't know what to do. I just know I have to protect you."

His desperation was so tangible that I pawed the grass and whined. It was unusual for him to show such vulnerability. If Shya caught a whiff of it, he would use it as a weapon against Arys.

Our eyes locked, and I peered into my vampire with hope that he would see how much his concern meant to me. Arys had always put my safety first. Unfortunately, that often meant hiding things from me or doing things without my knowledge. I did my share of things without making him aware, like I had tonight, but it was going to catch up to us eventually.

"I know you think I'm wrong about this, but Shya knows things that could help us. He has abilities we don't. And, he wants the same thing we do." The hardness was back in Arys's enchanting gaze. "I made a deal with him, Alexa."

That did it. That was all I had to hear; I couldn't keep quiet anymore. I shifted so fast it hurt. In a fluid, smooth motion, I was standing there naked before him. Crossing my arms, I fixed him with my best take no shit expression.

"Are you out of your damn mind?" I asked in disbelief. "Please tell me that was just a ploy to get me to shift."

"No, it wasn't." Arys's gaze travelled over me, taking in my nudity with appraising interest. "I told him we'd co-operate with him until Lilah can be dealt with. We all play nice until we get rid of her. That's it."

"Too easy. There's no way that's it." I shook my head vigorously. "He's a demon, Arys. He can twist your words, take them literally or figuratively. Whatever. He can't be trusted. Bottom line."

"He offered protection for you, Alexa. Shya doesn't want Lilah getting her hands on your blood either. It can be useful."

I stared at him, incredulous. "Have you forgotten he's the idiot that told her my blood would break her curse? That blew up in his face when she refused him. Now, he wants to save his own ass. This isn't about you or me. Shya is in it only for himself. Trusting him would be stupid. This isn't like you, Arys."

Arys rose and came to stand before me. The spark between us flashed at his sudden close proximity. "I don't trust him. In fact, I wish there was a way to kill two birds with one stone. Shya's been pulling strings behind the scenes for so long. Now, he's stepping out front and center, and that doesn't sit well with me. If we get close to him, we can find out what he's up to."

Again, he looked me over, lingering where my arms covered my breasts. I was ready to argue now so oozing sensuality wasn't going to work in his favor just yet. I stood my ground, prepared to let him have it.

"I can't help but notice you keep saying we," I observed. "I didn't agree to pal around with Shya. You did."

"That's right. I did." He nodded, fire smoldering in his eyes. "I told you I would do anything to make sure you're safe, and you are not going to make me feel bad about it."

Frustration shook me. I was ticked that he had gone behind my back to talk to Shya. After the night I'd just had, not to mention my week so far, this was the last thing I wanted.

"Safe? Until Lilah's out of the way, and then what? Then he follows through with that little promise to kill me. Did you forget about that?" My words came fast and furious.

I remembered the demon's sly threat very well. Shya was uneasy with me being the light half of a twin flame union. He threatened to kill me, so I would rise as a vampire, so Arys's darkness would tip the precarious balance between us. Maybe there was more to it.

"Of course not." Arys scowled. "You should really stop underestimating me, Alexa. I always get what I want. That won't be any different with Shya."

"Your cocky attitude is going to get us into trouble. One of these days," I warned, "you won't be right. And then, you'll be sorry."

We stared into one another with fierce intensity. Arys reached to brush the hair back from my face. A mischievous smile graced his lips.

"One of these days," he echoed in a low murmur. Then he dropped to his knees before me and pressed his lips to the intimate place between my legs.

My breath caught. A rush of sudden desire thrilled through me. What a crafty way to end an argument. "This doesn't mean you automatically win."

"Doesn't it?" His mouth moved against me, stirring my arousal.

The touch of his tongue sent jolts of electricity through me. Instinctively, I buried my hands in his soft tousle of hair. My knees weakened, and he gripped my hips to steady me.

"You play dirty, Arys." My throaty whisper coaxed a chuckle from him.

He flicked his tongue over me, hitting that sensitive spot that had my breath coming fast. I shuddered and clung tighter to him. The way he touched me was softer than usual, a gentleness that was rare for Arys.

"You love it," he said, guiding me down to the grass.

It was cold against my back but felt nice due to the heat flooding my limbs. I stretched languorously on the soft cushion of green. Arys kept up his tender worship of my body. He lifted one of my legs, propping it over his shoulder so he lay nestled between my thighs. Holding my hips tight, he licked me with a persistence that had me crying out.

Our fights could be downright scary, but there was always that wild element of eroticism to it. This was different. Instead of the fiery coupling we so often enjoyed, this was a delicate expression of love rooted in a deeper place. It was as strong as it was intimidating.

The dizzying explosion of climax had me seeing stars. Arys brought me over the edge to bliss. I watched through a pleasure-filled haze as he stripped off his clothing and aligned his body with mine.

Gazing into my eyes, he said, "I love you, my beautiful wolf. No matter what happens, don't forget that."

As much as I loved to hear endearments from my dark vampire, this one struck me as cryptic. Kale's forceful actions, I was certain, had truly frightened Arys. Before I could over-think it, Arys gathered me close and slipped inside me with a gentle thrust. He decorated my face in fevered kisses. I held tight to him as we moved together, uniting as one.

The power rose between us, fuelled by the passion of our actions. Arys guided our rhythm with slow, steady strokes. Buried deep within me, he claimed me with total abandon. The guard Arys held firmly in place shattered, exposing his rarely seen tender side.

A sense of anguish was in his energy; the tortured desperation in the way he held me conveyed something that he would never let out in words. I could feel it as if it were my own, crushing and almost painful. Tears welled up in my eyes as it overwhelmed me.

I felt it deep in my core, a twinge of the fragile humanity he'd once had but now knew only through his link to me. The kind of love Arys had for me came from a place of light that had gone dark long ago. The trace of me that he carried inside him always, that was his weakness. In that moment of desperate lovemaking, I was certain that Shya knew it, too.

Arys rolled us over so I was on top, disrupting my thoughts. He pulled me down hard, thrusting up to force a cry from me. He touched my chin, drawing my gaze to his. Raw, unbridled need shone in his eyes. The power spiralled around us, trapping us in the eye of the tornado. I moved atop him, instinctively matching his stride. White noise built to a deafening roar.

Many times, I resisted how solid our connection had become. However, moments like this made it undeniable. I was completely his.

I threw my head back to stare up at the sky. The darkness had thinned as dawn approached. It wasn't far now. Soon, it would chase us indoors. I closed my eyes and focused on the way Arys felt inside me. Each slick stroke brought me closer to ecstasy. For a brief time, nothing else mattered.

Collapsing on his chest, I gasped for air as the waves of climax swept me away. His arms went around me, holding me with a possessiveness I'd come to know well. I relaxed into it with his name on my lips.

"I trust you," I whispered, pressing tiny kisses to his chest and neck. "But, I don't trust any deal you make with that demon. He's dangerous, Arys. Maybe more so than Lilah in some ways."

"Don't let him ruin this moment." Arys ran a hand through my hair, stroking it lovingly.

I swallowed hard. I couldn't help but say what I was feeling.

"Don't let him ruin us."

Chapter Nine

"You know I would never let anything happen to you." Arys's voice thundered through the house. "You can't punish me for doing what I feel is best."

"I'm not trying to punish you, Arys. I'm trying to warn you." I moved around the kitchen in my bathrobe, making a much-needed latte. Sunrise had driven us inside where our argument had picked up right where it had left off, much to my dismay.

Arys sat at the island watching me. His glower was both sexy and frightening. This was going to be a hell of a long day if we were at each other's throats the entire time.

"And, I'm trying to make you see that right now we need to choose the lesser of two evils. And, that is Shya. We can bargain with him. There's no hope of bargaining with a woman who has already killed to get to you."

The afterglow had been short lived. No amount of sensual lovemaking could eliminate the ever-burning conflict we shared. In light of everything that had gone on lately, I wanted to feel united with Arys. It wasn't happening.

Shirtless, his hair standing up in disarray from our backyard romp, Arys flipped through a newspaper flyer. He turned the pages angrily, as if the paper itself had dared to defy him. Stifling a sigh, I turned back to the coffee machine, tapping my fingers on the counter as a stream of steamed milk filled a mug. I found it increasingly difficult to suppress my growing irritation.

"There is no lesser of two evils," I said quietly. "Not this time."

Darker

"It's better to have Shya working with us rather than against us. You've got to pick your battles, Alexa. This is not the time to battle him."

I stirred a splash of Irish cream into my coffee and lifted the cup to my lips for a sip. Heavenly. I would miss many things when I became a vampire. Caffeine and liquor would be high on that list.

"What about battling each other?" I quipped. "When does that stop?"

Arys ignored my question, feigning interest in a flyer for a furniture sale. "Shya won't harm you. He swore not to."

"Oh yeah? What did you have to promise him in return for that oath?"

"It's nothing. Don't worry about it." His evasiveness worried me. Hiding things wasn't new for Arys, but it was rarely ever good.

"Don't play this game with me." My temper flared. The urge to smack him with my coffee mug was strong.

Arys dragged his gaze to mine. It was guarded, impossible to read as he decided how much to tell me.

"I promised to torture some information out of someone for him." He tried to come off as flippant, like it was no big deal. It didn't work on me. I've been inside Arys's mind. I knew how he worked.

"Who?"

I drank my coffee, staring at him over the rim of the cup. Tension had me gripping it a little too tightly, and I had to force myself to relax.

"Bianca," he said with a shrug. "I can't imagine why you'd have a problem with that."

I was conflicted. She was one of the few people I truly despised. I would have the image of her atop Shaz burned forever in my memory. Still, it felt wrong to stand back and allow Arys to do horrible things to her.

"She saved my ass from Kale," I uttered the words in a hollow tone.

"So what? She also fucked and bled your wolf. Several times." Arys laughed bitterly. "Too little too late. Isn't that what you said to Briggs? Some actions can never be forgiven."

My gaze dropped to the granite counter top. I didn't know what to say. Too much had gone on recently. With Shaz's indiscretions, my own rash actions and Arys's readiness to kill without a second thought, forgiveness was a touchy subject. One we ultimately had to accept, or live always with walls between us.

I walked over to the heavily draped patio door and split the blinds apart an inch with a finger. Arys was far from where the beam of light fell inside the kitchen. I peered out at the sunlit backyard. Sparrows and chickadees fluttered about the patio, ducking into the small birdhouse filled with seeds. It had been Kylarai's idea.

I watched as a squirrel scampered up, lacking stealth but making up for it with speed. It swiped some seeds from the bird feeder and disappeared across the lawn with several birds chirping harshly at its retreating form. The sense of calm I got just from watching the activity of nature out my door was instant. I took a deep breath before turning back to Arys.

"What information does Shya want from Bianca?"

"He's looking for something. He thinks the FPA knows where it is. That's all I know. I didn't ask a lot of questions. He didn't volunteer a lot of answers."

That triggered a memory of Lilah not so long ago searching Veryl's office for a mystery item. Now, I was intrigued. If it was something everyone wanted, there had to be a good reason. My gaze darted to the laptop on the table. Veryl's files might shed some light on this mystery.

"You should know better," I scolded. "You could be helping him get his hands on something he should never have."

"Honestly, as long as it doesn't affect us, I don't give a damn what Shya does."

I grumbled obscenities under my breath. With coffee in hand, I sat down in front of the laptop and turned it on. I could feel Arys watching me.

"Always on the hunt for answers," he observed. "You're going to drive yourself crazy."

"Already halfway there," I tossed back. "Every time I find answers, I only end up with more questions. I can't stop looking. I'm sick of being in the dark. Especially now that I know my parents worked for the FPA."

Arys's noise of surprise gave me some satisfaction… Until he followed it up with a snotty remark.

"That explains so much, although it doesn't explain why the hell you would willingly walk back into that building if you knew that. You're reckless, Alexa. I get that. I grudgingly accept it. But, when did you become such a fool?"

"Did you just call me stupid?" I spun in my chair to face him, a growl rumbling in my throat.

A smirk curved his lips. "I did no such thing. Are you looking for a fight, my love? You know I'm always happy to comply."

"I noticed." With a scowl, I turned back to the laptop. I was touchy and temperamental. I was mad at him for making a deal with Shya, certain it would come back to haunt us.

"Are you really that pissed off at me? I only want to protect you." His tone was serious; all sense of playfulness had vanished.

"I feel betrayed," I confessed. "You warned me about Shya. You gave me shit for accepting the Dragon Claw from him. Now, you're making deals with him. It's shady. It makes me ill."

The silence hung heavy and long. I stared at my laptop. I was afraid to see what expression he wore. The truth was I felt insecure. I'd already lost Shaz. Kale had gone from forbidden lover to murderous enemy. Arys was mine in the deepest sense, yet the promise of trial and conflict between twin flames had me worried. We weren't meant to live happily ever after.

There was a squeak as Arys slid off the island stool. He joined me at the table, dragging a chair close to mine. "What is it you're not saying?"

"I miss Shaz like crazy." I sighed; those words carried a heavy weight. "I watched us fall apart, and I was helpless to stop it. I can't go through that again. Not with you."

"That will never happen," he insisted, but I could see the doubt in his eyes. He knew as well as I did that being bound to one another didn't guarantee us anything. Arys was quiet, thoughtful. After a minute he added, "Shaz misses you like crazy too, you know."

I stiffened. The files momentarily forgotten, I turned to him in shock. "Has he been in touch with you?"

Arys froze. If the vampire could have paled, he would have. Realizing the error of his words, he shook his head and swore.

"He's called a few times." The admittance fell from his lips like acid. It burned. "He needed to know you were ok."

"Then why didn't he call me?" It stung that Shaz would stay in touch with the man he could barely stand but not with me. "And, why the hell didn't you tell me?"

Arys reached to take my hand, but I stood up and walked away from the table. I felt betrayed by both of them. How many other things were the two of them hiding from me? Maybe I was blowing it up bigger than it was. I'd been missing Shaz for weeks now, fearing that he would never come back. This hurt.

"He asked me not to tell you. He knew if he called you, he wouldn't be able to stay away. It's killing him not to be here with you, but he's feeling better now. The urges, the need for a fix, it's not consuming him anymore."

My shoulders slumped and I sighed. "That's good. I'm happy to hear that. I'm just feeling sorry for myself. And, it irks me when you guys talk about me. It's stupid, I know."

I felt remorseful. I couldn't begrudge Shaz the time and space he needed. I owed him the same understanding he'd shown me so many times.

"You don't want us fighting, but you don't want us talking." Arys forced a dramatic sigh. "Make up your mind, woman."

I smiled, a painfully tight action. "Yeah. Good luck with that."

Knowing Shaz was doing well would go a long way in helping me sleep easier. It didn't erase the irritation I felt toward Arys for hiding the information. He knew how desperately I'd been missing my wolf mate. He'd had the ability to ease my mind, but he chose not to.

My phone rang before I could further vent my frustration. The fast-paced strains of "Gangnam Style" filled the room, and I flipped Arys the bird. He made no attempt to hide his glee. The bastard was always changing my ringtone to the most ridiculous songs. He'd do anything to embarrass or annoy me.

It was Brogan, not entirely unexpected but possibly worrisome. "Brogan, hey," I answered. "Everything ok?"

"Fine. I didn't wake you, did I? I wasn't sure if you'd be asleep or not."

"Nope. Not yet. What's up?"

Her voice was tight, pitched a little higher than normal. "Gabriel's mother called. She said he never came home last night. I'm worried about him."

"Shit," I cursed. "Any idea where he may be?"

"At the moment? No. But, I know his buddy's band is playing a gig tonight at The Spirit Room. I think there's a good chance he'll be there." There was hesitation on the line. "Would you mind coming with me to check it out? I know you have more pressing things to deal with. No worries if you can't make it."

I didn't have to consider it for long. Gabriel was practically a kid but a powerful one. Shya wanted him; therefore, I wanted to make sure Shya never got him. Plus, I still had to put the squeeze on Gabriel myself. He had a vision when he touched me, and I damn well wanted to know what it was.

"I can make it. No problem. What time should I meet you there?"

When I hung up, Arys was giving me the look that meant he was going to shadow me all night while ridiculing my decision.

"Don't start with me, Arys." I held up a hand, cutting him off before he could speak the words that accompanied the look.

"I wouldn't dream of it." The look he shot me oozed the sarcasm his tone did not convey. "Just be careful, ok? I know you want to save the kid, but don't forget you need some saving yourself."

I laughed scathingly; I wasn't willingly playing the victim. Between Lilah's sick attempt to force my hand and Kale's blatant abuse, I was done with it.

"Wrong. Maybe it's time for everybody else to need a little saving from me," I snarled, angry with no one in particular but angry just the same. "I'm sick of pretending I'm not one of the monsters. Maybe it's time to start acting like one."

A frown blended with a scowl to adorn Arys's face in a dark expression. "Careful what you say, love. We both know you don't mean that."

"Like hell I don't."

Arys left the table, coming to pull me into his arms. I tensed at first out of sheer stubbornness, but I could never resist him. Sinking into the comfort of his embrace, I sought something deeper, something permanent. There was no such thing. We lived moment to moment, and I had to be grateful for that. I was, but looking ahead, fearing what had yet to come and might never come, it was breaking me down. I would face Lilah when the time was right. Until then I intended to protect people like Gabriel from the demons and the FPA.

"Come on," he guided me toward the stairs. "Let's go to bed. You need to sleep once in a while."

"You go ahead." I cast a longing glance at the laptop. "I'll be up in a few minutes. Promise."

Arys's gaze strayed warily to the computer. "Alright. Don't be long. Or, I'll come down here and carry you off over my shoulder. Caveman style."

I waited until he'd gone up to my bedroom to grab the laptop off the table and slip out onto the patio. Settling myself in a chair where I could watch the birds, I opened up a file and began to read about Kale's sadistic mental state when Veryl first recruited him. It hit too close for comfort, so I put it away for another day and opened a different folder instead.

I shielded my eyes from the bright morning rays. The sun didn't burn me as it would a vampire, but I was incredibly sensitive to it. Though I genuinely enjoyed its brightness and warmth, I couldn't handle it for long.

Veryl had done an impressive job compiling info on all of us. I was a little awed by his collection of tidbits on people who had outlived me by centuries. It would take time to peruse it all thoroughly. Since Arys was waiting for me, I skimmed through, marking parts to return to later.

I would have loved to spend all day reading the dirt Veryl kept on everybody, but fatigue was setting in. The events of my night caught up to me, and I yawned, exhausted. I had places to be later, and if I wanted to be of any use to Gabriel, I needed to sleep.

* * * *

A restless slumber had me tossing and turning. Every time I started to slip beneath the surface into unconsciousness, I would feel Kale's hands on me again. I'd awake with a jolt, safe in the confines of my darkened bedroom.

I lay there with Arys stretched out beside me. If the frown etched on his face was an indication, Arys's dreams were also less than pleasant. Closing my eyes, I snuggled in against him.

Darker

My thoughts strayed to Veryl's files. There was a lot to go through yet. So far, I had learned that Shya had promised Lilah protection if she would help him keep his demons in line. What I wanted to know was protection from whom?

The night she had given me the Dragon Claw, she told me Veryl was blackmailing her. His threats to expose her to someone had fueled her need to see him dead. That was where I came in. I had been the one to kill Veryl, and I wondered if I would regret it.

If I kill him, everything he has on me leaks to the people I want it kept from. That's what she said, her reason why I had to kill Veryl. So, Lilah did have a weakness. I just had to find out who it was. There's no time like the present. I started to sit up, and Arys's arms went around me, his grip tight.

"Don't even think about it," he muttered into his pillow. "There's at least three hours until sunset. Go back to sleep."

"I can't. I was just going to do some reading."

"No."

I lay back down and huffed, a dramatic exhalation of breath. "It's important. About Lilah."

"No." Arys pulled me closer, burying his face in my neck. "It can wait a few more hours."

"Fine." I didn't really want to argue. I was happy to stay put beside him. He was right. I needed to let things go for a while, at least long enough to get a decent sleep.

In Arys's arms I drifted back to sleep, finding peaceful rest this time instead of fitful dreams. When I woke again after sunset, I was just starting to feel rested. With a groan, I hugged my pillow closer. Would a sleep-in day be so wrong?

Against my will, I dragged myself out of bed and into the shower. I had time to peruse the files further before heading to the city.

"Come back to bed for a bit, Alexa." Arys beckoned me with a finger. "It's a wonder you even slept at all."

"I'm not tired. Besides, I want to read through the rest of those files before we go." I stood in the en suite bathroom dragging a brush through my long, wet hair.

"The files can wait. They've waited this long." The weight of his gaze was heavy upon me.

"No, they can't wait. The FPA used Raoul's affair with my mom to murder my parents. That's why they have Juliet. They would have me, too, if Veryl and Shya hadn't intervened." I met his eyes in the mirror. "That was in the files along with some info that may help me deal with Lilah. I need to read the rest."

I filled him in on the details I had while examining my reflection. I gave my head of ash blonde hair a shake. Maybe it was time for another change, something big.

"Maybe I should cut my hair," I mused. "What do you think?"

Arys shook his head vehemently. "I think you should read the files. Anything to keep you from hacking off that sexy mane."

I smiled. It was a small victory, but I'd take it. While Arys took over the shower, I hurriedly did my makeup. Dark, smoky liner outlined my brown eyes. A dash of mascara, a hint of blush, and I was done. I dressed in black leather pants and a cleavage-enhancing top. Then, I was off to the kitchen where I promptly got acquainted with a cup of coffee.

I was limited on time so again I scrolled through the files waiting for something to catch my eye. I needed a solid day to do nothing but read Veryl's meticulous notes. He'd gone to great lengths to obtain and keep some of this information. I was eager to dive in. Unfortunately, it wouldn't be tonight.

"Don't get obsessed, Alexa." Arys swept into the kitchen with the scent of shampoo trailing him. His hair was wet and he was shirtless.

"I'm not," I said, distracted by the sheer beauty of him. "Now that I have access to the files, I'm afraid not to take advantage of it."

Arys leaned down to kiss me. Cold drops of water fell from his hair to run down my chest. "Damn, you look sexy tonight. You'll have men falling at your feet. Think you can fight in those pants?"

"I'm hoping not to have to fight at all. But, I can fight in anything." I grinned. "If anyone has people falling at their feet, it will be you. I have yet to meet a woman that doesn't want to be your victim."

"Does that include you?" He nuzzled me, a wolfish gesture that spoke volumes as to the depths of our bond.

Darker

Reaching around me, Arys closed my laptop despite my protests. "We should go soon," he said. "If you want to be ready for anything, we should hunt first."

"No way." I slapped his hand away from the computer. "I don't want to. Just give me a stiff whiskey, and I'm good to go."

"Until the bloodlust hits you, and you lose your friggin' mind." Arys gave me a dark look.

Ignoring him, I gathered my things. I tossed my phone into my shoulder bag and swiped my car keys off the counter.

"Since you won't let me dig up dirt on Lilah, let's get going. If you want to suck some young thing dry, that's your business. I don't want any part of it tonight." I headed for the front entry to dig through my footwear. Arys was hot on my heels.

"When are you going to accept what you are?" He boldly swiped the shoe out of my hand and tossed it on the floor. "You're not human. You never will be again. Denying what you are will only hurt you in the long run."

With an indignant glare, I picked up a pair of boots and studied them. "I know what I am, Arys. I'm a werewolf. In case you've forgotten."

I slipped the black ankle boots on. They had enough heel to give my petite frame some additional height but were still low enough to run or fight in. It was a warm night. I was torn. If I wanted to carry the Dragon Claw, I'd have to wear a long coat.

"You're more than a werewolf. You're vampire too." Arys's tone was hard, unrelenting. "You can't run from that. Living in denial will drive you crazy. You can either accept it and stay sane or end up like Sinclair, a five-hundred-year-old basket case."

I zipped the boots up and turned to face him. "I get that you're having a hard time with this. I admit it; I'm scared shitless to become a vampire. It's not like I have a choice, but I'll deal with it my own way, in my own time. Back off."

The tension between us soared. We stared at one another, and I saw my anger reflected in his eyes. I didn't want to go head to head with him again. Not tonight.

Arys's energy was scorching hot. A muscle twitched in his jaw. I was dreading the tirade that was coming. He surprised me. Spinning on his heel, he stormed upstairs to finish getting dressed. His parting shot was deadly, a blade of words that sliced deep.

"Fine. You're on your own. When you lose your fucking mind and drown in a sea of blood, don't say I didn't warn you."

Chapter Ten

Music poured down the street from The Spirit Room. Hard rock serenaded the night. It put a little extra oomph in my step. I never could resist the sound of electric guitars.

I perused the line up at the door for Brogan and swaggered past a small group of leather clad, long-haired guys sharing a joint. Their whistles and catcalls brought a blush to my cheeks. Not one to normally seek out male attention, I couldn't help but be flattered. It wasn't often I had human men reacting to me that way. It was nice to know it had nothing to do with power or supernatural hungers.

"Alexa," Brogan called from near the front of the line. "Over here."

Her dirty blonde hair lay on her shoulders in soft waves. In tight blue jeans and an Aerosmith t-shirt, she was casual but hot. The guy in front of us kept tossing glances back her way while she pretended not to notice.

"Is Gabriel here? Have you seen him yet?" I asked after exchanging pleasantries.

"No. I'm sure he'll be here. His best friend's in the battle of the bands tonight. He wouldn't miss it." She leaned close and her tone dropped low. "Unless something happened to him."

"Stay positive," I replied, scanning the vicinity for anything unusual. "He's inexperienced but he's not helpless."

The queue inched forward until we finally got inside. The place was packed with rock n' rollers. It was a fair size, bigger than The Wicked Kiss, excluding the back rooms. A smoke machine filled the air with a haze that covered the crowd gathered near the stage.

Right away I recognized the all-girl band Crimson Sin. They'd played in my club recently. The lead singer was a werewolf. I could feel her wolf's energy, hot as fire and burning with passion for her craft. With her purple hair flying and a sexy growl into the mic, she had no problem holding the audience's attention.

We approached the bar where the bartender was a flurry of activity. As we waited for our turn to order, I scanned the building, feeling for anyone or anything supernatural. So far, it was just the werewolf on stage and us. Of course, when it came to demons and angels, they could lurk without being seen or felt, and the bastards could pop in out of nowhere. I hated that.

"I can't shake this bad feeling I have," Brogan shouted over the music. "Gabriel is young, and he probably feels invincible. I don't think he realizes how dangerous our world is."

I paid for our drinks, passed Brogan her beer and took a sip from my whiskey. "Hell, I'm still figuring that out myself."

The liquor burned as I swallowed. I couldn't help but think of Arys and the tangy scarlet nectar he was hunting down. Without me. All of a sudden, I became painfully aware of the scent of human blood. All around me were hundreds of beating hearts, pumping blood through the veins of so many would-be victims.

I took another drink, concentrating hard on the way it smelled and tasted. I hoped the alcohol would wipe away the thoughts of blood and prove Arys wrong. Instead, I had to control my urges with effort. I could master the bloodlust, I knew I could.

A commotion broke out in front of the stage. A heckler had messed with the wrong woman. A purple blur was all I could see of the Crimson Sin singer as she leaped into the crowd and began pummeling the guy. It didn't take much to set off that wolf temper. I craned my neck to get a better look. As long as she wasn't unleashing the fangs and claws, a little ass kicking wouldn't hurt the lippy jerk much in the long run.

A bouncer broke up the fight, and the show continued. The energy rolled off the crowd, an excitement-driven force that caused my skin to prickle. I pulled it into me, savoring the raw human essence. It was a rush.

As long as we were there, we might as well have a good time. We blended into the throng of people in front of the stage. The band was great, likely the only all-female group in this contest. I didn't need to hear the competition to know I wanted these ladies to win.

Though Brogan was unable to relax completely, I had no problem riding the high of the music and the crowd. I moved to the beat, but my gaze continuously swept the building. I kept expecting Falon to appear, and I wanted to be ready for it.

However, I didn't anticipate Juliet striding through the door in snug blue jeans and a cute little one-sleeved top. Red lipstick and long brown curls added to her badass appearance. I blinked a few times, unable to believe she had been the little girl I remembered from my childhood.

"What the fuck is she doing here?" I muttered. I was willing to bet the casually dressed man at Juliet's side was also FPA. Leaning into Brogan I said, "Maybe you should check outside for Gabriel while I talk to my sister. Something is up here, and I don't feel good about it."

It didn't take long for Juliet to spot me. I headed in her direction, and she leaned in to speak to her companion who quickly disappeared near the bar. She had a perfectly plastic looking smile plastered onto place when I approached.

"I didn't think this was your scene," I said lightly, attempting small talk.

She didn't bother to play along. "A little out of your element, too, wouldn't you say? Everyone here is human."

"What are you doing here, Juliet?" Fine. No small talk. We'd do it her way.

"It's confidential." Her eyes narrowed, and for just a moment, her wolf lurked behind her eyes. "Stay out of my way, and I'll stay out of yours. Agreed?"

I shook my head. "I can't make any promises. Not until I know why you're here."

"I'm looking for someone. That's all I'm sharing. I'm sorry, Alexa. I'd just rather not do this," she gestured from me to her, "if that's ok."

I was stunned. And, I'll admit, more than a little hurt. My sister was giving me the brush off.

"I'm not your enemy, Juliet. The FPA has poisoned your mind." My tone was snide, more so than intended. "Do you even think about the things they ask you to do?"

"Poisoned?" She spat. "They took me in when I had nowhere to go. They tried to help you, too."

"They recruited mom and dad to get to me." I shouted the words at her without a second thought. The loud music quickly swallowed them up, but she had heard. "You're just a walking, talking weapon to them, Juliet. You can't trust them."

Her irises began to bleed across the whites of her eyes. She fought back the wolf with a worrisome desperation. "Who I can't trust, is you. You kill monsters to keep a secret. We kill them to protect the public."

"Is that so?" I challenged, my wolf bristling for a fight. "Is that why the FPA is holding several of them in the basement? Along with humans. For the protection of the public? I suppose that's what the lab is for, too."

Juliet paled, her gaze darting around for her partner. "I don't know what you're talking about."

"Then maybe you'd better take a look in the basement sometime." I started to walk away, then paused for a parting comment. "If you're here for Gabriel, you're wasting your time."

She opened her mouth to respond, but I beat a hasty retreat outside to find Brogan. I'd just reached the door when I slammed into someone's chest and went down hard on my ass. Falon stood over me wearing an amused grin. Son of a bitch.

"Looking for the witch?" He extended a hand as if to help me up but pulled it away before I could accept. Stepping over me, he surveyed the room, his gaze landing on Juliet. "This will be interesting."

I scrambled to my feet and rushed after him. "Falon, did you do something to Brogan?"

"Of course not." He scowled at me as if I were a stain he'd suddenly noticed on his jacket. "I merely suggested that if she wanted to live through the night, she would be better off leaving well enough alone."

"Don't threaten Brogan," I snarled. When he walked away from me, I grabbed his arm and refused to be budged. "I'm talking to you, Falon."

His silver gaze dropped to my hand. He stiffened and I froze. Void of humanity, Falon's expression chilled me to the bone. If looks could kill, I'd have been dead several times over.

Darker

"Just because you're Shya's pet wolf doesn't mean I won't hurt you," he said, calm, cool and oozing menace. "I'd love a reason to. Go ahead and give me one."

My temper flared, and the power rose within me in response. "I'd love a reason to tell Shya that you've been fucking Lilah. Looks like you just gave me one."

I didn't know why the fallen angel wanted that tidbit of information kept from Shya. However, I was counting on Falon's secret to give me an advantage that a straight up power struggle wouldn't. I spun on my heel to go.

"Wait... bitch," he conceded. "What's it going to take to shut you up?"

I beamed a bright smile at him, confident in my victory. "Stay away from Gabriel."

"Out of the question."

"Fine." I turned away again, and this time he grabbed my arm hard enough to bruise.

"Shya needs him to work a spell. What am I supposed to tell him? That you wouldn't let me bring him?"

"Tell him the FPA was here looking for Gabriel, too, so you thought it best to lie low and wait." I was keenly aware of Juliet's eyes upon us. Watching me converse furiously with Falon wasn't going to change her opinion of me. "You know what? I don't care what you tell him. You owe me a favor. Leave Gabriel alone. Deal?"

Falon stared at me in disbelief. "I owe you a favor, and you want to call it in over some kid? You're going to regret that. You'll probably never get another chance like this."

I considered this. "You're right. I don't need to call in a favor over this. I'll just blackmail you. Stay away from Gabriel or I tell Shya you've been diddling the demon bitch. Works for me. Have a nice night, jackass."

It wasn't the most mature approach though it was effective. Falon let me go, watching me in silent fury. If he ever got his chance, I didn't doubt he'd make me very sorry for this. I couldn't afford to care just then; I'd made a vow to myself to do whatever I could to help people like Gabriel. People like me.

Neither the FPA nor Shya had our best interests in mind. They were in it for themselves. Lesser beings playing God, I wanted no part of it. Now, I had my own agenda, and it didn't include trusting either of them.

I found Brogan outside trying unsuccessfully to convince Gabriel to go home. He was clearly inebriated if his bloodshot eyes and slurred speech were any indication. Brogan's shoulders slumped in relief at my arrival.

"Listen to Alexa, Gabriel. She knows what she's talking about."

"Don't bother." He waved us off, reeking of liquor. "I can take care of myself. I'm here to have a good time with my friends. No big deal."

He made as if to shove past us, and I blocked his path. He threw his hands up and jerked backwards. The power spilled from him. It felt like he had a leak that couldn't be contained. Getting wasted had compromised his control. Been there, done that. Gabriel was bound to learn as I had, the hard way.

"Gabriel, you need to listen to us," I said, trying to calm him with a subtle push of my power. "There are people in there looking for you. You do not want to be found. If you stay here, you're putting yourself in danger."

Peering through his mop of long black hair, Gabriel eyed me suspiciously. "Whatever you're doing, please stop."

Again he shoved by. This time I grabbed him by the shoulders and forced him to stop. He shook me off with a sudden desperate panic.

"Don't touch me," he shouted. "I don't want to see that vision of you again."

Brogan stepped in between us. "Take it easy, Gabriel. We're here to protect you. What did you see?"

"Nothing. Forget it." He shook his head, the hair falling to hide his face again. "You've always been real nice to me, Brogan. Thank you. But, I don't want or need your help."

We let him go. What choice did we have? Short of kidnapping, our options were limited.

"Well, shit." I watched him disappear inside the club.

"I'm sorry, Alexa," Brogan sighed. "I shouldn't have dragged you into this."

"No worries. I'm happy to help. If I can. Maybe we can't make him leave, but he can't make us leave either."

Darker

There was no sign of Falon when we returned inside. That didn't mean he wasn't present. Crimson Sin had finished their set. An emcee shouted to the crowd, firing them up for the next band. Gabriel sat at a table with a group of friends. I did my best to fade into the shadows at the back of the club where I could watch everything.

"Why do I get the feeling we're waiting for something big to happen?" Brogan shifted uneasily from foot to foot.

"Because we are."

I could feel it. Something was going to go down, and I planned to be present when it did. We didn't have to wait long.

The next band launched into a loud number filled with the crash of drums and the scream of guitars. I made a mental note to book them at The Wicked Kiss. I didn't get beyond that thought before Juliet stood up and walked across the room.

Flanked by her male companion, Juliet sidled up to Gabriel. She had no problem getting his attention with a flirty smile. Whatever she said next didn't win her any points. His expression changed from intrigue to irritation. He shook his head and waved her away. She produced a badge identifying her as a government agent. The man with her flashed a glimpse of his gun.

Gabriel stood his ground. I felt it when he reached for his power, readying to defend himself. I tensed, ready to react but afraid to do so too soon.

Juliet's partner pulled out a set of cuffs, and that's when I moved. Crossing the room with Brogan at my side, I watched Gabriel's lips move and seconds later the male agent was flat on his back. That wasn't the end of it though. Blood bubbled up from his nose and lips. He clawed at his throat as if an unseen hand crushed his windpipe.

Juliet pulled her gun on Gabriel. Before she could take a shot or make a threat, Falon appeared beside her. He backhanded her with a superhuman force that sent her crashing into a nearby table.

I was acting on instinct when I threw a blast of power at Falon. I never would have expected to hurt an angel, yet his body jerked as if I had. People in the vicinity reacted fast, moving away from the scene. The rest of the club was unaware and unfazed.

"I warned you," I told Gabriel with an angry growl. "You're not safe here. Now stop whatever it is you're doing to that guy before you kill him."

101

I gestured to the agent flailing and bleeding on the floor. I was close enough to smell the scarlet fluid streaming from him. Close enough for the aroma to fill me with an urgent hunger. The bloodlust came hard and fast, crashing over me with no warning, rising from a whisper to a scream in seconds.

My conscious mind was silent when I lunged at the bleeding man. My hands were wet with blood, my focus so intent upon it that I saw nothing but my victim. Brogan shouted my name, but I paid no attention.

Juliet recovered from her fall. She came at me with the wolf's strength, trying to knock me away from her partner. I flung her backwards with a flick of my wrist. Shouts began to ring out around us. Everything was a blur. I was suddenly jerked away from my prey. My teeth rattled as Falon slammed me against the wall.

He held me in place with an arm across my throat. "You use your power on me again, and I'll tear your fucking head off your shoulders," he seethed. "Our job is to keep shit like this quiet. You just gave the FPA exactly what they wanted from you. A reason to take you out. Fucking stupid wolf."

"I'll try to make time to worry about them after I deal with your demon whore," I spat. "What do you care anyway?"

"Oh, I don't care. As far as I'm concerned, you're a threat that should have been eliminated at birth. Lucky you, I don't make those decisions."

I struggled until he let me go, but not without giving my head a good smack against the wall first. I made as if to push by him, but he stopped me with a shove. A growl rumbled in my throat, and I bared fangs at him.

"You're a liability. If only Shya would acknowledge that you're not worth the risk." Falon's tone dripped acid. "Better watch your step, Alexa."

He was shit talking me, like usual. Yet, he was also giving me some insight with those nasty words. If Shya was taking a risk by keeping me around and alive, I must be valuable to him. I interpreted that to mean there was something he needed from me. Something he could get only from me. *Thank you for that, Falon, you insipid shithead.*

Darker

I sucked the blood off my fingertips, smirking when Falon openly grimaced. I caught Juliet watching me with blatant disgust. Her partner swayed unsteadily but otherwise appeared fine. Gabriel stood sullenly beside her, silver cuffs adorning his wrists. Oh, hell no.

Falon was forgotten as I marched over to my sister. I shook a bloody finger in her face. "Get those fucking cuffs off him now."

"Get that finger out of my face, Lexi. Or, you'll be wearing the next pair." There was a stubborn set to her jaw, and her eyes glowed daringly.

"I'd like to see you try." I stared her down, refusing to be cowed by my little sister with her big girl government ID. "Go back to HQ and look in the basement. If that doesn't get through to you, nothing will. Until then, don't think for a minute I'll let you take him out of here. You'll have one hell of a fight on your hands."

We faced off as we had so many times as kids. Every time I saw her now, I felt the separation between us grow. I wasn't willing to back down. If I had to hurt Juliet to keep Gabriel from ending up in the FPA basement, I'd do it.

"You just attacked my partner. I should bring you in for that."

"Listen to me, Juliet. Dammit." I resisted the urge to shake her but just barely. "I've been in that basement. There are people down there, prisoners locked in concrete rooms, held against their will because they have power. I'd be down there with them if Briggs had his way."

"Bullshit," she snapped, but the uncertainty was there. The truth was undeniable.

"As much as I'd enjoy watching you mutts tear each other apart," Falon broke in with a condescending sneer. "I've got better things to do."

He yanked the FPA cuffs from Gabriel as if they were a plastic child's toy. Tossing them at Juliet, he followed up with a slap of power that toppled both of us into Brogan, sending all three of us crashing to the floor in a heap. By the time I was able to move again, he was long gone, with Gabriel.

"Good job, Juliet," I hissed, holding my head as I got to my feet. Falon's hit had left me dizzy and slightly disoriented. I caught hold of Brogan's hand, helping her up. She shook her head a few times and swore.

Juliet glowered at me. "You're blaming me? I have a job to do, Alexa. If you weren't here getting in my way, maybe I'd actually be able to do it."

"Your job? Your so-called job consists of imprisonment for those that don't deserve it. I don't know how you can live with yourself." My growing anger was filled with bitterness. It was more than just the fact that my sister was a government zombie. It hurt that she was ok with it.

"I protect the helpless, those that can't protect themselves. From people like you." Her tone was high and sharp. It was the tone she'd always used when calling for our dad, begging him to punish me for one petty thing or another.

I wanted to throttle her. I took a step toward her, hands raised, ready to do so. With fists ready, she invited my attack. Before we could pummel one another like angry kids, Brogan held up a hand and uttered a word in Latin. An energy wall sprang up between Juliet and me.

"Ladies," Brogan intervened. "This isn't the time or place for this."

The urge to collapse her wall was strong. I could do it. However, it was irrelevant. She was right. Pounding on Juliet wouldn't make me feel any better. It also wouldn't help me to catch up with Falon any faster.

Vibration in my pocket drew my attention to my phone. I pulled it out to find a text message from an unfamiliar number along with a photo that chilled me to the bone. It was a picture of Jez and her girlfriend, Zoey, taken without their knowledge. They were in bed together, locked in an intimate embrace.

Along with the photo was the simple but effective message: *Guess who's next?*

Chapter Eleven

"I've got to go." I turned and fled the building as if it were on fire. There was no time to explain. The further Brogan and Juliet stayed from this, the better.

With superhuman speed, I ran down the street to my car. I couldn't be concerned with who might see the unnatural display. Throwing myself in the driver's seat, I fumbled with my phone. As I started the car and threw it into gear, I prayed Jez would answer. No such luck.

With a squeal of tires, I tore out of the parking lot. I hit the gas so the engine roared as the Charger sped down the street. I said a silent prayer that I wouldn't see blue and red flashing lights in my rear view mirror.

I could have lived happily without that image of Zoey and Jez burned into my brain. It might be the last time I'd see one, or both, of them alive.

"No, no, no." I pounded a fist on the steering wheel when a red light had me slamming on the brakes. The thought occurred to me that it might be a trap designed to lure me, but I'd have to take that chance.

Jez lived on the south side. It would take me at least twenty minutes to get there. I recognized her leopard print blanket in the photo. For the first time, I almost envied the demons and fallen angels their ability to pop from one place to another. Jez could be fighting for her life right now, and I was trapped in traffic while it happened.

"Fuck. Shit. Damn." All useless words that made me feel equally useless.

The light turned green, and I hit the gas. It was a race against time. Lilah had to be stopped. Her desperation for my blood was killing those around me. She was forcing my hand and doing a damn good job of it. I'd already lost a wolf to her. I couldn't lose anyone else.

I finally crossed the river to the south side. Rather than subside, my panic increased. What if they were dead because of me? I maneuvered through traffic, cutting off more than a few people who honked or flipped me the bird.

It felt like much more than twenty-five minutes had passed since receiving Lilah's message. I parked across the street from Jez's swanky apartment building and killed the lights. Fear told me to rush inside; instinct demanded I take a moment to scope out the place.

A dim light shone in Jez's second floor living room window. I reached out metaphysically, feeling for vampires, for Lilah. Nothing. That didn't mean she wasn't here.

Exiting the Charger, I darted across the street and blended into the shadows beyond the glow of the street light. I cloaked my energy, hoping I hadn't been detected yet if she was in the vicinity. I held the Dragon Claw in a white-knuckled grip. If I had it my way, its blade would soon taste Lilah's blood.

I reached the lobby door without incident. With the stealth of the wolf, I slunk into the building. The fluorescent light inside hummed loud in the otherwise quiet entry. I focused on the lock, willing the deadbolt to turn. It was much simpler than the heavy-duty locks the FPA used. Just when I began to grow frustrated, there was a loud click, and I was in.

I took the stairs two at a time until I reached the second floor. The building was oddly quiet, not so much as muffled TV noise. I stepped into the hall and paused. Empty. I sprinted down the hall to Jez's door with the dagger held ready.

Hesitating with my hand hovering over the doorknob, I listened. Eerie silence greeted me. The raw energy of fear and death crept near. My stomach dropped, and holding my breath, I shoved the door open.

The scent of blood assaulted my nose. Fear mingled with it to produce a sickly sweet aroma. I was too late.

I moved through the small but immaculate kitchen toward the glow of light coming from the living room. There I found Jez huddled on the floor, shaking violently. She was wrapped in a throw blanket from the couch. Her face was wet with black streaks of mascara and tears. Her golden hair was a tousled mop of curls atop her shoulders. With blood smears on her hands and a cigarette clutched between her fingers, she gazed up at me as if unsure whether or not I was real.

"Jez?" I said tentatively, my gaze straying to the darkened bedroom. "Are you hurt?"

She took a long, shaky drag off the cigarette. Jez hadn't smoked in a year now. She must have had a pack stashed away. It took several attempts for her to get the words out.

"She killed Zoey."

"Where is she?" I was dumbstruck with disbelief. This couldn't be happening.

"Lilah? She's gone. Zoey? In there." Jez pointed to the bedroom and a fresh flood of tears emerged. She made no attempt to wipe them away.

A sick feeling gripped me as I made my way to Jez's room. I didn't want to see this, but I had no choice. The thick scent of blood grew as I drew closer. The faint light shining through the open blinds cast a silver glow on Zoey's prone form. My keen eyesight was more than good enough to see in the dimness, but I reached for the light switch anyway, needing the false comfort of the overhead light.

Pale yellow illumination bathed the room. I held my breath, unwilling to breathe in that sweet hybrid blood. What I saw was horrifying, and though he'd been dead for more than a year, my first thought was of Raoul. Because I had loved him despite what a pompous, selfish ass he was, I had promised myself I'd keep Zoey safe, for him.

Zoey lay sprawled on the bed. Two sets of vampire bites marred her carotid artery. Blood stained the pillow beneath her. She had bled out quickly. Her bright blue eyes, now dimmed in death, stared off toward the ceiling. Jez had thrown a blanket over her to hide her nudity. Otherwise, the scene was untouched.

I'm sorry, Raoul. Zoey had never been one of my favorite people. She had killed her father and hurt both Kylarai and Arys as well as an innocent man. Perhaps I should have left her in the woods as wolf, but I'd felt it my duty to restore her to human form. Not once did I see her as anything other than a liability I was forced to accept. That didn't mean she deserved to die.

Returning to the living room, I sank to my knees beside Jez. I laid the dagger on the carpet and pulled her into my arms. She sagged against me before throwing her arms around me and sobbing. I plucked the cigarette from her fingers and tossed it in a Coke can on the coffee table. The sizzle as it hit the contents was loud, poignant, accompanied by Jez's heartbreaking cries.

Tears filled my eyes; rage filled my heart. Two of my wolves had now died at Lilah's hand. She wasn't going to stop, not until I stopped her.

"I'm so sorry, Jez. I'm going to make her suffer for this. Somehow. I promise."

"It happened so fast," she said between sobs. "She didn't come alone. She brought some guys. They made me watch. I thought I was next, but she just killed Zoey and left."

Another flood of tears cut off her words. I glanced around the apartment, wondering what to do with Zoey. Ideally, I'd call Fox and have him bury her beside her father. Fox was a city wolf that provided medical services to werewolves. He would normally help me with the safe and proper burial of a wolf, but involving him in any way might jeopardize his safety. Vampires would have to take care of this.

"Why didn't she kill me, too?" Jez sniffled, wiping her eyes with the back of her hand. "She barely looked at me, except to tell me it wasn't personal. It's fucking personal now."

I released my hold on Jez to fetch her some tissue and a glass of water. I felt absolutely useless handing them to her. It was a poor substitute.

"Jez, I'm sorry. This is my fault. She's doing this to force me to come to her willingly. To give her my blood." I sniffed back the tears that threatened. Pulling my phone out, I called Arys who didn't answer. Great. Not only had he let me go off alone tonight, he had also made himself unavailable.

"No, Alexa, this isn't your fault." Jez moved from the floor to the couch and promptly lit another cigarette. "It's Shya's fault. He made the dumbass decision to bind her instead of driving a stake through the bitch's heart."

"I know," I sighed, infuriated. "He's also the one who told Lilah my blood would break her curse. Manipulative son of a bitch."

Unable to force myself to drag Zoey's body out of there, I concentrated on reaching Arys through our mental connection. His resistance wasn't what I expected. I took that to mean he didn't want me to know what he was doing, but I didn't have time to worry about him. Kale would have normally been the next person I'd call. So much for that. Hoping Shawn or Justin would be able to help, I called The Wicked Kiss.

"Justin is coming," I announced after hanging up. "You should get dressed. Want me to get you something?"

She looked forlornly at the bedroom and nodded. I didn't want to go back in there, but I sure as hell wasn't going to make Jez do it. I longed to ease the pain she exuded. Knowing that was impossible, I fetched some things from her closet, grabbing enough to last her a day or two. I wasn't leaving her here alone.

I paused to look at Zoey a final time. It was terrible what happened to her. Still, I couldn't shake the feeling that Lilah had saved me from one day having to kill Zoey myself. With her mental instability and irrational, sudden fits of violence, it was bound to happen eventually.

"Here." I handed Jez the pile of clothing and went to the bathroom to gather her toothbrush. "Anything you need in here? You're coming to my house for the day."

"I can do this. It's ok." She appeared in the doorway, clutching her blanket like a lifeline in a storm. With her smeared makeup and tear-stained cheeks, she looked like a lost little girl. I'd never seen Jez so fragile.

"Is there anything I can do?" I felt helpless and I hated it.

She shook her head slowly. "Just don't let her be dumped like some random victim. Please."

"I won't. I promise."

The bathroom door clicked shut, and I took the opportunity to slip out onto the balcony for some air while she got dressed. Sucking in a lungful of night air, I stared out at the traffic that went by. The city continued to move and thrive despite the horror that had gone on here tonight. It was so unfair.

I was jittery and uptight. It took a lot of concentration to focus on the earth so that I could balance my energy. I needed to be calm and collected for Jez; she needed me. The essence of murder and death sought to get past my shields. I wouldn't be manipulated by it. I refused. I was stronger than that. I had to be. Other people were counting on it.

It wasn't long until there was a soft knock on the door. I let Justin in, quickly briefing him on what happened. I led him to the bedroom where we wrapped Zoey completely in a sheet.

"That sadistic bitch just isn't going to stop, is she?" he asked, a sense of knowing in his dark eyes.

"Not until she gets what she wants from me." I wrinkled my nose at the pungent odor of cigarette smoke. "Or, until I send her to hell."

"Well if anyone can do it, you can. Especially if even half the rumors about you are true."

"I appreciate the vote of confidence. I'm not sure I want to know what they're saying about me."

Justin forced a strained smile. "Probably not."

"Look, I need you to take care of her." I nodded toward Zoey. "As proper a burial as possible outside the city. Marked grave. Please."

"Sure thing. No problem." Justin hoisted Zoey in his arms. His massive frame made her seem so much smaller than she was.

It was late. The chance of him running into someone was slim, but I accompanied him down to the back door of the building just in case.

"Be careful. Make sure you're not followed. And Justin, thank you." I had no words. He was going out of his way to help me. Though I knew he might be helping for no other reason than self-preservation, I was still grateful. Just because Justin believed me to be the bigger bad in the city didn't make it true, but I was thankful someone thought so.

When I returned to the apartment, Jez was standing in the doorway to the bedroom. With her green eyes fixed on the bloodstained bed, she hugged herself tight. I gave her a gentle squeeze.

"I'll clean this up. You don't have to." Before she could protest, I got busy gathering the remaining bloody blankets. It was the least I could do.

She watched me in silence while I scrubbed down the crimson spots and smears with bleach. The blankets, I would take home to burn. When the sharp bleach aroma had burned away the last trace of blood along with my sense of smell, I called it done and washed up.

Nearly two hours had passed since I received Lilah's message. Time still moved despite Jez's heartbreak. I coaxed her away from the bedroom and the many memories within it. Memories she would no doubt replay many times tonight.

"Come on." I tugged gently on her hand. "We should let this place air out. We'll head to my house. Unless you don't mind making a stop at Shya's."

For the first time all night, she looked at me with the spark of emerald fire I was used to seeing in her eyes. "Shya's? Let's go."

I was happy to escape the chemical laden, death-riddled confines of Jez's apartment. Wary and alert, I scanned the street for anything suspicious, including a double check of my car itself. Depositing the bloody bedding in the trunk, I got into the driver's seat with a hunger for vengeance.

"Are you sure you're up to this?" I asked. "We don't have to go."

"Oh, I want to go. I have a few things I'd like to say to him." Jez stared straight ahead, her expression stony.

Taking Jez to Shya's house might not be the best idea. Seeing the hard set to her jaw, feeling the hatred running hot through her, I knew it could get ugly. However, she had every right to face the demon she blamed for the death of her lover.

I filled her in on Gabriel as we drove through the city. She nodded here and there to show she was listening, but I knew she was a million miles away.

Pondering where to begin with Shya, I fell silent. Between his utter failure with Lilah and tonight's kidnapping of Gabriel, I was at the end of my rope with the demon. Shya had saved me from the FPA, something I was grateful for, but he'd done it for his own reason, whatever that was.

Lilah might be my current priority, but it was only a matter of time until whatever Shya was hiding came to light. If I wasn't ready, I'd be sorry.

I began to have doubts when I turned into the tree-lined driveway. Shya's modern style home was a sprawling display of luxury and sharp angles. Nothing good ever happened when I was here. I didn't expect that to change now.

"Are you sure you want to come in?" I glanced at Jez, finding her surprisingly focused and intense.

"This bastard has been the one behind the scenes all along," she mused. "I thought we were all working with Veryl, keeping a lid on things to avoid public exposure. But, I think it means something more. We were all recruited. Something about each of us sets us apart from other supernaturals. That can't be a coincidence."

"It's not. I think Veryl's files will shed more light on that." I parked the car and killed the engine. I was afraid of what we'd find inside. If Gabriel had been harmed, I would blame myself.

"I've been thinking about those files, what they said about me. I think that's why I was recruited. It's obvious why you were. So what about Kale? And, how many others does Shya have running around, doing his bidding?" Jez rubbed her eyes and stifled a sigh. "We need to figure this bastard out. Before more of us die."

"Maybe we shouldn't be here right now—" I started to say, but she was already getting out of the car.

Jez lit a cigarette on our way up the front steps. She took a few big drags before dropping it in the nearest flowerpot. I raised my hand to ring the bell. Before I could make contact, the air rippled, and Falon appeared.

"You never know when to give up, do you?" He towered over me, trying to look especially foreboding.

"Get out of my way, Falon. I want to talk to Shya, and I'm not particularly in the mood to look at your face right now." I tried to shove past him, but he blocked my way, going so far as to shove me into Jez.

His laughter pissed me off even as it made my skin crawl. "Look at the little wolf trying to be the big bad. It's cute."

"I said get out of my way," I hissed through gritted teeth as I lashed out at him with a slap of power. It was just enough to knock him aside, but I couldn't hide my pleasure.

I let myself into the house, calling Shya's name. Falon recovered fast. Grabbing my arm, he spun me around and backhanded me hard enough to throw me off my feet. I landed on my ass in the open foyer, momentarily stunned. My jaw throbbed and my temper flared.

Before I could get up, however, Jez's shortened fuse snapped. She grabbed Falon's arm and spun her body, flipping him over so he landed hard on the floor beside me. Placing a boot on his chest, she gazed at him with eyes that had gone pure wildcat.

"Don't fucking touch her again," she uttered, her voice dangerously calm. "Your whore killed the woman I love tonight. Why shouldn't I return the gesture with you?"

"You can't kill me, kitten," Falon grunted as she put more weight into pinning him.

"Let's confirm that theory." With a slash of claws across his throat, Jez unleashed her vengeful need.

Blood poured forth from the gaping wound she created. Falon's eyes widened. Grasping her leg, he shoved with a supernatural strength that sent her crashing into the opposite wall.

We all bounded to our feet, braced and ready. My hands burned with the dancing blue and gold flames of raw energy flowing through me. I ached to unleash it on Falon. Maybe I couldn't kill him, but making him suffer would be enough for me.

Then, the scent of his blood hit me, and I swooned. Goddamn, it was heavenly; no horrible pun intended. The sweetness of Falon's blood taunted my control.

"Alexa, how nice of you to drop by." Shya's voice echoed in the high ceilinged foyer.

I spun to face him, simultaneously aware of the cool vampire energy present. Shya stood there with arms crossed, his constantly amused grin perfectly in place. At his side, looking livid, was Arys.

I didn't see him move. Just that fast he was in Falon's face, throwing a punch the angel didn't see coming. He followed up with another, then banged Falon's head against the wall a few times.

Bloodlust had Arys's pupils dilating as he too reacted to the spilled angel blood. Baring fangs, Arys snarled into the fallen angel's face, "I don't need to kill you to make you sorry you touched her."

Shya watched this with glee. With his perfectly pressed suit and slick black hair in place, he looked as he always did. I was starting to see through his human façade.

Already healed from Jez's attack, Falon's blood ceased to flow. Angel or not, he had to have a weakness. I was determined to find it.

He stared into Arys's angry eyes, and for just a second, I thought I saw a trace of true fear. Then, it was gone, and Falon sneered, shoving Arys away. His wings flared out behind him, massive, silver and meant to be intimidating. Arys scowled, refusing to be impressed.

"Where's Gabriel?" I demanded. Turning my back on the asshole angel, I let Shya feel the brunt of my anger. "You can't expect me to believe that you need him that bad. You, oh so powerful demon, you."

My snide tone earned me a dark glare that, truth be told, did frighten me, but I'd be damned if I'd show it. Jez sidled up to me with a deadly swagger. I was worried about her mental state. Her pain had faded to be replaced with the need to hurt something, to kill. That urge could lead her to say or do something we'd both regret.

"Gabriel is here. He's fine. He's also absolutely none of your concern." Shya narrowed his eyes in warning. "Stay out of it, Alexa."

"I want to see him." I was insistent. It was hard to keep my focus intent on Shya when I wanted to snap at Arys. What the hell was he doing here?

Shya turned his attention to Jez, ignoring my demand. "I don't believe we've officially met. Veryl always spoke so highly of you. I can see why. You're a firecracker."

"Save it. I don't want to hear your manipulative drivel. Because of you someone I love is dead." Jez appeared calm, but her fangs and claws indicated otherwise. Her energy was strong with pure, venomous hatred.

"Is that so?" Shya's self-satisfied grin grew. "Do tell."

"Lilah killed my girlfriend tonight. She made me watch. You failed when you bound her power. You drove her to this. If you would have let Alexa kill her—"

"She would have failed," Shya interrupted, his tone short and clipped. "Alexa's power has limits. Sure, she may have been able to send Lilah back to imprisonment, but it would have been unlikely. Risky. Too risky while Lilah still had some of her power. I wasn't willing to lose Alexa over something so trivial."

"Trivial?" Jez raged, lunging forward to hiss angrily into the demon's face. "We're not pawns in your game of underworld chess. You don't get to decide who lives and who dies."

She was yelling loud enough to hurt my ears. I stood close, ready to grab her if she went for him. As entitled as she was to what she was feeling now, I couldn't let her do something crazy.

I was dying to address Shya's comment about being unwilling to lose me, but that wasn't what I was here for, not this time.

"Is that it? Are you finished?" Shya studied her, peering deep into her green eyes with his snake-like crimson ones. "Demon blood might run in your veins, but if you don't have the power that goes with it, it doesn't mean a thing, so watch your tongue, sweetheart. I'd hate to have to pull it out of that pretty face."

Jez recoiled in horror. Her face fell and she backed away. Unease slid through me. Shya watched her as if she were a wounded deer. Easy pickings. I cleared my throat in an attempt to draw his gaze back to me. It didn't work.

He stared into her with a drowning red intensity. Only when she finally dropped her gaze did he avert his. The temperature in the room seemed to rise by several degrees. Shya's strange otherworldly vibe resonated strong and hot. It was slightly painful.

Dismissing Jez, his attention swung to Falon. With a brow raised in interest he asked, "Now, what's this I hear about your whore? Is there something you want to tell me?"

Disappointment filled me. I was bummed out that I wasn't the one to expose Falon's secret. However, I was more than happy to be present for its exposure. This I wanted to see.

Falon met Shya's gaze evenly. He was unafraid, facing the demon with a stubborn set to his jaw. "I don't need your permission to take a lover, Shya."

"No, of course not. Who that lover happens to be, though, may affect your loyalties. I'm sure you've heard the human saying, don't shit where you eat. Be careful, Falon."

The two of them faced off, exchanging so much without saying a word. The tension was palpable, heavy enough to suffocate. If they didn't stop staring at each other like that, my head was going to explode.

"I want to see Gabriel," I repeated, risking Shya's wrath. "I'm not leaving until I know he's alive."

"Fine." Shya spun on his heel and motioned for me to follow. "Let's get this over with. Once you see he's alive and well, I expect you'll be on your way. I'm busy."

"I see that." Finally, I got my chance to shoot a questioning glance at Arys. I mouthed the words, 'What the fuck?'

I felt him, a light touch in my mind. 'We'll talk about this later.'

I didn't reply. Instead, I chose to give him my best dirty look. My night was so full of chaos and shit already, I didn't have the capacity for more. Whatever Arys was doing here with Shya, I wasn't going to like it.

Shya led us into the living room. It was open, attached to the kitchen. With a high ceiling and a second floor balcony overlooking, it felt much bigger than it actually was. The back walls were glass from floor to ceiling. They looked out onto the backyard with its pool and sprawling lawn.

Gabriel was out there, seated on the back patio couch. Several spellcasting items were spread on the small table before him. His back was to us. I watched as he added a sprinkle of something black and dusty to a chalice. Shya had wasted no time putting him to work.

"There, you see? He's fine. Happy, Alexa?" Shya's expression all but dared me to argue.

"I want to speak to him." I didn't wait for Shya's permission. I strode to the patio doors and let myself out into the backyard.

Gabriel raised his head, surprise registering on his face. His eyes were solid black. He was filled with the dark magic he performed.

"You shouldn't be here," he said, his lips curling in annoyance. "This is a delicate spell. You're ruining it."

"You shouldn't be here either. And, you sure as hell shouldn't be messing with dark forces. It's dangerous, Gabriel. If you get in too deep, it will never let you go."

"I guess you would know. Do you expect me to believe your power isn't rooted in darkness?" He reached for a bag of what looked like dried flowers and continued preparing his spell.

"It's not," I said softly. "Not all of it. My power is both dark and light. It's the balance in between."

I heard myself say it, but did I believe it? I still had so much to learn about what it meant to be a twin flame, not to mention what it meant to be a Hound of God. My fear of being an utter failure was deeply ingrained. But, what I feared most was becoming a monster that lived only for the kill and the thrill of the power that came with it.

"If you say so," he replied with a stoic nonchalance that struck me as worrisome. "Look, I get it. You feel the need to prove to yourself that you're not like everyone else here. That you're better than them.

It's cool. But, it doesn't mean you have to save me. In fact, I don't want to be saved."

"This is the power talking. Not you. You don't want to stay here with a demon. Come on, Gabriel. Brogan is worried sick about you. Your mom probably is, too."

He paused in his spellcasting. "I'm not a child. I can make my own decisions, and I choose to stay. Sorry. I don't want to be used to make you feel better about yourself."

Whoa. He was too far gone. Nothing I said would change his mind. The murky energy surrounding him was too thick, a possessive, manipulative entity. It had him firmly in its grasp.

"That's your choice." I nodded, accepting defeat. "Tell me one thing though. Tell me what you saw when you touched me at Brogan's shop."

He fixed me with a strange, detached stare. A shiver ran down my spine.

"I saw you as a vampire. And, it wasn't pretty."

Chapter Twelve

I stared at Gabriel, frozen in place. My mouth opened, and I muttered something unintelligible. Maybe I shouldn't have been surprised. It's not like I didn't know that's what my future held, after my death at Arys's hand. If Gabriel had merely reiterated the warnings of the other witches, I could have accepted it. Instead, he was confirming something I now realized I'd hoped might not come to pass. For the first time since forming the blood bond with my twin flame, I had to ask myself, would I rather be dead than be a vampire?

"You don't want details," Gabriel said. "I prefer not to give them. I'm not a walking, talking crystal ball. Things can always change. What I see isn't written in stone."

"Have you ever been wrong?" I asked nervously. "Has that ever happened that you know of? A change from what you saw?"

"Just once." Picking up a small dagger, Gabriel pressed the blade to the inside of his palm. "You should probably leave. I've seen enough of your bloodlust to know I don't want to spill any blood with you around."

I beat a hasty retreat back into the house. The quiet lull of conversation between Arys and Jez died. Falon was nowhere to be seen. I didn't doubt he'd run to tell Lilah their little secret had been revealed. It was time I paid the bitch a visit, too.

Shya spread his hands expectantly. "Satisfied? Gabriel and I had a little chat, and he's more than happy to be here. Now, unless you have other business, I'll have to ask you to leave."

"I know what you're doing, Shya." I closed the patio door and turned my full attention on the haughty demon. "You talk a good game.

You promise people things they didn't even know they wanted. For the most part, you're not so bad. Until you fail to get what you want."

"Your point?" He did his best to appear bored.

"Your sweet talk might work on someone as young and new to this world as Gabriel, but I see right through you. I won't be manipulated. I'll find out what you're up to, and when I'm done with Lilah, I'm coming back for you." Sure, those words put my ass on the line, but I was furious and ready to fight back.

A fiery burst of energy accompanied Shya's laughter. My instinctive reaction was to harden myself against it. It easily burned a hole in my shields. I made a split-second decision to pull the aggressive force through me, channeling it back out and into the earth beneath the foundation under my feet. It left me feeling uncomfortably hot inside but otherwise unharmed.

"I look forward to it," Shya quipped. Rather than the anger I'd anticipated, he seemed impressed, genuinely pleased. "Your stubborn wishful thinking is endearing. It's because of my so-called manipulation that you stand here right now. You could have been FPA property. Like your sister."

Letting him antagonize me would be playing right into his hands. He and I were long overdue for a good ol' fashioned knockdown, drag em out, ass kicking discussion. That day would come.

"You win," I snapped. "I'm leaving."

Jez fell into step beside me as I strode toward the door. I didn't spare a last look for Arys. The weight of his gaze was upon me. I was so many kinds of pissed at him I couldn't even think about it.

He caught up to me outside, as I knew he would. I reached for the car door handle, and he put out a hand to hold the door closed.

"Alexa, whatever you're thinking, it's wrong. I didn't tell you I was coming here because there was nothing to tell." He pressed close, forcing me to look up at him.

Jez got into the car, giving us the illusion of being alone. I refused to let go of the door. Arys could talk circles around himself if given the chance. I didn't want to hear it.

"I just finished cleaning up a murder scene at Jez's apartment. Another one of my wolves is dead. I am not in the mood to argue with you."

"I don't want you to be mad. I can't stand it when you give me that look." Arys reached to touch my face. I stepped back, avoiding the contact.

"You're always going to do whatever the hell you want to do regardless of how I feel. If you want to let that bastard pull your strings, so be it. That's your choice. Right now, I have bigger things to worry about, starting with my friend whose heart is breaking because of Shya's fuck up; he brought Lilah's wrath down on all of us." I jerked on the door handle until he finally released his hold on the door. "You're making a mistake by being here."

"I'm doing what I have to do in order to keep you safe. To keep us both safe," he insisted, his blue eyes blazing.

"Now who's being reckless?" I got into the car and slammed the door, cutting off his reply.

"Yikes," Jez said, holding an unlit cigarette between her fingers. "Trouble in vampire paradise?"

"What else is new?" I muttered bitterly as I backed the car up so I could turn around in the driveway.

Arys stood there stiffly, watching until my car disappeared from sight. His prior refusal to cooperate with Shya had made sense. This sudden change of heart, it didn't. Bad things would come of this.

"I thought you two were so well matched. In synch."

"We are. That's the problem. We're both too damn hotheaded, and neither of us is willing to back down." I cast a critical glance her way, tempted to yank the smoke from her hand. "Don't light that nasty thing in here."

She fiddled with it, putting it between her lips, then dropping it back in the pack. She was understandably restless. "He just wants to protect you, Lex. Is that so wrong?"

I maneuvered the Charger down the dark gravel road, back to the city. I couldn't wait to get home. "It could be. Arys has this halfwit idea that an alliance with Shya will benefit us both. I think it only benefits Shya. Arys is desperate. He's afraid to lose me."

"So you're punishing the guy for being head over heels in love with you? Damn. I'm glad we never dated. I'd have to kick your ass." Jez forced a wry smile that didn't quite reach her eyes.

Her comment made me pause and reconsider. Was I overreacting? Demons didn't make deals without ensuring they had something to gain. Until I knew what I meant to Shya's personal plans, it was a risk we couldn't afford to take.

I steered the conversation to a lighter topic, making idle chat as we crossed through the city and headed west toward home. Sunrise was creeping closer. The mental and emotional exhaustion began to take hold, but I'd get no rest anytime soon. I had to go through the rest of those files. I was certain Veryl had left something in there that would help me with Lilah.

As we entered my house, I asked Jez, "Are you hungry? I can toss a frozen pizza in the oven or something." I stopped in the front hall, feeling for anything amiss. It was clear. "Or, if you prefer, we can go for a run. Hunt something with a heartbeat."

"Thanks but I think I'm going to suck down a few cigarettes and take a bath. If you don't mind." Jez let herself out onto the back deck just off the kitchen. The flick of the lighter was quickly followed by a deep sigh.

I kicked off my boots and pulled out my phone. I wasn't sure if angels slept. I had a question for Willow that wouldn't wait, but first I had to call Kylarai and tell her about Zoey. It wasn't a call I wanted to make; telling her about Zak had been hard enough. She'd cried, then I'd cried. Now, I'd let her down again.

Informing the town pack that a vampire had murdered the daughter of their former Alpha wasn't going to win me any points. They already thought associating with me was dangerous. I was about to prove them right.

Kylarai cried again. I had expected that. As I told her what happened, I moved about my bedroom, shedding the leather pants and exchanging them for fuzzy PJs. I pulled my long hair into a ponytail, trying to get as close to relaxation as possible.

"It's just so sad," she sniffled, her voice loud over the speakerphone. "She was no saint, that's for sure, but she deserved better."

I didn't have the heart to tell her a part of me felt relieved. I doubted if I'd ever say the words aloud.

"I'm sorry it happened," I said instead. "I can't let Lilah hurt anyone else. I have to stop her."

"Don't get yourself killed, Alexa. Please." Kylarai's voice was thick with tears.

"I don't plan to. I've got to do something though, or she'll keep coming after you guys. And, I can't stand to lose anyone else. Be careful, ok? I'd die if anything happened to you."

"You know me. I won't go down without a hell of a fight. I'll take the bitch with me if I can." Passive aggressive and maybe a tad bipolar, Ky's wolf spoke through those words.

By the time we hung up, Kylarai had gone from tears to fury. She volunteered to tell the rest of the pack what was happening. Two wolves had died in just a few days, and they wouldn't take this well. Our small town pack consisted of school teachers, car salesmen, stockbrokers, and other werewolves trying to maintain a semblance of normalcy. Vampires and demons were not part of their world, but I was changing that.

Returning to the kitchen, I found Jez leaning against the island. Her phone was in her hands, and she was scrolling through photos of her and Zoey. My chest tightened and guilt slapped me.

I didn't want to intrude on her moment. Words didn't exist for what she was going through. Nothing I could say would make things better, so I got busy making a pot of coffee. I was going to need it to get through Veryl's files.

"Are you sure you don't want anything?" I asked. "Coffee? Liquor? Something to eat? I think I have some leftover chicken breast."

She shook her head, never taking her eyes off the phone. "No, thanks. Maybe just some juice or something."

I dug through the fridge, finding some pineapple smoothie stuff. I hated that my friend was in pain because of me, and even more, I hated that I could do nothing to change that. She didn't blame me, but I blamed myself.

"There are clean towels in the hall closet upstairs." I set a glass of smoothie in front of her. "You can use the main tub if you want, but the one in my bedroom has jets. Take your pick."

She sipped from the glass. Selecting a specific picture, she handed me the phone. "I took that photo yesterday, when she was sleeping. Isn't she beautiful?"

I gazed down at the photo. Zoey's jet-black hair fanned across the pillow. She appeared peaceful in sleep, sane even. Except, the curve of her jaw reminded me of Raoul. I would forever remember the night she killed him, the night I failed to stop her.

"Yeah, she's beautiful." Swallowing the year-old pain of losing the first man I'd ever loved, I handed the phone back and turned away, busying myself with the coffee pot.

I waited until Jez went upstairs before calling Willow. While my laptop fired up, I sipped my coffee and hoped he would answer. Just as it was about to go to voicemail, his smooth voice came on the line, and I was crushed with relief.

He listened attentively while I again told the events of the night. I finished by asking, "Tell me, is there anything that will harm a fallen angel? Anything I can use against Falon to get him to tell me where she is."

"Silver," he replied calmly. "Pure silver will harm him as it will demons. Do you have a plan? If you allow your emotion to drive your decisions, it could backfire."

"My emotion is what will get me through this. I can't let her continue this killing spree. I'd rather hand myself over to her than watch more people die."

"Let's not get hasty. That's exactly what she wants. I'm sorry to say this Alexa, but if she breaks her curse, so many more will die. Starting with you, I'm sure." The clink of bottles in the background made me wonder if he was out drinking. It seemed to be the norm for him.

"I think I might have something I can use against her. I'll fill you in when I know for sure. Is there a way for me to summon Falon? To force him to come to me?" I could almost feel his hesitation on the other end.

"In a manner of speaking, yes. But, you don't want to do that, Alexa. It's dangerous. He would seek revenge."

A thought struck me. Lilah had messaged my phone. If the number she used was from a burner phone, I'd be screwed. If it wasn't, however, it would be traceable right to her.

"I'm going to find Lilah, and as a last resort, I'll use Falon to do it whether you tell me or not, Willow," I declared, the wheels in my brain turning. "I have to confront her. The sooner the better."

"Fine. I'm going to be there if you summon him."

He wouldn't be swayed despite my reluctance. It couldn't hurt to have someone like Willow watching my back. I'd seen Falon's power; fallen angels were not to be tangled with lightly. Yet, I didn't feel right about bringing another person into my battle.

As we debated, I clicked around on the laptop and opened Veryl's main folder. So many files were still unread. Until I'd absorbed every damn word in every damn file, I was determined to find that golden nugget of information, the gem that made Veryl's death mean something. Otherwise, I'd killed him just to get my rocks off, which is what it essentially had been.

"I'll call you back," I said, distracted. "Don't worry. I won't get myself killed without my loaded guardian angel there to drunkenly back me up."

"Hey," Willow protested with a laugh. "I'm not always drunk. I just like to take the edge off."

"Whatever you say."

I ended the call and gave my full attention to the screen before me. With coffee in hand, I readied myself for as many hours as it took to weed through every word. I found something almost immediately that had me spewing coffee in shock.

Kale Sinclair's brief history as a werewolf gives him a natural ability to understand the beasts. He knows their strengths and weaknesses. Though his mental stability is at times questionable, his loyalty is sound. His only flaw is his obsession with his sire. Given enough time, he shows much promise in assisting us with integrating shifters into the fold.

I reread the passage several times before it sank in. The tears I'd been fighting all night burst forth in an ugly crimson flood. Blood stained my hands as I raced to wipe them away. It didn't make any sense. It just didn't.

You never should have done this. The blood bond is not meant for one as free spirited as you. Kale's words from almost a year ago echoed inside my head. I struggled to accept what I'd just read. Had the change to vampire destroyed his wolf?

"Why didn't you tell me, you motherfucker?" I cursed as the blood tears streamed silently down my face.

So many things fell into place. Kale had been my partner since Veryl recruited me. Now, it seemed obvious why. He was babysitting

Darker

the new wolf, keeping an eye on me because he used to be one. When I rose as a vampire, I was going to lose my wolf.

I shook my head vigorously, praying that it wasn't true. Suspicions flitted through my mind. I'd attributed Kale's attraction to a metaphysical lure based on vampire power and energy manipulation. Perhaps it was his wolf all along. Maybe he saw in me what had been stolen from him.

The file went on to describe how Kale had been a military-infected werewolf used in espionage and black ops. Governments had been doing such things a long time it seemed. Then, he was sent to spy on a woman who happened to be a powerful vampiress. She changed him forever. No wonder Kale was barely sane.

Veryl hadn't recorded nearly enough details. Having heard only bits and pieces of Kale's past, I was flooded with questions. The shock took a long time to wear off. In the meantime, I stared at the screen until the words began to blur together.

The blood tears dried in macabre red lines beneath my eyes. A cold calm settled over me as denial took hold. I wasn't going to lose my wolf; I couldn't accept that.

Stiffly, I returned to the coffee pot for a refill. I stared down into the mug, watching as the cream swirled through the black liquid. As badly as I wanted to obsess over what I'd just read, I needed to bring Lilah down. I steeled myself for the return to the computer. Veryl had blackmail material on her, and I was going to find it.

Sunrise came and went. Arys never showed, but I was only mildly surprised. After the way I'd left things between us, he was likely fuming. Well, I wasn't too thrilled either.

The sound of water rushing through the pipes broke the silence. Jez was finished with her bath. I restrained myself from running to tell her what I'd found on Kale. We had time for that later; the poor girl needed to rest.

I found many more things, though, from Lena and Brogan's relation to one of the most powerful witch families in North America to bios and tidbits on people I'd never met. Fatigue pulled at my eyelids as worry nagged my thoughts. As I neared the end of the files, a sense of dread developed.

Then, I found Lilah's file. I held my breath as I devoured everything in it. Cha-ching! I hit the jackpot.

"Thank you, Veryl," I muttered aloud. "Your information hoarding has paid off."

If I were Lilah, I'd have been worried, too. Veryl had some juicy dirt on her. Unfortunately, it wasn't enough.

She was in hiding, fleeing a particular angel, Salem. I didn't know a lot about angel and demon politics, but I knew that whatever it was, it couldn't have been in Lilah's best personal interest.

Veryl had no record of exactly why she'd been imprisoned, but being confined in the angelic cage made her vulnerable and desperate. Soon, she manipulated an angel into freeing her; however, without blood from a creature of the light, she was still only a vampire. On the run ever since, she constantly sought a way to free herself and reclaim her former glory before being found by those hunting her.

When I couldn't fight the fatigue anymore, I shut down the computer. I had a lot to think about but enough information to play some cards during a confrontation with Lilah. Satisfied, I climbed the stairs toward bed.

Halfway up, I walked into a cloud of pain. Heavy and negative, it almost stopped me in my tracks. I shielded against the overwhelming sensation. The sound of muffled sobs drew me to the master bedroom where Jez lay curled in the fetal position in the middle of my bed. Her shoulders shook, and her hair fell across her face.

My worries faded when I saw her there. Jez needed me. That mattered more right now.

I sat on the edge of the bed and touched her arm. She grabbed my hand and squeezed, a small action laced with emotion. I swallowed hard as hot tears stung my eyes. Jez's agony was strong, and I loved her so much. It was impossible not to feel her breaking.

We sat in silence for several minutes. I couldn't say anything that would ease her pain, and I didn't want to cheapen the moment with phony words.

"You can sleep in my bed. I'll take the couch." I finally said. "Can I get you an extra pillow? Anything?"

"Will you stay? I don't want to be alone." Jez's voice was hoarse. Her grip tightened around my hand.

I climbed onto the bed beside her. The strong earthy scent of Were filled my nostrils. Curling myself around her, I hugged her close. The wolf within considered her pack. After missing Shaz so desperately, I found a sense of familial comfort in Jez. The affectionate touch of another Were gave me a soothing reassurance that was all about animal and pack. It felt natural. Right.

A cold panic gripped me. I was going to lose my wolf. My heart raced, and I had to concentrate hard on staying calm. I didn't want Jez to smell my fear. This was no time to be self-centered. Her pain came first; my worry could wait.

I held tight to Jez, burying my face in her gold locks. Only after she fell asleep did I let myself fall into a fitful slumber. In my dreams, I was still holding her, but as a victim instead. Her scent was no longer that of a kindred being but of my prey. I saw only blood, tasted only death.

I awoke with my heart thundering in my ears. Even in my dreams, I couldn't escape from the future I so desperately feared.

Chapter Thirteen

I woke up with a smile. It was just past sunset when the dream-world images of Shaz faded and I came back to myself. At least not all of my dreams were unpleasant, but waking up to realize it wasn't real was somewhat of a burn.

Jez was gone from the bed. Only her scent remained to indicate she'd been there. I found her in the kitchen with a bottle of wine in one hand and an unlit cigarette in the other. She leaned back in a chair at the table, my laptop open in front of her.

"Hey." She raised the bottle in greeting. Shadows lined her eyes. She clearly hadn't slept well. "You should probably put a password on this thing. Anyone could read this shit."

The bottle was almost empty. Jez had moved quickly from the crying stage to the drinking stage. It worried me. This stage was brutal; I'd been there myself.

"I'm destroying them once I read every last word. But, you're right." I stared into the fridge out of habit before deciding I didn't have much of an appetite. "So, what do you think?"

"I think if you've found out who exactly Lilah is hiding from, we've solved that problem. I also think you read the part about Kale and freaked out, which would explain why you came to bed stinking like fear." Tipping the bottle to her lips, she drained the last of it in one long swallow. "You were born to be a wolf, Alexa. The vampire thing happened by chance. Don't worry. You'll figure this out."

I forced a tight smile. "I hope so. I'm going to talk to Brogan and Willow about it, see if they know anything that will help. Until then, I'm going to take my mind off it by beating some answers out of

Falon. I want to have a little chat with Lilah, and he's going to tell me how to find her."

"I'm coming. I owe that smarmy angel a boot in the face. At the very least," Jez proclaimed, frowning at the empty wine bottle. "Where do you keep the hard stuff?"

"No way." I plucked the cigarette out of her hand and tossed it in the sink. "If you're with me tonight, then there will be none of this. No drinking. No smoking."

"But I—,"

"No, Jez. I know it's easier to escape than it is to deal, but if you come, you need to have your shit together. Beat some ass now. Drown your sorrows later."

She groaned and cast her eyes down to the floor. She was struggling to contain the rage and hurt that dominated her. It was difficult to refrain from responding to the strength of such emotion.

"Don't feel like you need to do this," I said.

"I can't stay here brooding. I need to feel like I'm doing something to avenge Zoey. I can't let Lilah get away with it." With a hard set to Jez's jaw, tears filled her bright green eyes, but they didn't fall. When she met my gaze, the predator inside her peered out at me.

Jez was hungry for vengeance; Zoey's death had broken her. Their relationship had meant more than I'd realized. They had only been together a couple months, but I understood how easily a bond could be forged. To have it broken so quickly had devastated her.

The doorbell rang, startling us both. I hadn't left the house yet, and already I was jumpy. Anticipation for what I planned to do with my night had me on edge. I ran down the long hallway to the front door, pleasantly surprised to find Kylarai on the other side, but she didn't look happy.

"Come on in." I stood back. "I was just about to get ready to head out. What's up?"

Kylarai peered out at me from behind a fringe of dark brown bangs. Her hair lay atop her shoulders in trendy layers that made her grey eyes stand out in contrast. Wearing butt-hugging blue jeans and a long, form-fitting sweater, Ky looked both professional and hot. Her energy was messy and scattered. It betrayed her fashionably well put together appearance.

"Sorry to just drop in," she said, anxiously tucking a lock of hair behind her ear. "I need to talk to you. About the pack."

"What about them? Did something else happen?" My pulse quickened. Lilah was susceptible to sunlight. Could she have hurt someone else so soon?

"No, nothing like that," she assured me. "I saw them earlier today. We had somewhat of a pack meeting. About you."

She spit out that last bit like it hurt her to say it. I realized where this was going; part of me had been expecting it.

I led the way back to the kitchen and waited patiently for Kylarai to give her condolences to Jez. I wouldn't trust me either, but I wasn't in a rush to hear that my pack didn't trust me with their safety.

"Go on." I gestured for her to continue when she looked uncertainly from me to Jez. "Tell me what the pack had to say. Since they're meeting without me, I can only assume it means one thing."

Kylarai sucked in a breath. She was having a hard time making eye contact. It didn't seem fair that she had to be the one to speak for them all. Of course, she was one of my best friends, so it made sense.

"They want you out, Alexa." Her words were rushed. Though she was nervously fidgeting with a stray penny lying on the counter top, her eyes were finally on me. "We've lost two wolves this week and Julian not so long ago. They think you bring danger to us all. They think you're more vampire now than wolf. Nobody trusts you."

The silence was deafening. Jez regarded me with wide eyes, awaiting my reaction. Kylarai was miserable. I could see this was the last thing she wanted to be doing right now.

"Fair enough," I said, my voice hollow, lacking emotion. The vampire remark stung especially deep after what I'd recently learned.

"I'm sorry." Kylarai's soft declaration was pained. "I love you like a sister, Lex, but you and I both know they're right. Things have changed for you. It's not safe for us anymore."

I nodded, having a hard time finding the words. "Fine. I'm out. No argument here. So who takes over? You?"

"Yeah. At least until Shaz gets back."

The urge to punch something was strong. My anger wasn't directed at Kylarai. This wasn't her fault; it was mine. If I lost my wolf because of my blood bond with Arys, that would be my fault, too. I was doing a fantastic job of fucking things up. If I didn't stay mad, I might cry. So, I chose to nurture the growing ire. It would come in handy later.

"You know what? You should be Alpha, Kylarai. Not me. I'm cool with this. Really. You can tell everyone I'll keep my distance." Being cast out of my pack hurt like a bitch, yet I couldn't deny the truth. "They're better off without me."

"I feel like an ass," Kylarai said, staring across the living room at a vase filled with fake flowers. "I'm so sorry. I didn't want to do this."

"Stop apologizing. Only a true leader can kick a friend out for the good of all. I respect you, Ky. That will never change."

She grabbed me in a big hug, crushing the air from my lungs. "If you need me, really need me, I've got your back. You know that, right?"

"Of course."

Kylarai had been there for me through some bad times. Back when Raoul was playing with both my head and my heart, before Shaz and I were anything but friends, she had been the mother hen of our pack, taking care of those in need. Recently, she had found love after a few failed relationships. She deserved to be happy and safe.

"Watch your back, ok? Lilah shouldn't be a problem much longer, but in the meantime, stay safe. Don't let your guard down." I was confident Kylarai could take care of herself. Hell, she'd torn her abusive husband's throat out and fought at my side many times. She would make a great pack leader.

"I should go. Coby's waiting for me in the car." She returned to the front door, casting apologetic glances my way. "We need to have that housewarming party you keep putting off."

"Oh, we will," Jez piped up from the kitchen. "I won't let her get out of it again."

Kylarai smiled, and though it held sadness, it still lit up her face. "I'll come by one night soon. We'll go for a run. It's been a while."

I smiled and nodded, doing my best to squelch the growing urge to scream. After a few more insistent hugs and promises to see me soon, Kylarai made her way to her Escalade in the driveway.

I closed the door and leaned against it. "Well, my night is off to a fucking great start."

Jez appeared at the end of the hall. "I'm not going to insult you by asking if you're ok. I imagine it feels kind of like being picked last in gym class. Nobody wants you on their team."

I laughed, a bitter sound that resonated through the empty corridor. "Nice try, Jez. Don't expect me to believe you were picked last."

"No, but I know what it's like to walk alone."

We stood at opposite ends of the hall, staring at one another. Jez was the only werecat I knew. I imagined that came with its share of loneliness. Cats might be solitary creatures, but they too craved love and affection.

"I feel like I've lost my wolf and my pack all in one day," I said, waiting for the emotion to hit me. Instead, I was numb. A hollow sense of calm always overcame me when I needed to shut down and escape. It would help me now, but I'd pay for it later when the floodgates broke open.

I stared at Jez, noting the predatory glint in her eyes. She had lost so much more, yet there she stood, ready to fight back.

Determination gripped me. I shoved away from the door with a bounce in my step. "Let's get ready. We have some ass to kick."

* * * *

"Are you sure? Once you do this, he won't ever forget it. He'll hold a grudge." Willow's warning went in one ear and out the other.

"He already hates me. I might as well give him a reason."

I watched Willow pour a salt circle on the floor of Harley's old room. In jeans and a t-shirt, he looked so casual. With his silver wings absent from sight, there was no indication of his angelic nature.

The Wicked Kiss seemed like the safest place to summon a creature of darkness. Falon could make all the noise he wanted, and nobody would give a damn.

"Are you sure that circle will hold him?" Jez asked, a brow raised in skepticism. Makeup hid the dark circles under her eyes. With her trademark red lipstick and skinny jeans, she hid her pain well, projecting a normal outward appearance.

"As long as nobody outside the circle breaks it, it will hold." Willow glanced my way, a mischievous glint in his gold-flecked green eyes. "You have something silver?"

"Will this work?" I pulled the silver cross Kale had given me out of my pocket and handed it to Willow.

He held up his hands in refusal, unwilling or unable to touch it, and I swore something almost wistful crossed his face. "Yeah, that works just fine."

"Are you ready? This is your last chance to change your mind."

"I don't have a choice. I can't track Lilah through the number she messaged me from, and I've gotta find her before she targets another person I care about." A nervous flutter started in my stomach. I was excited, looking forward to getting tough with Falon. In the back of my mind, I almost hoped he was hard to break.

I shrugged out of the long jacket that hid my dagger; I didn't need it or the dagger for this. In a black tank top and jeans, I was ready for a fight should one come my way.

Tossing my hair back, I stared at the cross, briefly struck with concern for Kale. Maybe I shouldn't be worried after what he'd done to me. Still, I needed to know he made it out of the FPA basement.

"Alright, let's do this," I said, my mind made up.

"You're doing it," Willow replied. "I'll guide you."

We stood outside the circle, careful not to get too close. Willow spoke slowly, the Latin rolling off his tongue with ease. It was just two lines, but it took me a few tries to get right.

"There are several ways to summon a demon, but Falon is in-between so calling him by name and offering an exchange of blood is most likely to work." Willow held up a knife with a golden hilt. "Whenever you're ready."

I stared at the circle. It crawled with negativity, the promise of dark things. Taking a deep breath, I spoke the summons, enunciating carefully. Then, I held my hand out to Willow. Grasping my wrist, he held my hand over the circle and sliced into my palm. The blood ran down to stain the carpet with bright red blotches. I tensed, waiting for something to happen.

At first nothing did. I thought it had failed. Then a strange, burnt metal smell filled the room, followed by a growing mist in the center of the circle. It materialized into Falon, who stood there disoriented. His pale gaze went from me to Willow. Realization struck and rage filled his eyes.

"You stupid fucking animal," he seethed. "You've gotten too cocky for your own good. And you," he directed his anger at Willow, "I should have known you'd turn up. And, with a Hound of all of things. I suppose you think by helping her you can earn your way back in."

"We're not here to talk about me." Willow shrugged, unaffected.

"Falon, I want to know how to find Lilah. Where is she?" I got right to the point, refusing to respond to his insults.

His sneer was expected. "No need to worry about that. She'll find you when she's ready."

"Where the hell is she? You're not getting out of that circle until you tell us." Jez approached with hands clenched into fists. I stopped her from getting too close, afraid she would step in the salt line.

Falon grinned. "You are a feisty one, aren't you?"

Jez growled and shot him a vicious glare. I cut in before she snapped. Palming the cross, I stood as close to the circle as I could safely get. I knew I might have to cross it and even hoped it would come to that.

"I'm going to find her, Falon," I said, my gaze locked on his. "You're going to help me. I know who Lilah's hiding from. I'll do whatever it takes to lead him to her. Are you willing to do what it takes to keep him from finding her? What's she really worth to you?"

His gaze narrowed. His substantial wings flared out behind him, hitting the invisible wall of the ten-foot summoning circle.

"You don't know anything," he spoke through clenched teeth. "Now, let me out of this circle, and just maybe, I won't tear your head off your shoulders."

I smiled, pleased with his anger. "I know she was promised to someone. And, I know that someone isn't you."

"So you know it all, do you? I bet you're feeling pretty proud. Well, since you are doing such a great job digging up information, find Lilah yourself."

Falon's expression was stone cold. Crossing his arms, he did his best to stare me down. His taller frame might have given the illusion that it was working, but even a fallen angel can't stare down a wolf.

The cross was warm in my hand. I wrapped the chain around my fist and held tight.

Willow caught my elbow before I could make a move. "Remember, once you enter the circle, you're trapped inside until someone on the outside breaks it."

I nodded, braced myself and stepped carefully over the salt line. There was resistance, like walking through water. Then I was through, and the circle closed behind me as strong as if it had been a concrete wall. Fascinating.

Falon stood his ground in the center, refusing to back up even a little. He held his hands up to keep me at arm's length. "You really are a crazy bit—"

I clasped his hands in mine, slipping my fingers between his and holding tight. The cross was lodged firmly between our joined hands. Falon's insult immediately became a scream.

Connecting with Falon opened me up to his energy. It ran over me like a waterfall soaking me in his essence. It was pain and pleasure twisted into a delightful rush that I both loved and hated. I tasted all that he was in that moment, discovering the depths of his power. He was an impressive creature, but he had weaknesses. I was determined to exploit them.

With a push of power, I drove him to his knees. A venomous hatred flashed in his eyes as he gazed up at me. I wouldn't always have the advantage with Falon; I needed to make the most of it.

"Get off me," Falon grunted, trying to pull his hands from mine.

I held tight, refusing to lose the connection. "Talk fast, or I'm just getting started."

I gasped then as our energy aligned. His became pliant, easily bent to my will. A deafening roar washed out all other sound. I stared into his silver eyes and saw my reflection. He was mine, a dark entity bound to the will of the light. For the first time, I felt my light, simmering deep in my core. Brightness filled me, bursting forth in response to the fallen angel in my grasp.

"Told you so," Willow said, but it was muffled, sounding far away. "You are definitely a Hound."

"Where is Lilah?" With each word, I sent another pulse of power into Falon.

He struggled hard to free the hand that I held against the cross. I knew damn well it was the silver allowing me the edge over Falon. Without it, he'd have kicked my ass well and good already. Still, it was impossible not to enjoy the high that came from having him at my mercy.

"I have no part in your conflict with her. Leave me out of it."

Despite his weakened state, Falon never once showed fear. He was rigid in his contempt. Having him on his knees before me was satisfying, but unless he was afraid, it just wasn't enough.

"It's too late for that."

It wasn't easy to hold him. My arms shook with the effort. The pressure began to build inside my head. No way was I letting him go yet, not without an answer.

Falon saw my exertion. He raised a brow in consideration. Unpredictable and unruly, it was impossible to know what he would try.

"You know, Shya may not let me kill you, but there are so many other things I can do to you."

"Funny," I replied with a growl. "I was just thinking something similar about you."

"Alright then." Falon smiled through the pain. "Ladies first."

I blinked, and my eyes were wolf. My fangs sprang forth and claws protruded from my fingertips. I held tight to Falon and let him feel my wrath. Focusing on the silver that joined us, I twisted its power over him with my own and shoved it deep inside him.

My temper was short. All I wanted was to make him hurt. After listening to his snarky comments and hateful insults for the past few months, my patience had run out.

Much to my disappointment, Falon's anguished cry was offset by his wicked laughter. Smoke rose up from our hands. I expected some form of retaliation. Falon was way ahead of me, and the bastard was clever.

"Your first mistake was thinking you could control me just because you summoned me," he said between clenched teeth. "But, where you really went wrong was when you were stupid enough to step into this circle. Do you really believe a tiny piece of silver is enough to overpower me?"

I bared my fangs in a snarl and ignored the growing pressure in my head. It took great effort to hold him. Unfortunately, I too have weaknesses. Rather than trying to outstrength me, Falon targeted my greatest one.

In a swift motion, he jerked my hand hard, slashing my claws across his neck. Blood blossomed up from a wound beneath his ear. The scent hit me, and I shuddered; that crimson spill promised absolute rapture. I resisted the immediate urge to run my tongue over that pumping fount.

The bloodlust smashed into me like a Mack truck. It left me dizzy, and my concentration broke. The connection between us was lost. Falon didn't hesitate. He jerked his hands from mine, swiped a finger through the blood from his healing cut and smeared it on my lips.

"What the fuck?" I muttered in confusion.

Falon's blood tasted like nothing I'd known. If power had a taste, this would be it. I ran my tongue over my lips, and that was it for me. The hunger swallowed me whole, and I was lost in it.

Because he made no attempt to fight me off, my attack was more forceful than was necessary. I heard Willow shouting for me to stop, but it was an irritation I ignored. Knocking Falon down, I ravaged his neck with a vicious bite. It wasn't just blood but power as well. I drank him in with a rabid appetite to feast on everything he had to give.

The tangy taste of him fed my lust for more. I pressed him to the floor and straddled him. I bit again, frustrated with his impeccable ability to heal so quickly. The power rose to a dangerous level as I took his into me and fed upon it. I needed more. I had to devour him.

I ground my groin against his, creating a push and pull of power as I did. A pulsing, throbbing storm filled the circle to capacity. Falon pulled me close, encouraging me to feed from his body and power. In my crazed state, I didn't think to question it.

Cursing beneath his breath, Falon grew hard beneath me. It encouraged the succubus nature of my vampire side, and I bit him again. The rest of the room fell away, and all I saw was the angel bleeding for me. It was ecstasy. Nothing else mattered.

Like the moment a fabulous dream is shattered by wakefulness, the blissful illusion was shattered when Willow destroyed the circle. He practically threw me across the room where I landed in a heap against the door.

The sound of wind rushing through the trees filled my ears. Blood dripped from my nose. More power than I could handle flowed through me, threatening what little remained of my sanity. Everything played out in a blur before me as I sought to catch my breath.

Now free of the circle, Falon came out fighting. He tossed Willow aside with little effort and turned toward me. Jez was there, ready with a silver dagger. She plunged it into Falon's midsection, holding it pressed to the hilt. Smoke rose from the wound, and he doubled over.

"How's that for a tiny piece of silver?" She hissed between bared fangs.

Falon's wings flared out, and with a great flap, he filled the room with an ear-piercing sound. It drove Jez back. She grabbed her head, trying to shut out the noise. Falon pulled her dagger free and held it high.

"I hope you learned a valuable lesson here, wolf," he said, scowling at me. "Your power is no match for me."

"Yeah," I gasped out through the pain filling my head. "I learned that you get a hard on from the power of an unnatural Hound like me. How does that make you feel, Falon?"

He crouched down in front of me so we were eye to eye. Turning the bloody dagger over in his hand, he said, "Don't flatter yourself, sweetheart. That kind of thing would happen to any heterosexual male with a woman wriggling around on top of him. I'm as disgusted by it as you are."

Grinning, he rose and tossed the dagger so it stuck in the carpet beside Jez. He shot a warning look at Willow and wagged a finger in scolding. To me he added, "I'm sure you'll never make a mistake like this again. Enjoy the ride, bitch."

He was gone, just like that. The horrible sound faded away, but the strange sensations continued to overwhelm me. My head felt like it might pop. It was a floaty, light-headed feeling accompanied by the overwhelming pressure of foreign energy. I tried to channel it back out, into the earth, the building, anything. It was no use. Falon's strange power roiled around inside me like a tornado on a path of destruction.

"Alexa?" Jez was at my side, lifting my chin so she could peer into my eyes. What she saw made her own grow wide in terror. "Willow, what the hell did he do to her?"

Willow pulled me to my feet and looked me over. "He purposely dosed her."

"What does that mean?" I squeezed my eyes shut as the room began to spin.

"He used your bloodlust against you, knowing you'd take power as well as blood. You can't handle immortal power like ours. He could have killed you, but since Shya won't let him, he let you take enough to really knock you on your ass for a while."

"I don't understand." I shook my head, and the room spun faster. It was hard to focus on either one of them.

"My God, Alexa, your eyes are silver," Jez breathed, a hand over her mouth.

"In basic human speak, he got you stoned off your ass," Willow explained. "Your power is life and death. What Falon and I are, it has never been human. It's beyond life and death. You can't control it. It will run rampant through you. You'll have facets of Falon's power. They will likely overwhelm you. It won't kill you, but it might feel like it."

I pulled out my phone, using the camera on the front so I could see my reflection. I gasped and dropped the phone, unable to take a closer look. My eyes were indeed the same pale silver as Falon's. The pupils were dilated, a wide and drowning black. Blood stained my lips.

A soft murmur of what sounded like a hundred voices all talking at once began inside my head. It steadily grew louder until it was just a cacophony of noise, each voice seeking to be the loudest. With my hands on each side of my head, I gave a frustrated cry. The power shifted inside me, and the voices fell silent.

My hands shook, and I had to sit down on the end of the bed. "Should be fine? What exactly does that mean?"

Willow looked from me to Jez and back again. With an awkward shrug, he said, "Either you manage to ride it out, or it drives you absolutely crazy."

Chapter Fourteen

Crazy was putting it lightly. It all hit me at once. The shaky unease gave way to a resurgence of stamina and strength that made me feel like I could scale a mountain. My awareness of every creature in the building, both human and supernatural, was heightened.

"It feels like everyone in the city is inside my head. I can hear them. Ugh."

"You can hear the freely given thoughts. The more attention you pay them, the worse it gets. I know it's hard, but try not to listen." Willow put a hand on my arm. He looked worried. "I'm sorry. I shouldn't have let you go into the circle."

"No, it's my fault. I underestimated him." I took a deep breath and tried to silence the voices again. "This isn't going to stop me from finding Lilah."

"Let me get this straight," Jez thoughtfully chewed a long fingernail. "He forced his power into you. So, can't you use it for your own purpose as long as you have it?"

Willow nodded. "In theory, yes. If it can be controlled."

"So why not just go into the club and pick through the thoughts of the vampires in there? Someone will know where she is."

Jez had a good point. I was glad one of us was still able to think straight. After locking up Harley's room, we headed for the heart of the club. My feet touched the floor, but if I didn't know better, I'd have thought I walked on air.

I shoved open the door that divided the club from the back hall, and it burst into flames. I shrieked and panicked. Willow waved a hand, and the fire went out.

Darker

"Careful," he warned. "Fire is just one of many things we can manipulate."

I ducked into the bathroom to clean up quickly. Jez hovered close, a watchful eye always upon me. I avoided looking at myself in the mirror. It was impossible to get used to the force trapped inside me. It felt foreign, immense and frightening.

Falon's blood might have easily been wiped from my face, but it was running hot through my veins. I wouldn't forget the taste for a very long time, if ever. Even as his power drove my wolf nuts and held me prisoner in my own body, I wanted to taste him again.

Returning to the club, I kept my hands close to my body as I walked through the crowd. As I passed each vampire present, an onslaught of thoughts and feelings swarmed me. They were all thinking about blood and sex, some more than others. I searched for Lilah in each of them. I found nothing until I passed a lone vampire standing near the door watching the rest of us.

Lilah was strong in his mind. She'd sent him to watch the place. Where was she? I turned my silver gaze on him and pinned him with a deadly stare.

I was suddenly there before him with no recollection of having moved. Before he could react, I placed both hands on his head and saw everything so clearly. Lilah was staying in a heavily guarded house on the south side of the city. It was a ritzy neighborhood in a private area. Both vampires and demons patrolled the premises. However, they weren't watching for Shya or me.

The vampire reached to throw me off. The power went out from me, and his head exploded into flames. I jerked my hands back in time to be covered with the ash and dust of his corpse.

Everyone around me stopped dancing, grinding and drinking. A few shrieks rang out from the human patrons. The vampires watched, waiting to see if I'd come for one of them next.

"Alexa, did you get anything?" Jez asked, watching me with uncertainty.

"I know where she is. We have to go in just before sunrise. She has too many guards."

The voices started up again, all fighting to be the loudest. The pressure swelled in my head, and blood dripped from my nose. I turned to leave, and the candle burning on the nearest table burst into a giant flame.

I frantically looked around for Willow who was at the bar with an upended bottle in hand. He came to my rescue without spilling a drop. Jez pressed a tissue into my hand. I dabbed my nose and swore. I couldn't take much more of this.

"How long is this going to last?" I clutched Willow's arm with more force than intended. My claws drew blood, and I jerked back, gushing a series of apologies.

"It's hard to say for sure. Either until you burn it off, or it burns you out." Willow swigged from the bottle of scotch.

He gave the impression he was just a regular guy with a drinking problem. With Falon's power commanding my senses, I could feel Willow's power in ways I never had before. It was vast and deep. He was ready to do damage if anyone gave him a reason.

I stared at my hands, willing the wolf to back down. For the first time in years, I couldn't repress the fangs and claws; too much power was wreaking havoc inside me. Thinking about the wolf made me think about losing it. Grabbing the bottle from Willow's hand, I downed a few good swallows. It didn't help.

A cool breeze lifted my hair. I felt Arys before he entered the building. We hadn't spoken since I left him standing outside Shya's house. My anger had long since faded. After everything that had taken place since last night, I had no interest in fighting with him.

"Arys is here." I glanced anxiously toward the door. "I don't want him to see me like this."

"You two need to talk," Jez said, giving my arm an affectionate pat. "We'll go sit down. You talk to Arys, and if you need us, we'll be right here."

"Whatever you do," Willow added. "Don't lose your temper. You could burn the whole building down."

Don't lose my temper? That was easier said than done as far as Arys was concerned. Willow and Jez left me standing there feeling helpless, though I was far from it. I didn't want Arys to see me there, amid the partygoers, filled to capacity with power that didn't belong to me. Drifting into the corner behind the bar, I waited.

He strode into The Wicked Kiss looking like an animal on the prowl. With his perfectly messed black hair and tight black jeans, Arys never ceased to make my knees weak. It seemed the more he drove me nuts, the more I wanted him. I anticipated the moment he would look my way.

Those midnight blue eyes landed upon me lurking in the corner. My stomach clenched when he came my way. Were we destined to always be this way? Growing more desperately in love with one another as the conflict between us also grew.

"What happened to you, beautiful wolf?" Arys took my face in his hands and gazed into my eyes. "I can feel your wolf's unrest."

His mention of my wolf brought forth a sadness I thought I'd buried. I shook my head and searched for the right words.

"It's my fault. I underestimated Falon." I went on to explain my poor attempt to manipulate information out of the fallen angel. I wanted to tell him what I'd learned about my wolf but couldn't bring myself to put it into words. Not yet.

"I'm sorry, Alexa." Arys pressed his lips to mine in a tender kiss. "About Shya. I shouldn't hide things from you. I just want to protect you."

"Look at me, Arys." I kissed him back, nibbling his bottom lip. "You can't protect me from everything. You can't even protect me from yourself."

He stiffened and pulled away. "I can damn well try."

Irritation took hold, and I huffed in annoyance. Arys needed to accept that I could handle myself. His insecurities were not my weaknesses. They were his. I grabbed a candle from the closest empty table and blew out the flame. Concentrating on the foreign entity inside me, I waved a hand over the candle, and the wick ignited.

Arys's eyes widened, and he appeared mildly impressed. I couldn't be too self-satisfied; that simple use of Falon's power had my head throbbing.

"I hate to say it, but I'm kind of glad it was you and not me," Arys admitted with a grin. "I've entertained the thought of sinking fangs into him more than once. How bad does it hurt?"

I had to pull out the tissue Jez had given me and dab the blood from my nose again. "Like a bitch."

Then, I noticed that I hadn't detected the slightest thought from him since his arrival. I stared at him, trying to pull something from him. Nothing.

"I can hear the thoughts of most of the people in here, but I can't hear yours."

"That's the plan. I keep my thoughts guarded. Many things can read minds, and I take no chances. You should do the same. It's no different than when you close me out of your mind. Same idea."

"Why are we not superheroes with abilities like this?" I joked. "Seems to me, we'd be pretty close to unstoppable."

Arys dropped his gaze, but not before I saw the worry flash through his eyes. Taking the tissue from me, he gently dabbed the blood that dripped from my nose. Maybe it was a very good thing that I couldn't hear his thoughts. I didn't think I wanted to know what was going on in his head right then.

"Some people think we are just about unstoppable. They may be right." He pulled me into his arms and kissed my forehead. Reaching to touch me metaphysically, I felt him shudder in response to what he felt thundering inside me. "You smell like wolf, but you feel like him. That fucking useless angel."

I didn't need to be inside Arys's head to know he would never stop blaming himself for condemning me to a future I now dreaded with every part of me. I needed him to know and to understand that it wasn't his fault. He had to accept it. Until he did, he would forever hold us both hostage to his misery.

A couple sat a few tables away, the only other people in the darkened corner. They were both human. Their hands were clasped across the table. Very clearly, I heard him wonder if she were really in love with the vampire she'd been shacking up with here or if she was under his influence. She stared at their hands and wondered why he had to make this so difficult; couldn't he just accept her choice?

She was breaking up with him, and I had to listen to her selfish thoughts as she did so. He was human. What could he offer her that would compare to the promise of eternity? Maybe some people were happy to settle for a "normal" life, but she had the chance to discover something extraordinary. Her mind was made up.

"You're making a huge mistake," I whispered beneath my breath. I wanted to grab her, to shake her and tell her she didn't know what she was getting into. *Get out while you still can.*

Arys followed my gaze to the couple. "Is something wrong?"

Darker

The couple's voices became just two of many as the barrage of thoughts started up again. The pain in my head worsened, and I felt like I couldn't breathe.

"I can't listen to this anymore." A hand to my head, I squeezed my eyes shut, but it only served to increase the volume. "Can we talk outside?"

"Of course."

With a hand on my lower back, he steered me toward the exit. The noise inside my head grew to a deafening crescendo. Sharp knives of pain pierced my skull. A storm of thoughts assaulted me, but one voice stood out above the rest. That one voice I knew well.

I felt the touch of his energy before I saw him. A honey sweet essence that called to the undying hunger I would always possess for him. We never reached the door. Arys stopped dead beside me, and I looked up to find Kale standing there, his gorgeous eyes fixed upon me.

For a moment none of us moved. It wasn't hard to tell that Kale wasn't himself. Madness caused his brown and blue eyes to glitter dangerously. The cacophony of noise fell away once Kale captured my full attention. He took one step toward me, and Arys snapped.

Arys was a blur of speed as he crossed the distance. Without hesitation, he threw a punch. It connected with Kale's jaw, and he stumbled back a few steps. Rubbing his chin, Kale turned to Arys with a malicious smile.

"I'm sure you can do better than that," he taunted, holding up both hands in invitation.

"Arys, don't!"

My shout went unheeded. Arys grabbed the other vampire by his collar and threw him. Kale crashed into a table and went down along with those seated at it. They had barely scrambled out of the way before Arys was there, dragging Kale to his feet.

"That's right." Kale spat blood. His grin was still in place. "I didn't play so nice with your girl last time. Do what you've gotta do."

"I should fucking kill you," Arys snarled. "She trusted you and you violated her. Like just another victim."

Kale's gaze passed over me. I saw no sign of the Kale I'd known, only the monster that had brutally tried to kill me in the FPA basement. It was like a knife to my heart. Sure, he'd been walking on the edge of sanity for a long time. I'd been ignorant enough to believe he wouldn't fall over into the abyss of bloodlust driven madness.

Staring into Arys's angry eyes, Kale laughed. "She is just another victim. Stop pretending you don't kill her yourself in your mind, every time you taste the power in her blood."

Kale might not have known it, but he was cutting too near the bone for Arys. Without warning, Arys lashed out with a right hook that opened up a cut above Kale's eye. I stood there knowing I had to do something, uncertain what that should be.

I threw my hands up, intending to separate them. Falon's power dominated my own, and instead of a simple separation, I threw them hard in opposite directions. I caught Jez's eye across the room. She shook her head and shrugged. Apparently, Arys wasn't the only one who thought Kale deserved an ass kicking.

Arys recovered fast. He was at my side, ready to do more damage. I grabbed his arm and forced him to look at me.

"Please don't do this," I pleaded.

"I can't let him get away with what he did to you."

Kale got up from where he'd fallen among the crowd gathered around the dance floor. Brushing himself off, he gave his short dark locks a toss and slowly made his way back for more. He paid Arys no mind; his gaze was on me.

I stepped between them with my hands up in surrender. "Just stop, Kale. Ok? It doesn't have to be like this."

"Doesn't it?" He kept coming. "You heard the man. He needs to defend your honor. Can't blame him for that."

"We can talk about this. Nobody has to get hurt." Try as I might to preach peace to them, it was incredibly difficult with the skull-bashing agony that threatened to bring me down.

Kale cocked his head to the side, studying me. "What happened, Alexa? Did you seduce one of the angels, too?"

My temper flared at the cheap shot. I almost blasted him with Falon's power but caught myself before I made a fatal mistake. Shaking with the effort it took to hold back, I sought out Willow's watchful gaze.

He stood close without getting involved. With his arms crossed and a casual stance, he gave the impression that he didn't care what happened either way. A quick nod provided the reassurance I needed. This wasn't his fight, but he wouldn't let me set the place ablaze.

"This isn't you, Kale. Nothing you say can hurt me. I know you're better than this."

"Are you still naive enough to think that? Haven't you been paying attention? This is what I am."

Kale's words echoed in my ears. Kale, who had once been wolf for such a short time, was now this monster, hell bent on destroying someone he once claimed to love. That would one day be me, too. It was too much for me to take.

"It's not always what you were," I said, the words tumbling out on their accord. "You were like me once. Wolf." Surprise flashed through his eyes at my words, so I bravely continued. "Why didn't you tell me?"

The shock was gone from his face as quickly as it had come. The twisted smile was back in place. "I suppose that was bound to come out eventually. Better be careful, Alexa. Nobody likes a snoop."

"Why didn't you tell me?" I repeated. Arys stood beside me, frowning at this latest revelation.

"You didn't need to know." Kale came closer, each step an unspoken promise.

"Why, goddammit?" My temper surged, and my hands burst into flames. It didn't hurt, but it scared the shit out of me.

Willow waved a hand from where he stood, and the flames went out. I'd have to be grateful later. Right then, it was Kale that mattered.

We faced off like the enemies we were never meant to be. Kale's expression was carefully vacant, impossible to read. "Because it doesn't matter. That time of my life was short. Almost non-existent compared to my years as a vampire. It meant nothing."

"It means something to me. You could have told me I'd lose the wolf. You could have…" I fell silent, realizing I'd been about to say *you could have stopped me*. I was distinctly aware of the tension and anger thrumming through Arys.

"Could have what?" Kale snapped. "Could have warned you? It wouldn't have made a difference. Look at you. Your choices are driven by your lust for power."

I had an anguished urge to hurt him the way he was hurting me. The loss of my wolf was a devastating fate. I merely had the inclination to strike him, and it happened without having to lift a finger. The power went out from me in a rush that left me breathless. It knocked Kale off his feet, flipping him head over heels. I gasped. I didn't mean to do it.

"I see how it is," he said, getting to his feet with a shake of his head. "You have regrets. Does it really make you feel better to take it out on me? I can help if you like." He moved fast. Pressing close enough to touch, Kale made a show of inhaling my scent. "I promise, Alexa, I'm going to finish what I started with you."

My bravado fled. Kale was staring at me as if I were prey. With the memory of what he'd done to me so fresh, I froze in fear. I'd trusted him; in some way, I'd even loved him. Until he'd made me a victim, that is, and then everything had changed.

Arys was done waiting. His energy turned scalding hot to match his hate-filled rage. When he came at Kale this time, he didn't let up. Kale did his best to defend himself, but after several weeks of being locked up, he had weakened. On a good day, he wouldn't have been a match for Arys. On a bad day, he quickly got his ass kicked.

I watched in horror as Arys threw a flurry of punches that all found their mark. A number of shots to the face had Kale bruised and bloody. A well-timed kick knocked him down. Several patrons turned their attention to the fight, many of them looking on in surprise as a vampire most of them knew well took a beating.

It all happened so fast. Judging by Arys's fierce aggression, he had wanted to do this for longer than the past few days.

"You're never going to touch her again." Arys doubled his attack by throwing power at Kale along with every punch.

"That's enough, Arys," I cried. My high-running emotions fed the foreign power inside me.

"There's only one way to guarantee that." Kale's smile had faded.

He kept on rising, inviting every hit he took. The deranged glint in his eyes, wild and ruthless showed his total abandon. He wanted this.

Through the insanity of voices in my head, his stood out above the rest. *Do it, you bastard. Save her from me. Do what she couldn't.* As mind fucked as he was by the blood hunger, Kale still had enough coherency for that thought. It spurred me into action.

I targeted Arys without a second thought. The force drove me to my knees. A bright, blinding light exploded behind my eyes, tearing a shriek from me. I could project Falon's power, but I couldn't control it. It was a force bigger than I was, one that I was pretty sure could kill me.

It slammed into Arys. Not only did it stop him from throwing another hit, it lifted him right off his feet and pinned him against the ceiling. I panicked, unable to manipulate the force commanding me. Thinking fast, Arys slapped me with a psi ball the size of a basketball. I pitched ass over elbows, coming to a stop against Willow, who hauled me to my feet.

He eased Arys back to the floor before turning to me. "You should get out of here, away from the crowd."

"I can't leave them like this." My vision swam, and I reached out to grab Willow for support but missed entirely. I slid to the floor, vaguely aware of the sticky residue of a spilled drink beneath me. My temperature rose. My palms grew sweaty, and I gasped for a breath that didn't smell like humans, blood and sex.

I watched in a dizzy haze as Arys grabbed Kale by the collar and jerked him close. His lips moved, but I couldn't hear what he said. The noise inside my head was too loud. A spark of gold-tinted blue lit up the place. Arys drew on the power we shared, pulling energy from me. It hit Kale at point blank range. He flipped over the bar and crashed into the bottles stacked on the back shelves. A shower of broken glass and liquor rained down on his motionless form. I held my breath, waiting. He didn't get up, but I suspected he wouldn't be down for long. There were only a few ways to kill a vampire. A hell of a beating wasn't one of them.

"Come on, Alexa. We have to get you out of here," Willow insisted.

Arms slipped around me, but it wasn't Willow dragging me to my feet this time. I knew that touch well. Arys guided me outside as I struggled to be free of him. After what I'd just seen him do, I was enraged, or I would be as soon as my head cleared.

"Let me go," I snarled, shoving him away.

As I got further away from the nightclub, the voices in my head disappeared. Though I was lightheaded, the dizziness faded. I walked to the far end of the parking lot, near the rear door and the back of the building. When I could no longer hear a single thought but my own, I reached down and placed both hands on the ground.

I tried to push the excess energy into the earth, to ground myself and refocus the power in my core. However, the earth refused to accept my offering. The fallen angel's power was rejected, pushed back to me like an unwanted gift.

"Why, goddammit?" I shouted to no one in particular.

Arys stood behind me, waiting. I rose and turned to pin him with a fiery glare. With hands clenched at my sides, I reminded myself that I wanted to give him a verbal beating, not set him on fire.

"How could you do that to Kale?" My voice wavered as I struggled to speak calmly.

"Alexa, open your eyes, and see that son of a bitch for what he really is," Arys shouted. "What you should be asking is how he could do that to you. He's a killer. You're blind to it. I don't understand how you can still see him as anything else."

I was deep in denial, and I knew it. I sure as hell wasn't going to admit it though. Chewing my lip anxiously, I studied Arys. His hands were balled into fists, and he looked ready to tear someone limb from limb.

"I don't need you to tell me how unhealthy my attachment to Kale is," I said. "Don't think I don't know that."

"He violated you. What kind of man would I be if I didn't do something about that?" Arys held his hands up in a gesture of helplessness.

I shoved a lock of hair back from my face. The power dancing in my fingertips prickled along my scalp, and I shuddered. I shook my head sadly. "You've done enough. I won't let you kill him."

"You think you can stop me?"

There it was, the challenge. One of us was always bound to issue it with little regard for the consequences.

"I think I'll damn well try. Let it go, Arys."

"Have you lost your mind?" He raged, raising his hands to the sky. Thunder boomed overhead, and the ground rumbled beneath our feet. "You attacked me in there. With power you can't control. You're the one out of line here, Alexa."

"So killing him will make everything ok? I've seen enough people around me die lately. Why must you contribute to it? Will it really make you feel that much better?"

"It might."

We stared at one another, the power of our anger spilling hot energy into the atmosphere. There was no right and wrong here. We were both entitled to what we felt, and no matter how I wished we could reach an understanding, I knew it would never happen.

It wasn't just Kale. It was everything: our differences over Shya, my safety and my inevitable fate as a vampire. Arys and I had never seen eye to eye. According to twin flame lore, we never would. I suddenly felt deflated, hopeless. I heard myself say something that I never thought would pass my lips.

"I don't think I can do this anymore."

"What?" Arys's gaze grew shadowed as he hid what was going on inside him. "What are you saying?"

"I don't know." A surge of emotion choked off my reply. What the hell was I doing? "I can't handle the constant conflict anymore. It will keep getting worse; it does every time. At what point does it destroy us?"

"Don't talk like that," he admonished with a scowl. "It's not like we can escape each other."

I forced myself to look at him, really look at him. He was a reflection of me in so many ways. Where those similarities ended, a great divide began. I loved him with a desperation that could only lead to pain. What we were, it wasn't natural. I didn't want him to suffer any more than necessary. We'd already suffered so much torment.

"No, maybe we can't. That doesn't mean we have to be together."

I hated myself when his guard fell and pain flashed through his blue eyes. I kept telling myself this was for the best. It would save our sanity and maybe even our lives.

"I can't believe you're saying this. We share power, a purpose. You can't turn your back on that."

"I'm not. I just think we need some time apart. I need some time." A sob caught in my throat. God, I was really doing this. "My pack kicked me out tonight, and it doesn't even matter because I'm going to lose my wolf. With Shaz gone, it's so much harder to resist your darkness. It grows in me, Arys. Every night it grows."

He crossed the distance I'd put between us and grabbed my arms. He shook me in frustration, forcing me to look up into his eyes.

"That will never stop. We need each other, Alexa. How can you think otherwise? I love you."

"I know that. And, I love you." I blinked back the blood tears that blurred my vision. "That's why this has to be the last fight. It's best for both of us."

"No. I'm not going along with this." His grip tightened painfully. He kissed me, a hard, bruising kiss that screamed of his refusal. It left me quaking.

I kissed him back with a red-hot passion I felt to the tips of my toes. My heart was calling me every name in the book, but my head knew I was doing the right thing. For the last year, so much of who I was revolved around Arys. I accepted that we were created to be together, but I needed to find myself first.

"Please understand," I whispered. "I need to discover who I am apart from you. For the sake of my sanity, just give me some time."

"I knew this day would come. I didn't want to believe it, but I knew." Arys held me close, burying his face in my hair. "I'm sorry about your wolf. I'm sorry I drove you to this."

I shook my head as the blood-red tears spilled down my cheeks. My words were an emotional jumble. "This isn't your fault, Arys. We just don't know how to exist together."

"I don't know how to exist without you. I waited so long to find you." His voice grew thick with emotion. "I can't lose you now."

A fresh surge of tears shook me. "You're not losing me. Just letting go. For a while."

We stood there for what had to be a long time but didn't feel long enough. I was still wrestling the urge to take it all back when he kissed me one last time and walked away.

I watched him go, fading into the night to become someone's worst nightmare. I collapsed to my knees on the pavement and cried. It felt impulsive, but this had been building for months now. Despite our love, we had no qualms about turning on one another when the situation allowed it. We had to do this, to save ourselves. We had to.

As much as I told myself it was better this way, my heart wouldn't believe it. I gasped for breath in between sobs as I became utterly and completely broken.

Chapter Fifteen

"You did what you think is best. What matters is that you can live with it."

Jez popped the cork on a bottle of champagne and toasted to the coming dawn. We sat in an old graveyard twenty miles outside the city. The earth was, for the most part, undisturbed. Except for Zoey, nobody had been buried here for a long time.

Justin's directions had led us down a long country road I'd never traveled before. A few hours before sunrise, we pulled into the overgrown cemetery. We found the spot where the ground had recently been dug up. Only a small bouquet of flowers indicated the place where Zoey now rested.

We both cried, each of us grieving a personal pain that no words could express. Then we sat against two headstones, facing one another, and talked.

"I didn't want to do it, Jez. I just knew I had to. I think I fucked up." I shook my head when she offered me the bottle. The only way I'd escape this pain was to finally accept Arys's darkness, but I wasn't going to give in until I couldn't take the resistance anymore.

"No, Lex, you're dealing with a lot. Needing some time to yourself is normal, healthy. Shaz is doing it, too. It's a good thing. When you come back together, you'll be strong enough to handle it."

"What if this is it? What if it's too late to come back from this?" I rolled my head back against the cold stone and stared up at the twinkling stars.

Jez sipped champagne and followed my gaze. "No time for what ifs. Don't force yourself to live in a moment that doesn't exist yet. Just getting through this moment, right now, that's hard enough."

"You're amazing, you know that?" I was awestruck by Jez. She had lost more than I had. She sat near her lover's grave and spoke encouraging words to me. It should have been the other way around.

"Well, yeah." She playfully rolled her eyes and grinned. The smile lacked genuine warmth though.

"Are you ready to do this? Feel free to change your mind. I wouldn't blame you." I raised a brow expectantly.

"Not a chance."

"Ready?"

Jez nodded. "Yeah. Can I just have a minute alone here?"

"No problem."

I pushed to my feet and walked through the long overgrown trail back to the road where I'd left the Charger. The power roiling about inside me caused my hair to float lightly, much like the effects of static. It wasn't as erratic as it had been a few hours earlier, though it was still testing the boundaries of my control.

I paused halfway to the car. If I could gain even a little control, I could use Falon's power when Jez and I stormed Lilah's house. I wasn't planning on a showdown; I wanted to talk to the bitch. If she knew that I possessed Veryl's info on her, she might be forced to back down. Of course, I had to be ready for anything.

Taking a deep breath, I released it slowly and focused on a dead tree stump. I willed it to ignite, but not so much as a spark appeared.

That was odd. I expected at least a flicker of a flame. I tried again, projecting my intent through thought as I would with my own power. I just didn't have that kind of ability with the borrowed force. Again, I tried to no avail.

"Fuck," I swore in sudden frustration and stomped my foot.

Immediately, the stump burst into flames. It climbed high into the sky, blindingly bright, then died down and went out. That was interesting. In The Wicked Kiss, the fire had seemed erratic. I couldn't be sure, but Falon's power seemed to react to my emotions. I'd have to test that further.

By the time Jez joined me at the car, I'd managed to ignite some brush on the side of the road and even float the Charger several feet off the ground. As good as my telekinetic ability to manipulate energy was, it wasn't quite that good. The car was easily more than four thousand pounds. Being able to toss around something that big would certainly have its perks.

Less than an hour later, we rolled into the swanky neighborhood where Lilah was hiding. The houses were huge; some of them easily made mansion status. Most of the properties were fenced off, giving the impression that the occupants wanted little to do with outsiders.

"Why do I get the feeling we're about to be very surprised?" Jez mused, her gaze passing over the millionaire homes.

"That's not the plan," I said with a soft laugh. "Lilah is the one about to be surprised."

"Here's hoping."

We passed the house I'd seen in the vampire's thoughts, and my stomach tightened. I circled the block and parked several houses away. I debated on whether or not to bring the Dragon Claw. I was hoping to have a discussion, not a fight. Packing a weapon like that might tip the scales toward violence. In the end, I left the dagger in the trunk of the car. If it came down to a fight, my best defenses were the ones I carried inside me.

Jez tucked her favorite ash wood stake into her boot and gave me a grim smile. "Ready when you are."

Willow wanted to accompany us. I'd asked him to keep an eye on Arys instead, to make sure he didn't do anything too worrisome.

The house was as massive as any other in the neighborhood. A twenty-foot concrete wall surrounded the perimeter, and an iron gate blocked the driveway. I made no attempt to hide my approach.

We scaled the wall with no trouble. Jez gave me a boost and climbed up after me, her lithe, cat-like grace making it appear effortless. I paused, reaching out metaphysically to feel the area. Vampires, I could feel their telltale aura easily. Nothing else registered, but some creatures had the ability to cloak their presence. I was one of them, and so were most demons.

"There could be just about anything in there," I observed.

"This should be fun then." Jez punched me lightly in the arm. "Let's go make this bitch sorry she ever met us."

We dropped down to the grass below and waited. It was too quiet. I knew it couldn't be this simple, and I was right.

Two seconds later, a pack of dogs came barreling around the back corner of the house. *Dogs* was hardly the right term. Beasts, monsters, things, all of those were a better fit.

"Hellhounds," gasped Jez. "I thought they were a myth."

"Just tell me we can kill them." I was both horrified and mystified by the beasts. If I was a Hound of God and they were Hounds of Hell, then this might just be fun. My wolf tensed, ready for the fight.

"I guess we're about to find out."

As the four ugly dogs came raging toward us, Jez and I stood side by side and braced for the attack. Each dog was huge, standing over waist high on all fours, easily weighing a few hundred pounds. Slobbering and snarling, they bared a mouthful of razor sharp fangs. Black with red eyes that glowed in the dark, they were dreadful things.

Though I was ready with fangs and claws, I didn't plan to let the monsters close enough to use them. Sweeping a hand before me, I threw a psi ball that spread out in a haze of fire across the grass. It knocked three of the dogs back, but the fourth leapt over the flames and kept on coming.

Jez met it with a kick. The hound flew back but was up again immediately. I focused on launching him into the side of the house. Falon's power ripped through me with force that left me shaking and my head pounding. The hound burst into flames. The high-pitched sound he made hurt my ears, but it was over quickly.

The fire I'd thrown at the other three had gone out, and they were on us before we could blink. I went down hard with one on top of me, fangs snapping dangerously close to my face. I got my arm between us and somehow managed to hold him off. Powerful hind legs kicked into my midsection, opening up a wound. Gritting my teeth, I shoved my power at the hound, and it flew backwards to land hard against the concrete wall. The crunch of breaking limbs was audible, and it didn't get up.

The other two were on Jez, who was fighting hard. She slashed claws across the jugular of the hound fighting for her throat. Blood poured forth, bathing her in a crimson wave. I grabbed the other hound by the back legs and threw it. I followed up with another psi ball before it could recover.

When I was sure each hound was dead, I pulled Jez to her feet and looked her over. "Are you ok?"

"Not a scratch on me," she replied with a grin. "Yours looks superficial. Damn, that was a rush. I wouldn't be surprised if there are more."

I inspected the cut on my midsection. It was minor. I'd live.

We warily made our way up to the front door. Large white pillars stood off to either side. I expected something to leap out from behind them, but it never happened. I glanced at the doorbell.

"Do we ring the bell or just burst inside like some action movie?" I returned Jez's grin. Nothing about this was funny, but it was impossible not to get off a little on the excitement.

"Hey, she only murdered people we care about for her own gain," Jez said, heavy on the sarcasm. "No reason we can't be civil."

"Alrighty, then." With a shrug, I leaned on the doorbell longer than necessary. I gathered my power close, ready to use it. The pressure built fast thanks to the taint of fallen angel, which would not be easily held.

"I swear," I muttered. "If Falon opens this door I'm going to kick him in the damn-,"

The door cracked open, and I braced for whoever was on the other side. I wasn't expecting a human. Thin and exceptionally pale, she stared at us with eyes the size of dinner plates. Stinking of fear and blood, she glanced nervously at someone out of sight before speaking.

"Can I help you?"

I could feel a vampire or two nearby, no problem. I was more worried about the demons that I couldn't sense.

"Tell her we want to talk. That's all." *For now.*

I waited for a reaction, but the woman had none. I could smell the bites on her though I couldn't see them. Lilah certainly wasn't the first vampire to keep human cattle, but it was still sickening. For once, I didn't feel so bad about my ties to The Wicked Kiss, as owner or patron. At least our victims were willing.

"She will see you in the library." The frail woman turned and walked away, fully expecting us to follow.

Jez didn't hesitate. She entered the house without batting an eye at the elaborate decor or the two vampires standing in the shadows beyond the sun's reach. I approached more cautiously. One of the vamps I recognized right away—because the bastard worked for me.

Shawn was a wannabe tough guy who had tried to scare me into letting him taste my blood the first time we'd met. Upon learning I was Arys's wolf, he'd backed off so fast he almost burned a hole in the carpet. Since then he'd been an acquaintance and The Wicked Kiss employee, ready and willing to provide muscle where needed.

"Sorry, Alexa," he said, lifting one shoulder in a half-assed shrug.

"No worries," I replied with a cold smile. "You're fired."

The foyer was huge, complete with the largest spiral staircase I'd ever seen. Lilah's human led us behind it to a set of open double doors that revealed a library so magnificent I couldn't help but gawk. Still, my survival instinct was stronger than my awe. When a pair of hellhounds appeared in front of us, I threw up an energy barrier that crackled with fire.

"Stand down, boys." Lilah's command was immediately obeyed. The beasts sat down and shut up but never once took their vacant red eyes from us.

Books lined the room from floor to ceiling. Right away, I could tell human eyes had never seen many of the titles. I would have loved the chance to take a peek inside any of them.

The hardwood floors were smooth and shiny. Paintings depicting various historical scenes adorned the walls. I didn't take any time to study them; I had eyes only for Lilah.

She sat in front of an empty hearth. I did a double take; she barely looked like Lilah. With her flame-colored hair in long, loose waves that framed her face and a flowing black gown that pooled on the floor at her feet, she was almost pretty. A shiny silver crown sat upon her head. The front of it was a cobra's flared head. The body made up the rest of the crown.

A small harem of vampires and demons fell all over themselves, fawning over her in worship. They kissed her arms, her face, touching her with lusty caresses. She sat in the middle, eating up the attention, smiling in satisfaction.

Her human pet stood awkwardly nearby, awaiting further instruction. A pair of demons flanked Lilah, each standing on either side behind her chair. One of them was Brook. He stood protectively over her, watching with a cold, steely gaze that spoke of nightmares come true.

I was willing to bet there were others, currently unseen. I wondered if Falon was among them. A dozen vampires scattered about the library watched us with intrigue.

"Look at you." Lilah's burnt orange gaze traveled over me appraisingly. She shoved her men away and gave me her full attention. "Sucking up power like a sponge. I bet Willow thought he was doing you a favor by sending you in here like that."

She thought it was Willow's power raging through me? Interesting. I saw no reason to enlighten her.

"I didn't come for a fight, but I'm ready if you want to give me one." In a brazen move, I reached out psychically to test her, making sure she was still powerless. Shya's binding was still in place.

"Come on now, Alexa. Do you really think I'd resort to getting my hands dirty if I had access to any power?" Lilah asked with a small smirk. "As you can see, I don't let things like that slow me down. So, you say you want to talk? Let's talk then, ladies."

Lilah gestured to the big easy chairs across from her. She was going to play the gracious hostess and milk this thing for all it was worth. I wasn't in the mood to play games.

"Did I say talk? I meant threaten." I let the energy wall drop.

I kept expecting to feel some kind of fear or apprehension. Though I feared what she might do to others, I didn't fear what she had planned for me. I was ready to take her on.

She pressed the tips of her fingers together and looked at both Jez and me in turn. "That's more like it. There's no reason we can't all be honest with each other. I didn't think you came here leaking borrowed power just to talk. Go ahead, I'm listening."

It was weird to see Lilah so dressed up. I'd never seen her in anything but army fatigues and boots. She cleaned up well. Playing the role of demon queen spoke volumes in regards to her determination. She was ready and willing to do whatever it took to reclaim her throne.

"I know who you're hiding from," I said, watching her reaction. "I think it's time he finds you."

"So, you do have Veryl's information." Lilah nodded knowingly. "I figured as much. That's the problem with people like you and Veryl. You think knowledge is power. It isn't though. Knowledge can get you killed. Or worse. So, this is blackmail then?"

"Don't look so surprised," Jez spat. "You gave us no choice."

Lilah fixed Jez with a dark glare. "This was never personal, Jez. Why make it so? Besides, I did that hybrid a favor by putting her out of her misery."

Jez lunged forward, and I stopped her before the hellhounds did. I didn't blame her one bit for having murderous intentions. Knowing Lilah couldn't be killed drove me nuts; I wanted to make her beg for mercy.

The demons standing guard near Lilah didn't move, but I could sense that they held their power ready should one of us give them a reason to use it. I held tight to Jez's arm, hoping she wouldn't fight me. The hate-filled energy thrumming through her spilled over me, drawing my attention to the pure Were blood pumping hot through her veins.

"You didn't kill Zoey in an act of mercy, Lilah. You think you can force my hand by killing my wolves. It's a coward's tactic." I focused on staying calm when all I wanted to do was set the bitch on fire.

"Yes, well it worked, didn't it? Here you are." Lilah's wan smile made it clear that blackmail wouldn't be enough. It might buy me time, but it would never stop her.

"I won't give my blood to you. I'm here to tell you face to face that it's over. You have no shot at breaking the curse. Not with me." I tried to stifle the spark burning its way quickly through my short fuse. If I lost my precarious hold on the power testing my resistance, this would get ugly fast.

"So what now then?" Lilah rose, and the demons on each side moved closer. She waved them away with a scowl. "You take over where Veryl left off blackmailing me? We can call a truce, Alexa. I can make it worth your while."

"I don't want anything you can offer."

"I can change that."

"Save it," I snapped, and a vase filled with flowers went up in flames. Oops.

Lilah watched the fire die out with pursed lips and a raised brow. "That's the problem with being a mortal succubus. You can soak up all the power you touch, but that doesn't make it yours. I can help with that."

"You're used to dealing with power-hungry dirtbags like Shya, I get that," I said, the condescension heavy in my tone. "I'm not one of them, so instead of wasting time trying to coerce me into a deal, you should be telling me what you're willing to do to keep me from telling Salem where you are."

At the mention of his name, Lilah froze. Her demon guards watched me warily, with Brook staring a little more intently than I was comfortable with. The low, steady growl of the hounds was the only sound.

"Don't say that name." Lilah moved with purposeful strides, stopping when I raised a hand to blast her. "You should know better than anyone why I ran. I don't belong to any man, no matter what fancy fucking claim he thinks he has on me. I won't be controlled by a bond I have no say in."

With each word, Lilah's anger grew until it was palpable. She was suddenly furious, and in a swift motion, she threw the vase I'd scorched. It smashed all over the floor in a mess of scorched flower petals and glass. I'd never seen her anything but calm. Even when we'd fought outside Shya's house, she hadn't exhibited such sudden temper. Whoever this guy was, he got under Lilah's skin in a bad way.

"You killed Veryl," she shouted at me, pointing a finger at my face. "Now, you think you can take his place? I'll kill you before I let you hand me over to Salem, even if it means losing my chance to break the curse with your blood. I'll find another way."

I grabbed Jez's hand and formed a circle with us inside. The desperation in Lilah's eyes was both satisfying and worrisome. She was terrified of this guy and clearly prepared to escape him at any cost.

"What's with the sudden freak out?" Jez taunted. "This guy must be a pretty big deal to get your panties in such a knot."

"Oh shut up, Jez. What would you know about being born to exist alongside another, whether or not you want to? There's a reason twin flames are so rare. They are not a gift but a curse of the worst kind." Lilah approached my circle and placed her hands on it. She flashed a grim smile at me. "Veryl's files didn't say that, did they?"

"A curse?" I sputtered through the shock and denial. "A twin flame union only happens for a reason. It's meant to be. There's something special in that."

"Special?" She smirked. "Bound to another against your will. United through forces you cannot control. Unable to escape them no matter how far you go or how many names and faces you wear. To hate that person as much as you love them. Oh, and how you love them. So much you start to hate yourself. And, for what? To be manipulated into fulfilling some horror-filled destiny? Not a damn thing about that sounds special to me. The chosen ones, us, we're meant to suffer. This is no gift."

Her words struck a chord deep in me. She described so well things I had felt even when I hadn't been willing to admit it to myself. She knew. Still, she was wrong. She had to be.

"Don't listen to this bitch, Lex. She's a demon, otherwise known as a deceptive liar. She's trying to get inside your head." Jez squeezed my hand. The fierceness in her eyes reminded me why we'd come here.

"If it wasn't a curse, why would light and dark be joined to one another? They can never truly become one. One will always devour the other. What kind of sacred purpose would join a demon to an angel? Or, a vampire to a mortal?" Lilah looked at me pointedly, and for just a moment, I saw a flicker of the sadness I'd seen in her once before. "When love is always pain, it ceases to hold any meaning."

"I don't believe that." I shook my head, unwilling to accept it even as I heard the truth in her claim.

I couldn't let Lilah put doubts in my head. She wanted to appeal to any weakness I might have. I would not let her find one.

In a bold move that I didn't take the time to think through, I dropped the circle and hit Lilah square in the chest with a blast that sent her tripping over a hound. She recovered quickly, glowering at the demons who stood by watching.

"This isn't blackmail. I have nothing to gain from you. I don't care who he is to you or what you think of it. Stay away from me. Stay away from those I care about. Otherwise, either he comes for you, or I send you back to the cage where you belong."

Lilah adjusted the crown on her head and slapped the human girl attempting to smooth her skirt. "Incompetent idiots," she hissed at the demons. "Grab the wolf. I need her alive."

"No." My shout was accompanied by a surge of energy that struck each demon, only momentarily disabling them. The force was staggering as it left me. "Just you and me, Lilah. No power. If I come out on top, you're a prisoner. If you do, you get my blood."

Darker

Could a demon be manipulated by a mortal? I thought of Arys as the challenge left my lips. He was so busy trying to protect me from himself, he'd forgotten about the real threat.

The hounds barked, an ear splitting sound that echoed in the vast library. I couldn't stop the flood of angel power that oozed from me. It was uncontrollable. I was merely a vessel to be used. A blue flame engulfed both hounds and made short work of them.

One of the demon guards backed away muttering something about Shya's mark on my wrist. The other, Brook, watched Lilah, waiting for her decision. She looked me over, lingering on my silver eyes. I saw her consider it. I think she even believed she could take me, but something held her back. She wasn't willing to gamble with it, whatever it was.

With her long skirt sweeping out behind her, Lilah spun on a heel and uttered a loud command in Latin. I didn't have to be fluent to get the gist of it. She returned to her throne-like seat and crossed one leg over the other, watching with red-hot intensity as her vampires and demons advanced on us.

"Kill them both."

There was a pause, so small as to be near non-existent. Then, everyone started moving at once. In the melee, several vampires rushed me, separating me from Jez.

Most of them felt new; they hadn't been undead long. I met the first one with a kick that threw him into another. I spun to block a blow by another with my forearm while projecting a steady stream of power at a lunging female. She burst into ash and dust, followed by the next two I hit.

I caught sight of Jez swinging with stake in hand and bared fangs. I had no doubt she'd hold her own just fine. A fist connected with my jaw, and I saw stars. It didn't stop me from setting my attacker ablaze.

Every time I used the power, it grew more painful until I was crying out with each blast. My nose dripped blood steadily, and I regretted my choice to leave the Dragon Claw outside, a stupid decision. Yep, Arys was right; I was too reckless for my own good.

I punched a fist into the chest of a vampire who got closer to my throat than I should have allowed. Pulling his heart free, I tossed it so it slid to a bloody stop at Lilah's feet. I didn't have time to enjoy the glare she wore before another solid, undead fist connected with my face. Several of them piled on me, and I went down beneath them, the breath crushed from my lungs.

Though my brain felt like it might spontaneously combust, I forced my power into them, finding that undead essence within me that was all Arys and all dark. The last time I'd done this I'd inadvertently knocked down several other vampires as well, including Kale.

Despite the pain, I felt an immense sense of relief as Falon's power exploded forth along with my own. The more I used it, the less it retained its hold on me. It was fading. I could feel the heart of every vampire fighting to tear me apart. All at once they burst, showering me in blood, bone and ash.

Though I'd hoped Lilah would also be affected, she sat smugly, protected by a shield of demon magic. She waited patiently, soaking in the chaotic energy saturating the atmosphere while I burnt myself out trying to stay alive.

I rose from the pile of ashen vampire remains and sought out Jez. Blood smears marred her face, and her eyes blazed pure wildcat, but she stood ready for more.

"Really, Lilah," Jez said with an eye roll. "Did you honestly think that would work?"

Lilah didn't answer. She nodded to Brook who whispered something that sounded like no language I'd ever heard. A pack of hellhounds appeared between Jez and me. The pack split in half, backing each of us against a wall. I was bracing to go down under a flurry of snapping jaws. Between the killer headache and the power, I was crashing hard now, and knew I'd never have enough left in me to take on each hound.

Jez abandoned any notion of taking them on in human form. Using her last precious seconds wisely, she shifted to leopard and faced them snarling. Being wolf meant giving up my power, no matter how fast it was draining. It also meant, if we got out of here alive, we'd be running through the city streets in a form that would draw far too much attention once the sun rose.

I could draw on power through Arys. Alerting him to where I was and what I was doing didn't factor into this poorly thought out plan. I grasped for everything I had left in me and prepared to go down fighting.

Darker

The hounds leaped in unison, a well-oiled machine that knew how to hunt together. They came at me from each side. Jez was a blur of black and gold across the room as she battled the hellhounds. I kicked one hound in the face, satisfied with the resulting crunch. Another got a taste of my claws when I slashed its throat open.

They came too fast, and there were too many of them. Fangs sunk into my arms as I tried desperately to fend them off. I screamed, a sound that echoed inside my aching head.

The air rippled, and Shya appeared with a flourish of black wings and the stench of sulfur. Every hound snapped to attention, grovelling at his feet with ears laid back and tails tucked between their legs.

I slumped to the floor, breathing heavily. I didn't know if he was here as friend or foe, but I was happy to be freed of the hellhounds trying to rip my throat out.

"You've gone too far, Lilah," A rumble, like thunder in the distance, accompanied Shya's words. "You have no claim here. This is my territory now. Brook, you're dismissed. We'll be speaking soon."

Brook looked torn as he contemplated loyalty to his queen and obedience to the most powerful demon present. He disappeared with the sound of ruffling feathers. The other demons present were quick to follow suit.

Lilah sat stiffly in her chair. With her chin lifted in defiance, she appeared completely unafraid. She knew just as well as I did that Shya wouldn't be the one to send her back to her prison. Damn demon politics.

"How dare you enter my house uninvited? You're not welcome here. When you severed your ties with me, you knew what that meant." Lilah's voice was brittle, as if she was fighting very hard to keep her calm and cool appearance.

"You're a powerless queen with low ranking demons that serve you out of pity, not loyalty." Shya shook his head and tsked. "It's sad. You just can't accept that your time is over."

"My time has yet to come. You would be wise to remember that. I made you, and I can and will break you. You're everything you are because of me." Lilah's calm tone became a shout.

I shoved to my feet and applied pressure to the gushing punctures in my arm. It was bad. Those bites were going to hurt for a day or two.

"Perhaps." Shya gave a slight nod. "But, I owe you nothing now."

He turned to Jez and me, ushering us toward the door with his outstretched wings. He didn't waste another word on Lilah. She sat there stewing, a self-appointed queen with no kingdom to rule. It would have been sad if it weren't so downright disturbing. I knew her type; nothing would ever stop her.

"I need her blood, Shya," she called after us. "If I can't have her, I'll ensure that you can't either. You'll regret this foolish rebellion."

Shya paused, a strange smile on his face. "That is exactly why you don't deserve to rule."

Lilah didn't respond. With nobody left to protect her, I saw my chance and decided to go for it. I reached for my power, gritting my teeth against the unbearable agony. I'd draw from Arys if need be; it would be worth it if this worked.

I set my focus on her and let go. I could feel her vampire essence, and I knew it was mine to manipulate. Excitement surged through me. This was going to work.

…Or, it would have if Shya hadn't blocked my attack. With a sweep of his wings, he knocked me off my feet. I cleared the library, sprawling on the floor of the foyer.

"We've won this round, Alexa. Time to leave." Shya came to stand over me, watching as I dragged my exhausted self to my feet.

"Fuck that. I'm putting that bitch back where she belongs." I shot Shya a dark glare.

"Leave," he said, shoving me along with those impressive wings.

Jez followed with a growl rumbling in her throat. I saw no sign of Shawn or anyone else. He'd probably met his end in the library along with many others. Just as well, he'd proven that he couldn't be trusted.

The sky was still dark, but sunrise was close; I could feel it in my bones. Shya would be forced to leave with the dawn. Demons couldn't maintain form on the physical plane during daylight. I could wait.

Darker

After ushering us out, Shya waved a hand over the front door. A barrier snapped into place, and I swore.

"Why the fuck are you protecting her? She's killing my wolves. She tried to kill me and Jez." What little energy I had left, I poured into my anger. Shya was getting on my nerves.

Moving fast, he grabbed my wounded arm and pulled me dangerously close. "You'll get your chance. She is my queen. There are things I cannot do no matter how far her kingdom has fallen. I don't expect you to understand."

"Good because I don't. She's a washed up queen with a curse. She knows she's going down, and she wants to take as many of us with her as she can. I won't let it happen."

I tried to pull my arm from Shya's grasp, but he held tight. I winced but bit back a pained noise. Jez paced beside us, her emerald eyes flitting back and forth between us. Her beast had my wolf pushing to break free from my exhausted human body.

"You have many fine qualities, Alexa. Patience, unfortunately, isn't one of them. Work on that. Knowing when to wait it out can mean the difference between victory and death." He let go of me abruptly. "I'll be having a word with Falon about what he did to you tonight."

"Don't bother. I'm sure I had it coming. I trapped him in a circle and bullied him with silver."

"I'm aware. You should know that what he did can have a lasting effect on people like you. He crossed a line."

Fatigue made it hard to care enough to continue the conversation, but anger kept me going.

"If anyone has crossed a line, Shya, it's you," I said bitterly. "You have Arys convinced that you're some reliable ally. You and I both know that isn't true. You've got some kind of ill-conceived plan for me. Whatever that is, leave Arys out of it."

"I said I'd protect you; I just proved good on my word." Shya cast a glance toward the sky, gauging how much time remained. He turned back to me and said with a wink, "I'm going to unleash hell on this city, and you're going to help me."

With his bemused smirk firmly in place, he unfurled his wings and vanished. My lips twisted into a scowl. "That was unnecessarily dramatic."

Jez bumped her furry face against my hand. She was right. We needed to get back to the car before the neighborhood woke up. As eccentric as these rich types tended to be, walking a leopard through the streets likely wouldn't go over well.

"Nothing more we can do here, thanks to Shya. Let's get going. I'm feeling the need to get furry, too."

I wasn't going to react visibly in case Shya lingered unseen, but his words had chilled me to the bone. It left so much open to interpretation. Lilah's need for a little blood paled in comparison.

Chapter Sixteen

For the first time in a long while, I slept a deep, uninterrupted sleep. A night of power binging was enough to grant me a dreamless slumber. It was similar to the effects of a human booze binge but intensified several times over.

I flung my arm out at one point, searching for Arys and finding the rest of the bed empty. Disappointment crushed me. I rolled over and hugged my pillow, falling back into the depths of sleep. Then, I slipped into Arys's mind, and the bloodstained images flooded me with an unholy hunger.

Screams rang in my ears, accompanied by his wicked laughter. He wanted to make someone hurt the way he was hurting. He needed them to beg and cry so he could take pleasure in the torment. Only when he caused suffering did he himself cease to suffer. Arys saw nothing but the couple he had chosen to inflict his wrath upon.

If he felt my presence, he didn't acknowledge it. The scent of blood was so strong it choked me. I woke up with a start, sitting straight up in my bed. The screams faded, replaced with the pounding of my heart. The hunger remained.

I sat there shaking in my bed despite the heat that had me throwing off the sheets. I was thankful Jez had returned to her apartment. After making me promise several times not to go after Lilah again without her, she had bravely gone home to face an apartment filled with memories.

As I went through the motions of showering and brushing my teeth, I could focus only on one thing: the heady rush that came with taking blood. Ravenous and impatient, I rushed through my human activities. A solid eight-hour sleep and the meal I'd eaten before bed had helped, but it wasn't what I needed to be at full strength. That would only come from stealing the life force from another. As much as I hated it, I wouldn't be sated until I had.

My eyes glowed Arys's vampire blue. Absorbing another's power so it visibly showed was unsettling. It made me feel a little like a freak, though what didn't these days?

Bloodlust drove me. I didn't think; I just acted. Like an addict who feels no remorse until after they get a fix, I moved mechanically, need and buried hurt guiding me. I should have known how Arys would choose to deal with the pain I'd inflicted.

It hadn't been my intent. I was hurting, too. I didn't know how to be apart from him. I couldn't accept that I could no longer exist without him. Lilah's remark about the twin flame bond being a curse lingered, taunting me, telling me it was true.

"Lying fucking demon," I muttered, punching buttons on the radio in the Charger. The country station was out of the question. A Top 40 station playing a lost love ballad was quickly changed. I settled on a heavy metal satellite radio station and headed for the city with electric guitars screaming in my ears.

If I couldn't hand Lilah over to Salem, I would have no choice but to keep confronting her until one of us was no longer standing. First, I had a desperate hunger to take care of, whether I liked it or not. Unfortunately, I would like it, and I would hate that.

I found myself sitting in The Wicked Kiss parking lot half an hour later. What was I thinking? I shouldn't be here. Not only was it the one place I'd told myself I would never patronize, but Kale's classic Camaro was parked near the rear door. He'd moved it for the first time in weeks.

I watched those milling about the front entry smoking and talking. Their raucous laughter carried. I saw them all as prey, ready and willing victims just waiting for someone like me to choose them.

Where was Arys right now? Tearing apart the couple I saw in his mind? Or, had that been a memory? I gripped the steering wheel tight and fought back the bloody images that surfaced. If I went into the club, I might not be able to control myself. And, though I sure as hell couldn't avoid Kale forever, I just wasn't up to that tonight.

Darker

I left the car and breathed deeply of the crisp night air. It did nothing to clear the haze of bloodlust fogging my head. I had just one purpose.

The will to fight had left me. The blood hunger ruled, and I thought of nothing but appeasing it. In a black skirt that flowed around my knees and a red halter-top, I crossed the lot with a predatory gait.

Upon walking through the lobby into the club, I was hit with the dizzying rush of excited energy oozing from those inside. I embraced it, wrapping it around me like a blanket. I wasn't in the mood to wait out the right victim. I scanned the crowd for my chosen one.

Kale was near the dance floor with a tall brunette in his arms. He whispered in her ear. She blushed and threw her head back in laughter. He looked at me, and I redirected my gaze. I wasn't here for him.

I prowled through the club, careful to give Kale and his playmate a wide berth. A guy standing alone near the bar caught my eye. Judging by his heavy metal attire, consisting of leather and chains, he was here to party. A pretty boy with slick black hair, he would do just fine.

Once our eyes met, I knew he was mine. Crooking a finger, I invited him to come to me. I tilted my head and gave him a come-hither look he couldn't deny.

The anticipation was foreplay like no other. The build-up to that inevitable moment when he would be mine was a pleasure all its own. I couldn't wait to taste him. Nothing else mattered but that moment. Vampires existed for this alone; the hunt made all other thoughts disappear. Problems ceased to exist. For now, I was in control, and it felt damn good.

"Looking for a friend for the night?" He asked when we stood face to face. His dark eyes sparkled with intrigue.

"You could say that." I pulled him close and gazed deep into him. It wasn't hard to lure him in. I'd so often been the victim of a vampire's thrall that it felt liberating to be the one behind the manipulation.

"Go easy on me," he said with a boyish smile. "I'm a bit of a newbie."

I searched him; the innocence in his eyes almost stopped me. He wasn't yet immersed in this world of vicious lust and pleasure that always comes at a personal price.

"What brings you into a place like this?" My lips brushed his neck as I whispered in his ear.

"What else? The curiosity. The thrill. The chance to run into a woman like you." He nodded appreciatively, looking me over with a glazed expression evident of my influence. "What's your name?"

"No names," I said with a shake of my head. A grin tugged at my lips. Arys's vampiric essence flowed from me, entrapping my victim in an unseen force.

My patience wore thin. It was getting harder to keep from tearing into him like a rabid dog. That would be quick and gratuitous, a waste. I resisted only to draw out the moment, savoring every second of agonizing anticipation.

I shoved him against the wall in the small corridor that joined the club to the back hall. His heart raced sporadically, and fear mingled with his masculine human scent. My fangs sprang forth, and I growled.

He pushed against me, but I held him with no difficulty. Intrigue turned to panic, and he struggled harder. A small voice nagged me, my conscience, demanding to know how I could be the one that destroyed this innocent. He wasn't an evil doer. He wasn't even a blood whore. He didn't belong here.

I pressed my lips lightly to his, aligning his energy with mine. I could feel every beat of his heart. The blood rushing through his body was loud, an echo in my ears. I wanted to have him beneath me, screaming even as he begged for more.

"Come with me."

I led him along to the back hall and selected the closest empty room, two doors down from Kale's dirty little hole in the wall. Kale was the only vampire here to have his own regular room. I could only imagine how many nights he'd spent there, lost in the throes of bloodlust-fueled euphoria.

With just a thought, the door burst open, bouncing off the wall. I shoved the nameless man in first and kicked the door shut. He sat on the end of the bed, staring up at me in mesmerized wonder. I climbed into his lap and forced his head to the side. Running my tongue over the pulsing vein in his neck, I slid closer to the edge of the abyss.

His eyes were wide in fear, but his body responded to me with lust. I had no intention of following through with my seduction though I could have bathed in the waves of sensuality emanating from him.

I was running out of time. If I didn't stop now, I would kill him. I did my best to avoid killing innocents. I preferred to target the pimps and johns exploiting young girls or the gangsters that gunned each other down over the slightest dispute. Assholes with blood on their hands, they were my victims of choice. Otherwise, I couldn't live with myself.

"Don't stop," he pleaded when I pulled back. "Your touch feels like electricity."

"I can't do this," I said. "You shouldn't be here. You'll end up dead."

My words didn't match my actions. I shoved him back on the bed, pinning his arms to the bed. It would take just one bite to cause a fount of blood to burst forth. One bite would kill the ache inside me.

I dragged a claw lightly over his throat, careful not to puncture. It would be so easy to bleed him, but I couldn't. This was everything I dreaded about being a vampire. If I couldn't control myself now, I would end up like Kale and Arys, killing out of sheer joy.

"No," I said aloud to nobody in particular. "I won't do this."

Two opposing natures warred within me. Every part of me screamed to drain him of all his blood and energy; I needed it. I shouldn't have come here. I knew better. Allowing the bloodlust to make me a slave was no way to maintain control.

My victim's arms went around me. He tried to pull me closer. Caught up in my spell, he didn't have the sense to fear for his life. Though his heart beat in a fear-driven pattern, he acted according to the passion I'd stirred.

I panicked. I jerked back from his grasp and leaped off the bed as the door opened. Kale stood there with his female companion wearing a knowing smile and a black eye. Vampires heal fast, but Arys had inflicted a hell of a lot of damage.

In my hungry haze, Kale's saccharine energy immediately captivated me. He couldn't appease my need for human blood, but he always called to my power-hungry nature.

"Well, look who's treading on the dark side," Kale said with a brow raised in scrutiny. "Is this a private party, or is there room for two more?"

Before I could respond, he pushed the woman in ahead of him and closed the door behind him with a malicious grin lighting up his handsome face. I was conflicted, torn between longing to touch the shiner framing his brown eye and wanting to smack the smirk off his face.

"Get out of here, Kale," I said through bared fangs. "Stay away from me."

"I wish I could. You're too deep inside me now. I can't get rid of you. Your other half couldn't beat it out of me. So, here we are." Madness shone in his eyes. It was something I'd seen before, when his precarious hold on sanity had slipped.

I was instantly defensive. "We're not doing this."

Kale grabbed the woman and jerked her close. She gasped but melted into his embrace. He moved her hair to expose her neck. Then, he bit fast and deep. His fangs plunged through her flesh. She cried out, and her eyes rolled back in her head. He shoved her into me, bleeding and swooning.

"Looks like we are."

I felt myself slip, even as I desperately tried to grasp onto the ledge. I had been dangerously close to the edge since waking tonight. All it took was the scent of fresh blood to send me over the threshold.

Once I tasted the sweet scarlet nectar, I snapped. I tore into her viciously. My savage nature exploded in a violent storm. Even as I lost myself to the bliss moment, I thought of Arys and his warning that I would lose control. I knew I should feel ashamed, but right then, losing control felt so damn good.

The guy on the bed was no longer so disillusioned about us. He lunged for the door in an attempt to escape. Kale intercepted him. More blood flowed as Kale and I killed together yet again. Enablers, that's what we were to each other, an excuse, someone to blame for making it so easy to give in to the weakness again.

Devouring the life force of my victim caused my power to flare. I felt alive and free, ready for another round with Lilah and whatever lackeys she could throw at me. Shya might owe her allegiance, but I owed her nothing.

I sensed movement and threw a hand up to ward off Kale. Finished with his victim, he licked the blood from his lips. He stood between the door and me. Flying high on the rush of the kill, I watched his slow approach eagerly.

"And now, we're alone." Dressed head to toe in black, Kale was like a shadow gliding toward me. His energy called to me, tempting me.

I chose not to answer. Engaging with him further would lead to no good. It was hard to resist him when he so openly gave off what I was seeking. My succubus traits were deeply ingrained because of my link to Arys. Blood was only part of the feed. I gleaned as much power from the tantric energy of desire and lust, and Kale's energy spilled over with longing.

He couldn't be trusted. I had become someone he loathed only because I was someone he loved. What a bittersweet knife in the gut love could be.

Kale reached out to me metaphysically, luring me with the burning desire he couldn't hide. I tensed, fearful that any move I made would send me into his arms. He was a killer, drawing me in. It was working.

"You want it, don't you?" He asked. "You always do. You know how to get what you want from me. Isn't that right?"

I couldn't speak. My tongue felt heavy in my mouth. I did want him. Goddammit, I always did. He craved me in a way that was tangible. The passion he carried for me fed my succubus yearning for erotic energy.

"I don't want anything from you." I stood my ground. Backing away would only encourage him.

"Then, why do you keep going out of your way to save me?" He stopped just inches away. He used his height to tower over me in a domineering stance. "Shya. The FPA. Even your beloved Arys. Is there anyone you won't save me from?"

There was no correct response to that. My cheeks burned. I was tired of defending my choices to both Kale and Arys.

"Myself, maybe," I said, refusing to be cowed.

My temper flared, and my wolf rose to the surface, bristling at his close proximity. I tensed, ready to slap him with a psi ball. It was what he wanted. At least, I thought it was.

With careful yet brazen manipulations Kale created a gentle push and pull of power between us. It was daring and downright inappropriate. It was an intimate touch, lacking only a physical connection. He draped that honey sweet energy over me, and I groaned. The high from the kill beckoned me to chase the ecstasy he promised. Why stop now?

"You let your actions say the things that will never cross your lips." Kale's voice dropped low, a sensual sound. "You torment me, and I was broken so long ago."

He threw me up against the wall, trapping me with an arm on either side of my body. My teeth smacked together from the impact. I growled.

"I know what you're doing. Provoking me into a fight is not going to end the way you want it to."

I wrestled the urge to hit him with a shot hard enough to send him crashing through the door. I was curious. Could I do it? Knowing that he wanted a strong reaction from me kept me from giving him one.

Instead, I said, "I didn't break you, Kale. I'm not the one who made you so twisted."

I stiffened when he leaned in to lick a drop of blood off my lip, but I couldn't stop myself from nipping at him. The battle for control continued. I was high on the kill, and Kale was high on me. This could end badly in so many ways.

Kale laughed, a devious sound that told me I should be afraid, but I wasn't. Not yet. I was too caught up in the tidal wave of power between us. He was unpredictable and clearly up to no good, yet I couldn't resist him. I hadn't realized how much I'd missed this game between us, one we both sought to win.

"No, someone else created my hunger. But, tasting your blood brought it back to life. Vampire heroin, that's what you are. I wonder, will the hold you have on me break when you have breathed your last mortal breath?" Boldly, he laid a hand on my chest, watching it rise and fall.

"So, that's what this is about." Understanding settled in with the first cold spark of apprehension. "You kill me, you free yourself."

I raised a hand to throw him off, but he caught it and slammed it against the wall. His timing was impeccable tonight. He was running at full power. Clearly, he had been binging.

"Something like that." He ran his hand down my thigh, tugging up the hem of my skirt. "It doesn't have to be that way. Put me out of my misery."

Darker

Such bittersweet agony. Part of me despised him for what he'd done to me in the FPA basement. He had been an animal, seeing me as only a victim. It was a loveless attack. Here, with the high of the kill riding me and a memory of one night in the rain dancing through my head, I wanted to take what he was giving.

"I won't do it," I said through gritted teeth. "I'm sorry my blood is some madness-inducing vampire candy, but I'm not responsible for your suicidal tendency. No matter how you come to your end, Kale, I promise you, it will never be me."

I wanted to slap his hand away; I knew I should. Butterflies tickled my insides as his fingers slid over my skin. He brushed his lips ever so lightly against mine.

"Are you sure about that?"

His touch was seductive, painfully so. I knew I could devour him. I wasn't a prisoner this time, and he had no advantage. Though, I knew from experience, he would put up one hell of a fight.

Thinking too much would only succeed in furthering my role as his victim. Instinct was what made me kiss him. I pressed my lips to his, slipping my tongue inside his mouth to taste the human blood he'd consumed. I ran a hand through his hair, making a surprised sound when he bit my bottom lip. Sucking at the small cut, Kale held himself at a distance, his body shaking with the restraint.

The vampire's will to control and manipulate others drove my actions. It wanted what it wanted, and the human side of me had no say in that. I was lost inside myself, a prisoner in my own body as a force bigger than I was made a slave of me.

My bloodlust had been sated, but my hunger was just getting started. I drew on his lust, feeding off the smitten vampire's forbidden desires. The raw truth spilled from me as I whispered, "My love for you is selfish. It's built on weakness. I see in you what I hate in myself. I can't suffer alone. So, I choose you to suffer with me."

He shoved away from me then. "Why me? What did I ever do to deserve to be a slave for you?"

"You fell in love with me. I didn't manipulate your feelings. I didn't ask for this either, Kale. Do you think you suffer alone? Get your head out of your ass and look around you. There are two choices: submit or suffer." I advanced on him, going so far as to toss a little power at him.

He toppled over the foot of the bed, narrowly missing the fallen body of the brunette. He was on his feet with a flash of angry energy, lashing out with a hit that I blocked with a hand.

"Have you ever wanted someone you couldn't have?" he asked, the darkness seeping into his mismatched eyes. "There are no choices in that kind of love. There is only misery and madness."

Moving fast, he dropped for a leg sweep that knocked mine out from under me. I gazed up at him and waited for his next move. I was starting to get sick of Arys being right all the time, but in this case, he was. I would never again be safe with Kale.

He pulled me up off the floor and shoved me. I tripped on the leg of a corpse and caught myself before falling.

"The first man I ever loved was a liar, a womanizer and an egomaniac. He was my mother's lover. I've watched those I love desert me, betray me and die. You think I don't know pain?" My voice caught.

My fingers tingled from the power running through me. I held back, unwilling to lash out at him again. I didn't want to hurt him. I would never give him the true death he sought from me.

His eyes were hard to read. He remained silent for so long, a knot formed in my stomach. Slowly, he reached out to smooth the hair back from my face. His hand lingered; he caressed my cheek as though my skin was fire to the touch.

"I always knew making love to you would drive me mad," he said, his gaze on mine. "As much as I ache to touch you, I fear it as well."

I caught his hand in mine and pressed my lips to his palm. "Please, Kale, let me help you."

"They tortured me in there. The FPA. With blood and women, they drove me mad, and all I could think about was you."

"I came for you, Kale. Twice. I tried to get you out." There was a desperate note to my voice that made me flinch. "I tried."

"I know." His expression hardened. He grabbed my wrist tight, his fingers dug into the dragon etched in my flesh. "You made a deal with a demon that sealed both your fate and mine. I begged you not to."

"I did it because I love you," I shouted. "But, we can't be together. We are terrible for each other, Kale. Look at this." I gestured to the bloody room, the bodies on the floor. "We're the Mickey and

Darker

Mallory Knox of vampires. All we bring each other is more pain and misery. That's what we share. It's all we've ever shared."

"You're right. That will never change. But, I can't go on like this."

He draped me in his power, exuding a heady pull I couldn't resist. All of a sudden, he was kissing me with a desperate fervor, a dying man's last gasp for air. There was so much in his kiss: love, fear and, ultimately, abandon. Whatever thin threads remained on his tie to sanity weren't just snapping, he was cutting them. I understood. It's easier to give in.

"Kale, don't," I gasped between kisses. "Please, don't let go."

"I can't walk this line anymore." His mouth was warm on mine, his hands lost in my hair. "One day, you'll regret that you didn't kill me when you had your chance."

I should have stopped him. After worrying about him for weeks, to have him here, alive and in my arms, was a sinful dream come true. So, instead of beating the ass of the vampire who had violently abused me in a psychotic craze, I held him close while he surrendered to the calling darkness we all held inside.

"You want me." His lips moved upon mine as he spoke. "Right now, you want to consume every part of me. To devour my power until it is yours, to take all I am until there is nothing left but dust and to have me buried inside you as you do it."

I said nothing. By refusing to deny the truth, I was acknowledging it.

Kale slowly trailed a hand up my thigh, just barely touching. He circled around to stand behind me. I sighed at the heat of his mouth on the back of my neck.

"Perhaps you'd like me to take you from behind. You almost begged me to once." To accompany his words, he dragged fangs over my sensitive skin, careful not to break the surface, not yet.

Willpower had left the building long ago. I yearned for Kale. The recent weeks we had been apart had made me miss this feeling, this certainty that he was mine. I reveled in it now.

I spun to face him. "Actually, I'd prefer to ride you until you can't remember your own name. I want to look into those beautiful eyes while you beg me for more. And then, I want to make you hurt for it."

A mischievous grin lit up Kale's face. "If I could fall any harder for you, that would do it. We share something more than just weakness. You just didn't know it before."

"The wolf," I breathed.

"I have been both wolf and vampire, as you are and will be. That's one thing that neither of your men can claim." He nuzzled me then, a wolfish gesture that was so natural, like he'd been wolf just yesterday. I gazed at him in wonder, and he laughed. "It never leaves you, even when you wish it would. Like a hybrid, it's there but trapped inside. I'd hoped you would never know about me."

"Why?" I caught his face in my hands, peering deep into him. "Why didn't you tell me?"

"It doesn't matter now."

"Why, Kale?" A loud hum followed my demand as the electricity in the building surged along with my mood. "I'm terrified of losing my wolf. I don't want to rise as a vampire if that's what it means."

He pulled away, refusing to provide me the solace he once offered. "I didn't want to be the one to tell you. I couldn't bring myself to break your heart that way."

"You could have warned me," I sputtered as emotion overcame me. "I trusted you."

"You should know better than to trust any vampire," he snapped. "Including your other half. You think he didn't know you would lose the wolf?"

Angry energy spilled from me, and Kale reacted to it. His pupils dilated dangerously. I didn't want to talk about Arys with him. Instead, I targeted the rest of what he'd just said.

"Are you saying I was wrong to trust you all these years?" I wanted to reach for him but stopped mid-motion.

Kale leaned in close, fangs flashing threateningly. "Never trust a man that wants to bleed you as bad as he wants to fuck you."

I recoiled in horror. His vicious words stung. "Get out, Kale, before I find a way to take your misery to a whole new level."

His chuckle was like an icy hand on my spine. "I'm in you now, just as much as you're in me. That's why you can't let me go."

I was a mass of confusion. My body remained flushed with wanton heat for him. My heart was stone cold.

Kale pressed against me, close enough for me to feel his arousal. With a finger beneath my chin, he tipped my head back and bent to drag his tongue along the throbbing vein in my neck. I swooned, leaning into him despite the power I held ready.

"I am going to make you so crazy, Alexa, that the only way out will be to drive a stake through my heart." With that, he released me and left the room without a backward glance.

Chapter Seventeen

I stood there stunned. Then, with a surge of venomous rage, I went after him. I caught up to Kale in the hall and, without a second thought, slapped him with a psi ball heavy enough to take him down.

Kale lay on the floor in the hall, staring up at me with a combination of surprise and amusement. I stood over him, hands on fire with the power rippling through me.

"No fucking way. You don't get to pull the dramatic exit. I'm sick of you vampires and your dramatic friggin exits." My voice rose, and several light bulbs in the hall exploded in a shower of glass. "You can clean up the mess you helped me make. I get to make the unnecessarily over-the-top exit. Got it?"

I didn't wait for a reply. Instead, I stormed out the back door, ignoring those who surfaced to see who was making all the noise. I kicked the door open and raged through the parking lot. I was spoiling for a good fight. What I most needed was a good kill of the supernatural kind.

A basic vampire kill would do little to ease my appetite for violence. I wanted Lilah, but rushing back to her simply because Kale had pissed me off would be stupid. I needed to do a little planning first. So, I went to the next best place where I could let off a little steam and get my head together, a dance club down the street from The Wicked Kiss. With the bloodlust appeased, I was free to walk among the heavily packed human bodies and enjoy the energy that a crowd hopped up on booze and music gave off in abundance.

I wasn't yet ready to join my vampire brethren in drowning my sorrows in blood baths and mayhem, so letting loose human style was just fine with me. I told the bartender to keep the whiskey coming until my vision swam. Then, I slipped onto the dance floor and remembered what being human felt like.

The steady beats kept coming as the DJ successfully packed the dance floor with writhing bodies. A few guys approached me, seeking someone to take home. I merely smiled and shook my head before dancing away. They didn't know it, but I was the last woman in the building they wanted to go home with.

Music is a force as powerful as any other that goes unseen. Like love or the exhilarating sensation of leaping from a plane, it was one of those entities that might exist outside of you, but their real power was born from within. Though trendy dance beats weren't my general cup of musical tea, that night they set me free.

After an especially wild song ended, I slid onto a bar stool and signaled the bartender for another shot.

"You started without me," came a voice to my left. Willow clinked his beer bottle against my shot glass in cheers. "How the hell can you dance in those things with a bottle of whiskey in your veins?"

I followed his gaze to my heeled boots and laughed. "It's a talent possessed only by women—and some gay men."

"You look happy out there, being one of them." He nodded toward the dance floor. "Do you miss it?"

I watched the people dancing the night away, each one of them here to leave something behind as they did so. Being human didn't make one void of trouble or pain. If anything, it made those things worse.

"Yeah, I do. Mostly, I miss the ignorance, not knowing how bad things really are. I miss that."

Willow wore a sour expression. "I know what you mean. Seeing the dark from the inside is a fucking ugly experience."

"Why do you always show up when I'm miserable?" I asked, sucking on a lime wedge from the nearby dish.

Willow shrugged and drained the beer bottle dry. "Just lucky, I guess."

He ordered a round of tequila shots, his favorite. I curled a lip in disgust; the drink didn't agree with me.

"Did you come to talk me down? I didn't think I tapped enough power tonight to draw attention."

"You didn't." Sliding a tequila shot in front of me, he flashed a lopsided grin. "I dropped in at your club to talk about last night. You weren't there, but a couple of bodies were along with one hell of an angry vampire. I thought you could use some drunken shenanigans."

"Shenanigans," I repeated. "Funny word coming from an angel. What did you have in mind?"

He continued to nudge the tequila shot a little closer until it was bumping my hand. "We could start a bar fight. Or, steal a car off the Ferrari lot. Maybe even try some illicit narcotics and spend the rest of the night staring at our hands."

"Sounds like you've been watching a few too many teen party movies," I laughed, giving in and taking the stomach turning shot. "That crap will rot your brain."

"Good. I got you laughing. Now, tell me what's bothering you."

The alcohol-induced happiness dulled. Willow was easy to talk to. Telling him the horrible things I've done, confessing my dirty little secrets, I never felt judged. With him, I was able to share feelings no words could fully describe. He seemed to understand, always offering words of wisdom from a place beyond my reach. He was a genuine friend, and I didn't have many of those these days. Of course, the fact that our relationship was platonic helped. It allowed me a sense of liberty. I was able to expose my soul to him without fear.

I swirled my whiskey but pushed away the next tequila shot Willow placed in front of me. I considered the deep golden liquid in my glass, imagining it as red and warm, straight from the vein. Muttering obscenities under my breath, I drank down the liquor, finding it to be a poor substitute.

"I'm a wolf with no pack, a twin flame divided from my other half and a Hound who is one of the very things I'm supposed to kill." I slapped a few bills down for the bartender and smiled bitterly at Willow. "How much time do you have?"

"I've got all the time in the world. By all means, talk away."

"I'd rather not. I don't even want to think about it." With a teasing scowl, I grabbed the drink he continued to push closer and swallowed it with a grimace. "You know, for an angel, you're a terrible influence."

Willow snickered. His eyes shone with delight. "What can I say? I'm a rebel. So are you. That's why both monster and man wants to either control or kill you. It's a good thing."

I rolled my eyes but took his words to heart. "Oh yeah, it's fantastic."

"Seriously, Alexa, when the bad guys consider you a problem, it means you're doing something right. Even if at times you're one of them." Willow plucked a lime wedge from the dish and bit into the tart fruit.

I shook my head and snorted with derision. "What am I really though? Wolf, human, vampire? I don't fit in anywhere anymore."

"You're a Hound of God and the light half of a twin flame union. Those are good things. You exist to fight evil. Bottom line."

"Until I become it," I said with a frown. "Lilah said the twin flame bond is a curse. The worst part is that even though I know she's a liar, I agreed with her reasons why."

Willow appeared thoughtful. Even as he downed drink after drink, he was barely drunk. I would have been on the floor after that many.

"Remember, she's the dark half of her union. Your roles are not the same. There's good and there's evil. And, some creatures walk in both worlds. There is something powerful in being able to experience both the light and the dark. But ultimately, even you must choose a side."

He delivered that heavy verbal blow by crashing his glass against mine in cheers. My drink splashed over the edge, spilling a few drops in my lap. He received my dirty look with a smile and shoved another shot of tequila in front of me.

His words reverberated in my ears as I mulled them over. Willow was wise. He had a way of breaking things down so they were clear where before they had been confused.

"Stop making me think. I'm trying to drink away my sorrows here." I tossed a lime wedge at him, laughing when it struck him square on the chin. The newest Christina Aguilera song pounded out of the speakers, and I perked up. "I love this song. Come dance with me."

I jumped off the stool. Dancing the night away with whiskey in my blood and sweaty humans at my side likely wasn't the best way to spend my night, but I needed a break from reality. Jez's Vegas vacation idea looked better all the time. Since I couldn't skip town tonight with Lilah killing my wolves, dancing would have to do.

"Trust me. You don't want to see me dance. My talents are better spent right here." Willow waved me off, dismissing me when the bartender placed another half dozen shots in front of him.

I gravitated to the dance floor, watching as a tall redhead moved in on Willow within seconds of my absence. It didn't surprise me; he was a looker.

A pleasant warmth spread through my limbs from the alcohol. It was such a predictably human way of numbing out. The more I thought about it, the more aware I became of the pounding heartbeats all around me. So much blood to spill. A kill like that could create a high that would last for days. I licked my lips and reminded myself I was here to unwind, to leave that world behind. I never could though; I carried the darkness with me always.

I suddenly wasn't feeling so hot. Flushed with overwhelming heat, the bloodlust sprang forth. No way, I'd fed that hunger already.

I pushed through the crowd, seeking escape from the crush of lively human bodies. Every breath I took overwhelmed me with their heady aroma. I had to get out.

"I have to go before I slaughter these people," I said, grabbing Willow's arm. The redhead glared darkly and sauntered away. Willow took one look at my panic-stricken face and got to his feet.

The outside air was thankfully free of any strong human scent, overwhelmed by car exhaust and the faint aroma of summer rain in the distance. We stopped at a bench half a block away. I didn't sit down. Instead, I paced back and forth in front of it, feeling uncomfortable inside my own skin. My wolf was restless.

That was another area of concern. Veryl's files made it sound like the wolf was lost upon transformation to vampire. Kale said it was still there, trapped inside. I wasn't sure which was worse, losing my wolf or having it caged within me. They both sounded like a form of hell.

Emotion surged, and I kicked a pop can in misplaced anger. It only served to infuriate me further.

"Think you can keep your shit together?" Willow lounged on the bench, regarding me with casual curiosity.

"I don't know what happened in there. It came over me so fast. I feel a little better now." Scowling at the pop can, I picked it up and tossed it in a nearby trashcan. "It could be Arys. Sometimes, we can feel each other without trying to. It can be disorienting."

"Makes sense. How did that all go anyway?"

I watched a couple across the street walking hand in hand. They leaned into one another, talking animatedly. I envied them.

"Not so good. I told Arys I need some time apart. Things have been kind of strained between us lately. I don't know where I end and he begins; it's driving me crazy."

I dug through my shoulder bag, seeking normalcy in going through the motions of using lip balm and checking my cell phone. I almost didn't notice the weird look Willow gave me.

"It *will* drive you crazy," he said. "Being apart. You're not meant to be apart, not now that you've found each other."

I groaned and sat heavily next to him on the bench. "Don't tell me that."

"Sorry to break it to you, but you can't exist without him. You're not meant to."

"Maybe Lilah's right. It does sound like a curse."

Willow harrumphed and flicked my arm hard. "Don't make me slap that attitude out of you. Do you have any idea how many lonely people would give anything to be bound to another? To share something so sacred despite the hardship that accompanies it. I've seen the depths of sorrow-filled loneliness. If anything is a curse, it's that."

I rubbed my arm, feeling deservedly rebuked. "I know. I sound like a spoiled asshole. I wish I hadn't said that. I'm just confused. I don't know what purpose Arys and I share, and I'm afraid we'll destroy each other before we figure it out."

We sat there in quiet contemplation, watching the downtown traffic whiz by. In the distance, I heard sirens. A drunken whoop echoed from outside the club we'd just left. Typical sounds of the city engulfed us.

"Have a little faith, Alexa. These things tend to reveal themselves when the time is right. It won't be easy, but it will be worth it."

"Yeah, I'm sure you're right." I nodded, thinking about Arys. I hated myself for telling him I couldn't handle it. He had waited so long for me. Bailing out when things got tough was cowardice. I was stronger than that.

Noticing the shift in my mood, Willow nudged me playfully. "Ready to get back in there and drink ourselves into total stupidity? I might even get on the dance floor."

No sooner had the words left him than two black Escalades screeched to a stop at the curb in front of us. Several FPA agents spilled out like clowns tumbling from a polka-dotted coupe. Many of them pointed what appeared to be tranquilizer guns at me. Agent Thomas Briggs stepped out looking like a man with an agenda. I wasn't going to like whatever happened next.

Briggs sauntered up flashing the gun at his hip. He held his badge ready like some TV cop. A tensor bandage was visible beneath his jacket sleeve. It wasn't a cast though, so I must not have hurt his arm as badly as I'd hoped.

I stood up to face him, and all of the agents braced to fire their weapons. I held my hands up in a show of peace yet tapped my power. Being human, they couldn't see the crackle and color of the energy. Only a human with a strong sixth sense would even feel it.

"Briggs," I nodded curtly. "Are you tailing me?"

"I'm government, O'Brien. I tracked the GPS in your phone." His steely gaze was unwavering, his stride purposeful. "We need to talk."

"What do you want, Agent? Cut to the chase." I crossed my arms, doing my best to appear unaffected with so many guns trained on me. It would take only seconds for a tranquilizer to take me down.

Willow rose slowly, standing ready beside me. If Briggs didn't somehow know what he was, I'd like to ensure that it stayed that way. A few of the guns switched from me to him. I wondered briefly if a tranquilizer would have any effect on an immortal.

"I have a few questions for you. Bit of a delicate nature. I'm sure you understand." Briggs studied Willow closely, sizing him up. We all knew how deceiving looks could be.

"And, if I refuse?" I challenged. I needed to know how far Briggs planned to take this.

"You're the madam of a vampire whorehouse. That alone is reason enough for me to bring you in. You have ties to the headless body we found. You came uninvited into my facility. Your boyfriend roughed up one of my agents. Not to mention, you're already on our watch list. Do I need to go on?"

So, Arys had followed through with his intent to beat some info out of Bianca. Couldn't say I was sorry I missed it, though I was curious what, if anything, he'd gotten out of her.

Briggs had too much on me; I didn't see a way to get out of this chat.

"I'm not going back to that building," I said, visions of the FPA basement danced in my head. I hated that place. "We can talk in public. Right here."

"Let's take a drive." Briggs nodded toward the trucks. "Alone."

"By that, I assume you mean me alone and you surrounded by gun-toting morons." I glanced around at the agents flanking Briggs. They were mostly men, just a few women. Juliet was not among them.

"You assume correctly, though, I promise you, I don't work with morons." Briggs was patient, awaiting my decision.

I looked to Willow, finding him characteristically calm and cool. I focused on opening my thoughts to him. It was best for him to leave me with Briggs. I could handle it. Willow shouldn't be subjected to the FPA simply because he liked to get loaded in my company.

'Just go, but walk away. Don't let them see you poof. Check on Jez, if you don't mind. Make sure she's safe.' I pushed the thought to him, hoping it worked. Aloud I said, "I'm going to take a ride with Briggs. If you don't hear from me within an hour, tell Arys where I went."

The mention of Arys was more for Briggs's benefit than mine. I didn't want Arys to come riding to my so-called rescue, but if Briggs thought he might, this conversation would go a lot smoother.

Willow made a show of checking the time on his phone. "Ok, one hour. Talk to you soon."

He stood there with arms crossed, giving Briggs a guarded but invasive stare. He watched as I got into a vehicle with agents on every side of me. I managed to flash him a wave and an eye-roll before the doors closed and we pulled into traffic.

Right away, I had four guns in my face. Squeezed onto the seat between a male and female agent, I glowered at Briggs who turned in the front passenger seat to look at me.

"Alright, Briggs. You got your way," I said, holding the wolf back. "Now, get those things out of my face and treat me with some respect. I'm not asking."

"Is that a threat?" He asked, wary and stern.

"Does it have to be? If I wanted to taste that rich, arrogant blood, I would have done it last time we spoke." I raised a brow and smirked. We all knew I was the monster here; if they forced me to act like it, I would.

Briggs regarded me with thinly veiled distaste. The feeling was mutual. After a minute, he waved a hand, and the agents withdrew their guns. I didn't move a muscle, just beamed a sickly sweet smile at him.

"So, where's Juliet?" I inquired expectantly. "Let me guess. She doesn't know about this little meeting. Just like she didn't know about the people you're holding hostage in the basement of that scary ass hospital."

"She took the night off. And, you don't know jack shit about those people."

"I know what I saw. Is that where you'd like to see me, Briggs? Locked in a cold little stone room, never again to see the light of day?"

A muscle twitched in his jaw. "It does have its appeal. However, I think you underestimate the respect I have for you, O'Brien. I knew your parents; I worked with them. I assure you, I have no ill intentions toward you."

The driver guided the vehicle through the busy downtown core. The second Escalade followed, shadowing every turn and lane change. I wasn't sure how to take advantage of the opportunity I faced.

"I'm aware of my parents' involvement with you. I know you expected me to grow up to be a good little agent like my sister. Sorry about that." I settled in against the seat. There was no telling how long this would take, so I might as well get comfortable.

"I'll be honest," Briggs nodded, tugging at his seat belt so he could turn more in his seat. "We'd hoped you would join the FPA, but we can't force you. Although, we would certainly still be interested in working with you."

He let that hang between us. I considered the many ways I could respond. My instant reaction was to tell him to shove it up his ass. Anger didn't make wise choices though.

"If this is about Shya, you can save your breath. I told you already, I don't know shit about his plans. I kill for him to keep a secret. That's all."

"A secret? Meaning the supernatural activity in this city?" Briggs's dark eyes searched me. He was keenly observant, taking note of my every blink and breath.

"That's right. I kill other supernaturals, the idiots that don't know how to keep a low profile. There's no more or less to it."

"To avoid public exposure."

"Obviously." I knew he was trying to figure out how that could benefit Shya. I would certainly never tell Briggs about Shya's belief that keeping the public in the dark about us gave us more power over them and kept us safe. It was a belief I shared.

"Sure, that's your story," he replied with skepticism. "We both know there's more to it. You're one of several unique, powerful types in Shya's arsenal. I'm sure he doesn't need that kind of power to police the idiots. But, who am I to say?"

I was growing increasingly uncomfortable. Somehow, I managed to sit still, giving Briggs a disaffected stare.

"Come on, Briggs. This can't be why you tracked my phone and hauled my ass in here," I said, trying to steer the conversation in a new direction. "What do you want?"

He appeared pensive, choosing his words. "I want you to replace Veryl Armstrong as our informant."

I wasn't sure what to think of that. Laughter was my initial reaction. Briggs glowered at me, waiting for me to get it out of my system.

"Now, why the hell would I want to do that?" I asked, sobering quickly.

"Well for one, it would make me a whole lot more likely to turn a blind eye toward your dirty little whorehouse and what goes on inside." Raising a dark brow, Briggs pinned me with an arrogant sneer. "Besides, it seems only fitting, seeing as you're the one who killed him."

My lips twitched into a hint of a smirk. Briggs really thought he knew it all. I still wasn't sure how I felt about killing Veryl. He had hidden so much from me. I still felt the bitter sting of betrayal. Yet, as I continued to uncover pieces of the puzzle, it became clear that there was more to Veryl's actions than I'd first thought. I was starting to think he might have been trying to protect me all along.

"I sure did. I had my reasons. When it becomes illegal to kill a vampire, maybe I'll share them with you. You might want to try something else. That tactic isn't going to work."

"I'm trying to protect this city, O'Brien. It would be nice if you'd like to do the same. Then, we could come to some kind of agreement." Briggs spread his hands as if trying to appeal to my common sense. "I'm not your enemy. I have a job to do. For this city, this country. The world even. Supernatural shit isn't contained by borders. You know that. You have an opportunity to play an important role here."

"So, what are you saying? If I don't I'll be labelled some kind of supernatural terrorist threat? I bet you have some swanky government term for that. I'm not your enemy either, Agent. But, I have no interest in working for you."

"Then work *with* us." Briggs leaned forward, his voice rising in volume. "Look, Alexa, I have information on Shya. I think you have some, too. If you're not on the inside with him, then I think it's safe to assume you and I want the same things as far as he's concerned."

"And, what might that be?" My curiosity was piqued. If Briggs knew something about Shya that I didn't, I wanted to know what it was.

"To stop him from tearing innocent lives apart. Freedom from the wait. Never knowing what he's up to, but always knowing whatever it is, it's gonna be big and fucking bad." Anger flickered through his eyes, and he clenched his fists. "Do you share that burden, or am I alone in that?"

I met his gaze steadily, repressing the flicker of hope that leapt in my chest. Could it be possible that I could trust the FPA regarding Shya? It seemed too good to be true. It would be so damn nice to have someone on the outside who understood how dangerous the demon was.

"Yeah," I admitted. "I share that burden. More so these days than ever before."

I glanced out the tinted window, watching the buildings pass by. I disliked Briggs immensely. He was near the top of my shit list after what he'd done to Kale. I held him responsible for Kale's snap in sanity. Still, I needed someone on my side with this. It would be a risk to trust him but one that might be worth taking.

"I know he's had a heavy hand in controlling your life since your parents died," Briggs spoke softly. "I'm sorry about that. He's not here by accident. He chose this city for a reason. And you. But, I'm not sure how much I can share. I need to know I can trust you."

I swung my gaze back to Briggs, letting the wolf rise up to fill my eyes. He did a great job of maintaining his composure. Only the subtle increase of his pulse gave away his unease.

"Trust is a two way street, Briggs. How the hell am I supposed to trust a man who keeps people locked up like animals?"

"There's more to it than that." His response came fast, and for the first time, he couldn't meet my eyes. "Those people are dangerous. They are a threat to the general public. Every single one of them."

"Then why not just kill them?" I countered, my suspicions growing.

"It's not that simple. We need them."

I nodded, my suspicions confirmed. "Right. Stop the vehicle and let me out. We're done here."

The driver looked to Briggs for direction. He shook his head and waved off my demand.

"I don't call all the shots; I take orders from the top. What happens with those people is not my call. It's irrelevant to this discussion. Can you honestly say your moral track record is squeaky clean? You've killed humans. You recently turned one. If we let our personal business stand in the way, we will never have a hope in hell of stopping Shya."

The smell of so many humans was starting to get to me. Being confined in the Escalade with them was slowly becoming a true test. The hunger that struck me inside the dance club lurked, waiting for a chance to shatter my fragile control.

"So, if we put our heads together to figure out Shya, then you never get involved in my business or personal activity? Is that a guarantee?" I let my breath out slowly. My mind raced as I tried to think of anything to diminish the bloodlust's hold. I would not lose it in a car full of FPA agents.

"As long as you keep your activity quiet and stay away from my agents. I don't need a repeat of what happened with Bianca." Briggs snorted in disgust.

"What exactly did happen with her? I wasn't part of that."

Briggs was almost fuming. His cell phone beeped, stealing his attention. When he looked back at me, he forced a fake nonchalance.

"Arys roughed her up pretty badly. He made her talk. She told him about an item we've been looking for. One that Shya is also seeking. I don't know how much she told him, but it was enough. I had to kill her." He shrugged, as if taking out one of his own was all in a day's work.

Bianca was dead. That little bomb left me shaking on the inside. I should have been happy to hear the vampiress who had seduced my wolf mate was nothing but ash and dust, but I wasn't. I felt cheated because I hadn't been the one to do it.

"That's another thing," Briggs continued. "Arys Knight. Keep him away from my people. I can't afford to lose anyone else, especially not to a vampire doing Shya's dirty work."

"Alright," I said, my gaze narrowed and stern. "Same goes for you. Keep your agents out of my nightclub. Nobody touches another of my vampires or werewolves, either."

The Escalade circled around the downtown district, heading toward The Wicked Kiss. It was time to wrap this up. There was a moment of silence that quickly grew awkward. I could feel Briggs staring at me while I peered out the window.

"What, Briggs? Just spit out whatever's on your mind."

"You and Arys. You're not just lovers. I hear you're very powerful together. How does that work?"

I chuckled. So, Mr. Big Time Government Agent didn't know everything. "In order for me to tell you, I'd have to know the answer myself. Don't worry about it. We're none of your concern, I promise."

He didn't look convinced. "I guess I'll have to take your word for it."

We pulled to a stop in front of The Wicked Kiss. The doors opened, and the agents who were piled in next to me got out, moving so I could exit the vehicle. Briggs got out, too, waiting until every agent was back inside the Escalade.

"We need to share information. Somewhere private and safe." He cast a critical look at the nightclub, watching the patrons lingering near the door.

"I'd suggest consecrated ground. Everywhere else is suspect. Besides, until I know you have something serious to share, I'm not going to be too eager to play nice with you." I turned to go, dismissing him. Boldly, he grabbed my arm to stop me.

He quickly let go, but the heat from his hand lingered. "Shya stole information from us regarding an underworld artifact. It's hidden in a sealed chamber that's been closed off for over a thousand years. He wants to reopen it. If he gets his hands on that artifact, he'll rise through the ranks of the demon hierarchy. He'll be pretty much unstoppable." Briggs opened the passenger door of the truck and glanced back at me over his shoulder. "Is that serious enough for you?"

Chapter Eighteen

I was stunned. Yeah, that sounded pretty damn serious. It also answered a few questions.

"Hey, Briggs," I called before he could close the door. "Next time you want to talk, call me. Tracking my phone is tacky and shady."

I watched the government vehicles disappear down the street. When I turned to go into the club, Willow was standing right behind me. I jumped and swore.

"I'm really not a fan of this popping out of thin air thing you guys do." I ran a hand through my hair and tried to decide where to start. "I need to ask you about something Briggs just said."

"Sure, but first Alexa, I need to warn you. Something happened here while you were gone." He stopped me from proceeding. That's when I noticed the near empty parking lot.

"What now? It was Kale, wasn't it?" I shoved by Willow, running across the lot to the front doors.

I burst through the doors, expecting to find Kale in the middle of a blood bath. What I found was a demon. Brook stood in the middle of the club, his black wings outstretched. He held a yellow envelope in one hand.

"What the fuck are you doing here?" I didn't know if I should be afraid of him, but I wasn't. I'd watched him be tortured at Falon's hand and saw him act like a subservient manservant for Lilah; I would not be intimidated by him.

"Waiting for you." Brook's black eyes landed on Willow and seemed to grow darker. "I have something for you. I need to see that it gets directly into your hands."

Darker

"And, you had to make a scene and empty my club to do that? Lilah can't send her bottom feeding lackeys in here every time she wants to take a shot at me. That card has been played. Tell her to up her game or leave me the hell alone."

Brook smiled and held out the envelope to me. "Consider this her next move."

I approached him warily. The bitch hadn't waited long to make a move. Trepidation gripped me. I snatched the envelope from Brook's hand, careful not to touch him.

"It's in her hands," Willow said. "You've done your job. So get out."

"Not so fast." Brook shook his head and adjusted his wings. "I have to see her open it."

I tore open the envelope with a sudden surge of hatred. Perhaps I should have been grateful Lilah hadn't left me another body, but when I saw what was inside the envelope, I went cold.

I pulled out an invitation. One that stated my attendance was required for a special event the following evening. There was something else. An item that assured I would be there whether I wanted to or not. A lock of blood-spattered curly brown hair, Juliet's hair.

"She has my sister?" My voice was deadly calm, a direct contrast to the storm building inside me.

"She does," Brook confirmed. "She's alive. For now. I'm sure I don't have to give you the rest of this song and dance."

"No. You don't. Tell Lilah I'll be there. And, if she lays another hand on Juliet, I'll guarantee she suffers in ways that will make her wish for a death that won't come." I hauled off and punched Brook square in the nose. "Pass that along, too."

Blood streamed from the demon's nose. He reached to touch his face, glowering when he saw the blood on his hands. There was little satisfaction in it, though; he would heal within minutes.

"Feisty little charge you've got here," he directed the comment to Willow. "They really made you pay for your indiscretion with the human."

Willow snapped. I never saw him move. He was on Brook, knocking me aside as he launched himself at the demon. He rained down blows that held the power of an immortal. Those wounds would likely linger.

I gaped as the two of them went hard at each other with both physical and unseen blows. The atmosphere quickly grew strained with the heavy, suffocating sensation of their immortal power. I backed away from the brawl, casting a glance about the room and finding the only other person present was Justin, who stood watch near the door.

This wasn't my fight, and I couldn't contribute in any meaningful way, so I watched. I was definitely intrigued by Brook's words, though; could watching over me be part of Willow's punishment?

He threw Willow off with a nice hit that had the fallen angel crashing into a table that promptly collapsed. Willow was up with a flare of silver wings and eyes shining with a strange light.

"She must have really got inside you. You're acting like an animal." Brook smiled, a taunting grin intended to provoke.

"That's right." Willow nodded, his expression filled with raw, untamed emotion. "I fell for love, not so I could act as a lapdog for one of Satan's mistresses. Forbidden love maybe, but it's what we are. Love. Have you forgotten the power of it? How it feels burning in every part of you? Or, has it been too long since the spark in you went out, demon?"

Brook's hand curled into a fist. A black wisp of smoke trickled between his fingers. "Still preaching after being cast out, Willow. Well aren't you the loyal one? No matter how you paint it, you're still one of us now. Guiding a Hound won't get you back in. Once you're out, you stay out. You know that."

Brook released the mist within his hand. It weaved an erratic path through the room, targeting not Willow but me instead. I braced for it, tapping my power, which did nothing to help. The murky demon assault burned its way through my energy shield and choked the breath from me. Brook's intent wasn't to kill by any means, merely to incite Willow's reaction.

He put himself in the path of Brook's attack, and the painful pressure quickly fell away. I could breathe again. The force that Willow exuded was as calming as it was strong.

The angel and demon faced off, a deadly staring match that bred palpable tension. Then, as fast as it had started, it was over. Brook backed off, hands raised in surrender.

"It's been nice catching up with you, Willow. I'd like to stay, but I have a cute little brunette werewolf to keep company." Brook grinned and winked at me. With the ruffle of feathers, he was gone before I could react.

"What the fuck was that?" I shouted, staring at the lock of hair I held in disbelief. "What is he going to do to my sister?"

Willow diverted his gaze, and that was enough of an answer for me. I stared at Juliet's bloody hair. Her wolfish scent wafted from it. Beneath that was the human scent of my sister. My baby sister.

Slowly, I crumpled, falling to my knees. My chest heaved as I struggled against the threatening panic attack. Targeting my wolves had been the perfect way to shake me up. Going after Juliet, this was how Lilah would destroy me, and she knew it.

Silent tears slid down my cheeks, falling to stain my hands red. I had no crushing pain, but I couldn't escape into safe numbness. Despair overwhelmed me with the certainty that I'd failed.

"Alexa, get up. You have to face this." Willow knelt before me. He gently took the envelope and its contents. "She's trying to cripple you. Don't let it work."

"Everyone talks about power. Who has it, who wants it. Harley, Shya, the goddamn FPA, they all said I have it, but I have nothing. A powerless demon has proven that everything I share with Arys doesn't mean a damn thing." As the words poured forth, I wiped at the tears, but they kept coming.

"That's not true." Willow pulled me up and sat me down in the closest chair. "There is nobody on this earth quite like you. Sometimes it's not about power or authority. It's simply about who wants it more. Lilah is desperate. She has nothing left to lose. You do. So, you have to want it more."

The truth rang in his words, but it didn't penetrate through the fog of desolation. I had no hold over this city. Evil ran rampant, and I was powerless to stop it. The voice in my head whispered my weakness and futility.

"I don't think I can do this," I said.

Willow took my hands in his and gave them a soft squeeze. "You have to. You can and you will. What you need to defeat her is already inside you. Trust that."

His green eyes searched me, and I saw the worry within them. His wings lay tucked against his back, the tips resting on the floor from the way he crouched before my chair. I reached tentatively to touch one of those silver feathers. In that moment, I saw an enchanting creature that I once believed never existed. I needed to know he was real, that this was all real.

My fingers brushed against a feather, and I gasped as a jolt of pure, beautiful energy shot through my hand to tickle my palm. The feather was soft but strong. Upon such close inspection, I saw that each fiber danced with the colors of the rainbow.

I dragged my gaze to Willow's; I needed to know. "What Brook said about me being your charge, is that true? Am I a job for you?"

"You're a friend," he replied, brushing a stray strand of hair off my face. "I don't have the power to be a guardian. Not anymore. But, that doesn't mean I don't honestly care about what happens to you. I'm happy to help in any way I can."

I nodded, swallowing hard. "Thank you, Willow. I appreciate that. I think I need to speak with Shya. He's the only one I know, other than Lilah, who has power over Brook. I can't let him touch my sister."

"I understand. You feel desperate. Don't let that desperation lock you into a deal. Lilah won't kill your sister. She knows it's the only way to make you walk back in there willing to compromise." Willow went to the bar and grabbed a glass. He returned with some ice water that he pressed into my hand.

I sipped the water. It should have been refreshing, but it wasn't what I wanted. I shoved the glass across the table in front of me and shook my head.

"Maybe you should go. I don't want to drag you into this mess." I pulled out my phone and opened the contact list. My gaze strayed to the dragon on my forearm. I was sure there was a way to use it to reach Shya but wasn't sure I wanted to know how. So, I hit the number I had for him and waited.

I got the voicemail. Both relief and disappointment crushed me. "Shya, it's Alexa. Lilah has my sister. I need to see you."

I hung up and stared at the phone. My mind ran through several people I could contact. Jez, Kylarai, Brogan. Only one stood out as the one I needed now. It would take the simplest act, a touch of my mind to his. I couldn't do it.

"You shouldn't be alone tonight, Alexa. You should be with Arys."

I tapped my nails against the table for a minute before shoving the chair back to stand. The screech of chair legs was loud in the quiet, empty nightclub.

"I don't know how to be with Arys anymore. Things are... complicated."

"Since when is that a reason to give up?" Willow challenged. He stuffed the invitation and Juliet's hair back into the envelope and tossed it to me. "If you need me, I'm here for you. But, you've got to figure your shit out. Take the rest of tonight, do what you need to do, whatever that is. Be ready tomorrow. I'll have your back. And, you'll walk out of there alive."

I chewed my lip, mulling it over. He was right; rushing in would not go my way. "Well, I'm glad one of us thinks so."

Willow seemed hesitant. "Do you want me to stay? We could hang out, go for a walk, share a bottle of the good stuff. Whatever you want."

"No. I need some time to meltdown. Alone. I'll be fine though. Really." I had a hard time meeting his eyes. I didn't want him to know what I planned to do.

Willow drew me close for a hug that enfolded me within his wings as well as his arms. There was so much warmth and comfort in that embrace I almost started to cry again.

"Alright," he said. "Think about contacting Arys. I'll see you soon. Remember, you don't have to do this alone."

I forced a smile so he would feel okay with leaving. He lingered as if unsure. Then, he was gone.

I shoved the envelope into my bag and headed for the door, pausing to talk to Justin. "Lock down the building. Anyone currently in the back can stay, but nobody else comes in."

He nodded, his ebony eyes taking in the dried blood tears on my face. "Just say the word, boss lady, and I'll be with you tomorrow night."

"Thank you, Justin. I'll keep you posted."

I crossed the parking lot to my car where I took a few minutes to clean the bloody smears from beneath my eyes. Digging around in my purse, I produced some red lipstick, which I generously applied. I tore my skirt shorter and finger combed my hair. A glance in the visor mirror revealed bloodshot blue eyes.

I didn't have to go far to find a seedy area ripe with the kind of activity I sought. I left my car in an empty grocery store parking lot and walked the few blocks from the decent streets of the downtown core to the filthy, crime heavy district. With an extra swing in my step and a toss of my hair, it didn't take long for the johns to roll up.

The first two I sent away with a shake of my head and a half-assed excuse that I was waiting for my pimp. I was looking for something specific. Wedding rings and families were not it. The third guy fell easily into my eyes, answering my questions almost hypnotically. No wife and no kids. He was disappointed that I was as old as I was. The pervert was cruising for underage girls. He was the one.

I got into his old pickup truck, wrinkling my nose at the smell of old McDonald's wrappers littering the floor. My chosen prey stank of booze and too much cheap cologne. It could have been worse. I directed him to the nearest sleazy motel, finding with each passing moment another trace of doubt had vanished.

"Take your clothes off," my victim said as soon as stepped inside the dark, dank motel room. "I want to watch you undress. Do it slowly."

The room was tiny and simple with one bed in the center. The blanket held old stains that could have been anything from food to blood. An adjoining bathroom that stank of mildew completed the suite. I would have preferred to be in a five star joint with a suit and tie kind of guy, but this would have to do.

I could have killed him in a matter of seconds, but half the fun was the build-up to the moment he would bleed for me. So, I played along.

I peeled my top off slowly, taking the opportunity to drape him in the lusty thrall of my hunger. His eyes took on a glazed, mesmerized glassiness. He was pushing fifty, a little on the thin side with a scraggly bit of beard. He watched me eagerly.

Sliding my skirt down my legs, I stood before him in my bra and panties. Without waiting for him to give me another command, I climbed into his lap, straddling him with a lascivious smile on my red lips.

Darker

"What's your name, gorgeous?" He mumbled into my cleavage. His hands were hot on my waist.

"Whatever you want it to be." I caught his hands before he could slip them any lower. Pushing him down on the bed, I ground my groin against him and leaned down to drag fangs across his jugular.

I half expected the erection he pushed against me to bring about an ill feeling. The surge of confident control and illicit desire felt rejuvenating. It was intoxicating, seducing me as I seduced him. I drew on the sex-charged energy vibrating through his deliciously human body.

My nails lengthened into claws, sharp points that poked into the flesh of his wrists. He stared up at me with a look of strange wonder, as if he were seeing something or someone else. I felt no hesitance. No second thought or regret. The sensual high was teasing, an indication of what came next. My succubus nature fanned the flames of his lust. Releasing my hold on him, I let him reach for my breasts. He wasn't going to live long enough to try anything else. My patience was thinning.

"Your eyes are fascinating," he said dazedly. "Has anyone ever told you that? It's like there's something weird there. Something..."

He trailed off, shaking his head slightly, unable to find the word. I brought his hand to my lips, turning it over to expose his wrist. Placing my lips to the pulse there, I breathed deeply of the scent of blood so close to the surface. Just a prick of fangs away.

"Inhuman," I supplied. I dragged my tongue over his skin, eliciting another rush of arousal to feast upon. "Yeah, I've heard that before."

Unable to hold back, I closed my eyes and bit into his wrist. The blood flowed and I sighed. A light flashed behind my eyes, and I felt myself fall into Arys's head. For a startling moment, my actions were exposed to him. I opened my eyes and found my victim grabbing hungrily for me. He either didn't know what I'd just done, or he didn't care. He was entirely under my thrall. All mine.

I knew Arys saw what I saw and felt what I felt. His presence was heavy in my head but quiet, watchful. I considered shoving him out, but the dark side of me entertained a naughty thought: What the hell, let him watch.

Dropping the john's arm, I rose up over him and pushed his head to the side. Exposing his neck brought a groan from me. I ran a claw over the pumping artery there. He would bleed out fast if I went for the carotid. Going for the jugular might give me a bit more time. I let the question echo in my mind. Arys's preference came in the form of a feeling rather than a clear thought. He wanted me to tear the guy apart.

The john tried to pull me in for a kiss. I teasingly shook my head and gave a coy smile. I wasn't sure if prostitutes really had a no kiss on the lips rule, but I didn't intend to let him touch me more than necessary. My head already spun with his lust, but that was the tip of the iceberg. I needed more. Blood and death.

The hand on my breast grew aggressive. He strained against me, demanding what he thought we'd come here for. Arys's tension permeated my thoughts. Again, I thought about shutting him out, but it was too late for that.

"Let's have a look at what you're hiding here." The john fumbled to get my bra off.

I grabbed his arms and roughly pinned him. "I know you're used to having your way with girls that should be home with their families. That ends here. So, try to enjoy what happens next."

I forced him to look directly in my eyes as I pulled him deeper under with my heady vampiric influence. Having him kicking and screaming would have been the icing on this madhouse cake. As easily as I'd pulled him under, I could set him free. He would fight and shriek. A thrill of excitement rocked me at the thought. Of course, having him beg for more while I killed him sounded pretty damn good, too.

'Decisions, decisions.' Arys's voice echoed in my head.

I ignored him, refusing to allow him to sway my choice. If I acknowledged his presence, the emotion bound within me might break free. I was here to escape that emotion, to find freedom from the torment. I would find that freedom in only one way.

I unleashed the short rein I had on my control. In a violent attack, I sunk fangs deep into the john's neck. He grunted, and his arms went around me. His blood spurted into my mouth, and I devoured it. The abyss of dark pleasure rose up to swallow me, and I leapt in head first.

I lost myself. Everything that happened next was a blur. I saw nothing but crimson, tasted nothing but ecstasy. I tore into the pervert beneath me, and he enjoyed every minute. Only when death approached did he snap out of my spell and begin to fight, far too late.

Arys's wicked satisfaction lingered inside. It fed my vicious hunger. When I finally came back to myself, I was sitting on the floor beside the bed, wiping blood from my mouth and trying to focus on the room around me.

A euphoric cloud lifted me, and I floated along it with a lazy grin plastered on my face. Then, I pushed Arys away. I closed my mind to him so as not to let him bring me down sooner than I'd like. I was going to ride out this high for all it was worth. Tonight, I would embrace the darkness, for tomorrow I would need to be the light. Somehow.

I washed the blood from my face and hands in the dingy bathroom. The tap only produced cold water, which was fine with me. It was refreshing.

Returning to the bedroom, I got dressed and surveyed the scene. The john's throat was a mess of punctures and tears. The bed beneath him was soaked in blood, filling the room with a sticky sweet aroma. Not so long ago, I'd gazed upon Zoey's prone form much like this. The meaning of this moment sank in deep. With a bitter string of expletives, I grabbed my bag and turned to go.

I smacked right into Shya who suddenly stood there looking both amused and quizzical.

"For fuck's sake, Shya," I cursed. "I know you like the element of surprise, but this is getting ridiculous."

His red eyes took in the motel room. "You called. I'm merely responding to your message. Did I catch you at a bad time?"

The dragon on my arm itched and burned. He had used it to find me. The thought was unsettling.

"Not at all. I was just leaving."

"Are you just going to leave him like this? For the police to find?" His tone held a note of warning, and he raised a brow, his expression disapproving.

"Yes. I highly doubt they'll walk in here and immediately assume a werewolf did it. You are aware of what century this is, right?"

I was snarky, and I wasn't sorry about it. The demon didn't share his business with me. Mine was certainly no concern of his.

"Veryl employed you to keep activity like this quiet."

I shoved by him and let myself out of the room, assuming he would follow. "Yeah, well Veryl's dead."

Shya fell into step beside me. Even with his wings absent from sight, he carried himself with an intimidating air. "And, if the FPA catches wind of this?"

"Then, it's their job to keep it quiet. They don't want the public to know about us anymore than you do." I headed down the street in the direction of my car. So much for enjoying the high, Shya was a real bring down. "Did you come here to lecture me or to talk about Lilah?"

"She didn't just take your sister; she's got Gabriel, too. I've been summoned to her sordid soirée tomorrow night. I believe she plans to force both you and me to make some hard choices."

I looked sharply at him. An ill sensation began in the pit of my stomach. "Why would she want Gabriel? How much leverage is he over you?"

Shya clasped his hands behind his back, a grave mask replacing his usual bemused grin. "She knows I need him. Grabbing him is her way of ensuring I show."

"What are we walking into, Shya? How bad is this going to be?"

"It's hard to say." He shrugged. "She's been targeting my demons, as she has been doing with your wolves. We are the two biggest threats to her throne. She wants us vulnerable. There's no telling what she will do to see us that way."

A shout followed by gunshots several blocks away accompanied us as we walked. I quickened my pace. I couldn't possibly get out of the crime-riddled neighborhood fast enough.

"What are you up to that has her so keen on bringing you down?" I asked, making no effort to hide my suspicion. "Aside from the obvious play for power. Why do you need people like Gabriel and me? What are we to you?"

Shya nodded appraisingly. "I admire you, Alexa; I do. I can feel the fear I instill in you, and still you never let it keep you from speaking your mind. There are demons that have existed since the beginning of time who are not so brave."

"You're not answering my question."

Darker

Our eyes met, and I saw within Shya a glimmer of pride. He was too confident with himself. It didn't sit well with me.

"I plan to overthrow Lilah's kingdom, to claim it as my own. I need something specific to do that. I need a coalition of those with exceptional skill to help me maintain a stronghold on this city and the power within it. The less you know, the better. It would be a shame if one of my foes were to torture information out of you." He said it as if it wouldn't be a shame at all, merely an inconvenience.

"And, why the hell would we want to help you? What makes this city so special?" I hoped he would keep talking. Even a little info from Shya could shed light on the mysteries of his plans.

"There's something here… a door that must be opened, if you will. You, Hound, will help me with that." He was being purposely vague, as if he enjoyed making me ask questions that he didn't intend to answer directly.

I was growing impatient. With a snarl I spat out, "Let me guess. My blood will open this door."

"No." He grinned, enjoying this moment. "Your death will."

I was dumbstruck. Breathless and stunned, I struggled for the words that disappeared on the tip of my tongue. "Sorry if I don't think that's as fucking funny as you do."

Shya's look changed to one of disdain. He so easily tired of my mortal antics. "If you had any sense at all, you'd know an opportunity when you see one. Once you die your mortal death and rise as a vampire, there will be no mortal constraints on your power. No headaches. No nosebleeds. No limits."

The bastard demon always had talked a good game. I wasn't buying it. "When I die, the balance shifts. Arys and I won't have the balance of light. We will just be dark. I get it. You're a demon. You like the dark. That's not my world."

"Ah, you silly mortal girl, it's always been your world."

Considering the scene I'd just made in the motel, it was hard to argue with him. My pulse raced, and my breath came fast. He was scaring me.

We reached the Charger, and I pulled the keys from my bag. "I won't be controlled. Not by you, not by Lilah and not by the goddamn FPA. I'm sick of you all telling me what to do and when to do it. I'm not a sixteen-year-old newbie wolf anymore. If I have as much pull in this city as you all think I do, then you should know better than to fuck with me."

The angry tirade spilled out. This shit had to stop. I was nobody's puppet.

Shya's expression grew absolutely venomous. His wings appeared with a loud snap, spread wide to intimidate. He shoved me hard against the car, closing in to trap me there.

"Is that so?" A pulse of scorching heat emanated from him. His mark on my arm throbbed in response, burning as if flames engulfed my flesh. "You know who shouldn't be fucked with? Someone who knows how to get inside the head of those who love you."

Logic told me to shut up, but the heady rush of the kill drove me to be bold. I wasn't backing down. "I know what you're doing with Arys. Taking advantage of his fear of losing me won't get you very far. He's not an idiot."

"No, just a man with a lot to lose. Everything in fact. And, the more he worries about keeping you safe, the more likely it becomes that he himself will destroy you." Shya leaned in dangerously close, searching me for something, weakness perhaps. "I promise you, I'll be there when he does."

This was not how I'd pictured our conversation. Shya knew too much. Had Gabriel also foreseen my death at Arys's hand? Is that how Shya knew?

"Even if you find a way to take advantage of my death, I will never help you. I won't lead vampires and wolves for you. I will, however, lead them against you."

Shya laughed in my face. He smelled of wine and roses. Faintly beneath that was the bitter stench of sulfur.

"I look forward to it," he said. "Now tell me, why did you really ask me here? I assume it wasn't to argue about petty details."

"Brook is working with Lilah. He delivered an invitation to me for tomorrow night. And, a chunk of my sister's hair. I need to know she's safe from him. That he won't do anything to her between now and then." Those petty details were my life and death, but he was right, I had called him because of concern for my sister. It was a risky call, and I knew he would take advantage of it.

"Oh I see." He stepped back a few paces, allowing me some room to move. "So, you expect me to do something about that."

"I know you have power over him," I offered lamely. I had a bad feeling I would regret this. Still, I couldn't leave Juliet in Brook's hands.

"What do you want me to do?" There was intrigue in his eyes.

My stomach turned. This would lead to nothing good. "I just don't want him to touch her in any way that would harm or violate her."

Shya nodded thoughtfully. Pinning me with a deep red stare, he pursed his lips in consideration. "I may be able to do something about that. Falon's recent indiscretions with Lilah have put him deeper in my debt. He's playing double agent now. I can have him speak with Brook."

Relief swept me.

"That's not going to come without a price, is it?" I was wary, afraid to hear his demands, but if it meant keeping Juliet safe, it would be worth it.

He pulled his wings in close so they hugged his back. Stroking a hand along the hood of my red Charger Daytona, Shya's grin was vicious. He tilted his head to the side and regarded me as if I were a prize, not a person.

"How about we negotiate on this whole leading vampires and werewolves issue? You are already Queen to Arys's King. Why not start acting like it?"

"I'm not going to pretend to know what you mean by that. You're too elusive, Shya. I can't agree to anything if you aren't straight up with me." I frowned when he sat on the hood of my car. I was ready for this night to end.

"Nobody has more power among vampires and werewolves than you two. I need the kind of power and muscle those creatures can provide. All you have to do is establish and maintain a position of respected authority. You have it. You just don't exercise it." When I glowered at him uncertainly, he added, "It wouldn't be so different from what you already do for me, what you did for Veryl. You'd just have more man power."

I searched him for a lie, hating that I couldn't smell one on a demon. "You want me to keep wiping out people that get in your way. FPA rats and such?"

"More or less." With a cocky smirk, he winked at me.

"That's what worries me. The more or less." I watched a car slow down as it rolled past us. The driver was smart to keep going. I said a small prayer that this wouldn't be a mistake that would come back to haunt me. "I'll do what I can to make connections with the vamps and Weres in this city. But, the Stony Plain wolves will be left out of it, and I won't force anyone to do anything. Their choice."

That was as close to giving him what he wanted as I was going to get. He knew it, too. The demon dragged out the moment, making me sweat while I awaited a response.

"Alright," Shya finally said after what felt like an hour. "That works. For now."

"Good. Now, can I please go home? I need to rest up so I can be bled by a vampiric demoness tomorrow night. Wouldn't want to be unprepared for that." Sarcasm dripped from my words. I reached for the car door handle, hoping Shya would take the hint.

He looked far too pleased with himself. A flicker of unease passed through his eyes. "Be ready for anything. It's going to get nasty. I'll see you there."

Shya vanished. I got into the car and started the engine. I kicked myself for being a hypocrite. Making a deal with the demon was stupid, but it was for Juliet.

As I headed out of the city, headed for home, I couldn't help but think that if Lilah bled me dry tomorrow, at least I wouldn't owe Shya a damn thing.

Chapter Nineteen

The sounds of the night were so different from my backyard patio than they were in the city. There was no traffic to ruin the peaceful quiet. No sirens. Small town living allowed me to see the stars glittering against the night sky. It called to my wolf.

I walked through the yard, taking in the scents of summer. It wouldn't be long until the warmth faded, and Fall moved in to strip the trees of their leaves and the grass of its green vitality. I couldn't help but wonder if Shaz would be back by then.

A chorus of howls broke the stillness. A shiver crept up my spine. Kylarai, Coby and the others were running tonight. They were miles away, but I could feel them as if they were right there with me. My wolf wanted to join them. That would probably never happen again.

It was tempting to shift, but the thought of running alone was depressing. I missed Shaz desperately. He would have had something reassuring to say, and for a little while, I might actually believe him. Too bad for me, he wasn't here. While I was here waiting for the clock to count down to my potential demise, Shaz was likely running through the mountains, at one with nature.

It was better that he wasn't here. I wouldn't want to risk him. His absence kept Lilah's attention off him. That was worth the pain I felt every time I thought about him.

Unable to listen to the pack's mournful cries any longer, I went inside and closed the patio door. The house felt big and empty. I didn't know what to do with myself. So, I poured another glass of whiskey and sat at the kitchen island.

I sipped the golden liquor and stared at my cell phone, watching the minutes change. It was a quarter past four. I needed to attempt sleep at some point. Being at full strength for Lilah's little shindig was essential. The thought of climbing into bed alone was painful. Maybe I'd crash on the couch instead.

"Only got yourself to blame," I muttered for no other reason than to break the silence.

I had no pack to call my own. My small town pack of everyday people had been a comfort, a sense of normalcy in an unusual world. The three men that I had ties to were all lost inside their own hell. Here I sat in mine.

I didn't cry. I only wished I could. The cleansing tears would have been a welcome relief from the hollow ache.

I decided to take the opportunity to leave a message for Kylarai while she was out. I wanted her to know where I would be the following evening, in case anything should happen, at least she would know. I called Jez after, happy to hear her alive and safe.

"I'm going with you," she insisted after I told her about Lilah's invitation. "You need back up, and I want to see the bitch go down."

"There's a huge chance it won't play out like that. I can't stop you from coming but don't take any hits for me, Jez. I mean it. Enough people have been hurt on my watch already." I refilled my glass and took a large swallow of whiskey. It burned in all the right ways. "How are you doing? You know, since Zoey…"

She sighed heavily into the phone. The crinkle of a chip bag was loud in the background. "I'm stuffing my face with pizza and Doritos. Does that answer your question? At this rate, I'll be obese in no time."

"Better than binging on blood and whiskey like I've been." I laughed despite my mood. "Besides, your scrawny ass could stand to gain a few pounds. You'll be fine."

"Laugh it up, blood fiend," she joked. I could hear the smile in her voice. Jez was broken now, but she would put the pieces back together. Maybe I could do the same.

A cold wind swept through me, capturing both my heart and my attention. Seconds later, there was a knock on the front door. I wasn't sure I could face Arys right now. He wasn't giving me a choice by arriving unannounced.

"Jez, I gotta go. I'll call you back later."

Darker

I set both the phone and my glass on the counter before creeping down the hall to the door. I grasped the deadbolt and started to turn it, pausing to second-guess the motion. I didn't want to fight with him. Could I keep the peace by refusing to open the door?

Groaning inwardly, I flipped the deadbolt and jerked the door open before I could change my mind. When I saw him standing there with a fire burning in his eyes and a bouquet of red roses in hand, I was smitten all over again.

I opened my mouth to speak, but he shoved inside and silenced me with a kiss. Kicking the door closed, Arys pushed the flowers into my hand and pulled me into his arms. The power sparked between us. For the first time since our fight outside The Wicked Kiss, I felt whole. In Arys's arms, the fear and despair faded, replaced by strength and confidence. I was complete again.

His tongue was soft on mine, exploring my mouth insistently. I was drowning in him. Every one of my senses were ablaze, ignited by his touch.

"Arys, what are you doing here?" I broke off the kiss to catch my breath. The roses in my hand were deep scarlet, reminding me of the blood I'd spilled earlier. That had to be why Arys was so worked up; he'd gotten off on it.

"What does it look like?" His lips moved on my neck as he kissed a warm path along my jugular. "I can't stay away from you. I tried. I wanted to do what you asked, but it's not going to happen."

A lump formed in my throat. I couldn't bring myself to push him away. With his scent tickling my nose and his mouth on my skin, there was no denying how desperately I craved him.

"We can't keep doing this," I said, a catch in my voice. I ran my free hand through his sexy shock of hair, holding him close. "The constant conflict is killing me."

"It's what we do. We fight. Then, we fuck. And, we both damn well love it." Arys knocked the flowers from my hand in his efforts to undress me. He peeled my top off and tossed it aside before burying his face in my cleavage. "You can't escape me, beautiful wolf. All it does is make the need stronger. We are meant to be together, and you will have to accept that, conflict and all."

The passion we shared crackled like lightning. Arys nuzzled my breasts, his hands worked to slide the skirt down my legs. A slave to the longing he stirred within me, I tugged at his shirt, seeking his bare chest.

He kissed me again. I sucked hungrily on his tongue and nipped at his lower lip. Running my hands over his hard body, I abandoned the sense of reason that tried to stop me. He was right. The bastard was always right.

"I never feel like me anymore unless I'm with you," I gasped out between kisses. "You're inside me all the time. I don't know how to live with that."

My bra and panties quickly joined the rest of my things on the floor. Arys's remaining clothes followed. He pressed me up against the wall in the hallway. His erection throbbed against my abdomen, and I licked my lips in anticipation.

Arys shook his head. Slipping a hand between my legs, he watched my face closely for a response. "That's not true. You just hate having absolutely no control over something. So you have no say in this, is that such a bad thing?"

To accompany his question, Arys glided a finger over me, teasing me with his feather soft touch. I groaned and reached for his swollen hard-on. He slapped my hand away with a wicked smile.

"Tell me you want me," he demanded, his touch growing aggressive. "You're mine and you know it. But, I want to hear you say it. Then, I'm going to make you scream for me."

A rush of heat made my cheeks tingle, among other places. Arys's possessive nature wouldn't be denied. He fully expected me to obey his command.

"I want you." My whisper became a soft moan. "You know I do."

Arys slid two fingers inside me, making my knees weaken. "Keep talking, baby."

I tried and failed to speak. He easily worked me into a frenzy, using the manipulation I had exerted over a man just hours ago to make me come undone. I loved every moment.

Arys grabbed my hand tightly and brought it to his lips. He kissed the inside of my wrist, hovering over the pumping artery there. I stiffened. The sharp sting of fangs followed, a light, teasing touch. Instead of puncturing my flesh, he continued up my arm to the sensitive inner curve of my elbow.

"Don't ever try to walk away from me again," he murmured, sucking at the pulsing blue vein beneath the surface of my skin. "I won't be so accommodating next time."

I shook my head vigorously. "I'm sorry, babe. I just feel so lost these days."

Every time he pressed fangs to my flesh, I moaned. I wanted to feel him inside me in every way. Knowing I longed for his bite, he purposely held out.

"You're never lost as long as I can find you." Arys kissed me once more, tenderly this time. A gentle brush of our lips accompanied the tiniest slip of tongue. "I can always find you."

I wrapped my arms around him and let my head fall back against the wall. The growing pleasure became an outlet for the pent up emotion I tried so hard to bury. The passion exploded forth. I kissed him with an aggression to rival the one building in Arys. A soft growl rumbled in my throat.

"I have to feel you inside me," I said, a pleading sound that earned me a low chuckle.

"Tell me what I want to hear. I need you to say it." There was a hard edge to his smooth as velvet voice. He slid his fingers from me, gliding them over the sensitive bud that had me writhing.

Arys's inner demons were not so different from mine. The insecurity and fear Shya sought to exploit was Arys's only true weakness. I couldn't allow the demon to twist that into a weapon to use against us.

"I'm yours," I said, seeing through a haze of love and desire. "Now, show me you really believe it, too. Claim me."

He snarled at me in a sexy show of fangs. Lifting me in his arms, he braced me against the wall and thrust inside me with a low, wolfish sound. With my legs around his waist, I held him close. Every slick stroke built the fire until it engulfed my entire body.

We fell into one another, sharing more than the union of our bodies. The power we shared soared. I could feel Arys in my head, his insatiable yearning as he filled me again and again. He pressed his face to my neck, moaning with each thrust. Gripping my hips, he plunged deep, forcing a cry from me.

Arys backed us up toward the staircase, collapsing onto the bottom few stairs. Landing on top, I quickly took control, impaling myself on his thick shaft. He buried his face in my breasts, clinging tightly to me. We moved together with perfect precision. The building waves of pleasure brought my buried feelings to the surface.

"Let me hear you, sweet wolf. Growl for me." To accompany his demand, Arys pulled down on my hips while simultaneously thrusting up. The force of the depth and impact brought a cry from me that bordered on a scream. He groaned and swore softly. "Dear God, do I ever love you."

I rode him with my focus on the finish line. The peak of climax loomed ever closer with each stroke. I savored the emotion-drenched energy surrounding Arys. These moments revealed the truth of things he might never say.

I swept my hair aside and bared my neck to him. He gazed at me with midnight blue eyes that were all wolf. It was eerie yet stunning.

Arys gently grasped the back of my neck and held firm. His bite was tender, delicate. The pain of fangs piercing my vein quickly gave way to joyous gratification. As my blood spilled, I plunged over the edge of ecstasy. I quivered atop my vampire, my inner muscles clenching him tight. In that brief moment of absolute rapture, I feared nothing. I felt vibrant, full of life. Being head over heels in love had a way of doing that. It was otherworldly.

The touch of his tongue against my wounded neck was warm and wet. My blood filled his mouth. He quickened our pace, driving fast and deep for those final few orgasmic thrusts.

It wasn't quite possible to collapse together and enjoy the afterglow. The stairs weren't afterglow friendly. So, I grabbed his hand and pulled him up the stairs to my bedroom.

After ensuring the heavy drapes covered every inch of the window, I crawled into bed to snuggle up with my vampire. We lay in the dark room, neither of us speaking for a long time. With my head on Arys's chest, I leisurely stroked a hand through his ebony hair. He held me close, his silence speaking louder than words.

"Wanna tell me what that was all about earlier tonight?" He asked in a lazy drawl. "You hunted that guy like an animal. I can't say it wasn't sexy as hell, but it wasn't quite your style."

"No," I agreed. "It was yours."

I recounted for him the events of the past two nights. Everything from my visit to Lilah's with Jez to discovering tonight that the demon bitch had my sister. He listened, attentive as I vented my anger with colorful words and curses. As I spoke, he dragged his fingertips up and down my back in a loving caress.

"I'm sure I don't need to tell you this, but I'm going to Lilah's with you."

I sat up to look at him, and the blanket slipped to my waist. "Arys, no. She has Juliet. If I go in with too many people or appear as a threat, there's no telling what Lilah will do. I can't risk anything happening to my sister."

I braced for the argument, certain it was coming, but Arys surprised me. He nodded and pulled me back down beside him.

"Fine," he said. "We'll do it your way, with a compromise. You go in without me but keep your mind open to me. If anything goes wrong, if it gets bad, I'm coming in."

It took me a minute to respond. I was shocked that he hadn't come back at me with a fight. It was a nice change, most likely a short-lived one as well. I'd enjoy it while I could.

"Alright. That works for me. But, follow my lead. No jumping the gun." I fell quiet for a moment, deciding how much crap I wanted to dig up. I didn't want to ruin the moment, but I had to ask. "The FPA killed Bianca. What did she tell you?"

Arys groaned and made a dramatic show of whining melodramatically in protest. "She didn't tell me a damn thing other than that she'd been sent to seduce either me or Shaz in order to find out more about you and what goes on inside The Wicked Kiss."

"Don't withhold shit from me, Arys," I warned. "Briggs said she gave you info that Shya wanted."

"She told me about a scroll, some kind of spell or something. Shya needs it. The FPA is trying to find it before he does. That's all she would say." Arys stretched and rolled us over so I was flat on my back beneath him. "I considered killing her. I thought you might be pissed if I did, so I let her go."

"After you kicked the shit out of her?" I stared up at him, worried that he would tell me something I didn't want to hear.

Arys's eyes glittered with the memory. He smirked before lowering his head to kiss my stomach. "I did what it took to make her talk. Don't judge, Alexa. It'll be you making that call one day."

My mind raced, putting the pieces together. I assumed Shya needed the missing spell for Gabriel who would then use it, along with my death, to open the chamber from hell. It was likely that Lilah sought the spell as well. Hopefully, she wouldn't be a problem much longer. I just needed to find the scroll before either Shya or the FPA did. Easy, right?

"I was hoping Bianca would know something we could use against Shya," Arys explained. "She didn't. But, she did confirm that the FPA doesn't have the scroll. Neither does Shya. As long as we get it first, we own his ass. Until then, he keeps every other big ugly bad away from you. I think it's as good a deal as we're going to get."

Arys shoved me back down beneath him. I pondered his logic, finding it sound. We didn't have many options as far as Shya was concerned. I was too impatient to wait for Shya to make a move; we had to find that scroll before the demon did.

Arys descended between my legs, interrupting my thoughts. The touch of his tongue stole my breath and left me grasping for words.

"We should talk about this," I said distractedly. "There's so much to consider."

"Not right now there isn't. There is only you and me. Everything else waits until nightfall. So, I suggest you stop talking, unless you're praising my wonderful performance." With a sinful laugh, he gripped my hips, holding me beneath him while he worshipped my body.

I didn't argue. Hell, he had a point. Until I walked into Lilah's, I just had to pass the time. Sleep would be a necessary factor in readying myself… after exhausting myself with my dark lover, of course.

Chapter Twenty

"Arys, get your ass out of that shower before I'm forced to flush the toilet and scald you out."

I swiped a hand through the steam layering the mirror, but my reflection was still hazy. I saw calm brown eyes staring back at me. My hair was long and loose, falling down my back in a wave of ash blonde. Smoky black liner and mascara was all the makeup I wore. It created a dramatic cat eye effect, just the start of the drama for the evening.

"Why don't you get your ass in here and soap up my... back?" he chuckled. "Don't make me rub one out without you."

"Alright, that's it." I reached over and flushed the toilet, giggling when Arys shouted a litany of curses.

"Not cool, Alexa."

Ignoring him, I left the bathroom and rifled through my closet. Yoga pants and a simple black tank top made up my casual but easy to move in outfit. I knew I'd be fighting for my life in a matter of hours and couldn't shake the sense of urgency. Having to wait until midnight to hit up Lilah's party of mayhem and doom was making me impatient. I wanted to rush in and save my sister. Unfortunately, it couldn't be that easy.

I took a slow, steady breath. Remaining calm and focused was in my best interest. It was just so damn tough.

Arys's notebook lay on the bedside table. I had woken up to the sound of a pencil scratching against paper. Arys's long buried artistic flare had recently come back to life. It was good for him; he needed an outlet that wasn't blood and death.

Curious, I picked up his notebook. He'd been drawing a wolf. It stared off into the distance, seeing something beyond the boundary of the page. The wistful expression it wore was painfully familiar. The wolf wasn't me; it was clearly Shaz.

"It's not my best work," Arys's voice came from behind me.

I turned to him with a smile. "It's beautiful. Really." And, it was. It also caused a pang of longing so fierce my chest ached.

Arys readied himself as I watched. In jeans and a t-shirt, he looked comfortable but prepared to fight. His wet hair had dried into the sexy mess it always was. The few silver piercings he often wore were absent, the jewelry left on the bathroom counter. I drank in the sight of him, wanting to hold on to one of our last moments alone together until this was all over.

"We have time for a quickie," he teased, poking the ticklish spot in my side until I laughed. He pulled me into his arms and kissed the top of my head. "Are you ready? I don't want to send you in there alone."

"Yeah, I'm ready. The wait is killing me. Besides, I won't be alone. Jez will be with me." I hugged him extra tight, and a small sigh escaped me.

The drive to the city was tense. I was tightly wound; the anxious energy building in my core had me vibrating with the need to unleash it on anyone who dared to harm my sister.

Jez and Willow were waiting for us outside The Wicked Kiss. Arys tentatively suggested that we go inside and find ourselves a willing victim, something to take the edge off, but I liked my edge right where it was. I wasn't hungry for blood tonight, only for vengeance.

"Should we say anything to Kale?" Jez asked, gesturing to his car in the lot.

"No," I shook my head and regarded the door cautiously. "He's got his own problems to deal with. I think he would be more of a liability than anything."

A shadow of absolute hate passed over Arys's face at the mention of Kale. I would definitely be doing all I could to keep them from having a further encounter.

I opened the Charger's trunk and stared at my dagger. The Dragon Claw, just a nick, was exactly what I needed to take out Lilah.

"There's no way she'll let me get in there with this," I mused.

"I'm going to try getting past her guards with this." Jez slid the hairpin out of her golden locks, showing me the blade attached. "It's pure silver."

"Nice." I nodded, regarding her with curiosity. "Does it hurt you at all?" I couldn't help but wonder. It would take some time to adjust to the idea of Jez being half demon.

Jez tucked the hairpin back into place and smoothed out a few loose tendrils. "Nope. That's the beauty of being mortal."

Sure she was mortal, but if someone got a hold of that thing and plunged it into her, what would it do then? I wasn't going to undermine Jez's choice to bring it; I just hoped that no one would use it against her.

"I can get that in to you." Willow pointed to the Dragon Claw. He had been relatively quiet. I wondered if it was because he was also relatively sober.

"Really? You can bring something like that when you do your little teleportation thing?" I wasn't sure if there was a more accurate term for what angels and demons did. They could pop from place to place and lurk unseen. Teleportation just didn't seem to fit.

Willow laughed, a musical sound that produced a sense of peace. "There are many terms for it, most of them fabricated or incorrect. Let's just call it a translocation jump. Seems to be the best way to describe it. And yes, I can take objects with me. Unfortunately, that's about all I can take. No live beings or anything like that."

"Perfect. Thank you." I lifted the dagger from its velvet-lined box and passed it to Willow, careful not to let it touch either Jez or Arys. "Wait until the right time, if you can figure out when that is. Too early or too late, and I'll never get a chance to use it."

"I'll stay out of sight until I feel I'm needed." Willow turned the dagger over, examining the demon blade with distaste. I handed him the scabbard, and he promptly slipped it inside before tucking it into his knee-length leather jacket.

"So, now we wait," I said, my impatience growing. I pulled out my phone to check the time, and it rang in my hand. The hard rock sound of Guns N' Roses was loud in the quiet parking lot. It was Briggs.

"Shit," I swore before answering. "What do you want, Briggs?"

"Have you heard from Juliet? When she didn't answer any of my calls I went by her place. There were signs of a struggle, and she's nowhere to be found."

I had a split second to decide between the truth and a lie. "Someone took her. Someone who wants to use her as leverage over me. She's alive. I won't let anything change that."

"If you know where she is, O'Brien, you'd better give me a little more information than that. I'll have a team ready in minutes." He covered the phone to bark orders at someone in the background.

"No deal. I'll handle this. Your people would only get her killed." I braced for the threat of government authority.

Briggs scoffed and swore. "Dammit, I am not in the mood to play these games with you. Not everything is a power trip. She's a member of my team, and I am genuinely concerned for her well-being."

"All things considered, I'm glad to hear that. You'll be the first to know when she's safe again." I hung up before he could reply. Having the FPA all over this would only increase the level of danger.

I stared at the phone, remembering Briggs boasting about tracking it. Turning it off should prevent that. Still, to be on the safe side, I would have to leave it here at the club.

When it was almost time to leave, Arys pulled me aside. "Be careful and most importantly, stay calm. Don't let her drive you to make decisions based on anger. Your short temper is dangerous."

"Who are you to talk?" I punched him playfully, trying to keep the moment from getting serious. It didn't work.

He kissed me with an intensity that stole my breath. "I promised Shaz I would keep you safe. Please don't do anything to make that a lie."

"I'll be fine." I touched his face, and he leaned into it, rubbing his cheek against my hand. "You're always with me, even when you're not actually with me. No worries, ok?"

By the time Jez and I clambered into her Jeep for the drive to Lilah's, I was frightfully calm. I'd awakened with fear and apprehension, but that faded, replaced by a solemn assurance that, no matter what happened, I was going to find a way to protect Juliet. The wolf paced restlessly inside me. It, too, was eager to make Lilah hurt.

"That worked too well," Jez commented with a smirk.

Darker

We watched as Arys drove away in my car, followed by a grey BMW sedan that pulled out of the grocery store lot across the street. Easing into traffic behind the Charger, it had to be the feds. Briggs thought he could send a tail after me? Please. He'd be sorry when Arys led them on a wild goose chase and sent them back with punctured veins, if he sent them back at all.

A few minutes later, we pulled into traffic, heading in the opposite direction. I watched closely in the side mirror for any sign of another FPA car. We were clear.

Turning in to Lilah's posh neighborhood got my pulse pounding. I clenched my fists and gathered my thoughts. The power boiled over inside, spilling out like a sieve despite my attempt to rein it in. I could do this. I had to.

"You need to tone that down, Lex," Jez remarked. "I think you're starting to give me static cling."

She patted her hair, smoothing it in jest. I focused hard on containing myself. Anticipation and wrath had me on overdrive.

We parked a block away and walked to the house. Guards waited for us at the edge of the property. The small group of muscle consisted of both vampires and a demon. The temptation to hit them all with a hell of a blast was great, but I resisted. They weren't worth it.

"You were supposed to come alone," grunted a vampire with a beefy build and an ugly sneer.

"The invitation didn't specify that. I doubt having a shifter at my side is going to make much difference. Lilah clearly has an arsenal here." I raised my arms and spread my feet when he started to frisk me; I had nothing to hide.

One of the other vamps frisked Jez while the demon present merely oversaw the process. Maybe they were ignorant or maybe they were just men, but nobody thought to check Jez's hairpiece.

They didn't hold us up with wannabe bad guy talk. However, they also wouldn't let us go further until sending and receiving word from Lilah that Jez could enter, too. Of course, she allowed Jez to pass. Lilah had something concrete on me. I could bring an army, but as long as the bitch had my sister, I'd have to play nice.

We continued down the stone walk to the front door. There were no hellhounds to greet us this time. No. It was far worse than that.

Falon swung the door open. He stood there with a self-righteous grin that didn't quite reach his ice-cold eyes. Dressed all in black with his silver wings flared, he stepped back and motioned for us to enter.

The doors slammed shut with a deafening bang. Immediately, several vampires flanked each of us. Again, a demon stood off to the side, just watching. I was beginning to think the demons weren't there for us but, rather, for Willow or others like him.

"I am going to enjoy this," Falon said. His smile had vanished, his expression now stony and unreadable. "Follow me."

He turned his back on us, expecting we'd follow. What choice did we have? I eyed the fallen angel suspiciously. He was playing a dangerous game here. I couldn't be sure if his loyalties lay with Shya or Lilah. Who was he here to help? His power would have a hand in determining the outcome of this little party.

Falon led us down a hall on the far side of the foyer, past the library we'd seen previously. The vampires were hot on our heels. I paused to give them all a once over. Unrecognizable, every one of them. I found some small relief in the fact that they were not patrons of my club.

At the end of the hall, a demon stood guard in front of a pair of closed double doors. He scowled at Falon but moved aside to let us through. Falon threw the doors open and strode through like he owned the place.

I hesitated in the doorway, peering inside. The vampires at my back shoved me over the threshold. I wasn't all that surprised by what I saw inside. The fact that I was growing accustomed to demon gatherings was troublesome.

The room was large even for a small mansion like Lilah's. The only windows were high up on either side of the arched ceiling, high enough to keep sunlight from hitting the lowest part of the room during the day. Careful design, fit for a vampire.

The hardwood floor shone as if freshly polished. The room was open with little clutter. In the center was a sunken circular couch. Several scantily clad bodies moved upon it, both men and women, human and vampire. They created a powerful energy that reeked of blood and lust.

I shielded against the onslaught of seductive energy. So, this was how Lilah enticed vampires into her fold. I had a sneaking suspicion the humans here were not present of their own free will but were instead victims of the vampire influence.

At the far end of the room stood three elaborate armchairs. Lilah sat in the middle with Gabriel and Juliet bound and seated on either side of her. My heart surged when I saw my sister, bruised but alive. Small cuts adorned her wrist and neck, evident of Lilah's curiosity. Juliet's blood hadn't worked. She wasn't a Hound.

Shya sat in a chair off to the side where he had an ample view of the entire room. Despite being bound in silver, he still wore his constantly amused smile. His grin broadened when he saw me, and a chill crept down my spine. Far too many demons were in this room for my liking.

I followed Falon around the couch, stopping in front of Lilah. Jez was at my side, tense but ready. Meeting Juliet's eyes, I nodded, hoping to encourage her. She stared back at me, expressionless.

"You came," Lilah said, crossing one leg over the other. "I've got to admit, I almost thought you might leave your sister to fend for herself."

"No, you didn't. But, why save her for last? Why kill Zak and Zoey?" I stared hard at Lilah, ignoring the demon that stood behind her but noting that Brook was not among those present.

Lilah did her best to look bored. It didn't work. She was thrilled to see me. "Because I wanted to. I only wish it had been easier to track down the white wolf."

I repressed the sudden surge of venomous hatred. I wanted so badly to slap her with a blast of power. Cool and calm. That's how I had to do this.

"So, what now? You bleed me and let my sister go?" I asked, indignant and refusing to show fear.

Lilah pretended to consider. She looked more like the Lilah I knew tonight. Her flame-colored hair was in a tight braid, and she was dressed to fight. I eyed her sturdy army boots, certain I'd take one in the face before the night was over.

"Are you in a hurry, Alexa? I'm not keeping you from anything, am I? Another hush-hush meeting with the FPA, perhaps." She shot a snide look Shya's way. He shrugged but remained silent.

"That's a pretty cheap tactic for someone as old and experienced as you. Isn't it?" There was a light touch on my mind from Arys. I let him in, seeking reassurance in his presence.

Lilah raised a hand to Falon, a wordless command. The asshole angel came to stand before me. It was so damn hard not to step away. His pale eyes were vacant of any emotion. Without laying a hand on me, he grasped my energy and jerked hard, stripping power from me.

The pain was immediate and agonizing. I screamed and went down hard on my knees. Falon grabbed my hand and pulled me up. The more solid connection intensified the pain. It felt like he was tearing me in half. Instead, he tore all the power that I'd gathered in readiness from me as if it were a limb from my body.

He whispered to me, using the sound of my shrieks to ensure nobody else heard. "You fucked up. I tried to help you."

I sagged against him, and he let me go. Jez caught me before I hit the floor again. I gasped for breath, drained to the point of exhaustion. The leopard inside Jez crawled to the surface where it tried to offer me some comfort. I drew on her energy, taking just enough to stay on my feet.

"How was that for a cheap tactic?" Lilah asked, her steely, burnt orange gaze upon me.

My mind raced as I tried to figure out what Falon had meant. When the hell did he ever try to help me?

'When he dosed you with his power,' Arys supplied. 'You came for her, and you failed.'

Shock settled in to fuel more questions. If that were the case, it would mean Falon wanted me to take out Lilah. I regarded him suspiciously, and he carefully avoided my eyes. As far as the angel was concerned, I couldn't afford to assume anything.

"Can we just get this over with? Or, do you plan on torturing me further?" Maybe I was asking for it, but if I could get Lilah busy kicking my ass, Willow might get his chance to pop in.

"Honey, I haven't even begun to torture you." Lilah rose and walked around my sister's chair, trailing her hand along Juliet's arm as she did so. "Where is your vampire, Alexa? Surely he wouldn't let you walk in here without him."

"He doesn't know I'm here. I'm not willing to risk my sister like that. Lilah, seriously, just take what you want from me and let Juliet go. Please."

"I gave you the opportunity to make an ally out of me. You chose Shya instead." Lilah's angry gaze landed on the demon who grinned, infuriating her further. "Naturally, I'm feeling a tad betrayed. I worked at your side for years. I saved your ass, yet you trusted him over me."

She was jealous of Shya? Really? I would have rolled my eyes if I hadn't been so sure she'd knock them out of my head.

"Hey, it's not personal. Remember?" I threw her own words at her. "I didn't come to stroke the ego of an insecure, washed up demon. Stop wasting my time."

Jez stiffened beside me and gave my arm a warning squeeze. Lilah's slow calculated actions were unnerving. I wanted to piss her off enough to shake her control, to throw her off her game somehow.

Lilah's eyes narrowed, but she held herself together. Without taking her eyes from me, she grabbed Juliet by the hair and jerked her head to the side. Dragging a sharp nail over Juliet's jugular, Lilah practically purred.

"It's personal now." She dug that nail in just enough to bring a bead of blood to the surface. Slow and languid, Lilah bent to run her tongue along Juliet's slender neck, capturing that drop of crimson.

I shuddered and bit back the urge to shout a useless stream of ugly curses at the demon bitch. The scent of my sister's blood wafted to tickle my nose with its heady Were aroma.

"You're a fucking nutcase," I said, clenching my fists at my sides. "You're completely mad, aren't you?"

A light went on as another puzzle piece fell into place. Lilah straightened up, shoving away from Juliet. She took a few steps toward me but kept a safe distance. I was aching on the inside from Falon stripping my power, yet she still feared me.

"I suppose that's a matter of perspective." A small smile played about her lips. "Aren't we all a little mad?"

I shook my head, doing my best to ignore the steady throb in my skull. "It's not that. It's him. The separation from your twin flame, it has driven you crazy, made you desperate. Because you know the longer you try to exist without him, the farther you'll fall into insanity."

She moved fast. The fist she threw landed like concrete, and I went down hard on my ass. This wolf knew how to take a few hits though, and I was back on my feet going after Lilah before I could rethink the reaction. Falon intercepted, throwing me back with little effort.

"Wrong, you presumptuous bitch," Lilah seethed, baring fangs. "See here's the thing about Salem. He and his angels, they were the ones who locked me in a cage. They ensured that if I ever got out, I'd be cursed into this godforsaken form. It was his pathetic attempt to control the way my darkness affected him. At full power, I'm a bigger force than he is. Battling the darkness was driving him mad. So, he took drastic measures."

I swiped a hand across my split lip, finding it bloody. Bleeding in a room with several unfamiliar vampires was not a good thing. If Kale's reaction to my blood was any indication of the effect it had on them, there was a chance they could lose control.

"And, you think getting your power back will change that?" I laughed bitterly. "Bleeding me might break your curse, but it will never break your tie to him."

Lilah's anger scorched the atmosphere. She seemed flustered. Turning away, she spoke quietly to a tall, brawny demon lingering near the captives. He vanished, leaving me to worry about where he had gone.

I considered reaching out to the vampires in the room, stealing their energy. I could take them all out and have a hell of a load of power to throw at Lilah. Except, until my sister was free, I couldn't risk it. Drawing on my link to Arys was possible, but his silence had grown, and I no longer felt him in my head. The first trickle of fear slithered through me.

I felt frustrated without any power, but I knew I could do this. I was a wolf, a Hound, whatever the hell that meant. I could do this powerless.

"You know, I hadn't intended to drag this out. That smart mouth of yours is making me reconsider." Lilah paced a slow line from Juliet's chair to Gabriel's and back again. Both captives stared straight ahead, unflinching and numb. I feared what might have happened to them already.

I stared at the demoness, steady and unafraid. As long as the bitch was talking, it bought us time to get out of this. I shrugged, running a tongue over my cut lip. It had swelled quickly.

"Do what you gotta do," I said.

Noise at the door drew everyone's attention. The demon who had just left dragged in an angry, curse spewing Arys.

Lilah's lips were pressed into a tight, thin line. "You're a terrible liar, Alexa. Did you expect me to believe your twin would not come? Now, he can watch you bleed."

Chapter Twenty-One

My heart dropped into my stomach like a stone. Arys was battered but otherwise fine. The demon pulled him through the room and forced him down on his knees in front of Lilah's chair, facing me. The demon held Arys's head in a vicelike grip, ready to remove it at Lilah's command.

Arys's blue eyes glittered with menace. He would not be broken no matter what they did to him, I knew that. Lilah knew better than anyone what the twin flame bond meant. So, she would break him by making him watch me suffer. It didn't take a psychologist to put this one together.

"Falon, I believe you owe Alexa some retribution for trapping you in a circle." Lilah nodded toward me.

"Are you kidding me?" I stared at her in shock. "You're getting Falon to beat on me for you? Why not do it yourself? I'm sure you want to."

Lilah crossed her arms and regarded me knowingly. "Why Alexa, I'd think you of all people would certainly understand how easy it is to gain power over a man simply by fucking him. Why get my hands dirty when I have someone to do it for me?"

Falon's wings ruffled ever so slightly. His carefully neutral expression didn't change. Without waiting for another command, he walked a slow circle around Jez and me. He shoved her away, effectively separating us.

My heart raced. Panic caused my words to rush forth. "Fuck the circle. That bastard purposely-,"

I saw stars before I finished my sentence. Falon's hit rocked me back on my heels. I struggled to stay upright. I looked fearfully to Shya as if he could save me. His face was a mask of cool composure, but fire burned in his red eyes.

"Is this worth it?" Lilah asked. It took me a moment to realize she addressed Arys. "Knowing you can't help her. That you can only watch as she suffers. Is it worth everything you share?"

Arys glared at Lilah with the power of a thousand burning suns. "You're afraid of her," he accused. "So afraid you don't even want to touch her. You see the light in her, and it terrifies you. I see right through you, demon bitch. Because I am you."

The two of them stared at each other, Arys with accusation and Lilah with uncertainty. Each of them part of the darkness, they shared something then that I would never understand. It momentarily crippled Lilah. She turned away from Arys, scoffing angrily.

"Get me the blade," she shouted at nobody in particular. "Let's bleed this wolf."

Falon pressed dangerously close. With wings flared wide, he trapped me, ensuring I didn't try anything. I had to do something, but my options were limited, almost nonexistent.

"Take your clothes off," he demanded. "You have to be wolf for this."

"Fuck you." I stood my ground. "This entire thing has been orchestrated for Lilah to throw her weight around, but she doesn't have any. You and I both know that."

"All I know is that you better start stripping. I'm sure a few of these guys would be happy to help you." Falon indicated the small throng of vampires watching the entertainment Lilah had promised them.

I gritted my teeth and fumed. Together Arys and I were powerful enough to wipe out every vampire present and maybe even beat back the demons, too. It wouldn't happen though. Stripped of my power, I felt weak. I needed time to bounce back from that. Even then, I wouldn't have access to my power in wolf form.

Lilah held up a shiny dagger with a sharp blade and a black stone pressed into the handle. She twirled it in her hands, eyeing me with a vindictive sneer.

"Tick tock," she said. Lilah moved between her hostages, lingering near each one of them. Stopping beside Arys, she held the dagger up for me to see. "Have you ever wanted to escape your twin, Alexa? Has anyone ever given you the opportunity to sever the tie?"

My entire body went cold. I shook my head, a vehement protest rising in my throat. "No. Don't. I'm undressing, ok? I'll shift, and you'll get your friggin' Hound blood. If you hurt anyone, that changes. I'll go down fighting, and I promise to take you with me."

The weight of so many eyes upon me was crushing. I kept my eyes on Arys, finding courage in his gaze. He could have fought back, could have escaped the demon's grasp on him. Yet, he didn't because my sister was still in danger. He was willing to hold tight and let me call the shots. If we got out of this alright, I'd make sure to show him my appreciation.

It was difficult to keep my hands moving. She wasn't just stripping me so I could shift; she was exposing me in a way that would sap my remaining strength. She wanted me vulnerable. I couldn't let that happen. I pulled my top off over my head and let it fall at my feet. My hands shook when I slid my pants down. They were vibrating when I reached to unhook my bra. Maybe I couldn't do this.

"Come on, wolf," Falon sneered. "I'd have thought you'd be used to public nudity, being a beast with two bodies. Don't tell me we're making you shy."

I was used to the nudity that came with running in a pack. It was natural, part of what we were. Being forced to strip down for the entertainment of others was not within my comfort zone.

"Actually, you are making me a little uncomfortable." I slid my gaze to Falon, searching him for some kind of truth. I couldn't figure the bastard out. "I'm not sure I want you this close, seeing as you've already had your erection between my legs."

He slapped me across the face, an open-handed smack that echoed in the large, open room. I tasted blood. My cheek stung, yet I couldn't help but grin. The fallen angel was ashamed of what had occurred between us despite the fact that it had been solely power driven.

That shame fueled his anger. Falon grabbed me and viciously tore off my underwear. My attempts to struggle were useless in comparison to his strength. When he had me naked and quaking, he grabbed my hair tight and forced me to the floor on my knees.

"Whenever you're ready," he said to Lilah.

I caught Juliet's eye and mouthed the words, 'I'm sorry.' I didn't know what else to do.

For the first time since I arrived, Lilah acknowledged Shya. She sidled up to him with a confident swagger. She tugged on the silver restraints holding him until she'd forced a sound of distress from him.

"Now it's your turn to play along, Shya." She bent down so she could stare straight into his face. "You need both the wolf and the kid. However, you can only have one. I'll let you leave here unharmed when this is all over. I don't need to kill Alexa to swipe a little blood. She can be all yours. Or, you can opt for the kid instead. Your call. You choose who lives and who dies."

"If you succeed in breaking your curse, there will be nothing to stop you from banishing me to the pits. Why should I believe you'd spare me? I know better." Shya showed no emotion. He was calm, possibly too calm.

"Come now. You know I've had a fondness for you. At least, I did until you tried to take advantage of my curse and claim my throne for yourself." Lilah tapped the dagger blade against the palm of her hand. She pointed it at Gabriel who glared hatefully at her. "I'm willing to spare you. After all, you have provided me with many comforts and protection over the years."

"Break your curse. Then I'll choose." Shya was so relaxed, he might as well have been in a recliner rather than a hard chair with chains. Did he truly fear nothing?

"You think I can't do it," she hissed accusingly.

"I know you won't do it." Shya's calculated grin revealed even white teeth. He was fucking with her, having his Cheshire Cat moment and loving it.

Lilah backed away with the dagger clutched in her grip. She spun around to face Gabriel, and I was certain in that moment he was dead. Then, she regained her composure and pinned me with her cold stare instead.

"Shift."

I was almost happy to if it meant escaping the leering gaze of the vampire muscle. I slapped at Falon until he stepped well out of my personal space. The shift was fast and fluid. All I had to do was embrace the wolf, to let her spill forth and take over. There was a brief moment of exquisite pain and then freedom. I was wolf.

The strength of the beast filled me. I bared my fangs in a snarl, daring Lilah to come at me with the blade. She regarded me with wariness but not enough caution.

"Try anything, and Falon kills your sister."

Like a good little minion, Falon moved to stand over Juliet, his pale eyes gleaming with anticipation. A growl rumbled in my throat. I glanced around, desperately seeking a way out of this. Jez stood stiffly nearby, watching with growing horror.

I touched Arys's mind, needing something from him. 'If I don't make it out of here I need you to make sure Juliet does.'

'You are making it out of here.'

'I need to know you'll keep her safe. Promise me.'

'I promise.'

Lilah held the dagger ready in case I lunged. It took all of my willpower to resist.

"Over there. By the couch." She circled around one side of the couch, waiting while I did the same opposite her.

As I drew closer, I realized that there was a circle. An energy circle, much like the one I had used to trap Falon, encompassed a giant pentagram on the floor. The people within the circle were confined, prisoners. They carried on with each other, completely oblivious. It dawned on me that they were the sacrifice.

An ugly sensation warmed my belly. This didn't feel right. Lilah would use my blood and their combined death to set herself free. Then what? We'd all have cookies and tea?

The tall demon shadowing Lilah stood at the edge of the circle, holding it in place. He produced a gold chalice and handed it to her. He stood between the two upper points of the inverted star. If Lilah broke the curse, we would all suffer. I was a wreck trying to see a way out.

Every other person in the room seemed to shrink back from the circle. I wished to be among them. The demon began to chant, low and Latin. My hackles rose as my fear grew.

Lilah advanced on me with a renewed ferocity. Eager, she rushed toward me, each step bringing her faster. I braced myself, unable to predict what she had in mind.

"Hold still and this will be over in minutes. A shallow cut, that's all I need," she said, the gleam in her twisted gaze growing brighter.

She came only as close as she had to. Resting the dagger blade against my neck, she shuddered with excitement. I stared at Arys and Juliet. I loved them both so much, though I still hadn't had a chance to reconnect with Juliet. If we got out of here, that would change.

The blade stung as it cut through my fur and flesh. The blood was warm as it seeped from the wound. Lilah was quick to capture it in the chalice. I tensed. This was it, the moment of truth.

Lilah lifted the chalice, sniffing its contents. I saw her consider tasting it. She resisted. Moving to stand at the bottom of the circle, near the point, she held the chalice ready, waiting. The demon continued to chant in a loud voice. Things were happening. I felt the earth tremble as dark powers in deep places began to stir.

A flash of silver drew my eye to Falon. He spread his wings wide and ruffled them, a potentially natural angel gesture. Something about it struck me as forced. He was trying to draw my attention to him. My eyes darted from Lilah to him and back. I couldn't chance taking my eyes off her at the wrong time.

The Latin stopped, and the silence that followed was deafening. Lilah tipped the chalice and began to drip blood onto each person within the circle. That's when Falon freed Juliet and all hell broke loose.

"Stop her," he shouted at me, already moving to release Shya from his bonds.

I froze, as did most of those present. After a heartbeat of confusion, everyone exploded into action. Shya was impossible to follow with the mortal eye. He went from his chair to the demon holding Arys, disabling him with ease. Arys was on his feet instantly, tossing vampires aside in his attempt to get to me.

The vampires were quick to spread out around the circle, doing their best to protect the outcast queen they had adopted. Several of them swamped Arys, trying to take him down. Pulling the blade from her golden hair, Jez leapt in to the fray, plunging the weapon into the heart of any vampire stupid enough to get in her way.

There was no time to think or plan. I lunged at Lilah, launching my full weight at her. She went down beneath me with a thump and a startled cry. The chalice fell from her hand and rolled across the floor, spilling the remainder of the blood as it went.

She still held the dagger so I sunk my fangs into her forearm, crushing bone between my jaws until she let go. Lilah fought back with the panicked desperation of one who knew her time was fast running out. With her free hand, she pounded her fist into the side of my head.

A heavy weight slammed into me. The Latin-chanting demon's power hit me like a runaway train. I was airborne, crashing hard into the vampire fight. The throng swallowed me. Disoriented and injured, I struggled to get my bearings and get out of the flail of limbs and smacks of power.

"Lexi!"

A familiar scent reached me as Juliet pulled me free of the chaos. Jez and Arys were back-to-back, taking on Lilah's vampires with skill and the love of the fight. Shya and Falon targeted the demons. Gabriel sat stiffly in his chair, free now, an amulet in his hands and his lips moving as he worked a spell. That left Lilah who was hastily trying to gather the spilled blood.

She cupped her hands, scooping it and throwing it into the circle. If dousing each human sacrifice in blood was the key to completing the ritual, I had to stop her from pulling it off in her crazed desperation.

A vampire with a football player's frame lumbered toward us with fangs bared. I left him to Juliet, confident in her ability as a wolf and a trained government agent. I wanted Lilah.

I dodged the vampire and bounded for the demoness. I leaped onto her back and bit her shoulder. With a shriek, she spun around trying to dislodge me. It worked. I hung back, judging my next attack.

"You could have left here alive," Lilah said, her voice low and uneven. "I won't let you take this from me. I will not be sent back to him."

She had reclaimed the fallen dagger. Wielding it with her one good hand, she advanced on me. I braced myself, ready to attack. My lips peeled back in a vicious snarl.

I avoided the first swing. The dagger blade sliced through the air inches from my face. I circled, forcing her to keep turning to face me. I lunged in close, snapping at her before moving back out of reach.

The wolf felt good. I had come to rely so heavily on my metaphysical power that the reminder of who and what I was, was refreshing. My power was not what defined me; I was so much more than that.

Lunging again, I knocked Lilah off her feet. She slid through the blood spill and gave an anguished cry. Before I could attack further, the air rippled and Willow appeared.

He pulled the Dragon Claw from his jacket, holding it uncertainly. I was in no position to take it from him. The only other person who could wield it was Juliet.

"Alexa, are you-," Willow's words died as Lilah plunged her dagger into his back. She pulled it free, and smoke rose from the wound. Silver.

Willow staggered back, trying to put space between them. The Dragon Claw fell from his grasp, hitting the floor. Lilah promptly kicked it away so it skittered across the hard surface. Then, she went after him again.

"Oh no you don't. You are not standing between me and my Hound." Blood ran from Lilah's shattered forearm where the bone lay exposed. Vampires healed fast. If I didn't do more damage, she would heal and make me pay for my mistake.

Willow beat her back with a slap of power, but the silver had weakened him. He slumped against the wall, wings spread for balance.

I touched Arys's thoughts, finding him enjoying the fight. He took on multiple vampires at once, using power and fists to take them out. Every one that burst into dust and ash fueled his fire.

'The Dragon Claw is here. Juliet has to get to it. She has to use it on Lilah. You've got to help her.'

There were no words, no thought to tell me he'd heard, but he had. I could feel it. I trusted Arys to make this happen. It was the only way.

I didn't hesitate or wait for the right moment. I attacked Lilah in a craze of snapping jaws. Driving her away from Willow, I threw myself at her, angling to take her down. She fell near the edge of the circle and tumbled inside.

The power holding it broke. So did the spell holding its occupants captive. I jumped in after Lilah, pinning her to the floor in the middle of the sofa circle. Everyone around us rushed to escape, screaming hysterically.

A burst of wind gusted over us as the carefully constructed circle lost all energy. It was useless now.

Lilah had lost.

The sheer insanity glowing in her flaming eyes was disturbing. I snarled down into her face, fighting for a shot at her throat. She fought hard to reach the blade she'd dropped just inches away. In a cheap but determined move, Lilah slashed my face with her sharp fingernails.

My left eye burned, and my vision blurred. The bitch tried to blind me. Infuriated and wild, I got my fangs around her throat, and I bit deep.

Her blood filled my mouth. It tasted like burnt sulfur. I held tight despite the horrid taste and smell. I gave her a rough shake and felt the tissue begin to tear. It didn't happen fast enough. Lilah got her fingers around the blade and, in a swift motion, buried it deep in my side.

I yelped, instinctively releasing my hold on Lilah. She withdrew the blade and swung hard for another blow. I scrambled out of reach, bounding across the sofa and out of the sunken circle. I didn't make it far; the pain was too much.

I collapsed near Willow where I involuntarily shifted back to human. Naked and bleeding, I lay there shaking. Willow moved to block me with his wings, sheltering me from further attack.

"Juliet," I gasped, my voice barely a croak. "Dragon Claw."

Willow nodded, searching frantically for my sister in the thinning crowd of flailing limbs. I saw Arys grab Juliet, his lips moving fast as he shoved her toward the fallen Dragon Claw. Then, he came for me, drawn by my suffering.

Arys fell to the floor beside me, his eyes wild with panic. He reached to touch me but hesitated as he took in the extent of my injuries. Blood seeped from my side. Every labored breath forced more from the wound.

Darkness threatened to pull me under into unconsciousness. I strained against it. This was one little stab wound. I'd taken a stake between the ribs; I could take this.

"This is bad, love." Arys pulled me gently into his arms, wincing at the pained sound I made. He clasped my hand in his, and the power sparked between us. "I think I can heal it. If there's not too much damage."

At his touch, my strength grew. I reached to touch his face, finding such sorrow there. "You know you can't lose me."

"I know you're not ready to be what I am," he said, wiping a scarlet smear from near my eye. "And, I don't think I'm ready for that either."

A scream rang out followed by Juliet's angry shout. I dragged my gaze to her, finding her grappling with Lilah. The demoness still had some fight left, though the tears in her throat clearly afflicted her. She grabbed Juliet's head and slammed it into the edge of the sunken circle.

Juliet's growl was audible over the din. She gave Lilah a head-butt that would have stunned the toughest opponent. She followed up fast with the Dragon Claw, plunging the massive blade into the vampire's chest.

The whole room fell silent, waiting. Lilah's eyes were wide as saucers. She opened her mouth, but no sound came out. Her body convulsed and exploded, raining down atop Juliet in a shower of ash.

Relief filled me. My baby sister saved the day. I couldn't have been more proud, even if I was bleeding out on the floor.

The remaining few vampires second-guessed their loyalty. They disengaged from combat with Jez and headed for the double doors. The sound of snarls and the snap of fangs came from outside the room, beyond my line of sight.

Just one demon remained. He knelt before Shya with head bowed. Tension eased from me, and I lay in Arys's arms, ready for whatever came next. Arys, however, did not share that acceptance.

He pushed healing energy into me, targeting the deadly hole in my side. I was dizzy. The room spun, and I struggled to focus. I tried to speak Arys's name, but nothing coherent came out. Maybe it was too late. Healing through energy manipulation has its limits. Perhaps I was beyond them.

A deep sadness hollowed out my insides. I didn't want the next time I faced Shaz to be as a vampire. He would cease to be the mate that made my wolf ache; he would only be food.

The light seemed to dim, and my vision swam. I was vaguely aware of the small group that gathered around me. Jez spoke soothing words in low tones to Juliet. They were both ok, and I couldn't have been happier.

"She's not going to make it," Willow spoke in a low, hushed tone. "It's a mortal wound."

"What about you? Can you do anything?" Arys's plea dripped with emotion.

"I'm sorry. I wish I could." Willow made a small sound of distress and eased away, trying to give Arys a respectful amount of space while I died in his arms.

My eyes closed, and the promise of escape drew near. The sound of my sister's sobs was especially loud. I slipped further into the approaching black, finding release from the pain there. The voices grew distant.

The last thing I heard distinctly was Shya's calm, disaffected tone. "There's something I can do. You might not like it."

Chapter Twenty-Two

I came awake with a scream. It echoed in the silence of the vast room. Disoriented and shaky, it took a moment for me to figure out where I was.

I was still inside Lilah's house. In fact, I was inside her circle. Sprawled beside me with eyes open in terror lay a man with his throat slit. One of Lilah's sacrificial humans, he was dead.

My breath came too hard and fast. I hyperventilated as a series of broken images flashed through my brain. Lena, Raoul, my parents. I had seen them in my dreams as I hovered between life and death. Nothing coherent had lingered.

"Calm down, Alexa. One breath at a time." Shya's voice startled me, and I turned to find him standing at the head of the pentagram.

I reached to touch my battered face and disheveled hair. I was solid, real and alive. No vampire fangs.

"What happened?" My voice cracked. My throat was sore and dry.

Arys's t-shirt covered me like a small blanket. I cast a glance about, seeking him. He crouched near the sunken circle, watching me with a fear in his blue gaze that I'd never seen before.

"What does it look like?" Shya looked especially pleased with himself. "I gave you an extension on that fragile mortal life you so desperately cling to."

I gaped at the body beside me. The circle, a sacrifice, I quickly pieced it together. The demon had exchanged another life for mine. What an ugly realization.

"But, why?" I asked no one in particular.

"Because, sweetheart." Shya extended a hand as if to help me up. "This world isn't yet ready for you to walk as a vampire."

I looked uncertainly to Arys. The room was empty save the three of us. I had so many questions. Where was my sister?

Arys bent to gather the clothing I had shed before the shift. That's when I saw the big black dragon etched into his back, its wings flared and tail disappearing beneath the hip of his jeans. Shock exploded through me, and I leaped at Shya with a venomous rage.

"What did you do to him?" I shrieked, slashing his face with clawed fingertips. "What the fuck did you do?"

Shya caught hold of my arm and threw me down at his feet. Standing over me with ebony wings spread wide, an inky swell of demon power oozed from him.

"I did what I do best. You are useless to me if you die before I find the scroll. Trust me, wolf, you don't want to be useless." His eyes flashed brighter red, the snake-like pupils shrunk to the tiniest slits. "Consider this a warning for sneaking around, talking to FPA agents. Be grateful. I let you live."

"What?" I shook my head, trying to understand. "I was never sneaking around."

Shya shoved me away and spun on his heel. "I'll let the two of you talk. Nice job tonight. You did well, all things considered." With that, he exited the room with a flap of wings. The faint scent of sulfur lingered in his place.

Arys pulled me into his embrace and just held me until I couldn't take it anymore. Something had happened while I was unconscious. I needed to know what it was.

"Tell me," I whispered against his bare chest.

"Shya doesn't trust us, Lex. He wasn't going to save you. As much as he needs you, he said he could do without. Find another way. I had to make him a promise."

I drew back to meet his gaze. A sinking sensation swallowed me whole. "Oh, Arys, you didn't."

"In exchange for your life, I had to agree to turn Gabriel. When it's done, he removes the mark." There was such anguish in Arys. It radiated from him in powerful waves.

"He lied, Arys." I took my clothes from him, passing back his shirt. I felt ill. "He wouldn't have let me die. I know it. That's what they do. Goddamn demons. They are deceivers."

"I couldn't take that chance. I was watching you die." He turned away and rubbed his eyes. The dragon burnt into his flesh mocked me. I didn't think I could hate anyone more than I hated Shya.

I got dressed, noting the stab wound in my side had healed immensely. It was an ugly pink scar now. Maybe being a vampire would have been better after all.

"It's more than that though, isn't it?" I touched Arys's arm, making him turn back to me. His eyes were red with blood tears he refused to let fall. "You had a chance to change the future. To change what the witch showed you. But, you didn't. Because you want it."

He stared at the floor as if seeing something I couldn't see. His shoulders shook with pent up emotion. I needed him to tell me I was right. His resistance only made it worse.

"You have to admit to yourself and to me that you want it," I demanded, growing angry. "You crave my death for yourself, and that's why you're putting us both through such hell."

Truth shone like a beacon in his eyes when he looked up. He tried to hide it, but I had already seen. After a strained moment he said, "I do. God I hate myself, but I want to be the one."

I expected to feel anger or maybe even sorrow. I just felt relieved. Kale had told me once that Arys would long for my death, to drain the life from me himself. He said it was the only way Arys would ever fulfill his need to consume me, to claim me in every way. I still didn't entirely understand; I wasn't sure I wanted to.

"You can't turn Gabriel," I said. "He's so young, and he has enough to deal with as it is. What's Shya thinking?"

"He needs Gabriel to work the spell he's been seeking. Making the kid a vampire makes him harder to kill." Arys sighed. "My concern is for you. I had no choice but to tell Shya what he wanted to hear."

"It's your bloodline," I whispered, feeling the urge to look over my shoulder. "Shya could have any vampire do it but to insist on you? The vampires in your bloodline are deadly. He's going to turn Gabriel into a black magic killing machine."

"And, use him to work the spell that will use your death to open the door." Arys's voice echoed through the room. The heat of his sudden anger scorched my insides. Just as fast as it rose, it dissipated. "Let's not discuss this right now. Your friends are waiting for you, and this isn't a safe place."

He slipped his t-shirt over his head and marched toward the door, pausing to hold a hand out to me. I hurried to catch up, wincing in pain. My bruised, battered body was stiff and sore.

Arys was more conflicted than I'd known, and he did a damn good job of hiding it. Worry gripped my heart in icy hands.

As we exited Lilah's sacrificial room from hell, Falon entered. He closed the double doors behind him. I imagined he would clean the place up, as if nothing had ever happened here. I owed him a kick in the nuts. Or two. Though he'd freed my sister, he had taken extra liberties by smacking me around. I wouldn't forget that.

Broken glass and debris from fallen paintings and photos littered the hall. We emerged in the foyer to find Jez, Juliet and Willow along with two brown wolves I recognized as Coby and Kylarai. My eyes filled with happy tears. They had come for me.

My sister was first to grab me in a hug. I savored her scent and the way she felt in my arms. FPA or not, I was not letting anything come between us again. A sob choked me, and I tightened my grip, wishing I never had to let go.

"Are you ok?" I smoothed a hand through her hair, searching her for serious injury. "Did anyone hurt you?"

"No, I'm fine. Thanks to Falon." She handed me the Dragon Claw. "Very impressive weapon."

"It's only as good as the one who wields it." I smiled through the tears.

We all had our share of injuries, even poor Willow with his silver wound. Nothing we wouldn't all survive though.

Kylarai and Coby had taken down the vampires guarding the exterior as well as those who tried to escape. It was no easy task, but one they had accomplished well together. Tongue lolling in joy despite an angry cut over one eye, Coby gave my hand an affectionate nuzzle.

"Everything ok?" Jez asked, a knowing look in her emerald eyes.

"Not as far as Shya is concerned, but overall, yeah, it's ok." I sighed, feeling weak and light-headed. A break from this life would be nice, even if just for a little while. "Hey, Jez, you know that Vegas trip you've been going on about? I think it's time we do that."

"Seriously?" She squealed with more energy than I could have mustered. "I can't wait to start planning."

Arys didn't approve. I could feel it. He was smart enough to say nothing.

"I need to get away. Just for a while. Besides, I'd like to see the Sin City version of The Wicked Kiss. It must be outrageous."

I was eager to leave Lilah's house. I wondered how long it would be before she found her way back. If Salem were smart, he would keep his twin flame close where she belonged. No sooner had that thought passed through my mind than Arys's voice followed. 'Never forget you just had that thought.'

I hadn't felt him in my head. Keeping my thoughts carefully neutral, I merely nodded.

Arys insisted I go with him when we left. After lavishing hugs and kisses on my companions, I accompanied him to my car where he'd parked it several blocks away. He tossed me the keys without a word. The entire walk to the car had been in silence.

I was tired and hungry, for more than one thing. Sliding onto the driver's seat, I put the key in the ignition and waited.

"Drive," Arys said.

"Talk. I know there's something you're not saying."

"Don't go to Vegas." Ah, there it was.

"I'm going. I need to get away from here. I need a break from this shit."

"Vegas is not the place to take a break." His anger had faded, replaced by defeat. "It's dangerous. There's a lot going on there, Lex. Stuff we don't need to get involved in."

I shrugged and started the car. "So we won't. I just want to go let off some steam. Drink, gamble, show Criss Angel how it's done. That kind of thing."

My joke did not earn me a smile from him. Instead, he shook his head and gazed out the window. "It won't be like that. The minute you step foot in that city, they will know you're there."

"Who is they?"

He reached over and captured my hand. Slipping his fingers through mine, he sighed. "You drive me crazy."

"Ditto, baby." What else could I say?

"I'm going with you."

"I wouldn't have expected otherwise."

He laughed then, a melodic sound that sent shivers down my spine. Nobody infuriated me the way Arys did. Nobody brought me to my knees quite the way he did either. As much as I wanted to thump him at times, I was head over heels for him. Being his twin flame didn't mean I had to love him. That blessing, however, would bring us through whatever lay ahead.

"You know how much I love you?" He echoed my thoughts.

"No," I teased. "How much?" I squeezed his hand, hoping that one small action conveyed the pulse-pounding emotion filling my heart.

"Turn the car off and get over here so I can show you." His seductive smile sent a tremor through me. I couldn't resist him.

We had to talk about so much. So many choices had to be made, and so many plans had to be laid. For now, I was where I wanted to be. With the vampire that had changed my life forever. Faith would carry us through. It had to.

Excitement had me shimmying out of my yoga pants. Car sex was never easy, but it was always fun. I climbed awkwardly over the center console, settling myself atop him. Arys freed himself from the confines of his jeans. He pulled me down on his lap, impaling me on his velvet-smooth erection. He erupted into laughter when I hit my head on the low car ceiling.

I held him inside me for a moment, savoring the way it felt when he filled me. Our eyes met, and a jolt of electricity joined us in a way beyond the physical. With every such encounter, my need for him grew. Bound on every level, I understood his need to go to all lengths to protect us. I even understood his craving to fulfill the witch's premonition, well almost.

For a long time, we'd wondered what our purpose was. Now, I was sure of it. We had to bring Shya down, somehow. Some way, we would stop the demon from rising to greater power, even if that meant I had to die to do it.

* * * *

Darker

The long awaited housewarming party was well under way. Just an hour past sunset, the evening was young and beautiful. The weather was perfect for the end of summer, warm and still. A faint pink glow shone ever so slightly on the horizon.

Coby manned the barbecue, serving up a variety of burgers and steaks that made my mouth water. Jez, Arys and I lounged on the patio, enjoying the calm and the presence of friends. I lay back in a lounge chair, a raspberry lemonade in one hand and a slice of watermelon in the other.

"Refills?" Kylarai stepped onto the patio from the kitchen, a fresh pitcher of lemonade in hand.

Jez sat up straighter in her chair, looking interested. "Did you put vodka in it this time?"

"Yes," Ky said with an eye roll.

It had been just a few days since everything went down at Lilah's. I felt a great sense of liberation knowing she wasn't out there, plotting my demise. No, I had Shya for that. Knowing Lilah was fleeing her twin flame made me see her in a whole new light. It also changed the way I saw myself.

Lilah and Arys were of the darkness. They saw the twin bond differently. It drove them both mad in their own way. One sought to escape the bond, the other, to protect it. Ultimately, they feared it because they couldn't control it.

It had tested my sanity, too. In some ways, it always would. The spark of Arys that I carried with me always ensured the darkness lived in me. But, I lived within him, too. As long as we had that balance, we were doing fine.

"Good Lord, that smells awful." Arys wrinkled his nose, watching Coby flip burgers. "The rest of you smell pretty good though. Especially the cat. That's a delicacy."

He chuckled, giving Jez a teasing wink. She regarded him through narrowed eyes, a hint of a smile on her ruby lips. "Watch it, vampire. I'll stab your eyes out."

The sound of their shared laughter was beautiful. What started out as a bittersweet gathering was fast becoming a lighthearted, joyful time. We all needed it.

"So," Arys exchanged a grin with Coby. "When does the strip poker start?"

"You're a poker master. None of us has had three hundred years to master the game. You're a bad boy, Arys." I shook my finger at him. "Besides, you know I barely understand how to play."

"Good," he quipped. "Then you'll be naked in no time."

Simultaneously, Jez said, "I'm in. Get the cards."

They shared another ridiculous laugh to which I rolled my eyes. I finished off the juicy piece of watermelon and considered having another. I glanced at Arys and wondered briefly what it was like to not only be unable to eat human food but to downright loathe even the smell.

"So, is all quiet on the demon front?" Jez asked, curiosity shining in her eyes.

"So far so good." I swirled the lemonade in my glass and took a sip.

Kylarai shuddered and made a noise of disgust. "If I never come face to face with a demon again, it will be too soon. I don't envy you, Alexa. In fact, I fear for you."

I didn't want to ruin the evening by discussing Shya. Doing my best to shrug off the concern, I shook my head, but Arys couldn't resist adding his two cents.

"Alexa isn't inferior to any of those rejects from hell. She's got leverage over Shya. He needs her." He spoke confidently without being haughty. That still didn't earn him any points with Kylarai.

She met Arys's eyes, frowning in disdain. "Right. Because of her tie to you. That's why she's valuable to him."

Arys and Kylarai stared at each other as if they were unaware of their audience. The two of them had never been close, but in the year since Arys and I had bonded, Kylarai had made it clear that she was not a fan of Arys in the least. She seemed to blame him for the dark side of me, but it wasn't his fault. He didn't create this union. He was as much a victim of it as I.

"Yes." Arys leaned back in his chair and crossed his arms, exuding disinterest. "So give her some credit for being able to hold her own with monsters like that."

"Monsters like you?" Kylarai clamped her lips shut as soon as the words left her mouth. It wasn't like her to pick a fight with anyone, though those close to her knew she was gentle and loving but a brutal killer beneath it all.

Darker

"So…" I gestured to Jez, seeking an ally in this little upset. "Who wants to play strip poker?"

"I do," Jez chimed in, raising her glass in an air toast.

Our lame attempt at changing the subject failed. The mood had shifted with such a brief exchange. Resentment tainted the air.

Arys's appearance was casual and relaxed, but I could feel the defensive fury spilling through him. "I think it's safe to say we're all monsters here. Is there no blood on your hands, Kylarai?"

Her face grew red. Grey eyes flashing angrily, she clutched a glass of vodka lemonade in a white-knuckled grip. Ky wasn't a big drinker. The lowering of her inhibitions was not going to help me play peacemaker.

I sought Coby's gaze. He stood quietly by the barbecue, watching the growing conflict with calm unease. He was the only person I'd ever turned. Though we weren't close by any means, we were learning to move past what I'd done to him.

"Wolf family meeting," I announced, standing up and descending the patio steps into the yard below.

Coby and Kylarai followed me to the empty fire pit in the middle of the backyard. I sat on the concrete edge, waiting for them to do the same.

"Ky, you are entitled to your opinions, and you know I love you for them, but you have to understand that Arys isn't to blame for anything that happens to me. He's a victim of circumstance, too. And anyway," I reached to touch her arm. "You're Alpha now. You need to focus on that. Don't worry about me."

Guilt slid over her face like a mask. "I'm sorry, Lex. I just worry. I know it's not his fault. And, I'm sorry about the pack. I've been meaning to talk to them about taking you back."

"Don't," I said, putting my arm around her shoulders. I pulled Ky close, resting my head against hers. "They're right about me. I've brought enough trouble to them. It's better for me to be on my own right now. Seriously. No hard feelings."

"Alright. I'll apologize to Arys," she relented. "But, I won't be happy about it."

"Fair enough."

She returned to the patio, leaving Coby and I behind. I expected him to follow her. Instead, he slid closer to me on the fire pit.

"Alexa," he began nervously. "I want to thank you. When we first met, I wasn't the nicest guy. You were so understanding. You took me in when I had nobody. I met Kylarai because of you, and I am insanely in love with her." He paused, and a blush spread across his cheeks. "The wolf fits now. It's become a part of me. I've learned that you are also a part of me. I wanted to tell you, if you ever need back up, anything at all, I'm here for you."

I was surprised and touched. I'd come to accept that Coby might always hate me for what I'd done to him. Never had I expected him to thank me.

"You have no idea how much that means to me." I leaned over for a casual hug. He took it a step further and pulled me in for a nuzzle. Rubbing his face alongside mine, it was an entirely wolfy action. It meant a lot to me.

"Hey wolf, hands off my woman," Arys called from the deck. It was nice to see him smiling, unaffected by the small rift with Ky.

I stood up to go, but Coby grabbed my hand. "Alexa, wait," he pleaded. "Um, would you uh, I don't know how to say this. Maybe it's too soon, but I know I want to marry Kylarai. Do you think she'll say yes?"

"Holy crap, Coby, you couldn't possibly be more adorable," I laughed. "I can't see why she wouldn't."

My heart squeezed in both joy and envy. I'd accepted that the picket fence life wasn't for me. At least, I thought I had. It was for Kylarai though, and now she had a chance to make it happen. I was thrilled for her.

It was hard to keep from crushing her in an excited hug when we returned to the patio. Somehow, I managed to keep myself contained. Jez prattled on about the upcoming Las Vegas trip while Coby dished out burgers. I was pouring a lemonade refill when the doorbell rang.

Immediately, I was concerned. Everyone I was expecting was already present. I glanced at Arys who shrugged, unaffected. That was weird.

I entered the house, crossing through the kitchen and down the long hall to the front door. I paused, reaching out metaphysically to sense who was on the other side. The earthy energy was strong and familiar. Werewolf.

Darker

I jerked the door open with my heart in my throat. I was a little lightheaded, unable to believe my eyes. There, with his platinum hair long enough to hang in his jade green eyes and a quirky little smile, stood Shaz.

"Hey, babe," he said. "Am I late for the party?"

I gawked at him like a moron, staring in stunned silence. If this was just a dream, I was going to be pissed when I woke up.

Before I could pinch myself, he stepped over the threshold and captured me in his warm embrace. The scent of wolf and pine filled my nostrils, scratching an itch I'd learned to live with. I ran my hands over him, down his lean body and up into his hair. No dream, this was real.

I tried to speak though no words could squeak past the knot of overwhelming emotion that choked me. I clung to him like a drowning woman to a life preserver. I wanted to say so many things that I must have mumbled something unintelligible.

"God, I missed you, Lex," he murmured, stroking my hair. "I never got used to being without you."

"When did you get back?" I finally managed to say. I held him tight, afraid to let go.

"Today. Just a few hours ago."

He kissed me, a tender press of his lips to mine that quickly grew into a passionate exhibit of frenzied love. My wolf leaped for joy at his touch. I couldn't get enough of the way he felt. I was ready to let go of the past, of the mistakes we had both made. He was here now; that was what mattered.

The sound of applause broke us apart. Jez stood in the kitchen, grinning from ear to ear. "Perfect timing. Dinner's ready. Although, it looks like you two are ready for dessert."

We followed her to the backyard where Kylarai also threw herself at Shaz in glee. Arys sat back looking pleased with himself.

There was a flurry of chatter as everyone threw questions at Shaz about where he had been and what he had done. Shaz laughed and ran a hand through his hair, one of his habits that I had dreadfully missed.

Arys rose to greet him with a handshake that became one of those loose guy hugs. The kind of hug that is brief and barely a hug at all but means more than either man will admit to.

"Welcome home, pup."

Epilogue

"You're going to Vegas? For how long?" Kale regarded me with skepticism. He sat across from me in a corner booth at The Wicked Kiss, drumming his fingers impatiently on the table.

"I'm not sure. A week or two I guess. Depends how much fun we're having." I swirled the whiskey in my glass before tossing it back and savoring the burn. This was the best place to speak with Kale. He had to know I'd be out of town; the club would be entirely his responsibility. So would everything and anything that happened inside it.

Kale leaned back, his lips pressed together. He sat stiffly, clearly as uncomfortable as I was. We hadn't spoken since the night he promised to drive me crazy. This meeting was awkward for me, too.

"You mean it depends how long it takes for someone to try to kill you," he scoffed.

"Would that really be a problem for you?" I asked snidely. I'd come to discuss the club, not to sling barbs at one another. "Besides, Arys and Shaz will be there. Jez, too."

"Ah, I see. So, your wolf came home. How very romantic. Must be nice having your little threesome back together." Shadows veiled Kale's mismatched eyes, and I couldn't read him. Even his energy felt tight and restrained. He didn't want to let me in.

Actually, our threesome had yet to resume. Perhaps it never would. Shaz had only been back a few days. Our time together had been spent talking and cuddling, simply finding joy in being together. I didn't know what the future held for Shaz and me. I was happy to take it a day at a time.

Darker

"Look, I just wanted to let you know I'd be gone for a while. I'm not interested in playing the game with you, Kale." I spun the empty glass, using it as a distraction. Maybe I should have just called him.

He chuckled, low and smooth. My pulse quickened, and I cursed inwardly, knowing he'd sense it. Raising a brow, he leaned across the table.

"Don't be coy. You love the game. You play it better than anyone I know." He reached out to drag a finger over the back of my hand. I froze, stopping the glass mid-spin. Before I could tell him off, he pulled back. "Relax, Alexa. I won't lose my shit and do anything too crazy while you're out of town."

I crossed my arms and sat back, far out of reach. "That's reassuring. Thanks." Sarcasm dripped from my words. "Call me if you really need to. If anything goes on here that I should know about."

"Will do, boss lady." He saluted and stood up. "Now, if you'll excuse me, there's a shy brunette waiting for me that likes it when I pull her hair while we're fucking."

Ouch. That, I did not need to hear. It shouldn't have bothered me, and I refused to let it show.

"Hey, Kale," I called as he exited the booth. "Why never a blonde?"

It was a mistake to ask; I knew the answer. Asking was just me being an asshole in response to his attitude.

He moved fast, sliding into my side of the booth, pinning me to the wall. He leaned in so close I could smell the leather of his duster.

"Do you really want an answer to that?" Kale brazenly twisted a lock of my hair around his finger. "The last blonde I've been inside was you. I could never take another to bed without it being you I saw. Is that what you want to hear?"

I felt the color drain from my face. Me and my big mouth. I couldn't possibly get any farther away from him. My back was to the wall.

"No," I said softly.

Kale studied me, even as I searched him, seeking a glimmer of the Kale I adored inside his brown and blue eyes. I didn't find him.

"Have a nice trip, beautiful. I'll be here when you get back." He placed a kiss on the back of my hand, lingering longer than appropriate.

Then, he was gone, moving through the crowd to find his playmate for the night.

I let my held breath out in a whoosh. Damn that had been intense. I was starting to give up hope that things would ever be ok again with Kale. He meant the world to me, but if he insisted on forcing this to a dangerous level, nothing would save him. Still, I wasn't ready to accept that just yet.

I stayed in the booth, watching the club activity. Getting away would be fabulous. I had no doubt that Sin City would be as dangerous as it was fascinating. Still, it couldn't be any worse than the mind-game playing demons and manipulative vampires here at home. Although, perhaps I shouldn't speak so soon.

Things would be changing around here soon enough. Shya had been right on one account; Arys and I had the ability to gather the vampires and werewolves of the city, to organize them. Their support would give us a stronghold, empower us for future events. It wasn't going to be the way Shya expected though, too bad for him. After the trip to Vegas, we would begin making moves to form alliances with the vamps and Weres of Edmonton. It was high time to take initiative. I was sick of being the only one with power who didn't utilize it fully. The time had come to make some changes.

Shya had been wise enough to leave me alone since Lilah's, though as far as I knew, Gabriel was still under his thumb. I wasn't telling Shya about my trip. Eventually he'd come creeping around again. Arys and I both owed him, and he'd make sure he got his payback. Before then, I had to find a way to outwit the bastard, or at the very least, outplay him.

I was counting on Veryl's files to give me some insight into Shya's end goal. Identifying the mystery artifact he sought would be nice too. I read and reread the files, convinced I was missing something hidden inside the documents. I couldn't bring myself to destroy them. Not yet.

Willow was back to his routine of drinking himself stupid. Anything to dull the pain, I guess. Poor bastard. I hurt for him. He was a good friend and a great guy. He deserved happiness.

I signaled the waitress for an ice water. I sipped it, watching Kale work his magic on the opposite side of the room. His brown-haired victim laughed as he whispered in her ear. If he ever set his sights on my brunette sister, I'd have him castrated.

Things with Juliet were better. I might even go so far as to say they were good. We'd recently had dinner. What had started as an awkward meeting developed into an easygoing visit complete with laughter and shared memories.

There were still a lot of issues to work through. We had grown up differently, become very different people. Being Lilah's captive had given Juliet some insight into the kinds of people and creatures I was dealing with. She had come away from that experience with a new respect for me, even if she didn't entirely understand my world.

We hugged it out and even promised to spend more time together. We could never go back to the past, to our lost innocence and ignorance. All we could do was work with what we had now. I invited her out to my place, to run with me on the full moon. The wolf was one thing we did share, something that could unite us regardless of what divided us.

Losing my wolf wasn't far from my thoughts. I was determined to find a way to deal with that; I had to. Having it trapped forever inside me when I became a vampire wasn't an option.

I still hadn't told Shaz about that. I had filled him in on everything important that Arys hadn't already told him. The wolf thing, though, I couldn't bring myself to say it. As ridiculous as I knew it was, part of me feared he would look at me differently if I lost the wolf.

No, it could wait. Now that I had decided to leave town, I couldn't wait to get moving. Jez had booked us a midnight flight. We were meeting at the airport. I had less than an hour to get there.

I finished my drink and rose to leave. The Wicked Kiss would thrive just fine without me, and so would Kale. He held his victim close, his lips on her neck. Our eyes met across the distance. With an evil grin, he sank his fangs.

My gut twisted. I didn't want to see this. More importantly, I didn't need this kind of influence an hour before I got on a plane filled with humans. Kale was taking this whole 'drive me crazy' thing seriously. And, he was right; I kind of did want to stake him.

I flipped him the bird and stalked out of the building. Kale could stay here and play vampire. I was heading to one of the wildest cities on the planet. Sin City, here I come.

My phone rang as I crossed the parking lot to my car. The incredibly funny but cheesy "Baby Got Back" streamed out of the speakers, and I rushed to silence it. I grumbled a curse and made a mental note to slap Arys.

"Where are you? You need time to go through security and all that jazz." Jez's excitement was palpable. I could hear airport noises in the background.

"I'm on my way. Getting in the car right now. Just had to stop by the club. I won't be long."

"Hurry up. Your boys are here already. Oh my gosh, I can't wait." She ended the call with that, and I laughed. Her enthusiasm was contagious.

Leaving The Wicked Kiss was liberating that night. It was someone else's problem for now, and that felt damn good. I wasn't just escaping the club; I was escaping reality, or at least, that was the plan. I was long overdue for a getaway.

My fingers tightened on the wheel, and my foot was heavy on the gas pedal.

I planned to leave my mark on Las Vegas. I didn't doubt that it would also leave its mark on me.

Author Note

I just want to take a moment to thank all of you for reading and supporting the series. It means the world to me to be able to share my world with you. I genuinely appreciate every moment you spend with Alexa. Time is precious and I value yours. Thank you so much for being part of this journey.

Check out TrinaMLee.com for information and excerpts from Freak Show, the upcoming 7th book in the Alexa O'Brien Huntress series.

About the Author

Trina M. Lee has walked in the darkness alongside vampires and werewolves since adolescence. Trina lives in Alberta, Canada with her fiancé and daughter, along with their 3 cats. She loves to hear from readers via email or twitter.

Printed in Great Britain
by Amazon.co.uk, Ltd.,
Marston Gate.